THE PRODIGAL SON

Anna was with Thora, comforting and consoling her, and pretending to be blind to what every eye could see.   Page 139.

The Prodigal Son.

The Prodigal Son

By HALL CAINE

Author of " THE MANXMAN," " THE DEEMSTER,"
" THE CHRISTIAN," " THE ETERNAL CITY,"
Etc., Etc.

Fredonia Books
Amsterdam, The Netherlands

The Prodigal Son

by
Hall Caine

ISBN: 1-58963-541-8

Reprinted from the 1904 edition

Fredonia Books
Amsterdam, The Netherlands
http://www.fredoniabooks.com

In order to make original editions of historical works available to scholars at an economical price, this facsimile of the original edition of 1904 is reproduced from the best available copy and has been digitally enhanced to improve legibility, but the text remains unaltered to retain historical authenticity.

⁶⁴ Then to the rolling Heav'n itself I cried,
Asking, 'What Lamp had Destiny to guide
Her little Children stumbling in the Dark?'
And—'A blind Understanding!' Heav'n replied

CONTENTS

THE PRODIGAL SON

PART I

*" The worldly hope men set their hearts upon
Turns ashes—or it prospers ; and anon
Like Snow upon the desert's dusty face
Lighting a little hour or two—is gone."*

I

ICELAND had never looked more wonderful. The stern old Northland, which in the daylight bears always and everywhere on its sphinx-like face the mutilating imprint of the burnt-out fires of ten thousand ages, and would seem to be dead but for the murmurings of volcanic life in its sulfurous womb, lay in the autumn moonlight like a great creature asleep—calm, august, and blue as the night.

The moon was still shining, and everything seemed to swim in the soft grace of its silvery light, houses, ships, fishing-boats, the fiord in front, the lake behind, the black moorland around, and the snow-tipped mountains beyond—when the little wooden capital began to stir in the morning.

It was the day appointed for the annual sheep-gathering at Thingvellir; the sheep-fold was thirty odd miles away; there were no railways or coaches, and few roads in Iceland, and hence the younger townspeople who intended to make a holiday of the event had to set out early on their little shaggy ponies.

As the clock struck four in the tower of the cathedral Thora Neilsen, the daughter of Factor Neilsen, awoke with a start, and leapt out of bed. She had drawn up her blinds the night before so that the daylight might waken her in the morning, but before she realized that it was the moonlight that had been playing upon her eyelids she was standing in the middle of the floor and crying in the ringing voice of youth and happiness:

"Aunt Margret! Auntie! I've overslept myself! I'll be late! Auntie! Auntie!"

Then the measured and sonorous breathing which had been coming through an open door from the adjoining room was interrupted by an older voice, a good-natured voice trying to be angry, and saying drowsily:

"Drat the girl, she'll waken the whole house."

This was followed by the creaking of a bed and the thud of bare feet on the floor, accompanied by a running fire of grumbling, in which the speaker reminded herself that she was not a cat, capable of sleeping in the daytime, and if she had to be called up in the dead of night she might at least be permitted to wash her face.

The girl listened for a moment and laughed—the light and joyous laugh of the soul that has never known sorrow. She was young and unusually fair. Her height was under rather than over the average height of woman, and if her face was not beautiful it produced the effect of beauty, being one of those soft-featured faces which have a smile always playing upon them, even when the owner does not know it to be there.

She lit her candles, dropped her venetians, and began to dress herself, humming a tune to show she was not concerned. By this time the rumbling artillery from the next apartment entered the room in the person of an elderly lady, who looked more than usually grotesque (if it is fair to take her at such a moment) in abbreviated underwear and small calico nightcap, with bobs of hair in papers about her forehead like barnacles on the figurehead of a ship that is fresh from a long service in foreign waters.

This was Aunt Margret, with goodness written on every line of her old face, but with a tongue that fell like a fountain on sharp stones and knew nothing of dry weather. The moment she set eyes on Thora in the preliminary stages of her toilet she cried:

"Silk? At this time in the morning? And who is to see them under your big boots, if you please?"

The girl laughed at this, as she laughed at everything,

and said: "Very well, give me the woollen ones then. But what a cross old thing you are, auntie. You knew I had to get up early, having a six hours' ride before me."

"But who wants you to have a six hours' ride, I wonder?" said Aunt Margret, bustling about breathlessly to get the girl ready.

"You know quite well who wants me, auntie—Magnus wants me. When they elected him mountain-king for the year I promised him faithfully that I would go to the sheep-gathering, and of course——"

"Don't try to fool an old fox, my dear, but come and wash in this water. It isn't because Magnus wants you at the sheep-gathering, but because somebody else is going to take you there."

"Auntie!" cried Thora, lifting a dripping face from the washbasin.

"Oh, you needn't color up like fire, my precious—I know it's the truth without that."

"How absurd you are, Aunt Margret! You know as well as I do that Magnus himself asked Oscar to take me. He wrote expressly from the farm, not having seen Oscar since he came from college, and wanting to kill two birds with one stone."

"The more fool he!" said Aunt Margret. "The man who expects to marry a girl and asks another man to look after her while he is away is a fool, and his friends ought to take care of him. It's only the simpleton who shuts the door with a bang behind him like that."

"What a nonsensical woman you are, auntie!" said Thora. "Oscar is Magnus's brother."

"Brother, indeed! So was Jacob the brother of Esau, and Cain was the brother of Abel, and those ten big beauties were the brothers of Joseph and Benjamin."

"Good gracious me, Aunt Margret, what a bad disposition you've got! That's the worst of you—you have got such a bad disposition. You talk of Oscar Stephenson as if he were a regular reprobate instead of the son of the Governor, and the idol of everybody."

"It's easy to defend some one whom nobody wants to strike. I don't say anything against Oscar."

"Of course, you don't, you cross old creature. You're fonder of him than anybody else, and I believe you want him for yourself, you jealous thing, because you think he is the brightest and cleverest and best-looking young man in Iceland."

"Many things glitter in the goldsmith's shop, but a sensible woman doesn't want to grab the whole of them."

"And do I, you silly?"

"It looks as if you do, my dear; but sit down here before the glass and let me brush your hair. You are to be married to Magnus, and your public betrothal is to take place the day after to-morrow in the presence of both the families, yet you've had Oscar here every day, and all day, since he came home from England a week ago, and now you are going to ride with him to Thingvellir. You'll make mischief, I promise you. Two dogs at the same bone seldom agree."

At that the girl was taken with a violent fit of laughing. "Auntie, what names you are calling us!"

"Better I should do so than somebody else! The people here are all ears, and Oscar is all mouth—he is always talking about you."

"Not always, auntie." Thora's pretty face was reddening in the glass in front of her.

"Always! Only yesterday he said, 'My future sister-in-law——'"

"Not 'future sister-in-law,' auntie."

"Did I speak, or did I not speak, Thora? 'My future sister-in-law is perfectly charming,' he said——"

"Now, I'm sure it wasn't 'charming,' auntie darling."

"Yes, it was, and hold your silly head quiet, miss—'perfectly charming,' he said, 'and I'm half jealous of old Magnus already.'"

The blue eyes in the glass were gleaming with delight, but the mouth said, "Well, of course, I should have been dreadfully vexed if I had heard him say that, but still it isn't my fault——"

"Fiddlesticks!" said Aunt Margret with a sniff of contempt. "Just take a cranky old woman's advice, my precious, and don't make trouble between two brothers."

Then the shining face in the glass became serious and thoughtful, and Thora said:

"How can you say such uncomfortable things, Aunt Margret? Merely because I am going to ride with Oscar to the sheep-gathering——"

"Oh, a little brook can start a big river. But what's the use of talking—a beast can be broken, but not a wilful woman."

Then seeing that the tears were in Thora's eyes Aunt Margret gave the girl's hair a softer smoothing, and said:

"Magnus may not be as clever as his brother, Thora, but he is twenty times as solid and steady, and he is just as able to take care of a girl, and quite as likely to make her happy. Besides, dear, it's all settled and done, and the made road is easiest to travel, you know. Your marriage with Magnus has been arranged between your father and the Governor; they have set their hearts on it, the contract is ready, and if anything should happen now——"

But Thora, who had been listening with head aslant to sounds outside the house, suddenly leapt to her feet, saying, "I do believe that's Silvertop's step."

There was a clatter of hoofs on the cobbles of the street, and at the next moment a silvery male voice under the window was crying,

"Helloa! Helloa! Helloa!"

Thora ran to the venetians, parted two blades of them, and said, with an air of surprise, "It's Oscar!" Then she tapped the window-pane, and cried "Presently" to the person outside, and stood for a moment to look down at him.

A young man of three-and-twenty sat on one pony and held another by its bridle. He was tall and slim, almost as fair as Thora herself, and he had a cluster of short curls under the Alpine hat which he raised to the moving blind. The moon had gone by this time; a greyish-pink light—the pioneer of the sun—was filtering through a vaporous atmosphere; the ships and fishing boats in the bay were breaking through a veil of mist, and vague shadows of men and women, muffled up to the throats, but chattering and laughing like children, were coming and going in the gloom of the streets.

"Quick, auntie, quick!" cried Thora, lowering her voice,

and while the women in the bedroom hustled about and
talked in whispers the young man waiting outside slapped
his leggings with his riding whip, and whistled and sang alternate lines of a love-song—

> " Drink to me only with thine eyes,
>   And I will pledge with mine."

" Must I wear these ugly——? "

" Certainly you must. They're warm and comfortable,
and it's not as if anybody could see——"

" Auntie, don't speak so loud, or people will hear."

> " Or leave a kiss within the cup,
>   And I'll not ask for wine."

" What a voice he has! I'm certain he'll make a success
some day."

" Maybe so, but people don't feed on voices—not in Iceland, anyway—here's your over-skirt."

" For goodness sake, Aunt Margret! "

> " The thirst that from the soul doth come
>   Doth ask a draught divine."

" Now for my hat! If I have to wear this old black riding
habit I must have something sweet on my head, at all events.
That one with the feather—no, this one and a veil. There!
Do I look nice? "

" Shockingly nice, if you ask me."

The girl laughed gaily, and said in a louder voice, " Then
let us go downstairs—the poor boy must be tired of waiting,
and anxious to be off."

" Not half so anxious as the poor girl, I'm thinking."

Then the smiling face became serious again, and Thora
said, " Don't say those dreadful things any more, there's a
dear soul! "

" Then don't forget my warning, and watch over your feelings, my precious."

The door to the street was being opened by this time, and
a rich barytone voice, mingled with the soft murmur of the
sea, came floating into the hall—

"But might I of Jove's nectar sip
I would not change——."

"Helloa! Good morning, Thora! Is that Aunt Margret?"

From behind the bulwark of the door ajar, with one eye and two curl papers visible in three inches of opening, Aunt Margret answered that it was, and told Oscar, as he lifted Thora to the saddle, to take care of her child and deliver her safely to Magnus.

Oscar laughed a little jauntily, and answered—not, she thought, with too much conviction—

"That'll be all right, auntie. Good-by!"

"Good-by!"

"Good-by, Aunt Margret!"

"Good-by, Thora! And remember!"

At the next moment the two young people had disappeared in the mists of morning, amid a cavalcade of similar shadows dying off in the same direction. Half an hour afterward the sun had risen and the little capital was going merrily.

II

THE father of Oscar Stephenson was Stephen Magnusson (according to his Icelandic patronymic), and he had been Governor-General of Iceland for more than twenty years. He was a man of the highest integrity and of the firmest mind. In his public character he was zealous and incorruptible, and his private life was without stain. His chief characteristics were dignity and pride.

The father of Thora was Oscar Neilsen, commonly called Factor Neilsen (of Icelandic birth, but Danish descent), and he was the chief merchant and one of the richest citizens of the capital. His business methods had often been a subject for discussion, and his domestic history a cause of gossip. He was a man of untiring industry and great frugality, amounting almost to greed.

These two men had been lifelong friends. Their friendship had not been founded on any hollow commercial league, but nevertheless it had been cemented by community of interest, and it was a common saying that the man who could break it could break the constitution. It was one of those friendships that are young after fifty years, and are constantly growing younger because they are always growing older—a peculiarity of all friendships that are true and constant, and the reason why new friendships can never take the place of old ones. Half a word explained a meaning, half a look provoked a laugh. Their friendship was the unwritten history of their past, a living obituary of memories and ideas that were dead. It began in boyhood, and notwithstanding varying fortunes, and some family differences, it had never been darkened by so much as the shadow of a cloud. But people said that if Stephen Magnusson and Oscar Neilsen ever ceased to be friends they would become the bitterest of enemies.

They went through the Latin School together as boys, and were two of four Icelandic students who were sent with stipends to the University at Copenhagen. That was in the days when student life was not so regular as it might have been, but three of them got through without serious damage, while the fourth made a slip which was perhaps the first cause of the present story.

When the time came to separate, one of the four went to Oxford as an assistant in the library, and became a University lecturer, and another went to London to be clerk in a bank, and rose to be manager. The other two remained faithful to their nationalities, and Stephen Magnusson returned to Iceland to practise law, while Oscar Neilsen stayed in Denmark to follow commerce.

Within ten years the friends had made rapid progress. Stephen had risen from advocate to assessor, from assessor to deputy-governor, and from deputy-governor to governor-general, while Neilsen had re-established himself in Iceland, first as factor for a firm in Copenhagen, and afterward as a merchant on his own responsibility.

In the meantime both men had married. The Governor married the daughter and only child of Grim, owner of the farm at Thingvellir, one of the largest farms in Iceland. The Factor, to everybody's surprise, married before he returned home, and nobody knew anything of his wife except that she came from Copenhagen. But scandal seldom loses its way in the dark, and it was whispered that the Factor's wife had been a little actress of the lighter sort, and had been compelled to marry.

The wife of the Governor had borne him two sons. He christened the first of them Magnus, after his father, but the second he called Oscar, after his friend, who had arrived in time to stand godfather at the baptism. In like manner the wife of the Factor had borne two daughters. She brought the eldest in her arms when she arrived in Iceland, and the Factor called her Thora, after his mother. The second, born soon afterward, he would have called Anna, after his friend's wife, but his own wife objected, and it was christened Helga, after herself. There were not many years between the births of the children, but Magnus was the eldest and Helga the youngest, while Oscar and Thora were almost of one age.

The wives of the two friends could hardly have been more unlike each other. Anna was homely in looks, dress, and habits. In practical matters she was a typical Iceland housewife, thrifty and economical. Although the position of Governor-General was one of considerable dignity it was far from a fat living, and Anna set her sail according to the draught of her husband's ship. She was shrewd, but not well educated, and wise, but not enlightened, and she governed the Governor by obeying him. Stephen found his wife his safest steward and most faithful counsellor. He had a profound respect for her instinct, but not too much reverence for her intellect. When in doubt he always consulted her, and while she told him what he ought to do he sat and listened attentively, but as soon as she began to explain her reasons he got up and fled.

The Factor's wife was distinctly comely, volatile, and vain, and her conduct on coming to Iceland might have been calculated to justify the scandal that was coupled with her name. She was extravagant in her dress, unthrifty in her home, restless in her habits, and romantic in her tastes, and after a while she began to gird at the monotony and dreariness of the life about her. A light wife makes a heavy hus-

2

band, and the Factor, who was not then rich, was made to realize that in marrying his Danish beauty he had bought a commodity which he could neither exchange nor return—a housekeeper who neglected his house, and a mother who cared little for his children.

The children were the first to feel their mother's loss of interest in Iceland, for while Government House was for-ever warm and joyous with some noisy festival—Magnus's first holiday or Oscar's last birthday—there were no holi-days or birthdays in their own home, which was always quiet and generally cold. But the mother's ear is thin, and across the gap that opened between the houses of the Governor and the Factor, Anna heard the hearts of the little girls and concocted schemes to get at them. The Factor's wife was nothing loth to be rid of her tiresome charges while she devoured dramatic newspapers and French novels, and thus it came to pass that Thora and Helga spent half of their early days with Anna, and that as long as they lived there-after hers was the mother's form that stood up in their memory when they looked back to the blue mountains of childhood and youth.

Gathered together under Anna's wing, what times the four children had of it! As long as they were little, Govern-ment House was like a nest of song-birds, and if at some moments it resembled more nearly a menagerie of monkeys, it was always alive and always happy. Except the Gover-nor's bureau, they took possession of the whole place, includ-ing the kitchen, for there was only one servant in those days, and she was as fond of them as her mistress. In summer time they ran wild over the home-field, and in winter they romped through every room in the house. Anna spoiled the whole of them, for she never knew how to be cross with children, and at Christmas and New Year she helped them to keep up their noisy customs—boiling the toffy which they pulled into twisted sticks amid shrieks of delighted laughter, and lighting the candles with which they marched in awe-some procession from chimney to coal-hole to find the hidden folk from the hills—and bad fairies who came to steal good children.

On such high days and holidays the Governor and the

Factor, smoking their long German pipes, would come from the bureau to the door of the kitchen to look on at the childish revels. And seeing Anna in the midst of them, like a fairy godmother grown middle-aged and matronly, but with the loveliness of love still shining over her homely face, the Governor would say to himself, " God bless her! " And the Factor would mutter, " God bless my motherless girls! " And then the two old friends would drop their heads, and go back to talk politics.

III

THE child grows, but his clothes do not, neither do his characteristics. What the children of the Governor and the Factor were at the beginning of their lives they remained to the end. Thora was always a merry little woman, with a constant smile on her comely face. She was usually following or clinging to somebody—generally Oscar—but she could sit for hours coaxing, scolding, and singing to her doll, for the instinct of motherhood was strong in her from the first.

Helga was at all points the opposite of her sister. She had black hair, a broad brow, large hazel eyes that were often half closed, a nose that was very slightly turned up at the tip, and a large mouth with thin, red lips which were generally a little awry. A witch may be found under a fair complexion, and an angel under a dark skin, but Helga did not belie her looks. She was as bright as a pebble of the brook, and just as hard and self-centered. Sufficient to herself, she clung to no one, but loved to have the eyes of everybody upon her. She sang like a throstle, and was fond of dressing herself up in grand disguises of paper crowns and coronets, being full of make-believe, and never quite able to distinguish fact from fiction.

The sons of the Governor were not less unlike each other. Magnus was a big, heavy, black-haired boy, silent and slow, and thought to be rather stupid. He found it hard to learn, and his face had often a puzzled expression, sometimes a gloomy and morose one. On the other hand, his moral character was as sensitive as his intellect was sluggish. If he borrowed a penny he would never rest until he had paid it back, and if any one lent him a pencil he would walk a mile to return it. As a consequence his sense of injustice was keen to the point of agony, and he suffered more from an unmerited rebuke than from a blow. He liked best to visit the family farm at Thingvellir, and when asked what he was going to be he plumped for being a farmer. Always fond of animals he filled the house with dogs, cats and white mice, and seemed to love nothing else except his mother. Not a lovable boy, and a rather surly and unhappy one, he was by no means a general favorite, but Anna was very fond of him.

Oscar was so totally unlike Magnus in every quality of mind and heart that it was difficult to believe they could be brothers. The fair-haired little fellow with the handsome face was as sweet-tempered as the sunshine, and as full of laughter as a running river. He could learn anything without an effort, and he had an extraordinary ear for music. Before he could speak properly he imitated the notes of any instrument from the organ to the guitar, and before he knew his alphabet he wrote mysterious musical hieroglyphics on scraps of paper, which the Governor carried off to his bureau and hoarded up like treasures more precious than gold. But in giving him something like genius Nature had taken away character—without which genius is a curse. The merry little soul did not seem to know right from wrong, or truth from a lie. He was always glancing from one thing to another like the sun on an April day. If crying one minute he was laughing the next. Nothing troubled him long, but, also, nothing seized and held him. He began by announcing that he intended to be a king; rather later he thought it would be grander to be a general, but going one evening with the organist of the cathedral to his weekly rehearsal, he finally concluded that to be organ-blower would be best of all.

Nobody loved him the less for his infirmities of character, for it is one of the whims of the human heart that the people who run most strictly within the laws of life find an irresistible fascination in the recklessness of those who kick

over the traces. Oscar was the privileged pet of everybody
and the idol of his father's eyes.

" Ah, Stephen, you'll never rear that boy," said the
Factor.

" Nonsense! Why shouldn't I ? "

" Whom the gods love die young, you know."

" That's only because they never grow old," said the
Governor.

From the first Oscar was fond of a pageant, and always
wanted to be marching in procession, like a victorious general, with the juvenile equivalents for banners and bands of
music. One day he was doing so, playing a tune of his own
composing on a comb, with Helga as an eager lieutenant,
Thora as a submissive soldier, and Magnus as a subservient
slave behind him, when coming to a river that crossed the
home-field a desire for carnage seized the general, and back-
ing suddenly on the narrow bridge he toppled his followers
into the water. Magnus and Helga escaped without serious
consequences, but, as nobody is anybody's brother in a game,
Thora, being dragged down by her sister, was drenched to
the skin.

The Governor came up at the moment when Magnus was
hauling Thora on to the bank, and he was angry.

" Was it an accident? " he asked, but the children did not
answer. " Then who did it? " he demanded, but Thora, to
whom he spoke, looked first at Oscar and then at Helga and
began to cry. " Was it you, Oscar? " Oscar hesitated for
an instant, but Helga touched his sleeve and he shook his
head. " Was it you, Helga? " Helga promptly answered,
" No." " Then it must have been you, Magnus," said the
Governor, and Magnus flushed crimson all over his face and
neck, but made no reply. " Was it you? " Magnus's mouth
quivered, but still he did not speak. " So it was you, sir,
and you can go indoors and to bed immediately."

Without a word or a tear, but with a look of defiance, Magnus wagged his head and turned toward the house. Seeing
him go, Oscar wanted to blurt out the truth, but his melting
eyes encountered Helga's, which held them fast, and he
said nothing.

It was one of Anna's many birthdays, and from the upper

room where all was silent and cold Magnus heard the children's voices below stairs, at first hushed and restrained, but after a while merry enough, with Oscar's voice amongst the rest, and Helga's above everybody's. The laughter and joking burnt into his soul, and at last he struck the table with his fist and burst into a flood of tears.

Then through the sound of his own sobs a thin whimper came from somewhere, whispering, " Magnus! Magnus!" It was Thora at the keyhole.

"Go away," said Magnus, gruffly, but Thora did not go.

"Magnus, shall I tell?" said Thora, and Magnus blinked several times as the big tears rained down his cheeks, but still he answered, " Go away, I tell you."

At that Thora fell to kissing the keyhole, and Magnus had stopped his sobbing to listen, when he heard another voice— Anna's voice—outside the door, and then the child was taken away.

As soon as the birthday party was over and the girls were gone, Oscar began to ask for Magnus, but the Governor patted his curly head and said Magnus had been naughty, and must sleep alone that night. Half an hour later Anna found him crying with his head under the bedclothes, and she said, " Hide nothing from your father, my child."

The Governor was sitting alone in his bureau when a little figure in a dressing gown came in, with swimming eyes and trembling lips, saying, " It wasn't Magnus, papa. It was——" and then a wild outburst of weeping.

The Governor was more touched by Oscar's confession than by Magnus's silence. He patted Oscar's head again and said, " That was very, very wrong of you, curly pate; but go and beg your brother's pardon and take him off to bed."

When Anna went upstairs again she found two heads on the pillow side by side—the dark as well as the fair one—and Magnus was listening and Oscar was talking, and both were laughing merrily.

As soon as the youngest of the children was fourteen winters old they were confirmed together. There was only one other candidate, little Neils, the Sheriff's son, whose mother was dead. In the preliminary examination it was expected that Oscar would come first, Helga second, Neils and Thora next, and Magnus last. The Rector examined them, and when the moment came to declare the order of the candidates he looked serious and even severe.

Oscar, with a sparkle in his eyes, was carrying himself gaily, and Helga was at her ease, while Thora and Neils were trembling with anxiety, and Magnus was nibbling his thumb nail, for he was in dread of not being accepted at all, and in that case, as his new black suit had been bought, he would be afraid to go home. But when the Rector had cleared his throat, and called for silence, he announced a great surprise.

"Magnus is first," he said, "Thora second, Neils third, Helga fourth, and Oscar—Oscar is last."

Then he turned to Oscar and said, "You are rightly served, my son, for you might have done better, and you took no trouble. Take an old man's word for it, Oscar—in the race of life it isn't always the rider who comes in first that was the last to put on his spurs!"

Oscar was crushed with shame, but he recovered himself in a moment, and while the others looked at him to see what he would do—Helga, with her mouth awry, and Thora, with eyes that could not see distinctly, and a throat that could not swallow—he swung about to where Magnus was standing with head down, blushing like a baby, and gripped and shook his hand.

It was a beautiful confirmation service. The cathedral was full of women, but the Governor was with Anna in their pew in the gallery, and the Factor, who was alone, sat in his seat below. The children knelt in a line on the lower step of the communion rail, the girls in muslin frocks and veils, and the boys in black suits and white gloves. The morning was bright and warm, and the sun was shining from the chancel windows on to the five drooping heads as the old Bishop laid his hands on them one by one.

When the little ones had made their vows the Bishop delivered an address: "Be true, be strong, be faithful! Think of the covenant you have made with God, and resist temptation. If Satan tempts you with the treasures of this life, remember that wealth and power are only for a day, while a dishonored name is for a thousand years. Love one another, my children! No one knows how soon the world may separate you, or with what sorrow and tears you may yet be torn asunder, but keep together as long as you can, and may God love and bless you all!"

The service ended with the confirmation hymn, which the children sang by themselves. Anna, the Governor, and the Factor were deeply affected. Ah! the sweet and happy time of childhood! If the children could only remain children! But there was nothing to foretell the future—nothing to be seen there except five innocent boys and girls kneeling side by side, with their faces toward the altar—nothing to be heard but their silvery voices floating up over the heads of the congregation to the blue roof studded with stars.

IV

Soon after that the children were separated. Helga was the first to go. The Factor had become rich, and his wife, who had only been waiting until she could claim a separate maintenance, parted from her husband and went back to Denmark, taking their younger daughter with her. Helga, who was then fifteen years of age, was glad to go, but it was a condition of the separation that at twenty-one she should return to Iceland if her father wished her to do so, or forfeit all interest in his will.

Little Neils Finsen was the next to leave, for his father had married again, and his stepmother had persuaded the Sheriff that the boy had a genius for the violin, and ought to be sent to London.

Oscar remained a few winters longer, trying to find out the profession he wished to follow, and deciding sometimes in favor of the law, sometimes in favor of the church. but generally in favor of music (which was vetoed by everybody as a beggarly business), and being finally despatched to the care of the Governor's college friend at Oxford as a first stage toward an English degree and the pursuit of a public career in Iceland.

Thus it happened that within four years of their confirmation only two of the five children were left at home, and it had come to pass that these two—Magnus and Thora—were living under the same roof.

Magnus having failed at the Latin School, the Rector had concluded that it would be waste of time to keep him there any longer, and the Governor had decided to send him to the farm, when the Factor volunteered to take him as an apprentice in his business and to receive him into his house.

The Factor's house was greatly changed by this time, the place of his wife being taken by his sister, a shrewd little body with a kindly heart but a sharp tongue, which kept everybody in order and reduced everything to rule. Under Margret's régime Magnus began as one of four apprentices who ate at the same table with the master and his family, but saw no more of them than they could see at meals.

He found it difficult to learn his master's business. It was business of barter, in which the farmers exchanged their wool for foreign products, and settlements were made on paper. Magnus made many blunders at the beginning, and was constantly being reproved. As time went on he grew to be big and powerful, and his fellow-apprentices christened him " Jumbo." The name stuck, and he was treated as a dullard.

Except twice a day—at dinner and at supper—he saw nothing of Thora now. Aunt Margret sent her to the Girls' High School, and if he met her in the street, coming or going, she would drop her head and smile and then run away. Magnus wanted to run too, and always in an opposite direction, for the secret of sex had begun to whisper to both of them.

Once a month in winter they met at a dancing class held at the Artisans' Institute. Why Magnus should go there, seeing he could never learn to dance, was a mystery to everybody, until one night the truth became obvious to all, and then nobody thought him a dullard any longer or dared to say " Jumbo " beneath his breath.

A sprightly young sailor named Hans Thomsen, lately home from a voyage, was carrying himself with extraordinary freedom. He was quick-witted, glib, and nimble, and partly for his merit as a dancer, but mainly for the glory of having "sailed," he was attracting the eyes of the girls. Seeing this, he did his best to make sport for them, and when other efforts had been exhausted he looked out for a butt for his ridicule, and seized upon Magnus. He called him "Jumbo" several times, and when this jibe began to fail he made a doggerel chorus, which he sung to a grotesque caricature of Magnus's elephantine steps:

"Slowly goes the cow in calf—
Jog along and do not laugh."

The laughter came in peals, yet Magnus did not speak, and the girls thought he was stupid. Encouraged by his success Hans wagered a group of his friends that he would take his pick of all the girls in the room, and to prove his word he strutted up to Thora—who was reputed to be the richest heiress in Iceland—and asked her to dance with him. But Thora, who had flushed up at the previous scene, said quietly, but in a voice tremulous with anger, "No, thank you," and turning aside she danced with Magnus.

Hans was at first speechless with amazement, but a man has to be hungry to eat his words in silence, and after a moment he winked to his friends and whispered "Wait."

The next dance was a cotillion, and in the first of its figures a girl had to sit blindfold on a chair placed at one end of the room while the boys raced from the other end to capture her. The one to reach her first had to lead her to the middle of the floor and kiss her—still blindfold—and then dance her round the room.

Hans whispered to the leader, Thora was chosen for the chair, and all the young men present—Magnus excepted—ran to catch her. Of course, Hans was the easy victor, and taking possession of his prize he led her to the appointed place, and then, while all were silent and everybody waited to see what he would do, he made a mock obeisance before her blindfolded face, as much as to say he did not wish to kiss her, and left her where she stood.

At that the girls began to giggle, and Thora, feeling that something was wrong, uncovered her eyes and found herself standing alone, and the sailor in his seat. Then the color rushed to her eyes again, but thrice redder and hotter than before, and, covered with confusion, she crept back to her place.

A moment afterward Hans was in the middle of the floor kicking his heels higher than a short man's head, when Magnus, pale as a ghost, stepped out and took hold of him.

"You must dance with me next," he said, and the sailor, feeling the grip of a lion about his waist, cried, half in earnest, half in jest:

"But it's no use dancing with a bull. Let go of me, will you?"

"Not till I show you how a bull would dance you," said Magnus, and before any one could know what was about to happen, the sailor had kicked the beam of the ceiling, filling the room with dust, and fallen with a crash to the floor.

Hans never went to sea again, and the Sheriff, who was a life-long rival of the Governor, fined Magnus a hundred crowns, after reading him a lecture on bad passions and the duty of parents to check them. The Factor paid the money and then stopped it, ten crowns a month for ten months, out of Magnus's salary. The salary was twenty crowns in all at that time, and Magnus took the other ten in secret to Hans himself. As long as Hans lived in Iceland Magnus paid him ten crowns a month, whatever his own earnings might be. Hans became a water-carrier and a drunkard.

V

AFTER that Aunt Margret invited Magnus to spend his evenings with her and Thora instead of going upstairs with the other apprentices. This led to the happiest period in his life. Thora played the guitar, while Aunt Margret knitted interminable stockings, and in order to find an excuse for his presence, Magnus began to learn the flute. He had no music in his nature, but he continued to scream and puff through his instrument like an express train through a ventilated tunnel. And when he had blown himself out of

breath, Thora, who was sweet and patient, would wait while
he wiped his forehead.

Those intervals in the harmony were always the dearest
part of the evenings to Magnus, for then he could talk to
Thora. The big silent fellow who rarely spoke to anybody
else would sometimes talk to her with a force and eloquence
which made Aunt Margret's closing eyes wink and open wide.
It was only about business, what he had done to-day or was
going to do to-morrow, but his face would light up, his eyes
would flash, his tongue would flow, and he would become
another being.

As time went on and Magnus passed out of his appren-
ticeship, he began to develop great schemes and ideas, and
he always tried them on Thora first. The barter business
would go to the dogs some day, and the fortunes of the future
would be made in the fishing. He was the richest man in
the world whose estate was in the sea, and if Icelanders had
the sense to see where their wealth was waiting for them
they would build luggers to replace their open boats, and buy
quick steamers to run their fish to England. That required
money, but Parliament ought to provide it, and some day—
who could know what might not happen?—Magnus himself
would enter Althing, and tell those talking automatons what
they ought to do.

The Factor heard of this project through Aunt Margret,
and he was much impressed by its foresight and practical
wisdom. One day, after smoking various pipes while turning the leaves of his ledger, he went over to the Governor
and said:

"Upon my soul, Stephen, that son of yours is no fool. He
has notions, and if he had capital as well, I don't know that
something mightn't come of him. But broad thighs want
broad breeches, and the question is what are we going to
do?"

"Lend the lad some money, and give him a chance," said
the Governor.

"And create a rival to crush me? No, no! Near is my
shirt, but nearer is my skin! But look here, old friend—why
shouldn't Magnus marry Thora?"

"Splendid! It has been the dream of my life to cement

our friendship in the second generation by a still closer bond."

"Let's come down to facts and figures, then, said the Factor, and within half an hour the marriage of Magnus and Thora was a settled matter.

Magnus heard of it from the Governor. "I've been talking with the Factor about you, Magnus, and ve think it would be a good thing if you and Thora made a match. He will make you his partner immediately, and in due time the heir to half he leaves behind. So if you agree ——"

"But Thora?" Magnus's eyes had lit up with a deep glow of delight. "Does Thora agree?"

"I must leave you to find that out for yourself," said the Governor.

Thora in her turn heard of the arrangement from Aunt Margret.

"Your father is growing old, my precious, and it's time he took a partner. Pity he hasn't a son for a place like that, but the next best thing is a son-in-law and if you or Helga would marry somebody who could carry on the business— somebody like Magnus——"

"But Magnus is like my brother, Aunt Margret."

"So much the easier to make him your husband, my honey."

"But surely it's necessary to love one's husband, auntie."

"Certainly it is necessary to love him, but that's easy enough with Magnus—such an old friend, and so devoted to the family."

There seemed to be nothing left except that Magnus should speak to Thora for himself, but that was a task of graver difficulty. The great creature who had broken the back of the swaggering bully began to tremble in the mere presence of the soft-voiced little lady, who dropped her blue eyes whenever he entered the room. The music lasted longer of an evening now, and the intervals were fewer and more brief.

But one day Magnus, who had been to Thingvellir on the business of the sheep-gathering, came back with a young pony and called Thora into the yard of her father's house to look at it. The four-year-old colt, which was prancing about for sheer joy of being alive, had faultless limbs, a glossy chestnut coat, and a silvery mane and tail.

"Is it a good one?" said Magnus.

"It's a beauty!" said Thora. "It's perfect! It's the loveliest thing that ever stepped! Whomever does it belong to?"

"It belongs to you," said Magnus, and when Thora gave him her hand to thank him he held it for a moment while he looked into her face, and then drew her to his side and kissed her.

"Is it to be so, Thora?" he whispered, and from somewhere in the depths of his breast Thora answered "Yes."

The world was going round him in a wild dance of joy when somebody touched him on the shoulder. It was the Factor, who had seen everything from the house.

"That's the best day's work you ever did in your life, my lad, and I'll take care you never rue it. But what's this they tell me—that you are Mountain-king at Thingvellir this year?"

"That is so," said Magnus.

"Well, well, I'm willing! Take ten days at your sheepgathering, and while you are away I'll have the contract written out and ready. Then we'll sign it the day after you come back, and the wedding can be when you please."

Thora and Magnus went into the house hand in hand like children, and Aunt Margret, who had been crying behind the kitchen door, fell on them and kissed them. Magnus thought he had never been so happy in his life, and though the sun had set it shone for him all night long. Next day he went back to Thingvellir, and scarcely two hours after he had gone word ran through the town that the steamer Laura had arrived in the fiord, and his brother Oscar had returned in her.

VI

OSCAR STEPHENSON carried everything before him. During the six years of his absence in England he had grown as straight as a poplar and as handsome as a young god. Both his dress and his manners seemed faultless in Iceland eyes, and each had a touch of individuality that was irresistible.

His spirits were as buoyant and boyish as before, and his gaiety captivated everybody.

It counted for nothing that his career abroad had been something like a failure; that his infirmities of character had followed him; that his father had forbidden him to return before in order to fix him at his studies; that he had left Oxford, nevertheless, without taking his degree, and that, removing to London at his own earnest entreaty, he had hitherto done nothing at the Academy of Music. He could and he would was all that anybody thought of this; and when he once began he would take the world by storm.

On landing from the steamer he ran up the street as light of foot as a reindeer, shouting salutations on every side, plunged into Government House, hugged his mother at intervals for five minutes, spoke so fast that she could not follow him, dashed into the Governor's bureau, kissed his father just as he used to do when he was a boy, talked for ten minutes, explained that he had not written to say that he was coming because he wanted to take everybody unawares; then said, " Now I must slip off to see my godfather," and vanished like a shaft of April sunshine, leaving the air of the room tingling like a candelabra, and the old people smiling into each other's faces with delighted surprise.

" Well! Oscar was always a master of surprise," said the Governor, and he took up his hat and followed him.

When Oscar reached the Factor's house, he came first upon Aunt Margret, and throwing his arms about her neck he held her so long that to recover her breath and to save her ringlets she had to beat him off with her fists. And then there stood Thora in her laced bodice and turned down collar, her hufa and tassel, and plaited hair, looking sideways out of her soft, blue eyes, and smiling with her rows of pure white teeth. He thought she was a picture of charming simplicity, and took both her hands in both of his, and so they stood for some moments, while she grew redder and redder every instant, and tried to get away.

" Can it be possible? " he said. " And this is Thora! When we were children she used to kiss me, but now——"

" Now she's going to be married, Oscar. Haven't you heard the news? Thora is to be married to Magnus."

"Then she belongs to the family, and I may kiss her in any case," said Oscar.

Thora escaped at last, and then the Factor came in, and Oscar had to turn round and round like a tee-totum, that his godfather might see what changes the world had made in him. He laughed and laughed again, inquiring about the business and the crops, and then tramped about the house asking what had become of this piece of furniture and what they had done with that.

"Everything seems to speak to me," he said, "and in my den at Oxford I used to hear that old Bornholme clock ticking away as plainly as I hear it now."

Then the Governor arrived, and Anna followed him, and while the old men smoked and Aunt Margret did the honors, Oscar poured out the foreign news in a stream of galloping words, and then asked what was going on at home. They told him of Magnus's ideas and schemes, but he did not approve them.

"Iceland will be Iceland no longer if you turn it into a little America," he said. "It is the country of song and story, of fire, frost, volcano, glacier, and of patriarchal methods of government and trade."

"Oscar is right," said the Factor. "Keep up the old order, I say."

And when Oscar had shot away like a meteor, the Factor said, "That young fellow has made me feel fifteen years younger. I must keep an eye on Magnus, though. He is no fool, but he can't reach with his hands where Oscar has his feet. Oscar's a boy!"

"He's a darling," said Aunt Margret, straightening her ringlets.

Thora hardly knew what she thought of him, except that he had left her very unhappy. When she went to bed that night she could not help comparing Magnus unfavorably with his brother—recalling little things like his hands and his nails and the discolored patches on his cheeks when he neglected to shave.

Next day Oscar distributed the presents he had brought from England—a brooch for Anna containing a place for his own portrait, a pin for Aunt Margret, a silver belt for

Thora, and something for nearly everybody. His unselfishness was a subject of general eulogy, and nobody remembered for the moment that the Governor had paid for everything.

In the afternoon he came again to the Factor's, and talked for an hour to Thora and Aunt Margret about London and the glory of its sights and scenes. "You must see them for yourself some day, Thora," he said. "But then I suppose old Magnus will never leave Iceland whatever happens."

Thora was more unhappy than ever when she went to bed that second night, thinking what a difference it made in a man if he had "sailed," and what a wondrous life the girl must live who was to marry Oscar. She was looking at her new belt in the glass, and standing off from it to admire her glorified waist when Silvertop winnied in the stable, and then she felt a little ashamed.

Oscar came the next day also, and, Aunt Margret being out on an errand of charity, he sat with Thora alone until it was quite dark, telling of the plays he had seen in England. There was a good deal about love in them, and one was of a girl beloved by two brothers. Her father had married her to the elder brother while she was still a child, but as soon as her heart awoke she loved the younger one, and her husband killed both of them. Thora cried for the two children who tried to be true, but could not, and she dreamt that night that she was Francesca, and Oscar was Paolo, and Magnus was Giovanni. The dream was painful, but the awakening was more painful still.

Oscar came the next day also, and then he played a number of songs he had composed on subjects in the Sagas. Thora thought she had never heard such playing; and do what she would she could not help laughing a little at the thought of Magnus's performances on the flute. "I'm sure he'll become a great composer," she said when Oscar had gone.

"Perhaps so, but no one can feed on honor," said Aunt Margret.

By this time Thora had begun to look for Oscar every day, and the next time he came he persuaded her to fetch out her guitar. She played some Iceland love songs, and

3

sang them in a sweet voice. Thora was like a flower that had grown under the snow, and was opening its eyes to the sun.

"I wonder whom Oscar will marry?" she said, and Aunt Margret answered:

"Some English miss with plenty of this world's goods and none of the next." And then Thora felt a tingling pain in her breast.

One day there came a note from Oscar, saying, "Glorious morning! What do you say to a few hours on the fiord? Will call for you immediately."

They took a boat belonging to the Factor and turned her head toward Engey, an island inhabited by ten thousand eider duck. Both were rowing when they left the jetty and the water foamed under their oars, but as soon as they were out of sight and hearing they dipped softly and drifted. The sea and sky were blue and quiet, like two mirrors face to face, each reflecting the other, and with the boat like a great bumble bee humming between.

Oscar was like a boy. He laughed and talked continually, telling stories of what they used to do when they were children. He was not very chivalrous then, he remembered, but when she pleaded pitifully he used to allow her to sit on his sledge and they went cracking and crashing through the crisp snow. They had tiffs, too, in those days, and people used to say, "Children who make a quarrel often live to make a match." Wise folks, were they not?

They landed on Engey and rambled about in search of the eider duck, but all the birds were gone, and there was nothing left in their empty nests but a few discolored eggs, and these were addled.

"We've come too late," said Oscar. "Haven't we come here too late, Thora?" he said again, stooping to look sideways into her face. And then Thora, who had been humming a tune, suddenly flushed as red as fire. Their eyes were sparkling, and they were quivering with excitement.

"How I wish we could be children again!" said Oscar. "Don't you, Thora?"

Before she was aware Thora answered "Yes," and then, becoming embarrassed, she turned back toward the boat. The ground was scored with narrow ruts which had been riven out of the grass by the frosts of winter, and Oscar said:

"We can't both walk in one rut, you know."

"You can catch me, then," said Thora, and she ran away laughing.

Oscar ran after her and caught her and held her by the belt, and then she became serious. After a moment she covered her face and began to cry.

"Have I hurt you?" asked Oscar.

"No, no! It's nothing. I'm silly! Catch me again!" said Thora, and snatching his cap off his head she flew over the ruts and had leapt back into the boat before he came up with her.

When they returned to the Factor's, Aunt Margret, who looked cool and thoughtful, gave Oscar a letter which his mother had left for him. It was from Magnus, and it ran:—

"Dear Oscar:—I am glad to hear you have come home, and I wish I had been there to welcome you. You come in a good hour, for you must have heard of my good fortune about Thora. It was long before I could bring myself to grasp my happiness, because she was such a happy little girl, and it seemed selfish to take her from her father's house and everybody there so fond of her. But now that I have got her I feel new strength and am doing the work of three. I am so happy that nothing goes wrong with me, and I am like the anvil that could not be made angry though it were to have the heaviest blow. But I am longing to see you, and I write to ask if you will come to the sheep-gathering and bring Thora with you. Now I must conclude, for we are camping in the mountains and it will take this letter all its work to reach you in time.—Your affectionate brother, Magnus Stephenson."

Oscar read the letter aloud, and when he had finished it Thora could not see him distinctly for the vapor which floated before her eyes—like the chilling thaw-cloud that comes down the valley on a bright winter's day and hides the shining fells. But after a moment Oscar laughed—a little nervously—and said:

"Let us go by all means. I'll have Silvertop ready and bring him round at five in the morning."

VII

NEXT day Magnus awoke on the mountains in the paling light of the moon and the early glimmering of the dawn, and thought of Thora. He always thought of Thora first on waking in the morning, and her face was the last he saw at night when he closed his eyes under the stars. Seven days before, when he had set his face toward the fells, with his forty shepherds and eighty ponies, he had found it hard to turn his back on the lowlands, because Thora was there. But when by daybreak the following morning they reached the ridge of the mountains which divides the north district from the south; and in the grey light and the running mist they met the shepherds who had come up from the other side, and hailed and saluted them, and exchanged snuff and drank healths with them, and then turned about and parted, and begun to descend the way they came, his spirits rose rapidly, because every step was taking him back to Thora.

Five days thereafter Magnus and his men scoured the mountains, gathering up the sheep that had strayed during the summer; and every night when they pitched their tents in some sheltered place where there was water and grass among the lava and screes, and every morning when they rose at the first glimpse of daylight, he told himself he was one day and one night nearer to Thora.

When he was midway down some one had brought him news of Oscar's return to Iceland, and after he had written his letter and despatched it, he was happy in the prospect of seeing his young brother after a long separation, but happier still in the thought of seeing Thora one day sooner than he had expected, because Oscar would bring her to meet him.

And now it was the last day of his duty, and as he and his shepherds came down the mountains, driving five thousand head of sheep before them, and the men began to talk of their wives and sweethearts, he thought surely nobody had ever loved anybody as he loved Thora, because there was only one Thora in the world.

The morning was bright and calm, and there was no sound in the clear air except the bleating of sheep, the barking of dogs, and the voices of shepherds calling to each other as they raced across the fells to keep their flocks together, but Magnus felt as if everything on earth and in heaven were talking to him of Thora.

He began to think of how they should meet, and he found it delightful to imagine what would happen. Oscar would say, " Have I brought her safely, Magnus ? " And then with one arm about Thora he would give his other hand to young Oscar and thank him for taking such good care of the sweet girl who was more to him than his own soul.

At eight o'clock they came in sight of the sheep-fold they were going to, lying in the valley like an inverted honeycomb, and then Magnus persuaded himself he could see through his field-glass a line of people like a train of ants coming over the plain beyond. He could hardly contain himself at the thought that Thora must be among them; and when, an hour afterward, he could plainly distinguish two riders galloping ahead, he was happy in the certainty that these were Oscar and Thora, and that they were hurrying to meet him.

By ten o'clock Magnus and his company had reached the sheep-fold, and there the farmers of the district were gathered to greet them, with snuff and health-drinking as before, but above the joy of that meeting was the delight of seeing a long cavalcade of the townspeople, who had come to make holiday, and were riding rapidly up the valley.

Half an hour later Magnus saw Oscar and Thora on the outside of the sheep-fold, but at that moment he was knee-deep in a palpitating and bleating sea of sheep, and he could only wave his hand and try to shout his salutations. He found he could not shout, for something had gripped him by the throat; but Oscar called to him, and he thought, " What a man he is now, and what a grown-up voice he has got ! "

During the next three hours Magnus was kept busy, separating the sheep, and settling disputes among the farmers; aut as he worked he saw the townspeople pitch their tents and light fires to boil their kettles. " Thora is there," he hought, and he was content.

By two o'clock in the afternoon the last of the sheep had

been separated; the shepherds were driving away their flocks in different directions; the bleating, barking, and shouting were dying off in the distance, and then Magnus—soiled, sunburnt and unshaven—turned his face toward the tents.

The townspeople had finished eating; their fires were smouldering out in the sunshine, and they were dancing to a guitar on a level piece of green, when Magnus went up to them and asked for Oscar, but looked for Thora. Somebody told him they had gone—gone for a walk somewhere—and Magnus was glad, because they could meet where they would be more alone.

He shaded his eyes and looked down the valley, and thinking he saw two figures at the foot of the hills, he leapt on the back of a pony that was grazing near, and rode off in that direction. He was humming a tune, for he was very happy.

After some minutes he was sure he saw Oscar and Thora, and began to call to them.

"Helloa!" he cried, but there came no answer.

"Helloa!" he cried again, but still there was no reply, and all was silent now save for the tinkling of the guitar behind him.

"Helloa! Helloa! Helloa!" but nothing came back to him but his own voice as it echoed in the hills.

Oscar and Thora were sitting on the sunny side of a rock which rose out of the foot of the mountain like a mound of black soil, but was really the mouth of an extinct volcano. Magnus thought he knew what they were doing—they were dropping stones down the crater and listening for the sound of their descent. That was why they had not heard him, although he had called so loud. Very well, he knew what he would do, he would play a practical joke upon them; he would take them by surprise; he would creep up on the opposite side of the rock and suddenly appear before them as if he had risen out of the pit.

With this intention Magnus made a circuit of the crater, and drew up on the shady side of it. He was then very close to the two who were sitting above, but still they did not hear him, so slipping from the saddle and throwing the reins over the pony's head he stole up softly and began to climb the rock as quietly as he could in his big boots over the rolling stones. The greater difficulty was to keep himself from laughing aloud at the thought of what their faces would be like when he stood up between them like a ghost that had sprung out of the earth.

Scrambling on hands and knees Magnus had climbed half way up the rock when he heard Oscar speaking, and he stopped to listen.

"But why did you consent?" said Oscar's voice.

Thora did not answer, and after a moment the voice of Oscar said again, "Why did you, Thora?"

There was a low murmur of indistinguishable words, and then the voice of Oscar said, "Because your father wished it? But surely you have to live your own life, Thora. However obedient a daughter should be to her father, she is a separate being, and the time comes when she has to fly with her own wings, as we say. Then, why did you consent?"

Magnus felt his fingers tighten their hold on the rock he was clinging to, and he leaned forward to catch Thora's reply. But there was only the same low murmur of indistinguishable words, and then Oscar's voice once more,

"Magnus? No doubt! I wouldn't say a word against Magnus—God forbid!—but love—mutual love—is the only basis of a true marriage, and if you do not love Magnus—not really and truly, as you say—why did you consent to marry him?"

Magnus felt the ground to be reeling under his knees. If he had not been clinging to the rock he must have rolled to the foot of it. All his soul seemed to listen, but he could hear nothing except the sound of Thora's voice breaking with sobs.

Then came Oscar's voice again, but lower and tenderer than before, "How hateful of me to make you cry, Thora! I didn't intend to do that, dear. But have you never asked yourself what will happen if you marry Magnus, and then find out when it is too late that you like somebody else?"

At that there came another note into Thora's weeping, a note of joy as well as sorrow, and Magnus—though he did not know it—clambered higher up the rock.

"What did you say, Thora? Tell me, dear, tell me—did you say you had found out already?"

And then at last came Thora's voice in a burst of passionate tears, "You know I have, Oscar," and after that there
was a startled cry.

Thora had risen and was moving toward Oscar, who was
already on his feet and holding out his arms to her, when
behind him she saw Magnus with a terrible face—eyes staring, lips parted, and breath coming and going in gusts. Oscar turned to see what it was that Thora looked at and,
seeing Magnus, his whole body seemed to shrink in an instant, and he felt like a little man.

"Is it—you—really?" he faltered, and he smiled a sickly
smile, but Magnus neither saw nor heard him.

Magnus heard nothing, saw nothing, and knew nothing at
that first moment except that he, a man of awful strength
and passion, was standing at the mouth of a pit as deep as
hell and as silent as the grave, with two who had 'been dearer
to him than any others in the world, and they had deceived
and betrayed him. But at the next moment he saw a look
in Thora's face that made him remember Hans, the sailor,
for it was the same look that he had seen there the instant
after he had thrown the man on his back, and then a ghostly
hand seemed to touch him on the shoulder and the fearful
impulse passed.

There was silence for some moments, in which nothing
was heard but the quick breathing of the three, and then
Magnus found his voice—a choking utterance—and he fell
on Thora with loud reproaches.

"What does this mean?" he said. "It is only six days
since I parted from you, and now I find you like this! Speak!
Can't you speak?"

But Thora could only gasp and moan; and Oscar, who
had struggled to recover himself, stepped out to defend her.
"It's not Thora's fault, Magnus. It's mine, if it is anybody's, and if you have anything to say you must speak to
me."

"You!" cried Magnus, wheeling round on him. "What
are you, I'd like to know? A man who betrays his own
brother! Is that what you came home to do—to make mischief and strife and break up everything? In the name of
God why didn't you stay where you came from?"

"Magnus," said Oscar, trying to hold himself in, "you must not speak to me like that. You must not talk as if I had stolen Thora's affections away from you, because——"

"Then what *have* you done? If you haven't done that, what *have* you done?"

"Because Thora never loved you—never—though I am sorry to say it—very sorry——"

"Damn your sorry!" said Magnus.

"And damn your insolence!" cried Oscar. "And if you won't hear the truth in sorrow, then hear it in scorn—Thora's engagement to you is nothing but a miserable commercial bargain between her father and our father by which she has been bought and sold like a slave."

The blow went home; Magnus felt the truth of it; he tried to speak, and at first he could not do so; at length he stammered:

"I know nothing about that. I only know that I was to marry Thora, and that in two days' time we were to be betrothed."

Then Thora said nervously, with quivering lips and voice, "It wasn't altogether my fault, Magnus—you know it was not. It was all done by other people, and I had nothing to say in the matter. I was never asked—never consulted."

"But I asked you myself, Thora."

"That was when everything had been settled and arranged, Magnus."

"But if you had told me even then, Thora—if you had told me that you did not wish it—that you could not care for me——"

"I didn't know at that time, Magnus."

"You didn't know, Thora?"

"I didn't know that the love I felt for you was not the right love—that there was another kind of love altogether, and that before a girl should bind herself to any one for better or worse until death parts them, she ought to love him with all her heart and soul and strength."

"And do you know that kind of love now, Thora?" asked Magnus, and Thora faltered, "Yes."

That word was like a death-knell to Magnus. He stared

blankly before him and muttered beneath his breath, "My God! My God!" and then Thora broke down utterly.

No one spoke for some moments. Magnus was going through a terrible struggle. He was telling himself that, after all, these two had something to say for themselves. They had their excuse, their justification. They loved each other, and perhaps they could not avoid doing what they had done, while he—he who had thought himself the injured person—was really the one who was in the way.

When Thora's weeping ceased. Magnus looked up and said, in a voice that was pitifully hoarse and husky,

"So it's all over, it seems, and there's no help for it?"

No one spoke, and Magnus said again, "Well, a man's heart does not break. I suppose, so I daresay I shall get over it."

Still the others said nothing, and Magnus looked from Oscar to Thora and said, quite simply, "But what is to be done? If it is all over between Thora and me, what is to be done now?"

Neither of them answered him, so he turned to Thora and said, "Your father was to have the contract ready by the time of our return—can you ask him to destroy it?"

She did not reply. "You can't—I know you can't—your father would never forgive you—never."

Then he turned to Oscar: "The Governor has plans about the partnership—can you fulfil them if I should fail?—No? Is it impossible?"

Oscar gave no sign, and after a moment Magnus said, "Then I must be the first to move, I suppose. But perhaps that is only right, since I am the one who has to get out of the way."

"Don't say that, Magnus," cried Thora.

"Why not? Better a sour truth than a sweet lie, Thora."

Thora dropped her eyes; Oscar turned aside; they heard Magnus's foot on the stones as if he were moving away, but they dared not look lest they should see his face. After a moment he stopped and spoke again:

"When I was coming down the mountain I thought we might go home together—all three together—but perhaps we had better not. Besides, if I have to move first in that matter, I have my work cut out for me, and I must be alone to think of it."

"What are you going to do?" asked Oscar.

"God knows!" said Magnus. "He has got us into a knot. He must get us out of it."

They heard his heavy boots on the sliding stones as he stepped down the rock; they heard him speak cheerfully to his pony as he swung to the saddle; they heard the crack of his long reins as he slashed them above the pony's head, and then—as well as they could for the tears that were blinding them—they saw him bent double and flying across the plain.

VIII

EARLY next day Magnus called at Government House and went up to Oscar's room. He found Oscar sitting at a desk with a pen in his hand, a blank sheet of paper before him, and sundry torn scraps lying about, as if he had been trying in vain to write a letter. The brothers greeted each other with constraint, and during the greater part of their interview neither of them looked into the other's face.

"I have come to tell you," said Magnus, sitting by the side of the desk and fixing his eyes on the carpet at his feet, "I have come to tell you that I see a way—I think I see a way out of our difficulty."

"What is it?" asked Oscar, looking steadfastly at the blank sheet of paper before him.

"It is a plan which does not involve Thora at all, or in any way reflect upon you, therefore you need not ask me what it is. I expect to try it to-morrow, and if it succeeds the consequences will be mine—mine only—and nobody else will be blamed or affected."

Oscar bowed his head over the blank sheet of paper and said nothing.

"But before I take the step I am thinking of, I want to be sure it will be worth taking, and have the results I expect. That's why I am here now—I am here to ask you certain questions."

"What are they?" said Oscar.

"They are very intimate and personal questions, but I think I have a right to ask them, seeing what I intend to do," said Magnus, and then, in a firmer voice, "and a right to have them answered, also."

"Ask them," said Oscar.

"I want to know, first, whether, if I can liberate Thora from her promise to me, you will marry her?"

"Indeed, yes—if she will have me—yes!"

"You said yesterday, you remember, that love—mutual love—was the only basis of a true marriage. Perhaps I forgot that in my own case, but I must not forget it now. So it is not sufficient that Thora should love you; it is necessary that you should love Thora—you do love her?"

"Indeed I do."

"Your attachment is a brief one—are you sure it is not a passing fancy?"

"Quite sure."

"It is a solemn thing that two human beings should bind themselves together, as Thora said, for better or worse, until death parts them—you are not afraid of that?"

"No."

"You will always love her?"

"Always," said Oscar.

"You have counted the cost, all the consequences?"

"I know nothing of costs and consequences, Magnus. I only know that I love Thora with all my heart and soul, and that if you will liberate her, and she will consent to marry me, I will consecrate my whole life to make her happy."

Magnus shifted in his seat, cleared his throat, and began again.

"Thora is a sweet, good girl," he said, "the best and sweetest girl in the world, but she is a simple Iceland maiden who has never been out of her own country. She is not like you, and if you take her to England she will not be like your friends there. Have you thought of that? Are you ready to make allowances for her upbringing and education? Will your love bear all the strain of such a marriage?"

It was now Oscar's turn to move restlessly in his seat. "Why should you ask me a question like that, Magnus?"

"Will it?" repeated Magnus more firmly.

"I certainly think it will."

"But will it?" said Magnus still more firmly.

"It will," said Oscar.

There was a short pause and then Magnus said quietly:

"There are two or three other questions I wish to ask of you, and I ask them for your sake as much as Thora's."

"Go on," said Oscar.

"Thora is practically her father's only daughter now, and he is old and very fond of her. If he should wish her to remain in Iceland after her marriage, you would be willing to live here for the rest of your life?"

"If he made it a condition—yes."

"Naturally the Governor has certain plans for you, having spent so much on your education, and you have your own aims and ambitions also, but if these should clash with your love for Thora, if they should tempt you away from her, you would be ready to give them up?"

"Certainly I would."

"You are sure of that?"

"I am sure of it—that is to say—it would be hard, no doubt—to abandon the aims and ambitions of one's whole life—but if they ever clashed, as you say, with my love for Thora, ever tempted me away from her—tempted me to leave her to go to England for example——"

"Or to any other country, or any other woman?"

"That is not possible, Magnus."

"But if it were possible?"

"I would not go," said Oscar.

"So that if I give Thora up and she consents to marry you, nothing and nobody will be allowed to disturb her happiness?"

"Nothing and nobody," said Oscar.

"Then write that," said Magnus, tapping the paper on the desk.

"Write it?"

"To her, not to me. If you are sure of all this, you cannot be afraid to put it in black and white."

"I'm not afraid, but it's of no use writing it to Thora."

"Why not?"

"Because when you left us yesterday she told me that, though her heart was mine, she had given her word to you, and she would be compelled to keep it."

"She told you that?"

"She did."

Magnus hesitated for a moment, and then said in the husky voice of yesterday, "Write it, nevertheless, and let me take the letter."

"You mean that, Magnus?"

"Yes."

"That you will give her back her word, and speak to her for me?"

"Write your letter," said Magnus huskily.

"What a good fellow you are! You make me feel as if I had behaved odiously and wish to heaven I had never come back from England. I cannot wish that, though, for Thora's love is everything on earth to me now, and I would do anything to hold on to it. But if I have done wrong to you I know of no better way of expressing my regret than by placing my dearest interests in your hands. I will write the letter at once, Magnus. I tried to write it twenty times and couldn't, but now I can, and I will."

While Oscar's pen flew over the blank sheet of paper Magnus sat with head down, digging at the pattern in the carpet. A fierce fight was going on in his heart even yet, for the devil seemed to be whispering in his ear, "What are you doing? Didn't you hear what he said—that Thora had decided to keep her word to you? Are you going to persuade her not to do so? You'll never get over it—never!"

When Oscar had finished his letter he gave it to Magnus and said: "Here it is. I think it says all we talked about, if less than a fraction of what I feel. She'll listen to you, though, I feel sure of that; but if she does not—if she sends me the same answer——"

"What will you do then?" asked Magnus, pausing at the door.

"Then I will take the first steamer back to England, and ask you to say nothing to anybody of what has happened."

A bright light came into Magnus's face, and then slowly died away.

"But I cannot think of that yet, Magnus; not till I hear the result of your errand. See her, speak to her, tell her she is not responsible for her father's contract; beg of her not to ruin her own life and mine. Will you?"

"I will."

"God bless you, old fellow! You are the best brother a man ever had. Don't be too long away. I shall hardly live until you return. Put me out of suspense as quickly as you can, Magnus. If you only knew how awfully I love the little girl and how much her answer means to me——"

But Magnus's tortured face had disappeared behind the door.

At the bottom of the stairs his mother met him, and she said: "So you've been up with Oscar all the time! Your father and the Factor were looking for you everywhere. They had the lawyers with them all the morning, and wanted to consult you about something. It's settled now, I think, so there's no need to trouble. But, goodness gracious, Magnus, how white and worn you look! That work on the mountains hasn't suited you, and you must do no more of it."

Magnus excused himself to Anna and hastened away to the Factor's. As he passed through the streets with Oscar's letter to Thora in his side pocket, and his nervous fingers clutching it, the devilish voice that had tempted him before seemed to speak to him again and say: "Destroy it! Didn't you hear him say that he would go away? Let him go! Nobody but yourself will know anything about the letter! Even Thora will never know! And when Oscar is gone, Thora will fulfil her promise to you! Let her fulfil it! If she does not love you now, she will come to love you later on. And if she never comes to love you, she will be yours; you will have her, and who has a better right? Destroy it! Destroy it!"

But his good angel seemed to answer and say:

"What's the use of having a woman's body if you cannot have her soul? That's lust, not love; and it's too late to think of it anyway. The question you have to decide is simple enough—do you love yourself better than you love Thora, or Thora better than yourself?"

And then the devil seemed to whisper again and say,

"What a fool's errand you are going upon! If you win you lose; if you lose you win. If you persuade Thora to preserve her own happiness you destroy your own! If you do not persuade her to marry Oscar she will marry you! Are you a man? Is there an ounce of hot blood in you?"

The fight was fierce, but Magnus decided in favor of the girl's happiness against his own, and he said to himself at every step, "Go on; you want Thora to be happy, then carry it through; it is hard, but go on; go on!"

When he reached the Factor's his great limbs could hardly support themselves and his ashen face was covered with sweat.

IX

The Factor's house was full of the sweet smell of the baking of cakes, and Thora and Aunt Margret were in the kitchen with the fronts of their gowns tucked up to their waists, their sleeves turned back, and rolling-pins in their hands, behind a table laden with soft dough and sprinkled with flour.

"Here's Magnus at last!" said Aunt Margret, "and perhaps he can tell me how it happened that you came home without him yesterday."

Magnus did his best to laugh it off. "That's a long story, auntie," he said. "A horse's shoe isn't made at a blow, and I want to speak to Thora."

"Mind you don't keep her long, then. If we're to be ready for all the people who are coming to-morrow there's work here to-day for a baker's dozen."

Magnus went up to the little sitting-room with the Barnholme clock in it, and Thora followed. There were dark rings under her eyes, and her manner was nervous and restless.

"I am ashamed of what happened yesterday," she said, "and I ask you to forgive and forget."

"I cannot do either," said Magnus, "that is to say, not yet, and in the way you mean."

Thora's eyes began to fill. "Don't be too hard on me, Magnus. I'm trying to make amends, and it isn't very easy."

"I'm not so hard on you as you are on yourself, Thora, and I'm here to tell you not to do yourself an injustice."

Thora thought for a moment, and then said, "If you mean that you have come to say that after all I must fulfil my promise, it is unnecessary, because I intend to do so."

"Will that be right, Thora?"

"It may not be right to Oscar, perhaps, or to myself——"

"I'm not thinking about Oscar now, and I'm not thinking about you—I'm thinking about myself—will it be right to me?"

"What more can I do, Magnus? It wasn't altogether my fault that I gave you my word, but I did give it, and I am trying to keep it."

"Would it be right to marry me—seeing, as you said yourself, you do not care for me?"

Thora dropped her head.

"You said yesterday that before a girl should marry a man she ought to love him with all her heart and soul and strength. Wouldn't it be wrong to marry me while you loved somebody else like that? Is that what you call making amends, Thora?"

"I was only trying to do what was right, Magnus; but if you think it would be wrong to marry you, then I will never marry at all. Never!"

"What good will that be to me, Thora? Five years, ten years, twenty years hence, what good will it be to me that because you had given me your word, and could not keep it, you are living a lonely life somewhere?"

Thora covered her face with her hands.

"What sort of a poor whisp of a man do you suppose I am, Thora?"

"I didn't intend to insult you, Magnus. But if I can neither marry you nor remain unmarried, what am I to do?"

"You know quite well what you are to do, Thora."

Thora uncovered her face; her eyes were shining.

"You mean that I must marry Oscar?"

"That depends upon whether you love him."

The shining eyes were very bright in spite of the tears that swam in them.

"Do you love him?"

4

"Don't ask me that, Magnus."

"But I do ask you, Thora. I have a right to ask you. Do you love Oscar?"

"I admire and esteem him, Magnus."

"But do you love him?"

"Everybody loves Oscar."

"Do *you* love him, Thora?"

"Yes," said Thora softly, and for some moments after that there was no sound in the room but the ticking of the clock.

"Then, as he loves you, and wishes to marry you, it is your duty to marry him," said Magnus.

"But I have given my word to you, Magnus."

"I give you back your word, Thora."

The shining eyes were shedding tears of joy by this time, but while love fought for Oscar, duty and honor struggled for Magnus.

"But I have told him it is impossible," said Thora.

"He asks you again, Thora. Here is his letter," said Magnus.

"He gave it to you to deliver?"

"I asked for it."

"And you came to speak for him?"

"I came for myself as well."

"How good you are to me, Magnus!"

"Read your letter," said Magnus, and with trembling hands Thora opened the envelope.

The fight was short but fierce. Magnus watched every expression of Thora's face. If there had been one ray of love for him in her looks of gratitude and remorse he would have clung to the hope that the time would come when all would be well; but love for Oscar shone in her eyes, broke from her lips, betrayed itself in the very insistence with which she meant to marry Magnus, and there remained no hope for him anywhere.

Thora looked up from her letter, and said:

"How splendid! How noble! That's what I *do* call brotherly! Oscar tells me that you think you can put the contract aside without involving me or reflecting upon him. You are too good—too generous—too forgiving—how can I thank you?"

" By giving me Oscar's letter," said Magnus.

" What do you want with it?"

" I want to have it in my pocket when I do my work to-morrow. That's only fair—that while I am doing my part I hold Oscar's written assurance that he intends to do his."

" You wouldn't produce it to Oscar's injury?"

" Many a man sharpens his axe who never uses it," said Magnus.

Thora returned the letter to Magnus, and he put it back in his pocket.

" Now you must answer it," said Magnus.

" Not yet, not immediately," said Thora.

" Immediately," said Magnus, and taking pen and paper from a sideboard, he put them before her.

The power of the man mastered her, and she sat at the table and took up the pen.

" But why should I write to-day?" she said. " Why not to-morrow?"

" To-morrow is the day fixed for the betrothal, and if I am to do anything then I must have everything in black and white."

" But let me have one engagement ended before the other is begun, Magnus."

" If Oscar does not receive your answer within an hour he will take the first ship back to England, and you will never see him again."

" He said so?"

" Yes."

" You will break my heart, Magnus. I don't know what to say to you."

" Write," said Magnus.

" I cannot. You have driven everything out of my head."

" Then write to my dictation: ' My dear Oscar '——"

" ' My dear Oscar '——"

" ' I have received the letter you sent by Magnus '——"

" ' Sent by Magnus '——"

" ' And I reciprocate all you say '——"

" ' All you say '——"

" ' I believe you love me very dearly, and that you will never allow anything or anybody to come between us '——"

" ' To come between us '——"

" ' Magnus has given me back my word because I do not love him '——"

" Must I say that, Magnus?"

" ' And because he wishes to make me happy '——"

" I cannot, Magnus, I really cannot——"

" Go on, Thora. ' Therefore, if he can satisfy my father and yours '——"

" ' My father and yours '——"

" ' I will marry you when and where you please, because '——"

" ' Because '——"

" ' Because I love you with all my heart and soul and strength.' "

Thora was crying when she came to the end of the letter.

" Sign it," said Magnus, and she signed it.

" Address it," he said, and she addressed it.

" Seal it," he said, and she sealed it.

" Now give it to me," said Magnus, and he took the letter off the table and put it in his breast pocket.

" What are you going to do with it?" asked Thora.

" Deliver it myself," said Magnus.

" No, no!" cried Thora. " At least let me keep it for half an hour—a quarter of an hour."

" I cannot trust you, Thora," said Magnus, and he made for the door.

" Give it me back! Give it me! Give it me!"

She threw her arms about him to detain him, and for a moment he stood trembling in the temptation of her embrace. Then he put her gently aside and fled out of the house.

While he was hurrying through the streets the warmth of Thora's soft flesh was still tingling on his neck and cheek, and the devilish voice was saying in his ear, " What a fool you were! In another moment her sweet body would have been in your strong arms and she would have been yours for ever."

He tried not to hear it, but the voice went on: " She may still be yours if you're half a man! Keep back Thora's letter and return his own to Oscar! Why not? What better does he deserve of you?"

Magnus walked fast, but the voice followed him. It told him how happy he had been when he thought Thora loved him; how he had left her for the mountains with his heart full of joy; how Oscar had come and everything was at an end.

"Keep it back! Return his own!" said the voice in his ear; and to make sure of Thora's happiness and to cure himself of all hope, he took Thora's letter out of his pocket and ran with it in his hand.

Oscar was at the top of the stairs, being too eager to wait in his bedroom. "So you have brought it! She has sent me an answer! Give it me!"

"Take it," said Magnus.

But having Thora's letter in his hands at last Oscar was afraid to open it. "Is it all right?" he asked.

"See for yourself," said Magnus, and he dropped into the seat by the desk.

As Oscar read the letter the expression of his face changed from fear to joy, and from joy to rapture. Without looking up from the paper he cried out like a happy boy, "It's all right! She agrees! God bless her! Shall I read you what she says? Yet, no! That wouldn't be fair to Thora! But it's as right as can be! How beautiful! Talk of education—nobody in the world could have put things better! The darling!"

He read the letter twice and put it in his pocket; then took it out and read it again and kissed it, forgetting in his selfish happiness that anybody else was there.

Magnus sat and watched him. The fight was almost over, but he was nearly breaking down at last.

"What an age you seemed to be away!" said Oscar. "Yet you have run hard, for you are still quite breathless. But there is nothing more to do now except what you promised to do to-morrow. You think you *can* do it?"

"I think I can," said Magnus.

"It will be a stiff job, though. To persuade two old men who don't wish to be persuaded! Nobody wants to see his schemes upset and his contracts broken, and with all the good-will in the world to me——"

"Wait!" said Magnus, rising—his unshaven face had

suddenly grown hard and ugly. "We have talked of you and Thora, and of the Factor and the Governor, but there is somebody who has not been too much mentioned—myself!"

"Don't suppose I am forgetting you, though," said Oscar. "I can never do that—and neither can Thora—never!"

"If I am to stand back, and take the consequences, there is something you owe me—you owe me your silence!"

"Assuredly," said Oscar.

"Whatever I do or say to-morrow," said Magnus, "you must never allow it to be seen that you know my object. Is it a promise?"

"Certainly!" said Oscar. "Silence is inevitable if I am to save Thora from her father's anger, and I *will* save her from that and from every sorrow."

Magnus walked to the door, and then, for the first time, Oscar looked at him.

"But what a brute I am—always talking of myself!" said Oscar, following his brother to the landing. "When everything is satisfactorily settled, what is to happen to you, Magnus?"

"God knows!" said Magnus, with his foot on the stair. "Everybody has his own wounds to bandage."

"Well, God bless you in any case, old fellow!" said Oscar, patting Magnus on the shoulder. And then he returned to his room and took out Thora's letter and read it over again.

X

THE betrothal was fixed for five o'clock on the following afternoon. Aunt Margret had had women in to clean the house down, and everything was like a new pin. The large sitting-room, looking toward the town, was prepared for the legal part of the ceremony, with pens and ink on the round table, and the smaller sitting-room, divided from it by a plush curtain and overlooking the lake, was laid out with a long dining table, covered with cakes and cups and saucers and surrounded by high-backed chairs.

These rooms were standing quiet and solemn when at half-past four Aunt Margret came down in her best black silk and with ringlets newly curled, to have a last look round. She was doing a little final dusting when the first of her guests arrived. This was Anna, also in black silk, and, being already on her company manners, Aunt Margret kissed her.

"But where's Oscar, and where's the Governor?" asked Aunt Margret.

"Stephen is coming," said Anna, "but far be it from me to say where Oscar is! The boy is here and there and everywhere."

"That reminds me of something," said Aunt Margret. "Can you tell me how it came to pass that the young folks missed each other at Thingvellir yesterday, and Magnus came home alone?"

"Goodness knows! It wouldn't be Magnus's fault, that's certain. Magnus is like my poor father—as sure to be in his place as a mill-horse on the tread, but Oscar is as hard to hold as a puff of wind. It's his nature, he can't help it, but it makes me anxious when I think of it, Margret."

"Don't be afraid for Oscar, Anna! He'll come out all right. And if he is restless and unsettled, God is good to such, weak heart. He never asks more than He gives, you know."

The Factor came downstairs—a tall man, clean-shaven, bald-headed, and a little hard and angular, wearing evening dress and a skull-cap, and carrying a long German pipe in his hand.

"No smoking yet!" cried Aunt Margret. and with a grunt and a laugh the Factor laid his pipe on the mantelpiece.

"And how's Anna to-day?" he said. "No need to ask that though, our Anna is as fresh and young as ever. Upon my word, Margret, it only seems like yesterday that we were doing all this for Anna herself."

"She was a different Anna in those days, Oscar," said Anna.

"Not a bit of it! There's a little more Anna now—that's the only difference."

The Governor came in next—a broad-set man of medium height, with a beard but no mustache, and wearing his official uniform, bright with gold braid. He saluted the Factor and said:

"I have taken the liberty to ask the Bishop, the Rector of the Latin School, and the Sheriff to join us—I trust you don't object?"

"Quite right, old friend," said the Factor. "The most important acts of life ought always to be done in the presence of witnesses."

"And how's Margret? As busy as usual, I see! All days don't come on the same date; we must get ready for you next, you know!"

"For Margret!" laughed the Factor. "She'll have to be quick, or she'll be late then—people don't hatch many chickens at Christmas."

"Late, indeed!" said Aunt Margret, with a toss of her ringlets. "If I couldn't catch up to you folks with your pair of chicks apiece, I shouldn't think it worth while to begin."

The men laughed, and Anna said, "Well, two children would be enough for me if I could only keep them. But that's the worst of having boys—they marry and leave you. A mother can always keep her girls——"

"Until somebody else's boys come and carry them off, and then she sees no more of either," said Aunt Margret.

"That depends on circumstances," said the Governor— "the marriage contract, for example—eh, old friend?"

"Exactly!" said the Factor. "You can generally keep the bull about the place if you have the cow locked up in the cow-house."

The men laughed again, and then the Bishop and the Rector arrived—the Bishop a saintly patriarch with a soft face and a white beard, and the Rector—as became the schoolmaster—sharper, if not more severe.

"I was surprised when I heard it was Magnus," said the Rector. "Oscar has beaten his brother in most things, and I thought he would beat him in getting a wife. And then Thora and he are such friends, too, and so like each other!"

"They get on worst together who are most like each other," said Anna; and Aunt Margret said:

"Stuff! A dark man's a jewel in a fair woman's eye, and what does Thora want with a fair one?"

"But where is Thora?" asked the Bishop.

"She's dressing," said Aunt Margret. "Let us go and fetch her down, Anna," and the two women went up-stairs.

"Magnus ought to be here, too," said the Governor. "Where is he, I wonder?"

"Were you asking for Magnus?" said a voice from the hall. It was the Sheriff—a small man with a sly face, wearing a gold-braided uniform like the Governor's.

"He's at the warehouse, isn't he? Or is he still at the jetty?" asked the Factor.

"No," said the Sheriff entering. "To tell you the truth, when I passed the hotel he was sitting in the smoking-room."

"The smoking-room of the hotel?" said the Governor.

The Factor laughed. "Treating his friends in advance of the event, I suppose! It's bad to let the sledge go ahead of the horse, though."

"No," said the Sheriff again. "To tell you the truth, he was quite alone."

"Drinking?" asked the Governor.

"Nonsense, Stephen! Magnus does not drink," said the Factor.

"I hope not, but I'm always afraid of it. His grandfather on the maternal side, you know——"

"Ah, nobody knows what is inside another's coat," said the Bishop. "Anna's father had some trouble in his head—must have had."

"Even diseases are inherited," said the Governor.

"But the old man drank after he buried his wife, not before he married her," said the Rector.

And then Aunt Margret and Anna returned to the room saying, "Here she is at last!" bringing Thora in her simple velvet costume called the kirtle, with silver belt, bell sleeves, and white lace about the neck.

The Governor took Thora in his arms and kissed her. "But how pale, my child!" he said.

"You may well say so, Governor," said Aunt Margret. "She has been crying since early morning."

"Crying?" said the Factor. "Now, I never can understand why a woman must always cry when she is going to be married; it's such a bad compliment to her husband."

"But I agree with Thora," said the Governor. "If ever there is a time to cry, or, at least, to feel grave and anxious, it is just that moment of life when it is customary to dance and sing as if you were setting out on a triumphal procession instead of taking a leap into the dark."

"And I agree with the Governor," said the Bishop. "When I see a bride crying so bitterly at the altar that she can hardly utter the responses, I generally know she is going to be a happy wife."

"Thora might wait until the wedding, though," said Aunt Margret, and then Oscar came dashing into the room.

"Out walking—lost count of the time—only six minutes to dress—did it in five," he said, in breathless gasps.

"He's another pale one," laughed the Rector. "Has there been a frost overnight that has nipped all our rose-buds?"

"Been running to get here," said Oscar, "but I've raced Magnus it seems."

"Magnus has raced you in another way, my boy," said the Rector, nodding his head toward Thora, who was blushing and looking down; whereupon the Governor muttered:

"Oscar must not dream of marriage yet awhile. He has his career to think about, and he has not been too earnest about it hitherto."

"Well, my experience in business," said the Factor, "is that when a woman marries she slackens off, but when a man marries he tightens up."

At that the Sheriff nudged the Rector, who whispered:

"The Factor has still another daughter, Rector."

"What if he has?" said the Factor. "A man can't have two sisters-in-law to one brother."

"No, but he can give his brother a sister-in-law, too," said the Rector, and then everybody laughed.

"That reminds me," said the Factor, "Helga sent us a photograph the other day. Where is it, Thora?"

"Here it is," said Thora, taking a photograph out of a drawer. Oscar held out his hand for it, and looked at it long and earnestly.

"How fine! I've scarcely ever seen such a splendid face! Quite grown up, too! Is Helga coming home soon, Factor?"

"Not very soon," said the Factor.

And then the lawyer came in with a large portfolio of papers and laid them on the table.

"Ha, ha!" laughed the Rector. "A rich man's child needs a careful christening, it seems!"

"You're right, Rector, and it has taken my clerk the entire day to engross the contract, but it was not that which kept me until now—it was this!"

"The rings!" cried the two elder women, as the lawyer took a small plush box from his pocket.

"Yes, you may remember that when the rings had to be ordered yesterday morning, Magnus could not be found anywhere, so I was compelled to order them myself. Well, I thought I gave careful instructions, but the idea is abroad in the town, do you know, that it is Oscar, not Magnus, who is to marry Thora—nobody believes anything else—so what does Olaf, the silversmith, do but write 'Oscar' on the inside of one of the rings!"

"Never!" said Oscar, trying to laugh with the others.

"Yes, indeed, and the error was not discovered until the very last moment, and then all I could do, as you see, was to have 'Oscar' erased—it was too late to have 'Magnus' inscribed instead."

"Where is Magnus, I wonder?" said the Governor, walking restlessly before the window.

"Don't be anxious about Magnus, Stephen," said Anna. "He grows more and more like my poor father. If father promised to be somewhere at a certain time he would turn up to the minute if he had to kill a couple of ponies in getting there."

The cathedral clock struck five at that moment, and sure enough before the clang of the last stroke had died away Magnus walked into the room. He looked slack and almost untidy in his pea jacket and long boots, and was the only person in the room who had not troubled to dress for the occasion. The Governor's face darkened at sight of him, and the Factor said in a tone of vexation:

"Well, let us get to work and have it over—I've been spoiling for a smoke this half-hour."

The lawyer opened his portfolio, and the company gathered about the table, whereupon Aunt Margret cried:

"Magnus, do you allow of this? Here's Oscar sitting beside Thora."

"Don't disturb him," said Magnus. "This is good enough for me," and he took a low seat by the side of his mother.

"Now, come," said the Factor, "let the one who has the best voice start the singing."

"It must be the lawyer, then," said the Rector, "for every lawyer has a voice of silver—passes it for silver anyway."

And then, amid the general laughter, the lawyer opened the marriage contract and began to read.

XI

THE company listened intently, and at the close of every clause the Governor, who was resting his head on his hand and his elbow on the table, said: "Good!" "Very good!" "Generous!" "Most generous!"

When the lawyer had finished, the other old people leaned back and drew long breaths of satisfaction, but the Governor rose and crossed to the Factor and shook hands with him, saying: "Just like you, old friend!"

The Factor was gratified by the reception of the document and became bright and almost humorous. Imitating the manner of the auctioneer, he cried: "Anybody bid higher? Then going—going—go——"

"Wait!" said the Governor. "Hadn't we better ask the opinion of the young people themselves? After all, they are the persons ultimately concerned, and though a cow seldom kicks when you are carrying her clover——"

There was a general titter, a nodding of many heads and muttered responses of "Just so!" "Just a matter of form!"

"Very well! Thora, what do *you* say?" said the Factor, expecting a burst of rapturous approval, but Thora only answered timidly:

"I don't know. Hadn't you better ask Magnus first?"

"Certainly, my dear—Magnus first, as a matter of course. What do you say, Magnus? Any suggestion to make? Any little improvement? How do you like the contract?"

There was an awkward silence which astonished the older people, and then came a great surprise. Magnus, who had been sitting with his head down, raised a white and firm-set face and answered:

"I do not like the contract at all, Factor, and I cannot sign it."

At this there were looks of bewilderment among the older people, who seemed to be uncertain if they had heard aright, while Thora and Oscar, who partly understood, seemed to be struggling to catch their breath. The Factor was the first to recover his self-possession, and he said, with a slightly supercilious accent:

"Is that so? I thought I knew something of these matters; but if you think you can draw up a better document, Magnus——"

But then the Governor interposed: "Some trifle, no doubt," he said suavely. "Magnus will explain. What is the point you object to, my son?"

There was another moment of tense silence, and then Magnus said in a harsh voice:

"By this contract I am required to live in Iceland all my life—that's slavery, and I will not submit to it."

"But, my dear Magnus," said Anna, "don't you see the reason for that? To all intents and purposes Thora is the Factor's only daughter—his only child—and if she goes away, who is to cheer him up and make home bright for him? Be reasonable, Magnus!"

"Anna, hadn't we better let the young man finish?" said the Factor. "He may have other objections. Have you?"

"Yes," said Magnus. "According to this contract I am to be taken into partnership on marrying Thora, but only on a quarter share. Partnership is partnership, and where there are two partners it should be half and half—I must have half."

The company listened in consternation, and the Factor began to laugh. "Why not?" he said in a cynical tone.

"Everything is hay in hard weather. I'm so hard up for a son-in-law that I shouldn't stick at a trifle."

"Old friend," said the Governor, "let us not be too hasty. Perhaps Magnus has not made himself quite plain."

"As plain as a pikestaff. He wants an equal partnership. But perhaps that is not all. Is there anything else?"

"Yes, there is, sir," said Magnus, in a rather aggressive manner. "By this deed, when you retire I am to take over the business, but I am only to have one-third share of the profits. I must have two-thirds."

"In—deed!" said the Factor. "Do you know I thought if I allowed you to come into the business that I had made, and to work it with my plant and my capital, one-third was generous."

"Most generous!" said the Governor, mopping his forehead. "But Magnus is slow—slow both of thought and speech. He must have some explanation. What do you mean, Magnus? Take your time and speak plainly."

"I mean, sir," said Magnus, "that the barter business in Iceland will break up before long. When the Factor retires—perhaps before—his business will be worth nothing—not even the name, for that will be less than nothing. A new business will have to be created, and if I am to create it I must have two-thirds of the profits, leaving one-third for the use of the Factor's money."

The Factor was losing his temper. "Why any at all?" he said. "Why not kick me out altogether? No use beating a dog with a cheese when a whip is handy."

The company were murmuring at Magnus, when the Governor interposed again. "Magnus," he said, "to say I'm astonished is to say nothing. The Factor has treated you with boundless liberality, but no well is so deep that it can't be emptied, and if you go any farther——"

"Go any farther!" said the Factor. "Why shouldn't he go farther? It isn't fair play between the wind and a straw, but why shouldn't he beat me about a little more? Anything else to ask, sir?"

"Yes," said Magnus, without the change of a muscle. "By this contract my wife is to inherit half her father's fortune at his death—she must inherit the whole of it."

" Good Lord!"

The exclamation seemed to come from everybody in the general chorus of condemnation which followed.

"Are you dreaming?" cried the Governor. "Do you forget that the Factor has another daughter?"

"No, sir, I do not forget it," said Magnus. "But the other daughter has gone away with her mother; she may never come back; and after Thora has spent her life by her father's side—cheering him up and making his home bright, as mother says—and, perhaps, nursing him in his last days— is somebody else, who has done nothing, to sweep off half of all he leaves behind? No! My wife—if I marry—must have everything!"

The older people, both strangers and members of the family, broke into loud expressions of dissent, while the Factor looked round at them, and said, "An eagle isn't displeased with a dead sheep, is it? And so, Mr. Governor's son," he said, wheeling about on Magnus, "these are the only terms on which you will do me the honor to marry my daughter?"

Without noticing the sneer, Magnus answered "Yes."

"Well, I must say I'm deceived in Magnus," said Aunt Margret. "I didn't think he had a selfish thought in his heart."

"I didn't think," said the Factor, who was not laughing any longer, "I didn't think the son of anybody in Iceland could afford to turn up his nose at a daughter of mine."

"Neilsen," said the Governor, firmly, "we have been friends since we were boys, and neither of us knows which will bury the other—don't let us quarrel now over the conduct of our children."

The company murmured approval, and then the Governor turned once more to Magnus.

"My son—for you *are* my son, though I'm at a loss to understand it—you are making a breach between two families by asking these utterly impossible terms! Don't you see they are impossible? Have you taken leave of your senses? Are you quite mad? Or is it true that you have been drinking—that you are drunk? Good God!"

Magnus made no answer, but the painful silence which followed the Governor's outburst was broken by a pitiful cry,

It came from Thora. She understood everything at last; she knew what Magnus was doing for her and the price he was going to pay for it; and she wanted to cry out, but could not; so she dropped her head on Aunt Margret's shoulder and wept bitterly.

Anna mistook Thora's tears for shame and humiliation, and turning to Magnus she said:

"My dear son, you haven't thought of things in the right way or you couldn't do what you are doing. I don't like these marriage contracts myself. It seems like a tempting of Providence to talk about money and business just when two souls who love one another are joining themselves together and becoming one. But you are making it worse, Magnus—you are making it a mere bargain. And, then, think of Thora! If you refuse her father's offer everybody will hear of it, and the poor girl will be shamed. Do you want to see that, Magnus? I'm sure you do not! So come now, for Thora's sake—even though you don't quite like the Factor's conditions, for Thora's sake, Magnus—will you not?"

Everybody waited for Magnus's reply, and even Thora raised her head.

"No," said Magnus, in a voice like a growl, and then he sat with a stolid face while the condemnation of the company fell upon him in a chorus of denunciation. "Infamous!" "Hateful!" "Execrable!" "Damnable!" "The man's heart must be as black as a raven."

Oscar could bear no more. He had been sitting silent, with head down, as if trying to hide his agitated face, while turning Helga's photograph over and over in his restless fingers; but now he rose, walked to the curtains, which divided the front room from the back, parted them with a trembling hand, and looked out over the lake on which the sun was setting.

"Don't go away, Oscar," cried the Governor. "I know you are disgusted with your brother's turpitude; but I want you to speak to him for all that. It is hardly likely that having refused to pay attention to his mother or me, he should listen to you or anybody else, but try him. For the honor of the family, tell him that if he adheres to the attitude he has taken up, he will be an object of hatred and contempt. As long as he lives people will despise him, and his family will be ashamed to acknowledge his name. If he has no love for Thora, see if he has any respect for himself. Speak to your brother, Oscar, for mercy's sake, speak to him."

Oscar's hand on the curtain shook visibly, and he said, with an effort, while all listened without breathing, and Thora's parted lips quivered:

"I cannot do that, father. I do not feel that I have any right. No doubt Magnus knows as well as we do what he is doing, and has counted all the consequences. Everybody has to live his own life."

At this there was a murmur of disappointment, and the Governor, turning away, walked to the window. Then Oscar stepped back to the table, and said, more firmly, yet with as much emotion:

"But if I cannot appeal to Magnus, there is something I can do—I can offer to take Magnus's place. If you and the Factor will consent I can accept the conditions of the contract just as they are, and be only too proud to marry Thora if she will accept me."

At first there were looks of blank amazement about the table, then a general sigh of relief, and everybody seemed to be saying at once, "Good!" "Splendid!" "The very thing!"

"Yes," said the voice of the Governor, husky with emotion, "it is just like Oscar—always doing the great thing! But in a matter which so intimately concerns the boy's future welfare I cannot allow a momentary impulse of generosity——"

"It isn't a momentary impulse, father. Since I came home from England I have learnt to love Thora. But she was engaged to my brother, and I couldn't speak until Magnus had spoken——"

"Honorable!" "Most honorable!" said several voices, and it was with difficulty that Oscar could go on.

"But now—if it is understood that Magnus retires, that is to say, refuses to marry Thora——"

"He does, undoubtedly he does," said the Factor.

"And if Thora will take me——"

Every eye looked toward Thora; she hesitated for a

5

moment, then rose from her chair and timidly held out her hand. Oscar grasped it eagerly and there was a chorus of congratulation.

"But we cannot allow Thora, either, to be carried away by a momentary impulse," said Aunt Margret, who was vigorously wiping her eyes, "and if she's only doing this to escape from a shameful position——"

"I'm not, auntie," said Thora. "I only consented to marry Magnus because my father wished it, but I love Oscar, and if father will agree——"

The Factor's eyes were sparkling with the light of triumph, and he cried across to the Governor, "What do *you* say, Stephen?"

"Well, I must say it's fast ambling—too fast," said the Governor, "but if the young people are satisfied, and if Oscar is content to give up his career in England—his music and his studies—and live in Iceland all his life, it may save a breach between our families and tide us over an ugly reef——"

"Then so be it, godson," cried the Factor, slapping Oscar on the back, "and as for England, I'll take care of that!"

This was received with a shout of approval from the strangers, and then the Factor called to the lawyer to alter the names in the contract and get it signed without delay.

"As for you, sir," he said, turning to Magnus, and snapping his fingers in his face, "your ugly chickens have come home to roost. You thought you could corner me, but your selfishness and worldliness have done the work that everybody seems to have wanted. Ha, ha, ha! he laughs best who laughs last! There's nothing I like better than to dish a man who tries to dish me, and I'll go to bed happy to-night."

Magnus had risen from his low seat and was standing with his head down and his hands on his hips while the storm beat over him, and thinking he was still unmoved the Factor burst upon him again in a tone of biting raillery:

"But if the barter trade is going to the dogs, hadn't you better cut it before the crash comes? Heavy is the fall, you know, when an old man tumbles, and I might crush you coming down. I'll trouble you to leave my house, sir, without a day's delay."

"Father!" cried Thora, and she stepped between them, but the Factor brushed her aside.

"You get away, Thora. If a daughter of mine had done to me what he has tried to do to-day she wouldn't have a roof to cover her to-night."

"Neither shall a son of mine—not in this town, at all events," said the Governor. "Magnus Stephenson——"

"Stephen! Stephen!" said Anna, and Oscar, in the same quivering voice as before, cried out to his father.

"Hold your tongue, Anna! Oscar, be quiet, you've done enough for one day! Magnus Stephenson, when you leave the Factor's house you will go to Thingvellir, and stay there, and thank your stars if for the rest of your life you are allowed to earn your bread by the sweat of your brow."

"The amended contract is ready for the signatures," said the lawyer, and then everybody save one turned back to the table, and there was a cackle of cheerful voices. When the names were all signed and witnessed, the rings were exchanged, and there was some joking and happy laughter.

"All's well that ends well," said the Bishop. "That will do as a pledge between you until you come to me to be made man and wife."

"Supper is ready," cried Aunt Margret, drawing the curtains of the inner room, and then seeing a photograph on the floor beneath them, she said, "but who's been treading on poor Helga's portrait?"

"That's Oscar," said Thora. "He had it in his hand when he got up."

When the company were seated about the supper table it was seen that there was one chair too many, and the Governor pushed it back with an impatient hand. Magnus had gone—no one had seen him go.

XII

ALONE and forgotten, a prey to the devilish voices which had tortured him in the time of his temptation, angry and unsatisfied although he had carried out his purpose and triumphed as he had intended, Magnus was in his room at the top of the house gathering up his belongings by the light of a candle.

They were few and not valuable—a little money, two or three suits of clothes, two or three pairs of riding, fishing, and snow boots, some musical exercise books, the "Book of Job," "The Pilgrim's Progress" (having illustrations of Apollyon with horns), and the precious flute with which he had beguiled those blessed evenings that now seemed to belong to another existence. He had sent for two ponies to take him to the farm—a saddle pony and a pack pony—and two small boxes held everything. When all was packed he came upon the remains of a bottle of brandy which he had kept in his bedroom as medicine, and he drank the spirit and threw the bottle away.

During that short hour of pain and degradation he heard at intervals the various noises of the company at supper below—sometimes in single voices, sometimes in climbing cries like the sounds of a geyser, sometimes in peals of joyous laughter—and his heart grew bitter. He could plainly distinguish Oscar's voice among the rest, at first quiet enough, but afterward loud and hilarious, and his very soul sickened.

"You fool!" said the other voices at his ear. "What did you expect? Did you think he would be overwhelmed with sorrow? He is glad; he'll walk over your head, and over Thora's head, too! Listen to him already—the sweet, unselfish, privileged pet of everybody!"

After the boxes had been sent down-stairs Magnus took a last look round, and then he tried to shut out all bitter thoughts and evil passions, for he believed that he was leaving that room for ever. It had been his home through seven long years, and some of them had been bad years, but some of them had been good, and the good ones filled the little place with memories of many visions.

The slooping roof, the dormer window, the deal furniture, the sheep's skin on the bare floor, and the sunflower pattern on the wall-paper were all ghosts of the dreams he had dreamt there. Some were dreams of the great things he was going to do for Iceland, but more were dreams of Thora, and remembering that both sorts were dead now, and that Thora belonged to Oscar, to save himself from further repining and to crush down the riot that was rising within, he blew out the candle and that chapter of his life was at an end.

But the devilish voices were not yet done with him. Going down-stairs he had to pass the door of the front room on the first landing, and he went by it on tiptoe. For years he had always passed that door on tiptoe, for it was the door to Thora's room, a holy place, half nursery, half sanctuary, as Thora herself had grown to be half saint to him and half child; but he was not thinking of that this time. He was thinking he must get out of the house without seeing her again, for she belonged to Oscar now, and if they were to meet and she began to thank him for giving her to Oscar—but God forbid!

Thora's door was closed, but the next room stood open. It was Aunt Margret's bedroom, and Magnus knew that a photograph of Thora was on the chest of drawers near the door. He had often envied it, and now he stooped to look at it for the last time, and the voices at his ear seemed to say, "Take it; it's all you are going to carry away of her."

Going down the last flight of stairs he heard the two sitting-rooms buzzing like the mill-house, and knew that others must have joined the party; but above all other sounds he heard the sound of Oscar's voice, clear as a flute, saluting people as they came in. "Listen to him! The darling!" said the mocking voices by his side.

Coming to the hall, he encountered some of the women of the town in their feast-day dresses, and with garden flowers in their hands. Hardly any of them looked at him, but all passed into the sitting-room, where Oscar waited to welcome them.

The hat-stand in the hall had been cleared for the newcomers, therefore Magnus had to go to a rail under the stairs for his overcoat and riding-whip, and while he was there Aunt Margret opened the door of the back sitting-room to ventilate the crowded place. She did not see him, for she had taken off the spectacles she usually wore, and he was standing in the shadow, but he saw everybody in the room, and Thora among the rest.

Thora was sitting by the wall, and the townspeople were

going up to her one after another and offering their flowers and making congratulatory speeches. And she was thanking them in her soft voice and looking very happy.

Magnus was hurt by Thora's happiness. He had done all he could to make her happy; he had sacrificed everything; but now that he looked on her happiness he was hurt by it; and when Oscar went and stood by her chair, looking bright and proud, he felt hot with anger and hatred.

While he pulled on his overcoat he could not help hearing what was being said within the room. "Such an extraordinary thing, Thora," said one, "people in the town actually said it was Magnus you were going to marry!" "I heard that, too," said another. "I heard it at Olaf's, the silversmith's, when we were drinking coffee." "Such an idea!" said a third, "as if any girl would marry Magnus who could get Oscar!" And then Oscar's voice, large, expansive, indulgent, almost patronizing, "Tut, tut! You mustn't say anything against Magnus, Elisabet!" "But I hear Magnus insulted Thora this evening, and the Factor has turned him out for it." "Can it be possible? I saw him in the hall as I was coming in!" "No, no, not insulted—not insulted exactly," said Oscar's voice again, and then Magnus, sick and dizzy, turned away.

He was going out of the house with head down when the door of the front sitting-room opened and closed quickly, and he found himself face to face with Thora. She was trying to look sad, but the light of her happiness was still in her eyes, and her parted lips were smiling.

"I heard you were here," she said, "and I couldn't help coming out to see you. Oscar told me yesterday I was not to speak, whatever happened, but it seems so terrible that you should leave us like this."

"We made a mistake, and we had to get out of it somehow," said Magnus.

"I know," said Thora. "And of course I think it will be the best thing in the end. You would have had no joy of me, Magnus, and I should have been very unhappy."

"Perhaps you would," said Magnus.

"But it is a great grief to me that you will have to give up all the schemes you had set your heart upon, Magnus."

"I have given up more than that, Thora," said Magnus, and he tried to push past her and go.

The light of her smile died off her face, and with a wistful look, in a pleading voice, she said:

"I feel as if I am losing a friend, Magnus, and you are saying good-by to me for good."

"Not that exactly," said Magnus.

"Good-by, Magnus!"

"Good-by!"

They were standing with hands clasped in what they believed to be their last parting when the buzz of the inner room broke out upon them again, and a cheery voice cried:

"Thora! Thora! Where are you?—Oh, it's you, Magnus?"

It was Oscar, and at the next moment Thora had gone back, the door of the sitting-room had closed behind her, and Magnus and his brother were together in the hall.

"I meant to come out to you before, old fellow," said Oscar, "but they stuck to me like leeches, and I couldn't get away. I wanted to thank you for what you did for me this evening. It was too generous, too brotherly, and I can never be sufficiently grateful."

Magnus did not answer, so Oscar went on:

"You pledged me to silence, and you were right, plainly right; but, of course, I cannot allow the error about your motive to go much farther, and as soon as it is safe to do so I will set you right. People shall know the truth about what you did, and why you did it; and they will make amends for their mistake."

Still Magnus did not speak, so Oscar continued:

"It's too bad, though, that you should suffer in the meantime, and if there is anything I could do for you—in a material way, I mean—if you are in want of——"

But the dark fire that was rising in Magnus's face frightened him, and he could not finish what he wished to say.

"I don't care a straw what people think I did it for," said Magnus, "and I don't care a damn if they never make amends. *You* know what I did it for, and that's enough for me. I did it for the sake of Thora. I gave her up to you that you might love her and cherish her and make her happy, and be a better husband to her than I could be. But if you don't do it; if you ever neglect her or desert her or give her up for another woman, I'll take her back. Do you hear me?" —(Magnus swayed like a drunken man and laid hold of Oscar's arm)—"I'll take her back, and then—then, by God, I'll kill you!"

Saying this, he walked heavily out of the house, leaving Oscar with white cheeks and gibbering lips, alone in the hall.

His ponies were waiting for him in the street ready for the journey to Thingvellir. The night was dark, but the windows of the house were bright, for the blinds had been drawn and the sashes thrown open. A cackle of many voices came out of them, for the company within was now large and very merry. While Magnus tightened the girths somebody played a guitar, and as he was riding away Oscar began to sing.

PART II

" Impotent pieces of the game he plays
Upon this chequer-board of nights and days;
Hither and thither moves, and checks, and slays,
And one by one back in the closet lays."

I

OSCAR did his best to keep the fire burning in the inner sanctuary—the fire of love and duty—but oftener than he was aware it flickered, and seemed to be in danger of dying out. He tried to tell the truth about Magnus, but as frequently as he thought out a way of doing so he was confronted by the ugly question which would surely be asked: "Can it be possible that you stood passively aside while we condemned Magnus for a vice he was not guilty of, and praised you for a virtue you did not possess?" The humiliation of speech like that would be deeper than the degradation of silence, and from day to day Oscar postponed the painful confession. Thus a month passed, and he had said nothing.

His position would have been easier if he had been getting on better with his work—if he could have felt it impossible that the Factor could regret the loss of Magnus. Then he would have said, "After all, though na.urally you didn't think so at the time, everything has been for the best," whereupon the Factor would have said, "You are right, godson," and after that he would have told all.

But his work was going badly, and there was no blinking the fact that he was a poor business man. On first going into the Factor's, on the footing the contract gave him, he rambled from office to warehouse with aimless and shiftless uncertainty, dressed with Bohemian freedom, and looking like a butterfly in a back alley. Then the Factor said,

"Come, come, young fellow, we must be getting to work; choose a department and be responsible for it."

Oscar selected the export department. This brought him into relation with the farmers, and some of them cheated him unmercifully, concealing their inferior wool in the body of the packs he bought from them. Magnus would have rooted out both the bad stuff and the men who brought it, and they would have gone flying before his threatening face; but Oscar wished to stand well with everybody, and the firm suffered accordingly.

After a week he wished to change. He thought the import department would suit him better: "Very well," said the Factor. "Mistakes are made by the young as well as the old—buckle to at the imports, my boy."

The imports brought him into relation with the mates of steamers and trading ships, and they were quick to shuffle their responsibility for damaged freights onto Oscar's shoulders.

After another week he went back to the Factor and said, "I don't think a department is what suits me best, god-father—why not let me have a general supervision?" The Factor shrugged his shoulders, but replied, "I'm willing. You shall be my right-hand man, then, and I'll ease off as soon as you are ready."

But from that moment onward Oscar did nothing, good, bad, or indifferent. He was always running about like one out of breath, but he came at any hour in the morning and left at any time in the evening, and was always skipping off to see Thora. That little lady was entirely content, but the Factor was heard to say to Aunt Margret, "There was something in Magnus after all, Margret." And Aunt Margret was heard to answer, "Many a good sword is in a bad sheath, you know."

But one day Oscar came flying to the Factor in breathless haste with his mouth full of great news. The Member of Parliament for the town was dead, and the Radical party were already preparing to run a candidate—an out-and-out Socialist named Oddsson, an enemy of the old order in both politics and trade.

"Why shouldn't I go into Althing?" said Oscar. "I could

protect the business against these rascally revolutionaries, and help to preserve the old principles."

" Let me talk to your father first," said the Factor.

The old friends agreed that the scheme was a good one. Not only was the man Oddsson a believer in Magnus's doctrine about the barter trade, but he was the champion of an agitation for establishing a new constitution in Iceland, which would abolish the Governor and set up a Minister responsible to Parliament alone. He must be kept out. In self-defense they must fight the common enemy! Oscar would be a good candidate, being young and bright and clever, and a personal favorite.

" But I cannot appear in the contest," said the Governor.

" Leave it to me," said the Factor, and he went back and told Oscar, who shouted with delight and shot off to tell Thora.

By this time Thora had spent a long month in radiant happiness. If she thought sometimes of Magnus's position, she remembered that Oscar had said he would set things right, and the delay counted for little, because she measured existence by days no longer, but by emotions, and she was conscious of one emotion only—love for Oscar, and therefore for everybody and everything in the world.

As the year was growing elderly and its withering winds made further excursions to the islands of the fiord impossible, they remained at home and romped like children or played the guitar and piano. At such times Thora was not without certain backward thoughts of Magnus, for the room was the same and nothing was different except the hour of the day, but there was always the difference of its being Oscar.

He taught her some Icelandic love songs, and she sang them in a thin sweet treble, which Oscar cheered tumultuously. It did not hurt her in the least that Oscar never took her singing seriously—he did not take Thora herself seriously. He called her " Baby Thora," and she christened him the " Bad Boy."

The moment he had left her sight she would send a letter after him, like a handkerchief he had forgotten. He always replied, and his letters were full of affectionate banter, but perhaps at the bottom of her heart she was a little disappointed with them. They were not quite lover-like enough; there were scarcely any of them she could not read aloud to Aunt Margret; there was hardly one that was her very own.

But Oscar made up for every deficiency when he arrived himself, and on the day when he came with a hop, skip, and a jump into the sitting-room, and announced that he was to be member of Althing, she saw him for one moment great and glorious, like the top of a mountain when it has broken through the mist and the sun has flashed on to it, and then she said, " And now the Bad Boy must play with me—he hasn't played me blindman's buff since yesterday."

Thora was too happy to think of her happiness, but she told herself sometimes that there was only one thing wanted to make it complete—that Helga should come home to share it. She broached the subject to Oscar, but it was at a moment when he was immersed in his manifestoes, and he merely said, " Good idea! Splendid! Helga looks like a stunner! Send for her certainly if the Factor approves," and he went on with his tiresome politics.

She broached it next to Aunt Margret, who was less encouraging. Putting her spectacled face close to Thora's, she shook her ringlets, and said, " Don't be a ninny! Two's company, three's none! "

But Thora mentioned the matter to Anna also, and the motherly old thing was moved. " That would be beautiful if you could manage it, Thora," she said, " and if it should lead to bringing the others together, what a blessing it would be! "

After that Thora regarded herself in the light of the family peace-maker, and in this character she approached her father. The Factor listened to her with sympathy, for nature is stronger than lawyer's ink, and he had often told himself he had been foolish to part with his child. " Well, I don't see why she shouldn't," he said. " She might come for the wedding—or, say for a year—one year at all events. I'll write to the lawyer in Denmark."

By the same mail Thora wrote to Helga:

Dearest Helga:—Father is writing to the lawyer to ask him to send you back to Iceland. It is only for a year, so

I hope mamma will not object. I am sure *you* will not when I tell you what is to happen. There is to be a wedding, and, of course, a party, and great goings on.

Dear, I am to be married to Oscar Stephenson, who has come back from England, and is so handsome and so clever. If you could see him as he is now, you would fall in love with him instantly, but he is so fond of me, and I am so happy. I *was* to have married his brother Magnus, but the engagement broke down, and now I am very sorry for Magnus, and if ever you hear anything against him when you come home you are not to believe a word of it, because Magnus is as good as gold, only *I* could not care for him, so it was no use trying.

Dear, there are such lots of things I want to tell you, but I must save them until you come. We have had bad trade this summer, and Oscar has gone into father's business. I am weaving a web of cloth for father's Christmas suit, but it does not make much progress, because somebody is always interrupting, and when you are about to be married there is so much to do—isn't there?

Dearest Helga, I have no more to write about now, so give my love to mamma, and mind you come before long, for the wedding may be soon, although nothing is fixed yet.— Your affectionate sister, Thora.

P. S.—Come quickly. I am dying to introduce you to Oscar.

A fortnight later the Factor announced that he had heard from the lawyer in Denmark, and Helga was to come by the next steamer.

" The ' Laura,' and she's due on the first of November, and that's the day of the election! " said Oscar.

" What a good omen! " said Thora, and she sang her Iceland love songs all that evening through, for she was very happy.

II

ON the morning of the day when the " Laura " was due, there was no sign of her on the sea, but that was a matter of moment only to Thora, who had been up early and down at the jetty before breakfast. The rest of the little world in which she lived were immersed in preparations for the election and were going about like dogs on the leash before the hunt begins. Oscar was flying to and fro with red ribbons in his button-hole; ponies were coming and going with red ribbons in their bridles, and red flags were hanging all over the town; but, nevertheless, there was a sense of uncertainty everywhere and an atmosphere of intense excitement.

The day opened dull and rayless, with a pale sun behind a slaty sky like a white wafer on an old parchment. An hour before the polling booths opened the Governor called upon the Factor, under pretense of his morning's walk, and said:

"I'm doubtful of the result, Neilsen, and I now see that Oscar was the worst possible candidate to stand for our cause. Everybody who has a grievance against the Governor is going to vote against the Governor's son, and everybody who has a grievance against the Factor will vote against his son-in-law."

"Oh, I know the people, bless them," said the Factor. "Master when you want anything—slave when you don't. But we'll see, Stephen, we'll see!"

After finishing his breakfast comfortably the Factor walked leisurely to his counting-house and called for his ledger. It showed that nearly half of the electors of the town were indebted to him, some of them slightly, others deeply, and not a few beyond hope of payment without pressure or distraint. He counted up their total indebtedness, and it proved to be frightful. "But life is precious when death is at the door," he thought, and lighting his long German pipe, he put the leather-bound book under his arm and strolled quietly across to the polling-station.

As chairman of Oscar's committee the Factor had a right to sit inside the polling booth, but he merely asked to be allowed to take a chair outside the counter to which the voters would come up when they recorded their votes. "A low seat is often easy," he said, sitting with his face to the Sheriff and his back to the door.

When the doors were opened the Factor laid his ledger across his knees and took out a thick blue pencil. Then as each voter came up to the counter and his name was called and looked up in the register, the Factor was seen to turn up the voter's account in his own book and hold his blue pencil over it.

"Whom do you vote for?" asked the Sheriff, "Oscar Stephenson or Jon Oddsson?" and if the voter answered "Oscar Stephenson," the blue pencil was seen to descend in two broad strokes across the account as if cancelling it altogether; but if he answered "Jon Oddsson," it was seen to score the total with a double underline as if marking it for immediate recovery.

The opposition had entered in hot haste, but the effect was instantaneous. A voter would come swaggering up to the counter, call his name in a robustious voice, and then (while waiting for the verification of his right to vote) see the Factor sitting below with his own account open before him, and, understanding everything in a moment, would begin to answer the Sheriff with a faltering, "Odd——," then pause, tremble, mumble "Stephenson," and go stumbling out of doors.

Silently, hour after hour, from the beginning of the day to the end of it, the Factor sat at his task, never once looking up from his ledger and apparently doing nothing but checking, as he had a right to do, the Sheriff's record of the votes. Aunt Margret came to say that dinner was ready, but he answered that he was not hungry. Toward three in the afternoon Thora arrived in great excitement to say that the "Laura" had been sighted outside the head, but he told her to meet her sister herself, and tell her that he did not expect to be home before midnight.

When the cathedral clock struck four the Sheriff rose and ordered the shutting of the doors. The short winter's day had closed in by this time, and while the counting was going on with its monotonous beat in the silence of the breathless room, like the splashing of rain on the pavement—"Stephenson, Stephenson, Oddsson, Stephenson"—the Factor, who had lit his pipe, was pacing the corridor outside, like a man who walks in his orchard when the fruit is ripe.

When the counting was finished the Sheriff told the attendants to open the window, and then the deep hum of a crowd which had been cheering and singing outside, with a noise like the waves breaking on a bar far off, rose to a roar, like that of the sea running up a stony beach. At the next moment everybody was shaking hands with Oscar, a band was beginning to play in the street, and the Sheriff was stepping on to the balcony.

Meantime Thora, fluttering with excitement of another sort, had gone down to the jetty to meet Helga. As soon as the " Laura " had steamed up the fiord and cast anchor outside the town, she put off in her father's white boat and drew up alongside. It was now quite dark, but lights were burning on the steamer and the dark figures of a line of passengers were silhouetted against the sky as they leaned over the rail and shouted to the friends in little boats who had come out to meet them. Thora was sure that Helga must be there, and she wanted to call to her, but her heart was beating so fast that her voice would not answer. At length the ladder was let down, and Thora's boat swayed up to it, and then she climbed up the steamer's side.

" Helga! "

" Miss Helga is below," said a voice out of the darkness, and though she felt a pang of disappointment that Helga was not waiting, she ran down the stairs to the saloon. At the bottom she called " Helga " again, and the stewardess said:

" The young lady is in her cabin."

" Which? "

" Second to the left."

Feeling conscious of increasing disappointment, but still panting in her eagerness, Thora skipped off to the cabin, and then came a shock of surprise.

Somehow she had expected to find Helga a little thing, grown certainly, but still smaller than herself. In her dreams of their first meeting she had pictured herself stooping to kiss Helga, and then in a sisterly-motherly sort of way putting her arms about her waist. But the young lady who came leisurely out of the cabin with her veil down and buttoning her kid gloves, was much taller than Thora and quite dignified and stately.

" Thora! " said the girl.

" So it *is* you—really you? " said Thora.

"Really me," laughed Helga, and then it was Helga who stooped to kiss Thora, who had to lift up her face to her.

Thora's heart was in her mouth in both senses. She looked at Helga again by the dim light of the saloon lamp, and felt herself small and insignificant. Helga was beautiful, with fine features, large gray eyes and rich dark complexion, and Thora felt herself to be plain and commonplace. Helga was fashionably dressed in the Danish manner, with the soft silk things about the neck and bosom which give charm to a charming girl, and Thora felt herself to be dowdy and countrified in her Iceland hufa and stiff velvet cloak.

"Have you come alone?" asked Helga.

"Quite alone," said Thora.

"But hasn't father come with you? Or Aunt Margret? Or that wonderful Oscar? Is there nobody but you?"

"Nobody but me," said Thora, and then, though she felt crushed and small, she delivered the Factor's message and told about the election.

"So that was the meaning of the band we heard as we were sailing up?" said Helga, and at the first moment Thora thought perhaps Helga had hoped it was in honor of her own arrival, but at the next she felt ashamed and foolish.

"We might as well go, then," said Helga, and she swept up the stairs, leaving Thora to follow. It was all so different from what Thora had expected—so utterly different—that she would have given anything to run away and cry.

But going ashore in the boat, she sat at the helm side by side with Helga, and there, the lights being gone, and Thora no longer in awe of Helga's fashion and beauty, she slipped her arm about her sister's waist, as she had always intended to do, and after that they got on better.

When they touched the jetty there was much shouting and scrambling in the darkness, and Thora was nervous and excited, but Helga was quiet and even amused.

"No carriages in this benighted country yet, I suppose?" said Helga.

"No, but I've brought Silvertop to take you up," said Thora.

"And what is there for you?"

6

" Oh, I'll walk—I love walking."

The street at the top of the jetty was thronged with the people who were waiting outside the polling place to hear the result of the election, and when the girls came to the crowd, which was good-natured but boisterous, they found it difficult to plow their way through until a big man stepped before them and swept the people aside like ninepins.

" What a tremendous creature that was," said Helga. " He could have felled an ox, I fancy."

" But didn't you know him, Helga? It was Magnus Stephenson," said Thora.

" Magnus? Why didn't he speak, I wonder?"

They had reached the outskirts of the crowd and were crossing in front of the polling place when the people raised a great shout, for it was the moment when the Sheriff stepped on to the balcony.

" He's going to declare the poll. Shall we wait?" asked Thora.

" It might be amusing," said Helga.

As soon as there was silence the Sheriff read the figures. Oscar had been elected by three votes to one. At this there was another hurricane of cheers, with cries of " Oscar!" " Oscar!" and Thora said:

" Oscar will come next. Shall we wait and see him?"

" Why not? It will be good fun," said Helga, and in the interval Thora patted Silvertop to keep him quiet, and creeping closer to her sister squeezed her hand.

Then Oscar came bounding on to the balcony amidst a wild breaker of applause, and behind him came two men bearing torches, so that his figure and face were plainly visible to the crowd below—his slight, lithe form, his fair hair slightly ruffled, his sparkling eyes, his mobile mouth and the never-failing smile that captivated everybody.

It was thus that Helga saw him for the first time since he became a man, and her face, which had worn a playful expression, became grave.

" How fine!" she said.

Thora could hardly catch the words over the sibilation of the running cheers, but she said:

" He will speak—shall we wait to hear him?"

"Assuredly," said Helga, and when Oscar began with "Fellow townsmen and fellow countrymen," Thora felt Helga's hand shiver and heard her say, "The same voice!"

Oscar's speech was punctuated by applause at the end of every sentence, and when it was finished, and the speaker and the men with the torches had disappeared, Thora spoke to Helga again, but she answered at random, and sat in her saddle like one in a dream.

Somebody else came on to the balcony and had a mixed reception.

"It must be father," said Thora, and then the Factor's voice, utterly indifferent to hostile interruptions, was heard to say that a supper had been prepared at the hotel for the committee of the successful candidate, and they were to go there at once—the new member would follow presently.

With that the crowd broke up, and the girls went their way—Thora clinging closer than ever to her sister, for her heart was warm with love and pride.

"Well," she said, "what did you think of him?"

"Think of him? Oscar?" said Helga. She laughed uncomfortably, and then stooped from the saddle and whispered:

"Only to think that a little thing like you, dear, should capture a man like that!"

Thora laughed also, but she hardly knew whether she was pleased or hurt. A sudden chill had struck her. It was like the breath of the mountain snow which sometimes comes down in summer.

III

THE gods of riot were playing so hard a game with Thora that she was in a fever to introduce Oscar to Helga, and when he did not appear by noon of the following day she sent a letter across to Government House to order him to come forthwith. The "Bad Boy" was too full of his silly politics, while there was something far more charming and absorbing waiting for him there. But an answer came back from Anna to say that Oscar was still asleep, and after the excitement of the day before, and the late hour of the previous night, she was unwilling to waken him.

Early in the afternoon Anna herself came over expecting to see the first-fruits of the peace-making, and, while Aunt Margret was below stairs preparing chocolate for the company that was expected, the motherly old thing tried various artful ways of finding out from Helga what her upbringing had been in Denmark, and, particularly, what religious instruction and society her mother had given her. Helga saw through the device in a moment, and with her red lips a little awry she painted an alarming picture of theaters and concert-halls, and a flat in Copenhagen frequented by actors and actresses, especially on Sunday evenings, where everybody, including the ladies, smoked cigarettes and drank brandy.

Meanwhile Thora watched for Oscar out of the sidelight of the projecting window, and as soon as she saw him swinging down the road, she darted into the hall and threw herself into his arms and kissed him, whereupon, with his head full of his victory, he said:

"Congratulations, eh? The sweetest I've had yet," and pushed through toward the drawing-room.

"Wait, wait, wait! Somebody to show you!" cried Thora.

Then the poor victim of God knows what maleficent powers—not knowing what she did, but laughing merrily as if a song-bird had been imprisoned in her throat—began to play the old familiar trick of children; standing behind Oscar on tip-toe in order to reach, she put her hands over his eyes, and crying, "Forward, soldier!" marched him blindfold into the drawing-room and up to the place where Helga was waiting. Then, removing her hands sharply, she cried, "There!" and stood off to see the effect.

Oscar found himself face to face with a girl as unlike Thora as could be, tall, dark, with hair parted at the side and hanging over the forehead, dressed in a light silk blouse and silver-grey skirt, and having an odor of violets about her.

"Helga! Can it be possible?"

He stretched out his hand and Helga took it, and held it, and so they stood for some moments, while Thora, breathing rapidly, watched the changing lights in their faces: in Oscar's, astonishment, admiration, and rapture: in Helga's, curiosity, satisfaction, and delight. And Thora's own face, too—to the pitying angels who alone were looking at it— showed expressions just as various: pride, joy, then uneasiness, and finally a little twinge of secret pain.

To relieve this feeling, Thora burst into laughter, and then everybody laughed, and Aunt Margret came into the room with the chocolate and cakes.

"So you've brought them together again, Thora?" said Aunt Margret, and Thora swallowed a lump in her throat and answered, "Yes."

Then Oscar and Helga went over to the window and talked together with great animation. Thora heard snatches of their conversation as she carried round the cups. It was about things of which she knew nothing—Denmark, Copenhagen, England, London, Oxford, the English theater, the Danish theater, and, above all, music, music, music.

"How well they get along," said Thora.

"Trust them for that," said Aunt Margret.

Toward dusk the Factor returned home—not having altered his habit of work by a hair's breadth; and then came half the great people of the town—the Bishop, the Sheriff, the Rector of the Latin School, and finally the Governor. Helga moved among them with the quiet ease of one accustomed to company. Within an hour she had captured all the men, but the women were less sure of her.

"The minute I set eyes on her," whispered Aunt Margret to Anna, "I said to myself, 'Thora is a Neilsen out and out, but there's more of the stranger in this one.'"

"She's the living picture of what my wife was when I saw her first," said the Factor in a low tone to the Governor, who answered significantly, in the same low tone:

"Then I don't wonder, old friend—I say I don't wonder!"

"Helga's head and yours were nearer together when I laid my hand on them last," said the Bishop to Thora. "Take care! Your sister is running away from you, little one."

"Isn't she?" said Thora.

Thora did not feel quite so happy in Helga's visit as she had expected, but still struggling to show her off, she asked her to play something on the piano—she had played after breakfast and it was beautiful.

Helga played brilliantly, and Oscar, who turned over her music, applauded her boisterously.

"And now Oscar ought to play something," said the Governor. "From his earliest years he made us conceive the highest hopes that he might become a great musician."

"He will, too—my son Neils at the College of Music says he will," said the Sheriff.

"Nonsense!" said the Factor. "Oscar has something better to do now than to scrape catgut or blow his lungs through a steam-pipe."

"Still, an occasional flirtation with the muses," said the Rector, "you wouldn't object to that, Factor?"

"I would object to flirtations of all sorts," said the Factor, "and I should think the man a fool who put himself in the way of them."

"Surprising how many men do," said the Governor with a wink at the Rector. "Would you believe it—a certain friend of yours wrote a poem in the days of his youth!"

"Never!" cried the Rector, and while the old people laughed, the Factor said:

"When I was a child I behaved as a child, but when I became a man I put away childish things."

"Well, I so far agree with the Factor that I think a man can't have his heart in two places at once," said the Governor. "What do you say, Thora?"

"I suppose not," said Thora.

"Certainly not, any more than a man can love two women at the same time," said the Governor; and then Oscar began to play.

He played as the bird sings because the song is in the soul of it, and when he had finished, the company cheered him lustily, and Helga, putting her face close to his, said in a whisper:

"And *you* asked *me* to play—I who only play as I am taught, and you can play like that!"

Oscar was delighted with Helga's praises and suggested that they should play together. They played a difficult selection, full of flourishes, and the company declared they had never heard anything like it.

"Wonderful, wasn't it?" said somebody.

"Yes, wasn't it?" said Thora.

She was feeling utterly eclipsed and forgotten when Helga wheeled round on the music-stool and said:

"And now Thora must give us something on her guitar— Aunt Margret says she plays it beautifully."

"Indeed she does—beautifully!" said Aunt Margret.

But Thora begged off in alarm, saying, "No, indeed, no! I couldn't possibly play after playing like that."

So Oscar and Helga began again. This time it was an English ballad. Helga played the accompaniment, and Oscar sang the air, and there was a chorus which they gave together. The company were completely carried away. "Charming!" "Exquisite!" "But how well their voices harmonize!" "They might have been meant by nature to go together!"

"Might they not?" said Thora.

"But now Thora ought really to play her guitar," said Helga.

"Certainly! Thora and her guitar," said Oscar. "And let her sing one of her Iceland love songs to it."

It was cruel, it was heart-breaking, it was almost as if Helga were trying to humiliate her, as if Oscar were joining her, as if they were conspiring together to expose her inferiority.

"No, no, don't ask me, please don't," she pleaded.

But Helga continued to ask and Oscar to second her, and being able to bear the strain no longer, Thora burst into tears, and fled from the room.

"How extraordinary!" said Helga.

But Oscar followed Thora and coaxed and comforted her and brought her back with a smile on her face, although the tears were scarcely dry in her eyes.

"I was silly," she said. "I don't know what came over me."

"Perhaps it was the heat," said the Governor, and he opened one of the windows.

IV

DURING the next month Oscar was every day and nearly all day at the Factor's, to the total disregard of his public work and the complete neglect of business. But his visits were not always to Thora, who was ceasing to be "Baby Thora" either to him or to any one, and becoming a serious little figure with a wistful face. She never romped about the house now, but sat in a corner with a ball of wool in her lap and a crochet hook in her hand while Oscar and Helga played the piano and talked music.

It was music, music, always music at the Factor's in those days. Early in her visit Helga brought down a pile of the music of Wagner, and Oscar was completely carried away by it. Other composers produced beautiful harmonies, a subtle and clever combination of sweet sounds, but when Oscar played Wagner, the piano seemed to him to waken and weep, to burn the flame under his fingers.

"It's glorious!" he would say. "I can never thank you enough, Helga. It's a new world, a new revelation."

Helga had heard of Oscar's songs from the Sagas, and one day she said, "I wonder you don't try to compose something yourself, Oscar—something in the style of Wagner—I'm sure you could."

Then with diffidence and apologies Oscar produced his 'prentice efforts, and Helga praised them enthusiastically. "Do you know you are a born musician?" she said. "And you should never do anything except create music—never!"

Oscar was intoxicated by her applause, but he only laughed and said,

"Ah, that's impossible."

"Why impossible?"

"Parliament—public duties—and so forth."

"But, my dear Oscar, you don't mean to say you are going to waste your life like that?"

"Do you call it waste, Helga?"

"Not for everybody—not for a man like Magnus, for example—but for you, yes," said Helga, and then, with irresistible drollery, she mimicked the manners of Parliament, with its " Mr. Speaker, permit me to rise to a point of order," and " Will the honorable and learned member explain," and all the other inanities of a legislative assembly in a little country.

Oscar laughed until tears (from more springs than one) began to roll down his cheeks, and then he said—

" What an actress you would make, Helga! But principles, my dear girl, principles are the soul of politics, and if a man can guide his country in the higher paths, he can afford to forget the plains—don't you think so, Thora?"

And Thora, who had been feeling dizzy and faint, answered in a helpless way, " Yes, Oscar. But I forgot to tell you that father wished to see you on business."

" Business!" cried Helga. " That, too!"

" Then you object to business also?" asked Oscar.

" For you—certainly, because you are not fit for it," said Helga. " And if you go into business you'll be like a man who has married the wrong woman. She may be an excellent, thrifty soul, quite suitable to somebody else, but she was never meant for him."

" There's something in that, though it's wonderful how you know it," said Oscar. " I'm about the silliest beggar at a bargain that ever breathed out of an oyster shell."

" Of course you are, Oscar—you must be. Now, if Magnus had gone into business he might have got something out of it. But you—what in the world do *you* expect to get?"

" Ah, now you're wrong, Helga! I have got something out of it already—I've got Thora!"

" Thora?"

" Didn't you know? Thora was the prize I was bidding for when I took over that contract."

" So that was it—was it?" said Helga; and then Thora herself, feeling sick and ill, gathered up her work and stole out of the room.

Nevertheless the seed which Helga had sown had not fallen on stony ground. Within twenty-four hours Oscar appeared with a new composition in his hands.

" An idea came to me last night and I had to get it off," he said, and then he sat down to the piano and played.

"Beautiful!" cried Helga. "Really beautiful! But this subject suggests the organ—why not set it to that, and try it on the organ in the cathedral?"

"Splendid idea!" said Oscar. "Thora knows the curator and can get the key. What do you say, Thora?"

"If you would like to," said Thora, and next day they carried out their scheme.

Oscar and Helga sat together in the organ loft, while Thora was sent down the communion steps to report the effect at a distance. "How did that go, Thora?" cried Oscar, once or twice at the beginning, and Thora answered, "Very nicely, I think," but then the two in the organ loft forgot her altogether in the rapture of their rehearsal.

During the next two or three weeks Oscar and Helga went to the cathedral every day, and sometimes Thora went with them, but more frequently she remained at home. A sudden wave of energy seemed to lift Oscar out of himself, and he produced one composition after another. Helga applauded all of them, and her praises intoxicated him like glory.

"I can never be sufficiently grateful to you, Helga," he said, "for all the good things you have poured out on me since you came back to Iceland. You have given my life a new joy, a new splendor!"

"Nonsense!" said Helga. "I am nothing but a voice to awaken your genius. You were born to create music, and whatever happens you must never, never throw away a life which has the glory of a future like that."

To this, and such as this, he always answered "Ah, no!" or "Impossible!" or "It's past praying for," but Helga's words were as the very incense of the dreams which, in vaguer forms, he had been trying to forget since the day he engaged himself to Thora.

"Why shouldn't there be another Wagner, an Icelandic Wagner, a Wagner with a still grander scene and still greater stories—the Sagas and Eddas of this stern old land?"

About a month after Helga returned to Iceland she suggested to Oscar that he should write an anthem on a passage which she selected from one of the Sagas. It was that in which the old gods of the Pagan world, in anger with the family of man for permitting the establishment of Christianity, tore open the bowels of their fruitful valleys with earthquakes, and deluged them with molten lava, and how Christ came through the chaos saying, " Let there be peace! "

" Great! Glorious! A stunning subject! But can I do it? " said Oscar.

" You can, you must," said Helga, and from that moment a continual fever burned in Oscar's blood until the task was done. Thora saw nothing of him for days, except when he bounded in to run over a part of his score with Helga, and then away, without a word, to his work again. When the anthem was written and he was ready to try it on the organ, he said:

" Are *you* coming across to the cathedral to-day, Thora? No? Perhaps you had better not. We'll have to go over the thing again and again—it might be tiresome."

It was the afternoon of a dull week-day in the early winter, and some of the dreary noises of the work-a-day world followed Oscar into the cathedral. A vessel was unloading in the fiord—he could hear the rumble of the iron trolleys as they rolled up the paved jetty to the Factor's warehouse. A new house was being erected on the corner of the cathedral square—he could hear the thin clank of the mason's trowel. A steamer was on the stocks in the shipyard down the harbor—he could hear the sharp beat of the riveter's hammer.

But there was another atmosphere in the cathedral, and Oscar floated on it as on a flood—the silent sanctuary, the rows of empty pews going up to the chancel, the empty pulpit with its sounding-board, the empty altar with the Eastern subject painted above it, the marble font for the baptism of future generations, the marble monuments to the memory of past ones, and then the listening air, awakened by a whisper or a footfall, and full of the breath of dead prayer and vanished praise.

In this atmosphere of art and religion Oscar sat down at the organ, with Helga by his side, to try his anthem for the first time. The organ throbbed under his fingers, the empty cathedral shook like a sea-cave under the boom of his waves of sound, and when he came to the end of his first reading he was quivering with excitement and Helga was in a fever.

"What did I tell you?" she said. "Was I not right? Oh, if this could be heard in Denmark!"

"Or in England!" said Oscar.

They played the piece again and again, and at every fresh playing their excitement increased until it reached the point of hysteria, and their voices in that silent place became as shrill as the wind on the mountain top. At last they tried the words, and then their emotion knew no limit.

The organ trembled and throbbed again, and then on the top of all other sounds came the sound of Helga's voice, like a human cry above the thundering waves of nature, sometimes weeping, sometimes raging, sometimes crouching, sometimes springing out of the surge, and finally sinking down to the soft whisper of "Let there be peace!"

When the anthem was over and all was still, Oscar sat quiet for some moments while the unheard echo of the music seemed to roll through the silent air; and then the lightning-flash of joy or madness which comes to every man of genius once in his life came to him also, and his heart cried out, in its delirious happiness, "I, too, am a great composer!"

In the intoxication of that moment, Oscar's hand swung down and took Helga's hand and held it, and their fingers trembled together and they seemed to hear the beating of each other's heart. They looked at each other, and his eyes were bloodshot and hers were wet.

"Helga!" he cried.

"Oscar!" she answered, but at the next moment a window blew open on the staircase to the organ loft and Oscar heard again the dreary noises of the work-a-day world without— the rumble of the iron trolleys, the thin clank of the mason's trowel, and the quick beat of the riveter's hammer. It was like the wakening of a prisoner in his cell when the warder beats at the door and the dream of glory is gone and the prison walls close round him again.

Oscar's fingers slackened, and the next moment he heard Helga's rapid breathing behind him, and her voice saying with a strange bitterness:

"Is that Thora?"

He started and turned. "Where?" he asked.

"Down there by the communion steps—by the altar. No, I was mistaken. It's only a shadow. The light is fading."

Then with the same bitterness she said, "But I suppose she will be there soon, and you with her."

Oscar shuddered as if a wounded artery had been torn open, and Helga continued:

"Then you will go back to business, and Oscar—Oscar Stephenson, the musician—will be dead."

He fingered the organ stops fumblingly, and made no reply, whereupon Helga, with undisguised irony, began to picture the dull routine of the business life that was waiting for him after marriage—its calculations of discounts, its squabbles with farmers, its buying and selling of pots and pans.

"It is such a pity," she said.

"Don't torture me, Helga," he cried.

"But is there no way out of it?"

"No, no, no!"

"No way at all, Oscar?"

"Let us go," he said, and he had got down to the door before he remembered that he had left his hat behind him in the organ loft.

Thora had tea ready when they got back to the Factor's. She was kneeling before a cozy fire, making toast, after cutting the bread and butter, and she looked up at them as they entered with a nervous, questioning, tearful smile.

"Poor little soul! She must never know—never, never!" thought Oscar.

V

THORA knew already, and the big heart in her little breast was breaking. She had begun to think that what had happened to Magnus when Oscar came back was now happening to her—Oscar was falling in love with Helga, and she, like Magnus, was being left alone.

Yet she could not reconcile herself to this suspicion without a hard battle, and the first skirmish of the sweet heart was to fight for the enemy—Oscar had made a great, great sacrifice when he agreed to marry her; it was not to be wondered at if he had spasms of regret sometimes. She hinted as much to Aunt Margret in one of the long hours in which they were left together.

"Don't you think that Oscar was very unselfish when he signed that contract?" she said.

"Unselfish? I don't call it unselfishness to sign yourself into a fortune," said Aunt Margret.

"But he had to take up the business, you know."

"Certainly he had—the best business in Iceland."

"Helga seems to think it is a little beneath him, Aunt Margret."

"It's good enough for Helga's father, and he made it. Besides, Oscar had nothing else, and an ugly sheep is better than no mutton."

"Oh, yes, he had his music, auntie, and Helga thinks that was a good deal."

"Does she, indeed? People who are naked needn't go about mending other people's clothes. Oscar's music wouldn't have brought him a penny of profit, and as for honor—what about Althing, and all the other things he couldn't have got without being rich?"

"So you don't think Oscar sacrificed himself very much when he signed the contract?"

"Sacrificed himself? Perhaps the boot was on the other leg, if you ask me."

Thora was happy for days after this interview, and while Oscar and Helga played their Wagner, she went about the house singing her little love ditties, and thinking of the time when Parliament would begin its session, and Oscar would throw himself into politics, and become Speaker, and perhaps Governor, and it would all come of having married her.

But it was hard to sit for hours in the same room with people who were scarcely conscious of her presence, and though Thora tried to hide her pain lest Oscar should feel ashamed, she sometimes felt bitter about Helga, and wanted to burst out on her. The only thing which restrained her from doing so was a sweet doubt which she cherished in the most secret chamber of her heart that perhaps she was mistaken after all, and Oscar did not really care for Helga.

"Auntie," she said, "don't you think it's silly to be jealous?"

"Depends upon circumstances, Thora."

"If a wife—for example—fancies her husband is paying too much attention to another woman—don't you think she is silly to be jealous?"

"She's silly to show she is, my precious. It doesn't prevent the sting to bite the head off the serpent, and if a wife shows the husband she's jealous, she's just doing what the other woman wants."

"So you think she ought to be quiet and say nothing?"

"Certainly, I do. If the man is going to run away from her, she had better let him run, and if he isn't, he'll be the more ashamed because he thinks she doesn't know."

"You mean that if the man is only fascinated for a time——"

"Just so! Fascination may be good enough for a flirtation, but it's like bright metal—it soon gets tarnished in a damp cellar. You want gold for the dark places, my honey."

"That is to say, auntie dear, that love is the only thing for married life?"

"I should think so, indeed, with its crosses and disappointments, and children and croup, and all the rest of it. And when it comes to marrying, the silliest of the men know that, bless them!"

"What a lot you know about the men, auntie darling—I wonder you never married, yourself, dear."

"That's why, my precious!"

It was easier for Thora to veil her agonies with smiles after this conversation. She pictured to herself the time when her love would be everything to Oscar. In the secret places of her soul she thought of the days when children would come, and perhaps even sickness, and they would be drawn close—so close—together, because the dear clouds of life hung over both of them. She was not beautiful, she was only a homely and humble little thing, she was unworthy of Oscar, and there were so many things in which she was inferior, but oh, her love was wonderful! Nothing in the world was so wonderful as her love. It would work miracles, it would be stronger than death, it would stand by Oscar to the end.

But all the same it was hard to receive her wounds without a cry, and when Oscar and Helga went off to the cathedral and left her at home she told herself she was too ignorant to be Oscar's wife, and all her sweet, heroic love was wasted.

"Don't you think Helga is very clever, Aunt Margret?"

Aunt Margret lifted her eyes from her knitting, and blinked through her spectacles.

"Clever?—a girl who can't darn a stocking or boil a potato!"

"But see how she can talk, auntie."

"So can the parrot, my dear, and the raven is seldom sparing of his voice either."

"But surely a man wants his wife to be a companion, auntie—to be able to converse with him on the subjects he is interested in, and to criticise his work, perhaps."

"Does he? Perhaps he does, but it would be a crazy creature of a man who would rather marry a critic than a cook for all that."

Always after this Thora had tea ready when Oscar and Helga returned from the cathedral, and if her heart had its tremors, still she tried to take care that Oscar should never see a tear in her eyes. But many a time when she felt herself to be like an isthmus between the two, holding them together, yet keeping them apart, the strung bow of her will slackened and she was nearly breaking down. She waited day by day for Oscar's heart to speak to her, and when it did not speak she told herself it was because Helga was so beautiful.

"Isn't Helga beautiful, Aunt Margret?"

"Perhaps," said Aunt Margret.

"You *know* she is, auntie. You know she is the most beautiful girl in Iceland."

"Maybe I do—maybe I don't!"

"What an advantage beauty like Helga's gives to a girl—she gets everything and everybody. If a girl is only beautiful enough, she has all the men at her feet."

"They must be chiropodists, then, and there are not many of them in these parts. No, no, beauty isn't everything, Thora, and that's a mercy for some of us."

The color began to mount to Thora's eyes, and catching sight of this flag of distress, Aunt Margret continued:

"But fine feathers make fine birds, and I know some in Iceland dress would make Helga look small if they were done up in her Danish folderols."

Thora's blushing face began to shine like the sunrise.

"But what's the use? Beauty fills the eye, but not the belly."

"Auntie Margret, what plain things you say!"

"Do I? Then it's best to say them plainly. It isn't good to gild copper with gold, my honey."

After this talk with Aunt Margret, Thora was more the mistress of herself than before, because the dividing line between Helga and herself seemed less. She made up her mind that she would dress in the English manner, so that Oscar should not see so much difference.

She had money—the dress money her father gave her. It was not very much, but in previous years she had given away most of it, and this year she had intended to buy a Scotch overcoat for Hans, the sailor, who was losing all respect for himself and going about in cold weather with nothing over his shirt. But now she would be selfish, she would spend her money on herself, and that was only right since it was spending it on Oscar also.

It must be a secret, a great secret; it must come upon everybody as a surprise, because that would be half the battle. So she bought postal orders with her savings, and sent to Edinburgh for a costume such as she saw in the picture of a trade advertisement.

The costume came by a trading steamer, and she was like a child in her secrecy and joy, smuggling the big cardboard box up-stairs to her room, and answering the inquisitive questions of the Factor and Aunt Margret with mysterious little nods and subterfuges.

The day was crisp and frosty, and when Oscar, coming in the afternoon, suggested a walk to the lake to try the ice for skating, Helga responded readily, but Thora said no,

7

she had something to do, something important—a little surprise, they should see when they came back again.

As soon as Helga and Oscar had gone, and Aunt Margret had promised to make tea, Thora stole up to her room, locked the door, opened the box, and took out the new garments that were to work the wondrous change. They were beautiful, they were dreams, they were lovelier than anything of Helga's—a blue voile dress with a silk corsage and embroidered yoke. The pleated skirt was like the sun's rays over Hecla after a shower of summer rain, and the silk of the blouse was as beautiful as the ice of a glacier with the flowery bubbles of air in it.

Thora laughed for joy, and taking off her old Iceland costume she threw it aside as a thing she had done with—the granny skirt, the stiff treya, and the starchy brjest. She wondered how she could have worn them so long, and even told herself what she would do with them—she would give them to a young widow who had lately lost her child by diphtheria and joined the people at the Salvation shelter.

When she took up the new garments she had some doubt as to how they were to be put on, and almost wished she had inquired of Helga. The accordion skirt was easy enough, and its ample train made her feel tall and imposing, but the blouse was a besetting trouble. It fastened behind, and after despairing efforts to catch the hooks and eyes she was tempted to call Aunt Margret; but she thought no, that would never do, so she struggled on.

The room was cold, but when she had finished dressing her face was flushed and heated. She had put on her silver belt, because it was a present from Oscar, and brushed her hair sideways over the forehead, because that was how Helga wore it. Then looking at herself in the glass she laughed again, for she was proud and happy.

What would Oscar say when he saw her? He would say, "Why, this is Helga! Another Helga! Not quite so tall perhaps—but just—yes, really just as nice-looking!" And then Helga would be angry, and envious, and perhaps go back to Denmark.

She was walking to and fro on tiptoe, glancing with

sparkling eyes at her figure in the glass, when she heard voices in the hall below.

"Thora!" cried somebody from the foot of the stairs. It was Oscar.

"I'm coming," she answered.

"What about the great surprise?"

"Presently!" she cried.

She waited until she heard a door close below, and then, still laughing a little, but breathing rapidly, feeling sure of victory, yet with a fluttering at her heart, she went down the stairs, and sailed into the sitting-room.

Oscar was leaning on the marble stove, and Helga, sitting on a low seat, was warming her feet at the fire. They turned to Thora as she entered, and looked at her with wide eyes. There was a moment of chilling silence, and then Thora, breathing faster and faster, said:

"Well, what do you think of it?"

Helga began to laugh, first in a smothered titter, but finally in an outright roar, whereupon Oscar, who had struggled not to smile, caught the contagion and joined her.

Thora's pitiful face fell, and she said, with a crack in her voice:

"But what are you laughing at, Oscar?"

"My dear, dear child!" said Oscar; and Helga, who was still laughing, said:

"A little milliner! It makes her look like a little milliner!"

"No, no, not that," said Oscar. "But it's not Thora. Thora is a sweet, simple Iceland maiden whose charm is her simplicity, whereas this——"

"I see," said Thora, and with her heart in her mouth she turned to go.

Oscar stepped to the door to stop her, but with the shrill cry of a hare that is wounded to death she flung out at him and passed through. She went up-stairs with a slow step, took off her English costume, put it back in the cardboard box, and pushed it under the bed—crying a little and wiping her eyes.

She knew the truth at last—she knew where she stood in Oscar's mind. A simple Iceland maiden—that was all he had ever seen in her! It was she who had merely fascinated him, and Helga whom he loved!

When the door of the sitting-room closed on Thora, Oscar looked at Helga and said:

"Whatever has come over her?"

"Don't you see?" said Helga.

"Why, no—what is it?"

"How stupid these clever boys can be! I could tell you in three words."

"Tell me, then—tell me."

"Thora is jealous."

"You don't mean that?"

Helga's face flushed; she looked up at Oscar, and a mysterious thrill went through him. The great surprise had come indeed.

VI

OSCAR slept badly that night. For two months he had been moving in a garden of dreams, where the odor of sweet flowers overpower the senses, but he was awake at last, and was being dragged to trial in a tribunal of his own creating. In that court of conscience he was both righteous judge and guilty prisoner, and through the long hours of broken sleep, when he saw his life and motives as by flashes of lightning, he asked and answered some terrible questions:

Is Thora's jealousy justified?

No, yes! That is to say—I may have neglected her—thoughtlessly neglected her.

Do you love Helga?

It isn't necessary to think that. I admire her—I admire her beauty, and her intellect, but——

Then you do *not* love her?

I love her society—I love to be with her; she is bright and brilliant; we have many interests in common.

Then if you do not love Helga, why not cut her off rather than see Thora suffer?

I can't! I can't!

So you *do* love Helga?

Yes! Yes! I do love her.

Then what about Thora?

I am sorry for Thora—very sorry.

Have you ceased to love her?

Don't say that. My feeling for Thora is the same now as it has always been.

Then you have *never* loved her?

I thought I did—I sincerely thought I did.

So your feeling for Thora was an illusion?

A most unfortunate illusion, and I am troubled about her—I shall always be troubled about her.

But you are betrothed to her?

God help me, so I am!

What are you going to do now?

What am I going to do? I am—yes, I am going to obey the commandment of Nature. Accident and error and illusion have betrothed me to the wrong woman, but must I hold to her after I have found out that I do not love her? No! She is sweet and loving, and I have no fault to find with her, but I must obey the law of my heart, and who shall judge me if I do that?

But what about the law of the land—you have signed a contract to marry Thora?

Even so, is marriage like any other worldly transaction? Are you bound to go on merely because you have begun? Can human hearts be dealt with like so much merchandise?

So you do *not* intend to marry Thora?

I cannot—it is impossible—now that her sister has appeared before me, I see too well I do not love her.

But *she* loves *you!*

That is the pity of it. Poor Thora!

She thinks you are slipping away from her?

It is very pitiful—I see how I have made her suffer.

What will happen if you leave her altogether?

Her heart will break—her tender, sweet, child heart will break.

Can you break Thora's heart?

No, no, no! Better break my own!

Then what are you going to do?

I must go on with the marriage. I see now that I must—it is my duty—there is no help for it.

Wait! There is something you have not thought about. If you go on with your contract and marry Thora, you must be prepared to live her life.

I know! I know! And I am not fit for it! Good or bad, I am not fit for it!

But if you break your contract, and do not marry Thora, you may live the life of Helga.

Yes, yes, and I am fitted for that life above everything else. It thrills me, it inspires me, it lifts me up.

The one is the lower life, while the other is the higher life.

I cannot bear to think of it.

You know that if you marry Thora you condemn yourself for ever to the lower life, and give up all hope and all thought of the higher one?

Don't torture me! Don't torture me!

But the higher life will be a life consecrated to self, whereas the lower life will be a life devoted to self-sacrifice—which is it to be?

That settles it—I must go on with the contract, whatever the consequences.

When Oscar awoke in the morning from his restless sleep he thought he saw his way clearly. There was only one solution of the hard problem of his iron destiny—he must sacrifice himself! He was betrothed to Thora, and he must go on with the marriage. He loved Helga, but he must tear her out of his heart. He wished to be a musician, and to live the higher life, but he must be content with the lower life and do his duty.

A few irresistible pangs of regret, a few tears which he could not quite keep back, and then, feeling a certain satisfaction with himself, a certain pride in his self-sacrifice, Oscar went early to his work.

It was the autumn caravan time, when the farmers come with the last of the year's tallow and wool to have their accounts made up and settled. The offices and warehouses were like a market-place, and there was work for everybody. Oscar threw himself into the day's doings with astonishing energy, and when the Factor returned from breakfast he bantered him on his industry. "Better late than never, though," said the Factor, " and a good day in the autumn is worth two in the spring."

Oscar spent the morning in the office helping at the accounts. His part was to reconcile the farmers to their balances, for many of them were dissatisfied, and nearly all were in the Factor's debt. Some grumbled at the rate they received for their produce, others at the price they paid for foreign goods. Oscar's task was to persuade, cajole, and comfort them, and finally to draft the notes of hand on the bankers with which they discharged their debts. He felt mean and miserable.

Toward noon Helga sent a messenger to say that she hoped to rehearse some of the new music in the cathedral in the afternoon and to ask if Oscar would go with her. He answered that he could not, business was pressing, and he must stick to his work. It cost him a pang to send back this answer, but he had made his bed and he meant to lie on it.

He spent the afternoon in the warehouse, where the produce brought by the farmers was weighed and stacked away for the winter. The odor of the tallow and wool, mingling with the smell of the men's clothes and the reek of their bodies, made the atmosphere close and noisome, and to freshen the air Oscar ordered the big doors to be thrown open.

All at once through the clear, crisp winter air outside came the sound of the organ being played in the cathedral, and that was the last drop in his cup. It was like a voice calling him out of the lower world he lived in to the higher one he yearned for. It was like Helga beckoning to him in his unblessed surroundings, and through the roll of the music he could see her face.

For the first time Oscar was feeling bitterly about Thora, as if he were a prisoner and she were his jailer, when a man rode up to the warehouse door on a bright chestnut pony, with a line of pack ponies behind him. It was Magnus, and seeing him stand outside the counter, which he had formerly stood within, Oscar felt some qualms of shame, and called him into the scalesman's office.

The interview between the brothers was brief and commonplace, but every simple word seemed to throb and scorch like a flame. Oscar asked how Magnus was getting on at the farm, and if he had good servants, and Magnus answered "Yes"; he had always been fond of farming, and for servants he had only the old ones, and everything was as before. Oscar asked if the Governor had made satisfactory arrangements, and Magnus said he had, that the farm was his own now on terms of tenancy, and was to become his property at the old people's death.

"And how are you getting on here?" asked Magnus.

"I? Oh—pretty well, I think."

"You like the work?"

"Yes—well—not to say like, perhaps; I never expected to do that, you know; but I'm all right, I think."

They had to pause, for the din in the warehouse was louder than usual—some of the farmers were squabbling with the scalesmen.

"And Thora?" said Magnus after a moment.

"Thora? Oh, Thora is all right, too, I think. Yes, Thora is all right," said Oscar.

"Mother tells me she looks pale."

"Pale? Does she? I hadn't noticed it. Perhaps she does though, the weather is getting cold."

There was a painful pause in their conversation, and while they waited Oscar could hear the organ in the cathedral breaking into the opening notes of his own anthem.

"I hear that Helga has come home," said Magnus.

"Oh, yes, Helga has come home," said Oscar.

"They say she is handsome."

"Handsome? Yes, she's rather handsome, in fact, distinctly handsome—and musical—decidedly musical. Indeed, she has grown to be a very attractive girl—very!"

There was another awkward silence, in which the anthem pealed out over the jangling voices in the warehouse.

"I suppose the wedding will be soon," said Magnus.

"The wedding? Well, to tell you the truth, Magnus, nothing has been fixed yet."

"Not yet?"

"Nothing definite, I mean—no precise date. I don't know why, but——"

Oscar looked at his brother, and felt his tongue arrested.

Magnus was calm, his eyes were quiet, and his voice was soft, but there was something in his face which brought back a terrible memory. It was the memory of the night of the betrothal, the last time they talked together, when Magnus had said, " If you ever neglect or desert her or give her up for another woman, I'll take her back—do you hear me?—I'll take her back, and then, by God, I'll kill you!"

Oscar supped at the Factor's house that night. He was unusually solemn, and more than once during the meal Aunt Margret bantered him on his silence, but, at the end of it, while lighting a cigarette, he said:

" Godfather, I hope you'll consent to our having the wedding soon?"

Thora, who had been looking pale and nervous, colored up with a glad look, while Helga, who had been flushed and excited, grew white and rigid.

" What do you call soon, Oscar—Easter?" asked the Factor.

" Earlier, much earlier, say the middle of January at latest," said Oscar.

" But what does Thora say?"

Rising from her seat, with brightening eyes and heaving bosom, Thora crossed over to Oscar and kissed him.

" So that's what Thora says!" laughed the Factor. " Very well, I'm willing! The middle of January let it be then, and fix the date between you."

Helga's white face quivered. " So *that's* settled!" she cried, and leaping up she went across to the piano and began to play with great vigor. She played the wild " Ride of the Valkyries," becoming faster and louder at every bar.

Oscar was in torture, and he went home early. " What a mercy Helga does not know!" he thought. " If she did, I could not trust myself even yet! And if she loves me as I love her—good God!"

But Thora was very happy. Going to bed that night she thought, " How wrong I have been about Oscar; how cruelly, wickedly, shamefully wrong!"

VII

NEXT morning Oscar thought the battle was over, and his conscience had conquered, but the devil was not done with him yet. He had hardly settled to his work in the warehouse when a letter came from Helga, saying:

"The ice is perfect on the lake this morning, and in spite of business and every other botheration you must carry out your promise to take me to skate. Therefore come at two o'clock to the minute, and you will find me waiting to go with you."

It was the first letter he had received from Helga, and it seemed to burn his fingers. The scented note-paper and the free, bold handwriting gave him a physical thrill which he had never felt before.

Should he go? His soul said, "Certainly not! Why expose yourself to temptation, especially now, when you are as weak as water." But his heart said, "You must! To make any difference in your attitude toward Helga would be to run the risk of betraying your secret. And what about the future—can you always run away like that?" His heart won, and at the appointed time he was walking up to the Factor's.

Helga was standing by the door at the top of the steps. She was dressed in pale blue serge, a short skirt exposing the long tanned boots, a jersey revealing the flexible lines of her shapely figure, and a white woolen cap, like a chain helmet, covering half her forehead and closing under her chin, leaving her vivid face bare and beautiful as a young nun's in hood and bands.

Oscar was beginning to doubt himself already, and he asked where was Thora.

"I'm here," said a cheerful voice from the hall, and Thora came to the door bright and happy, but bareheaded, and sewing a piece of moleskin cloth.

"Not ready?" said Oscar.

"I'm not going, I can't skate," said Thora.

"Then we'll take a walk instead," said Oscar. But Thora would not hear of it. Helga had set her heart on skating, and she had set her heart on something else—making a sleeve waistcoat for Hans, the sailor.

"Well, if you really wish it," said Oscar.

"Really, truly! And I'll have tea ready for you at five o'clock."

"We'll be back before that," said Oscar, and then he and Helga went swinging down the road.

Helga, in her short skirt, walked with a spring, like a young horse in sharp weather, and Oscar, as he swung along by her side, sometimes touching her, felt his blood tingling, and every nerve tremblingly alive. This frightened him a little, and turning to look back he saw Thora waving to them from the house, and said, "God bless her, the dear little soul!" And then Helga glanced at him sideways and laughed.

The frost had filtered the air, and it was crisp and quivering with currents of electricity, which stimulated all their senses. Their voices crackled when they spoke, and when Helga laughed the sound was like that of dry sticks in a quick fire.

"What are you laughing at, Helga?"

"I don't know," she said, and then they laughed together.

The ice of the lake was glorious—a broad mirror black as ink, for there had been no snow yet, the water had frozen as by first intention, and through five fathoms they could see the stones and pebbles at the bottom.

"What a pity Thora didn't come," said Oscar.

"Isn't it?" said Helga, and again she glanced at him sideways and laughed.

They sat on the bank to put on their skates, and while Helga fumbled at her straps, Oscar thought, "I must not, I will not!" But Helga looked across at him with a smile that seemed to ask a question, and at the next moment he was down on his knees in front of her, with one of her skates and one of her long tanned boots in his quivering hands.

Oscar thought Helga's skating was wonderful. It was divine, it was devilish, it intoxicated him, he could not trust himself to look at it alone, and seeing a number of skaters at the farther side of the lake, where there was an island of lava rocks, he said:

"Let us go over to the others."

Hours passed, the exercise and the air warmed his blood, his tremors left him, and he forgot about Thora. At length the sun began to set over the sea in a flood of glory, and Oscar said, "Time to go home."

"Not yet," said Helga, and they went round and round the island, sometimes apart, sometimes with clasped hands, sometimes side by side with arms interlaced across their breasts.

The sun went down, and both sea and land became gray and cold, but still the tops of the mountains were golden.

"Tea will be waiting," said Oscar.

"A little longer!" said Helga, and nothing loath, Oscar went round and round with her again.

The night came striding up from the plain behind, and somebody lit a fire on the island.

"Too late for tea now," said Helga, and once again Oscar went round and round with her. It seemed to him that Helga's face flashed with electric flame as she swirled out of the darkness into the red glow from the fire, and back again into the darkness.

One of the skaters started the Elf-song, others joined him, and then it was a scene of complete enchantment. The frost had laid its hand on the falls that fed the lake, and they were quiet; it had stroked the streams, and they were still; but if the voices of the waters were silent, the voices of the skaters rippled and rang in the crisp night air.

> "Dance by night and dance by day,
> Life and Time will pass away:
> Love alone will last alway."

Oscar was enraptured. The humming of the skates, the swaying of the ice, the music of the singers, the heat, the glow, the sinuous movement, and above all the girl by his side, so bright, so beautiful, so full of life and laughter, carried away every sense, and flesh and blood were afire.

Then the moon rose, a brilliant moon, and it was reflected full and round and white in the black mirror of the ice, with its streamers going off from it, as if it had been a comet that had fallen to the earth, and lay there at their feet.

"Look! Let us cut across it," cried Helga, and away they shot in the darkness, with the moon's reflection receding as they followed it, until they came to the limit of the lake, and then the skaters and the fire and the singing were far behind them.

"What a will o' the wisp she is! I could catch *you* quicker than I could catch her!" said Oscar.

"You couldn't!"

"I could!"

"Do it then!" cried Helga, and off she went, laughing at first, but afterward silent yet breathing fast, and at last panting audibly while she twisted and turned to escape from him, until he came down on her at length with outstretched arms and a cry of "Done!" And then, before he knew what he was doing, he was clasping her to his breast, and she was clinging to him lest she should fall, and he was beating kiss after kiss upon her lips.

At the next moment consciousness came back to him like an ice wind blowing in a furnace. His arms slackened away from Helga, and he said in a cold voice:

"I beg your pardon, Helga. It was wrong of me. I am very sorry."

Helga laughed, a nervous, broken laugh which seemed to say, "Are you sure you are thinking of me?"

"I am betrothed to your sister, and in less than two months I am to be married to her. I had no right to give way to my feelings like that," said Oscar.

The nervous, broken laugh came again, and it said, as plainly as words could speak, "Do you know what you are saying, Oscar?"

Oscar trembled like a withered leaf. He was like a man standing on the hot ground of the geysers, where the crust was thin and cracking under his feet.

"Let us go home," he said.

"Take off my skates then," said Helga.

She sat on the bank in the moonlight, and while he knelt at her feet and fumbled with the straps, his tongue went on with rambling sentences, but every word was tearing as at a torn tendon.

"When a man has engaged himself to a good woman, he ought to be true to her. It is his duty, and whatever the consequences to himself, he ought to do it. If he has to suffer, he *must* suffer, Helga, and if he has to sacrifice himself——"

A faint sound stopped him. Helga was crying. Her crying seemed to search his innermost thoughts, and to say, "But have you any right to sacrifice *me?*"

"Helga! Helga!" he cried, but she took no notice. She covered her face with her hands, and her crying became deep and long and inconsolable.

He wished to comfort her, but he dare not do so. He remembered Thora and Magnus, the Factor, and his father, and his thoughts danced about his naked soul like demons.

"Helga! Helga!" he cried again, but still Helga's weeping continued. If it had gone on a moment longer he must have taken her in his arms again and told her that he loved her; that his love for her was above all laws, all illusions, all conventions; it was the commandment of Nature, and he was compelled to obey it; and they must fly from Iceland and never return, whatever the waste of ruined lives they had to leave behind them.

But Helga's crying stopped suddenly, and throwing back her head she said fiercely, "Very well, if you are satisfied, so am I!"

Then she leapt to her feet, wiped her eyes vigorously and laughed—a short, hard, bitter laugh, and after that Oscar recovered control of himself.

"Let us be off," she said.

Going back by the road that skirts the lake, side by side, but neither touching the other, and both silent, Oscar thought, "Good heavens, what an escape! Another moment and what might not have happened! What a fool I was to expose myself to this temptation! Marriage is my only safeguard. It must be soon. Thora and I must go away. When we return, Helga may be back in Denmark, and then a scene like this will never occur again!"

When they reached the house at last, he felt like an adulterer coming home after his first offense, but Thora looked happy and unsuspicious.

"I knew you couldn't tear yourselves away from your skating, so I put the tea away, and now supper is nearly ready," she said.

After supper Oscar said, "Godfather, I wish you would permit me to alter the arrangement of last evening."

"You want to go back to Easter, eh?" said the Factor.

"No, sir, to come on to Christmas," said Oscar, and then he gave his reasons. Thora was looking pale—everybody thought so—she wanted a change—he would like to take her to England, perhaps to France, and even to Italy. They might stay away during the months of spring and come back for the first of summer, when Althing would open its session, and by that time Thora would be well, and he himself would be ready to set to work in earnest.

"But Christmas, my gracious!" cried Aunt Margret, "hardly time for the banns! And what about Thora's wedding-dress?"

But Thora herself was in raptures, and Aunt Margret's objections were borne down.

"Christmas let it be then," said the Factor, whereupon Thora gave a cry of joy, and Helga, whose eyes had passed with a quick glance from face to face, while her own grew paler and paler, leapt up, saying:

"And now let us have a dance to celebrate the happy event!"

"No, no, no," said Oscar.

"Yes, yes," said Helga, and sitting down to the piano she played a dance tune with a rapid and passionate touch. "Make him dance, Thora," she cried with an awful brightness in her eyes.

Thora took hold of Oscar and dragged him to his feet, saying laughingly, "Why not, Oscar?"

Tables and chairs were pulled aside, the Factor went off to smoke, and Oscar and Thora danced while Helga played, laughing loudly, and calling to them again and again.

"Helga! Helga! Not so fast! You'll kill us," cried Thora.

But Helga only laughed the louder and played the faster, with a fierceness that seemed to consume her like a fire.

Oscar went home that night with an aching heart, but Thora went to bed happy.

"How wrong I was about dear Helga, also!" she thought, and then drawing a deep breath she fell asleep.

VIII

To think yourself happy is to be happy, and Thora thought herself the happiest little woman in the world. The weeks before her wedding were the brightest period of her heart's existence. She counted the days backward from the day she was living in to the day of all days that was to come, and every morning, the moment she awoke, she said to herself, "Only nineteen now," and then eighteen, seventeen, and sixteen, until it became three, two, and one. "Our Thora is like a white mouse in a revolving cage—she can't make the world go round quickly enough," said Aunt Margret.

Hers was not the happiness that makes the heart afraid, and she had not a moment's misgiving about Oscar now. She never once saw him alone for more than two minutes together, but that did not trouble her at all. He came and went every day, always in a hurry, and always breathless, and she gave him the benevolence of a smile, and occasionally the charity of a kiss, when it could be done decently behind the dining-room door. But usually he had to be content to see her seated among her dressmakers and sewing-maids, and that suited him better than she knew.

There was nothing to tarnish the white simplicity of her happiness, and when Oscar could come with maps and tour lists to arrange about their journey she would say:

"Why don't you talk it over with Helga? She knows more about traveling."

And then Oscar would stammer a little and say, "Well, if you are willing to be guided by Helga's judgment, and Helga herself will——"

"Certainly I am, so be off to my bedroom and settle everything."

Whereupon Oscar would cry, "No, no, we're right enough here," and then Helga and he—the one trembling lest a word should betray him, the other going through the bitterness of looking at happiness through another's eyes—would discuss routes and railway journeys to the click of scissors and the buzz of the sewing machine.

"We'll go up by the Mont Cenis, eh?" "No, by the St. Gothard." "We'll come back by San Remo and Nice." "And Monte Carlo!" "Yes, of course—Monte Carlo."

"My gracious, it might be Helga who was going on her honeymoon," Aunt Margret would say.

"Mightn't it?" Thora would answer, and then she would laugh like a child.

In the Holy Land of her innocent heart she had only one thought about her sister—that she had done her the wrong of suspecting her. Helga might know nothing about that, but *she* knew, and she could never be quite satisfied until she had made amends. Time and again she thought of a way to do this, and at length an artful scheme occurred to her. It was a daring design, and asking herself when she could bring it to pass she concluded that it must be on her wedding-day, because she would be the queen of her own little kingdom then and nobody could deny her anything. Meantime it was to be her secret, and Helga was to hear nothing about it, and even Oscar himself was not to know.

There was only one other streak of alloy in Thora's happiness, and that was her memory of Magnus. The brave heart did not break and Magnus's despair might be dumb, but the thought of his suffering was the tang of iron in the sweet wine of Thora's life. To complete her happiness everybody had to share it, so when Oscar came one day she took him into the hall and said:

"Oscar, who is to be best man?" And Oscar stammered:

"Well, really, to tell you the truth, I hadn't—that is to say——"

"Why not Magnus?" said Thora.

"Magnus? I thought of that, but—" and then came the old difficulty—he had not yet set Magnus right on the subject of the betrothal, and until that could be done the old people would object to him.

"But why shouldn't you do it now, Oscar? Such a splendid moment to heal every sore and let bygones be bygones."

"Yes, certainly, that's so," said Oscar, but he went off

8

with a troubled face, and Thora heard no more from him on the subject until the day before the wedding, when he said:

"Oh, by the way, about the best man, that splendid scheme of yours was impossible, Thora."

"Impossible?"

"Mother tells me Magnus has gone to the Northlands—went away about a week ago, it seems."

"In the winter and on the eve of the wedding?"

"She thinks he'll be back for that, but, of course, we can't take risks, so Neils—you remember Neils Finsen, the Sheriff's son?—Neils came back in the last steamer, and he'll be best man, so that's settled."

"What a pity!" said Thora, and then Oscar, who had opened the door, cried:

"Helloa! Snowing! We're going to have a white wedding, Thora!" and with a nervous laugh he buttoned up his coat collar and went off without kissing her.

She remembered this again when she was going to bed, and, sitting on the great chair before the cheerful stove, with the curtains drawn and all so sweet and cozy, she reflected that it was the last time she was to sleep in her father's house. The three weeks were almost gone at last, and so was her girlhood; and now that both were nearly over they seemed to have vanished like a dream. She was happy still, but it would have taken very little to turn her happiness into pain. It was a pity Oscar had forgotten to kiss her, and it was a pity Magnus would not be present at the wedding.

Toward the mirk of night she went to bed, and then the snow was still falling. She thought of Magnus traveling over the desert, and wondered why he had gone away just then. Perhaps it was because he could not bear to look upon their happiness—hers and Oscar's! Poor Magnus!

But the memory of Magnus was whirled away in a cloud of other thoughts—the wedding, the wedding presents, the wedding-feast, and Oscar, always Oscar—and then the tired eyelids of her mind closed in peace and good-will with all the world, and she slept the last sleep of her maidenhood.

IX

"THORA! Thora! Well, I declare! The girl is still sleeping!"

"On her wedding-day, too. Thora! Thora!"

Thora awoke with a start at the calling and knocking at her door. Leaping out of bed she ran to the window and parted the curtains. It was broad morning, the sun was shining brightly over the snow, and all the world was white.

She opened the door, the sewing-maids and dressmakers trooped into the room, and from that moment onward for several hours the universe was a chaos without form and void, in which all talked at once and everybody ran up against everybody else, and Thora ate her breakfast while walking about or being "fitted on."

But the dress and the dressing were finished at length, and Aunt Margret was called up to look. Nobody in Iceland had ever seen such a bridal costume—the silk kirtle, the silver-gilt crown, the faldur, the veil, and the blue plush cloak.

"Isn't she beautiful, Margret?" said the maids, whereupon Aunt Margret, whose eyes were glistening behind her spectacles, said:

"Talk about Helga—tut!"

Then the cathedral bells began to ring and a hush fell on everybody. Thora went slowly down-stairs and found her father (looking taller than ever in a new silk hat) waiting for her in the hall, and Silvertop standing ready in the street, with a side-saddle of red plush and gilt. There were a few jests, a few laughs, a few furtive tears, and then they started off. The snow underfoot was as dry and soft as flour, and it was with difficulty that the pony could be made to walk sedately.

From the moment they reached the cathedral it was all like a dream to Thora, a beautiful day-dream, such as she had dreamt sometimes when she thought she was dead and her happy soul was entering heaven.

The bridesmaids were waiting in the porch—Helga looking wondrously beautiful in an English dress, and two former school-fellows in Iceland costume.

Thora, who was moving as in a vision, felt somebody taking off her plush cloak, and then the bells stopped and the organ began. At the next moment the choir was singing a hymn—the usual hymn, "When God the Father led the first of brides"—and then she was going up the aisle, leaning on her father's arm.

She had never seen so many faces since the day she was confirmed. They seemed to move past her, and they made her almost dizzy. She remembered how at other weddings the congregation had watched for the bride and looked at her as if she had been a supernatural thing. "She's coming!" "Here she comes!" She herself was the bride now, and the people were craning their necks to see her.

Thora could feel their smiling faces, and she knew that her own face was smiling. She could hear what the people were saying as she passed them: "Dear Thora!" "How lovely she looks!" "I'm satisfied now, and I don't care if I go—I only wanted to see how Thora looked in the kirtle." And meanwhile the voices of the choir were coming down from the gallery as from the sky and floating round and round her.

At the top of the nave Oscar was waiting—so perfectly dressed, so handsome, so noble-looking—with a fair young man on his right hand, and on his left the Governor, very solemn and stately with his iron-grey hair and beard.

The hymn came to an end, the organ died down, and Thora found herself standing by Oscar's side at the foot of the chancel steps, with the old Bishop in his pleated black gown and white ruff at the top of them. There was a rustle behind her, then there was silence, and the Bishop began to speak.

"My children," he said, "when long ago God the Father led the first of brides to the first of men in the beautiful garden of Eden he linked their hands together in love, and that was the first marriage. Since then He has carried on the human story by the same sweet means, and love is still the bond that binds man to woman, and woman to man."

"My children," said the Bishop again—he was speaking to her and Oscar—"you come here to be made man and wife, and because you love one another God is willing to join your hands in holy wedlock, for He blesses and sanctifies no other union, whether of wealth or worldly advantage or any other interest whatsoever.

"We know you both, my children; we who are gathered here have watched the flower of your affection bud and bloom, and now we pray to God that you may be true to the vows you are to make to-day, always bearing each other's burdens, forgiving each other's faults, and cherishing the human love that is a symbol of the love divine.

"My daughter, love him who is to be your husband; let him find on your breast his solace for every sorrow, whatever the world may do to him, and whatever the world may say.

"My son, love her who is to be your wife. There is nothing nobler in this imperfect existence, no sight more sweet and heavenly, than when a good girl leaves the father who loves her, and the home where she has been happy, and says to him who is to be her husband: 'The past was beautiful, but I trust the future all to you.' Be worthy of that trust, my son, be strong, be brave, be faithful, and He who knows our weaknesses, having trodden the earth before us, will bear you up if your feet should falter.

"Be companions to each other in the journey of this world, my dear ones, and if it should please God to give you children let them be bonds to bind you closer together. Above all, love one another, for that is the first commandment, and may He who gave it guard and guide you through all the thorny paths of life."

The Bishop's voice became tremulous toward the end, and when he finished there was some coughing and blowing of noses among the congregation. Oscar, too, was breathing heavily by Thora's side, and Helga was trampling on her train, but Thora herself was as calm as a trustful child.

At the next moment she was kneeling by Oscar's side on the communion steps—just where they had knelt as children to be confirmed—and the Bishop was administering the vows. There was a breathless hush in the crowded cathedral during this solemn and beautiful ceremony—a ceremony for ever new, for ever old, for ever awful—the consecration of the man to the woman, the woman to the man, for better or for worse, in sickness and in health, "till death us do part."

Oscar was still breathing heavily, but Thora felt too happy to be agitated, too sure to be afraid. When the Bishop put their hands together, and laid his own hand on the top of them, she felt Oscar's hand tremble and his pulse throb, and she wanted to calm and comfort him. But it was all over in a moment, for they had risen to their feet, and one of the assistant clergy was giving out a hymn.

> " Guide Thy children, Father, guide them,
>   Through the thorny paths of life."

The choir began it, but the congregation joined in, and all the voices seemed to quiver with emotion. Thora felt herself carried away, far away, but still she was holding Oscar's hand. She thought she could hear Magnus's voice among the voices behind her—the deep voice she used to hear on those evenings so long ago. Poor Magnus! But then he could have had no joy of her, so it was better even for him.

It was something of a descent when the hymn ended and the Bishop shook hands with her, and the Governor followed his example, and the bridesmaids came up and kissed her in the presence of the whole congregation. But Oscar gave her his arm, and as they moved down the nave the organ and choir began again:

> " O Perfect Love, all human thought transcending,
>   Lowly we kneel in prayer before Thy throne."

She was now sure she could hear Magnus, and looking up at the organ loft she saw him. Yes, he was there; he was in the choir; he had come back from the Northlands to sing at her wedding.

> " That theirs may be the joy that knows no ending,
>   Whom Thou for evermore dost join in one—"

She had only one glance at his face, but she saw it plainly. She had never seen it like that before—so broken up, and so soft, yet so strong and brave. His eyes were steadfastly fixed on his music book, and he was swaying a little and singing as with all his might.

> " Grant them the joy which brightens earthly sorrow,
> Grant them the peace which calms all earthly strife—"

But Magnus was whirled away from her in a moment, for the people whispered as she was going past. " Dear Thora! God bless our Thora! "

Oscar was bowing on both sides of the aisle, and the people were talking to him also. " How handsome he looks! " " He looks as if he could take care of her, too! " " Take care of her, Oscar! "

They were back in the porch at length, and somebody was putting her plush cloak over her shoulders. Silvertop was standing outside, and Hans the sailor (in his new sleeve waistcoat) was giving him water out of his pail.

Oscar lifted her to the saddle, and they turned their faces homeward. The bells began to ring again—a merry peal—and then, at last, Thora's tears began to flow. How good everybody had been to her! It was all for Oscar's sake! How sweet to think they were good to her for the sake of Oscar! Thank God for Oscar!

X

ANNA and Aunt Margret were at the door of the Factor's house to receive them. They kissed Thora, and called her " Mrs. Stephenson," and then took her up-stairs to change. When she came down again the friends invited to the wedding feast were coming in quickly, taking off their snowshoes, shaking hands with Oscar, and talking all at once.

The table was laid in the double sitting-room which had been the scene of the betrothal. The Factor sat at the head with Oscar on his right (just in the place where he had trodden on Helga's photograph), and Thora on his left (where Magnus had sat on the low seat beside his mother), while the Governor faced the Factor, with Anna and Aunt Margret at either side of him, and the Bishop, the Sheriff, and the Doctor between. Helga sat midway down the table, with Neils Finsen on one side of her and the Rector on the other.

Thora was bashful but bright, reddening a little with maidenly reserve when pointed remarks were made to her, but filling the room with musical laughter. During the meal nearly everybody raised his glass to her, and at the end of it the Governor rose, bowed to her down the table with a stately grace, and began to speak.

"I rise," said the Governor, "to propose the health of the bride and bridegroom. We are all happy in the marriage which has just been celebrated, and no one can be more happy than myself. It had been for many years the dearest hope of my heart that the life-long friendship between Factor Neilsen and myself might be cemented in our children by a still closer bond."

"Your health, old friend," interrupted the Factor, raising his glass, and the Governor stopped to drink with him.

"Time was, perhaps," he continued, "when I feared lest this hope might be frustrated."

"No, no!" said the Factor, while Thora dropped her head, Anna sighed audibly, and there was silence for a moment, as if the spirit of some one who was not present had passed through the room.

"But sweet is the bliss that follows bale," said the Governor, "and thank God we are now of one mind and one family."

When the glasses of the company had ceased to jingle, the Governor went on to speak of Thora. "She has always been like a daughter in our house, and now she is our daughter indeed. We have loved her all her life, and to-day we have given her the best we had to give to any one—our son, our favorite son, the idol of our hopes and the pride of our hearts. God bless both of them!"

As soon as the Factor had done wiping his eyes with his print handkerchief he rose with a laugh and said:

"Stem before stern when the sea gets up, and I'm not much used to pulling backward, but I'm with the Governor in thanking God that the storm that threatened has blown over and we are sailing in smooth water. As for Oscar, he has been my godson ever since he was anything; and to-day he has become my son, and I could not wish for a better.

"And now," said the Factor, as soon as he was allowed to go on, "a small promise kept is better than a big one forgotten, and I'm going to keep a little promise which I made on the day of the betrothal. Perhaps some of you wouldn't think it, but I believe in young people enjoying their youth while they've got any. I managed to miss mine somehow, and it's been work, work, work with me all my days. The same with the Governor; it's been work, work, work with him too, and we haven't had a holiday between us. But we are going to have a holiday now—we're going to travel to the sunny south lands, where the ground and the sea aren't white like this and that." (The Factor waved his hands toward the windows front and back.) "Yes, we're going to see the world in our old age, the Governor and I, but it's got to be with eyes that are better than ours are now—the eyes of our children."

"What's more," continued the Factor, when the company were again quiet, "we're not going to grudge the expense either, and if Oscar will look under his bottom plate he'll find a little oil that will grease the wheels on the way."

Oscar lifted his fruit plate and took up two checks, and when the toast had been honored he rose to reply. Nobody had ever before seen him so pale, so nervous, or so serious.

"I thank the Governor and the Factor," he said, "for the splendid present they have given us—so much more than we can possibly require on our journey. I thank you all for coming to our wedding—it is so pleasant to be surrounded by the people who have known us all our lives. 'Find your wife among your friends,' says one of our Sagas. I have found mine almost in my family, and I trust the two branches now made one may never be divided as the result of what we have done this morning."

There was some applause, and when Oscar began again his voice faltered and broke.

"I thank the Bishop, too," he said, "for the words—the wise and touching words—he spoke in marrying us. I know that love—love is the only foundation of a true marriage, and I—I trust my marriage is a true one. I do not love my

wife as much as I ought—as much as she deserves. I can
never do that; it is impossible, but I hope to love her more
and more as time goes on, and to fly from every temptation
to love her less. I know I am not worthy of the dear good
girl who has given herself to me to-day, but I will try so
to live that she may never regret it. Often forgive the
woman's faults, says another of our Sagas, but a truer word
in this case would be forgive the man's, and I pray God my
wife may never have too much to forgive."

When Oscar sat down the men thought his speech had
been a little affected and far-fetched, but there was not a
woman in the room who did not want to leap up and kiss
him. Thora was openly wiping her eyes, but her face was
one high noon of enjoyment, and in the buzz which followed
the silence Aunt Margret called across to her.

"Mrs. Stephenson, you had better take care of your husband or some of these young women will run away with him."

There were other toasts, "The Governor," "The Factor,"
and finally, "The Bridesmaids," proposed by the Rector in
a playful speech.

"They say a kiss isn't the same thing from all women,"
he said, "and being an old bachelor I know nothing about
that; but the young fellow on my left" (the Rector indicated
Neils Finsen), "who has a right to consider himself the best
man in Iceland to-day, has confessed to me in a whisper that
he finds one of the bridesmaids so charming and beautiful
that if he had been in Oscar's place, and compelled by a
narrow-minded law to choose between the Factor's two daughters, he would have cut off to some eastern country where he
could have married both."

Everybody laughed and looked at Helga, who had herself
been laughing rather hysterically, and looking at Oscar all
through dinner. And then Thora, who was overflowing
with happiness, glanced down at her sister, and remembered the great scheme she had conceived to make amends
for mistrusting and suspecting her. Now was the moment
to carry it into effect—now that she was queen in her little
kingdom—and, half bold, half shy, she rose from her seat,
put her arms about her father's neck, and whispered something in his ear.

The Factor's face straightened for a moment, then broadened again, and he said, "But what does Oscar say?"

"Oscar will be *sure* to agree," said Thora, and she whispered in her father's ear again.

"Well, I'm not going back on my word; I'm willing; but you must ask Oscar."

Then, laughing and reddening, Thora crept up behind Oscar and whispered in his ear also, while looking sideways down at Helga. As Oscar listened his face became serious and he said:

"But you are quite sure that you wish it, Thora?"

"Yes, yes, yes," said Thora, laughing and blushing, for now the eyes of the whole company were on her.

"Let us talk of it to-morrow," said Oscar.

"No, no, now," said Thora.

"But perhaps Helga herself—" began Oscar, and then he stopped, whereupon Helga, hearing her own name, said with a nervous laugh:

"What is that about Helga?"

"Yes, what is it?" said several voices at once, and then the Factor explained.

"Thora wants to have her sister to accompany them on their tour, and she is trying to persuade Oscar."

There were some unconvincing cries of "Why not?" and "Splendid!" and then there was silence, broken only by Thora's voice saying:

"Please, Oscar, please!"

It was the last thing Oscar could have expected—to have temptation thrown in his way at the moment when he was trying to escape from it; to have the flood-gate of passion opened afresh after he had struggled so hard to dam it—and to have this done by Thora herself, in her blind unselfishness and innocent joy, as if the powers of hell were making game of her.

But the company were waiting for Oscar's answer; and, not to betray himself, he tried to escape by banter. "I'm not like Neils—I don't want both of you," he said; but still the pleading, coaxing voice was at his ear, saying:

"Please, Oscar, please, please!" And when Oscar continued to hesitate the Rector said:

"Tut, tut, Oscar, refusing your wife's first request is a bad beginning."

"I'm not refusing," said Oscar, "and if Helga herself really and truly thinks she would like to go with us——"

"Would you like to go, Helga?" asked the Factor, and then there was another moment's hesitation, in which Helga, biting her lower lip with a fierceness which betrayed the struggle in her soul, looked across at Oscar as if trying to read in his face what her answer was to be.

"Tell her to say yes, Oscar," said Thora.

"Yes," said Helga, and at the next moment Thora was clapping her hands in triumphant delight and making the room ring with her laughter.

Neils Finsen had sat down to the piano and the servants were clearing the table to make way for dancing, when Anna came up behind Thora and whispered:

"Somebody outside wishes to see you, Thora."

"Is it perhaps——?"

"Yes, dear," said Anna, and Thora followed her out of the room.

XI

MAGNUS was waiting in the hall, dressed in snow stockings and a long cape overcoat, rough and worn and belted about the waist. His face was stamped with the deep lines which in a strong man stand for resignation and in a weak one for despair. Thora thought she had never seen him look so big and brawny, but his voice when he spoke to her was as soft as a woman's, and he broke into the sunniest of smiles. She closed the door of the sitting-room to shut out the sound of the piano, and then came forward and held out her hand, feeling little and weak in her kirtle and the bridal crown across her forehead.

"I came to say good-by and to wish you a good voyage," he said.

"I'm so glad you've come," said Thora. "I heard you had gone away, and I was afraid I was going to miss you."

"I've brought you this for a wedding present," said Magnus, taking up from the hall table a large white bear's skin which Thora had not noticed before.

"What a magnificent rug!" said Thora.

"Is it a good one?" said Magnus.

"It is perfectly beautiful. I have never seen anything like it. It must have cost you a fortune."

"No, not a great deal. I bought it in the Northlands."

"Then it was to get this that you went there?"

"Yes."

"In the winter, too—such a long, cold journey!"

"I am strong, Thora—I never feel the cold."

His sad eyes were glistening, and Thora's throat was thick.

"I shall use it on the ship and in the train and everywhere," she said. "And whenever I use it I will always think of you."

"Will you?"

"Indeed I will. But we are going south, you know."

"I know."

"To England and France—perhaps to Italy."

"It will do you good, Thora. The sun will do you good. And you will see the fruit and the flowers growing—it will be beautiful."

"Will it not?"

The piano was becoming louder, and there was a sound of shuffling feet—the people in the sitting-room were beginning to dance.

"And what do you think—Helga is going with us," said Thora.

"Helga!"

"Didn't Anna tell you?"

"Is Helga to go with you to Italy?"

"Oh, yes, and we are delighted to have her. She's so clever and bright—Oscar can never be dull for a moment while Helga is with us."

The grave face looked sideways for a moment, and then he said, in a still gentler voice:

"I hope you'll be happy on your journey, Thora."

"I'm sure I shall. We shall all be happy. We sail by the 'Laura' to-morrow morning."

"So mother told me—I've been taking your baggage aboard and seeing to your cabin."

"And you have been doing that while we——"

"I wanted to do something for you, Thora."

"But, Magnus, you ought to have been here by rights. Oscar always wished it. In fact he wanted you to be his best man."

"Oscar did?"

"Indeed he did, but you couldn't be found, because you had gone on your journey."

Over the sound of the music and the dancing the Governor's voice came from within, mingled with the Factor's hearty laughter.

"Perhaps it was just as well I was away," said Magnus. "The old people have never forgiven me for what I did, and if they ever came to suspect that somebody else was responsible——"

He stopped, and then Thora dropped her eyes and said:

"I was so glad you were in the cathedral."

"It was beautiful," said Magnus.

"You have no feeling against Oscar now?"

"Not now. When I saw you kneeling together at the communion rails I thought of the day when we all knelt there. And then—then Oscar was my little brother once again."

"Magnus—won't you—won't you kiss me?"

He hesitated for a moment, but she held her sweet face up to him—pure as a saint's and wet with tears—and he opened his great arms and gathered the little white figure to his breast and kissed her on the forehead under the bridal crown.

"Good-by, little girl, and God bless you and make you very happy. But if you ever want me say 'Come,' and I'll come to you—if it's to the farthest corner of the earth."

Thora began to cry audibly and Magnus bustled about and made for the door. He must be off, he had a long journey before him.

"And then Silvertop is outside—I must not keep him waiting.

"Silvertop?"

"Mother told me to take care of him until you return—so I'm taking him back to the farm."

"Let me say good-by to him," said Thora.

Magnus covered her from head to foot in the bear's skin and led her down the steps to the street. It was dark, but the stars were out and the northern lights were cleaving the sky as with the sweep of a mighty saber. All was white and silent, save for the deadened beat of the piano and the thud of the feet of the dancers. Two horses, saddled and bridled, stood quietly in the snow with their reins hanging over their heads, and Magnus, mounting one of them, said:

"This is Golden Mane—Silvertop's big brother."

Thora found her own pony, stroked its ears and kissed its nose, and then fled back to the door out of the frosty air.

"Good brothers go well together; we'll be home by midnight," cried Magnus.

Thora watched them go. A glittering shaft of the aurora lit up the three as they turned the corner of the road— Magnus riding Golden Mane, and Silvertop, with an empty saddle, running briskly beside him.

XII

WHEN Thora returned to the sitting-room Oscar and Helga, both with sparkling eyes and flushed faces, were waltzing vigorously. Then Thora herself danced with the Governor, the Factor, the Rector, and, of course, with Oscar. But the room grew hot and stuffy, too full of excitement, and after a while Thora became pale and faint. Seeing this, after Aunt Margret had called attention to it, Oscar began to say it was time to break up. The young men bantered him ("Want to get rid of us, eh?") and Helga, who grew more and more hysterical, protested that the evening was still young, but Oscar sent his bride up-stairs to prepare for the journey to her husband's house.

"Let us all take her home, then," said one of the bridesmaids, and when Thora reappeared, muffled up for her night walk, with only eyes, nose, and mouth visible, she was surrounded by a group of merry girls, similarly bandaged, and chirping over her like linnets in spring.

At last the final moment came when Thora had to leave her

father's house for good, and then Aunt Margret, whose face
had become grotesquely long and watery, broke down altogether.

"It's no use," she said. "I'm losing her, and I don't know
what they'll do with my precious now."

"Nonsense, Margret," said the Factor. "Oscar will take
care of her."

"He'd better, or I'll murder him," said Aunt Margret;
and the idea of Aunt Margret murdering anybody was so
amusing to the company that they broke up merrily.

The Factor's family went to the door to see them off, and
Helga, who was hot with dancing and excitement, but wore
no wraps, stood on the top of the steps holding a lamp above
her head to light them down the road. It was a paraffin
lamp with a glass reservoir, but she paid no heed to any
warning.

"Take care, Helga, do take care," said Oscar, but she
only cried:

"Good night, pleasant dreams!" and continued to wave
the flickering lamp above her head.

"Helga, for mercy's sake, Helga!" shouted Oscar, and
Thora said:

"Yes, dear, don't let us have an accident on our wedding-
day."

"The better the day the better the deed," cried Helga, and
she sent a ringing, hysterical laugh after them as they disappeared in the darkness.

The wedding party went off in two batches, Oscar in the
midst of the young men, whose arms were round his shoulders, and Thora in the midst of the young women, who were
holding her by the waist and stopping at intervals to whisper
mischievous messages in her ears. The crisp snow crackled
under their feet, and the starry sky, with its northern lights,
pulsed and throbbed like the hearts in their bosoms.

When they came to the gate of Government House somebody suggested that Oscar, as a zealous Sagaman, ought to
carry out the ancient custom of lifting his bride across the
threshold; and then to Thora's delight, amid a squealing
chorus of laughter, Oscar picked her up in his arms and
carried her into the house, where Anna (who had gone on

ahead) smuggled her up-stairs while the others went into the drawing-room to drink the last toast before parting.

A bright fire was burning in the bridal chamber, the curtains were drawn, the bed was laid open, and the room looked like a white nest of eiderdown when Thora, with a fluttering heart, stepped into it.

"What a day it has been!" she said.

"Hasn't it?" said Anna, closing the door behind them.

"Well, I can always say I had a wonderful wedding-day, can't I?"

"Indeed, you can. A woman has only two days in her life that are her own—her very own—and her wedding-day is one of them."

"And what is the other day, Anna?"

"The other? Oh, the other day is too far away for you to think about it yet, but all the days between belong to somebody else—her children or her husband."

"But how sweet! How beautiful! To live in your husband, to give up everything to him, your life, yourself, everything! There's happiness in that, isn't there, Anna?"

"Indeed, there is, my dear, and pain, too, perhaps. But there's something better in this life than happiness, Thora, and that's blessedness, you know."

This made Thora think of Magnus, but she heard Oscar laughing in the room below, and soon forgot everything else in a delicious shuddering which suddenly came over her. Anna helped her to undress, and when the crown and the kirtle were laid aside, she moved about for some moments without speaking. Then she said, softly:

"Will you go to bed now, dearest, or shall I give you your dressing-gown?"

"Give me my dressing-gown," said Thora faintly.

Anna moved about on tiptoe a moment or two longer, turning the lamp down and fixing the shade. Then she opened the door and stood for an instant on the threshold looking back at Thora where she sat combing out her hair before the stove. All at once her middle-aged, homely face became young and beautiful by the magic of a memory of her own, and going softly back she kissed Thora without saying a word, and then crept silently out of the room.

9

Left alone, Thora looked timidly around her, and seeing things of Oscar's lying among her own she felt a new and still more delicious sense of happiness. During the days preceding the wedding she had thought that as soon as the service in the cathedral had come to an end and she was Oscar's wife a mysterious change would come over her, but that had not been so, and all day long she had felt quite the same. But now it was different, and in this room she had become another being—not herself only, but Oscar also. It was very sweet and beautiful, but it was a little frightening, too, and to ease her fast-beating heart she got into bed and covered up her face.

She could hear the company breaking up below, and a little later she heard their footsteps crunching the snow under her window, which fronted the road. They stood there and sang a bridal song. It was the song of the "Two Roses."

The winter was cold and the ground was white, but two roses of love still grew in the garden of God. The frost could not freeze the two roses of love, for they were warmed by the air of heaven; the sun could not scorch the two roses of love, for they were watered from the well of life. Two roses of love on a single stem; two roses of love in two fond young hearts; two roses of love and joy!

When the song came to an end there was some merry giggling under the window, followed by shouts of "Good night, Thora!" "Happy dreams!" Then as the company went off they started the bridal song again, and in her mind's eye Thora could see them going back to the town, arm in arm, young girls and young men.

Thora listened to the voices dying down the street, and for a moment all life seemed to be set to the music of love; Oscar and she would be children always, never growing older, but rambling hand in hand through a flowery world where everybody loved them and they loved everybody, and there could be no real trouble because love was all in all.

But just then the cathedral clock struck eleven, and she remembered Magnus. She could see him crossing the desolate white heath under the shooting stream of the northern lights—a lonesome man riding one horse, while another, with an empty saddle, was running by his side. Poor Magnus! But there was no help for it!

The voices died away in the distance, and there was a moment of silence in the cozy nest—a warm, muffled, secret kind of silence, broken by nothing but the underthrob of the ceaseless sea. Thora closed her eyes and held her breath. How happy she was! She was trembling like a bird caught and held in the hand, but even her fear was full of happiness.

At the next moment there was a noiseless footstep on the floor, a sense of somebody in the room, and then—Oscar was leaning over her and kissing her on the lips.

PART III

Yet ah, that spring should vanish with the rose!
That youth's sweet-scented manuscript should close!
The nightingale that in the branches sang,
Ah, whence, and whither flown again, who knows ?

I

THE wedding being over, and the wedding party gone, Anna went on a visit to Magnus in order to bear him company during the first weeks of his first winter, and to see that his house was in order.

The farm was thirty-odd miles from the capital, not far from the scene of the sheep-gathering and in the middle of the great plain of Thingvellir—an historic spot, formerly the place of the Icelandic parliament, for the neglected Mount of Laws may still be seen there.

There were only two houses on the plain—the farmhouse and the parsonage, with its little church beside it. The farmhouse was the larger of the two, and being on the line of road from the capital to the chief market of the Northland it had become a resting place for travelers.

The Inn-farm had belonged to Anna's family for many generations and her father had been the last to hold it. He was a worthy man, silent and serious, much like Magnus in personal character, but he left the place badly embarrassed, having fallen into the hands of a defaulting factor. After his daughter married he lost his wife and then he died suddenly—people said of drink. Since then the estate had been twenty years in the hands of a steward, but the Governor had paid off the mortgage out of the savings of his salary and the farm was free.

It was an endless delight to Anna to bring the place back to its former condition. She began with the sleeping accommodation, for sin comes with a laugh, she said, but goes with

124

a cry. The shepherd and his wife she put in the upper bed-room (the Badstofa), the maids in the lower one, and the farm-boys in the loft. Each of the rooms was under its own roof, and the homestead as a whole was less like a single house than a group of houses, or like a gipsy encampment, with its peaked tents going off in different directions. The principal apartment was a large square hall, with two guest-rooms opening out of it. Magnus was to sleep in one of these guest rooms, except when both were wanted for trav-elers, and then he was to lie on a mattress stretched on the floor.

Anna inspected the kitchen (the Elt House) and the storehouse (the Skemma)—examined the winter's stock of potted meat and dried and salted cod and whale, and put a lock on the Bur, for seldom does the servant-maid starve in the larder, she said. Finally she turned her attention to the Hall, which was the general living room, and furnished it afresh with a settle, an armchair, a Bornhome clock, and a big German stove. As a finishing stroke she hung two large photographs on the walls, one of the Governor, the other of herself. The Governor was gorgeous in his gold-braided uniform, but she was homely in her black hufa, and on second thoughts she would have taken her own picture down but Magnus said something nice about it and she al-lowed it to remain.

Anna's visit was a long one, but as often as she prepared to go, saying home was the best place for the stupid, Magnus answered that in that case Gudrun must unpack her trunk, for the Governor could not be expecting her. In this way she stayed at Thingvellir until the snow began to be honey-combed by the thaw and the ribs of the landscape to be re-vealed again.

Meantime her life at the farm was simple and primitive and every day had its own duty. Before it was light in the morning she rang the bell in the hall which awakened the household, and sent the maids to the shippons and the boys to the beasts in their pens. And when the short day had closed in she rang the bell again for supper, and finally for prayers, when the house-father (Magnus now) gave out a hymn and read a lesson.

On Sunday she went to church, and met the fifty-odd people who had ridden over from the farms that bordered the plain. She sat in the seat in front of the communion rail, with its picture of Christ in white robes among warm eastern foliage. Magnus sat in the choir and put up the figures on the plate that gave the numbers of the hymns. He had little voice and no music, but Anna listened and was happy.

Though the nights were long the household was never idle. While the servants had to mend and make blankets in their own quarters, Magnus would weave on a loom he set up in the hall and his mother would spin or knit stockings. He was full of great projects again, and though his former schemes were impossible to him now he had others of equal consequence.

What Iceland wanted was roads; roads were the landmarks of civilization; without roads the most productive country in the world could not prosper, for what was the use of a cow that gave much milk if it kicked over the pail?

Night after night in the pauses of the loom Anna had to listen to this story and to assent to the schemes that were tied on to it. Yes, Magnus was going to be very comfortable and she could go home in content.

"After all, perhaps everything was for the best," she said, "and if there were only a mistress in the house——"

But Magnus rattled at the loom and nothing more was heard for some moments.

"John and Gudrun are very well, in their way, but it's thin blood that isn't thicker than water, and when I go back——"

The loom rattled still louder.

"But a young man who couldn't be satisfied with a girl like Thora isn't likely to find many to his liking."

And then the loom rattled louder than ever, and nothing more was said that night.

II

At intervals during Anna's visit to the farm there came news of the wedding party—the letters being sent on by the weekly post from Government House and from the Factor's.

The first to come was from England, and it was a joint letter to everybody written by all three of the wanderers. Oscar began it, wi h a playful review of their journey from the time of the departure of the " Laura."

" As soon as we set foot on the ship we were told that Captain Limsen had given up his own cabin to us, and from that hour to this everybody has shown us boundless hospitality, especially father's old college friends, the professor at Oxford and the banker here in London. Naturally we know we owe everything to the magic of the Governor's name, and consequently I am cultivating an extraordinary reverence for it, though I doubt if I shall ever find it more beautiful than I did on the morning of our wedding at the bottom of that splendid check."

" Ha, ha, the mouse knows where to come back for his cheese," said Anna.

Helga came next, with a glowing account of the London theaters, opera-houses, and picture-galleries.

" The half had not been told me, as the big Book says, and I wonder more than ever why a poor girl should be doomed to waste her life in a wilderness when she might live in a world of so many clever and beautiful people."

" M'm! It's poor work pouring water on a rock," said Anna.

Thora came last with a rather sad little note. It was all very wonderful, no doubt, but she was feeling just a wee bit home-sick. Did not care so very much for operas and picture-galleries, so Oscar had to take Helga by herself.

" I like best to sit in the window of the hotel and look at the crowds in the square. Such multitudes! Always going and coming and hardly anybody ever speaking to anybody else! That's what strikes you at first as most extraordinary. It is so strange to think that the people in the streets do not even know each other by sight, and that every young woman who goes by has her own family somewhere— her own husband and perhaps her own children—and that she is hurrying away to them. I don't know why, but it makes me feel so lonely, and then I almost want to be back in my dear, sweet, homely old Iceland."

Magnus had to read this letter aloud—for Anna was no

reader of handwriting—and when he came to Thora's part his voice thickened and broke.

The next letter came from Paris, and Helga wrote the whole of it.

"Such sights! Such luxury! Such gaiety! And such dreams of dresses! And then the opera—Chopin, Verdi, Wagner, Greig! We are at the opera every night—that is to say, Oscar and I are, Thora not caring very much for music. Thora's chief pleasure is to walk in the flower market by the Madeleine and watch the children playing, and look as if she wished she were one of them."

"Just like our Thora," said Anna.

"Neils is here—Neils Finsen you know. Neils has finished his course at the Musical College, and is connected in some way with Covent Garden and has come to Paris on managerial business. He seems to be getting along wonderfully and it makes me feel almost envious. Oh, to get on in life! To escape forever from that grey sky and all those freezing surroundings! What I would give to do it! Nothing should stand between me and success in life if I only saw the chance of it. And who knows—perhaps I may some day! Neils declares that my voice has improved wonderfully and I am practising constantly. But to have any real opportunity in music one ought to be here or in London or Dresden, and it is so expensive. I'm nearly penniless as it is, and I am so shockingly dowdy that if some one does not send me——"

The letter was to the Factor and he had cut away the end of it.

"M'm! M'm!" said Anna. "What the Miss is used to, the Misses keeps up." And then they ate their supper of smoked mutton and black bread in silence and rang the bell for prayers.

The third letter from the wedding party came from Italy, and it was written by Oscar only. The post that brought it had been delayed by a snow-storm, and had sheltered two nights on the Moss Fell Heath. At the Inn-farm the cattle-pens had been completely buried, and Magnus and the men

"The world will be white with you in Iceland, but here in Italy the roses are in bud, and the sky is blue and the air is balmy. What a time we have had of it! We came down from Venice, the city of silence and dream, through Florence, the city of sunshine, and Rome, the mother of cities, to Naples, the city of song. Italy seems to set all Europe to music! Lovely and beloved Italy! If only some one could do the same for Iceland! Rugged, gaunt, grand old Iceland! But wait—only wait—perhaps somebody will do it yet!"

"Ah, Oscar, Oscar," said Anna, "it's easier to count twelve mountains than to climb one."

"Helga is enjoying the trip tremendously. Out every minute of the day and making friends on every side. Thora does not seem so well, poor child, and she hardly cares to go about. We are going on to the Riviera next week and thence back to Iceland. I must, of course, be home for the opening of Althing, but Helga is grudging every day. It is now two o'clock in the morning and we have just returned from a Veglioni—that is to say a masque ball—this (yesterday) being the last of Lent. Flowers, streamers, confetti, and such dresses! Helga looked magnificent in a pale blue chiffon of the latest model and was, out of all comparison, the belle of the evening. Poor Thora did not care to go, so she stayed in the hotel and went to bed early."

Magnus and his mother also went to bed early on the night they read that letter. Anna rung the bell that hung from the ceiling of the hall, and the servants in their skin slippers and woolen stockings trooped in for prayers. The lesson was the story of the widow's cruise and the hymn was—

> "Meek and low, meek and low,
> I shall soon my Jesus know."

The last letter they received from the wanderers came on the first day of spring, when the thaw had set in, and the water was running down the discolored snow on the mountains like tears on a wrinkled face, and the sheep were beginning to lamb. It was from Monte Carlo and was written by Thora to Anna herself.

"This place is so beautiful, Anna, yet I do not think I like

it very much. The houses are all splendid palaces, but they
don't seem so comfortable as the little homes in Iceland. I
dare not say this to Oscar, lest he should think me ungrate-
ful, and certainly there is no fog or mist here, and no big
white waves, because the sea is always blue; and of course
the trees are so wonderful and the blossoms so beautiful!
Sometimes they have a carnival, and then wagon-loads of
flowers are flung about everywhere; but next day it is quite
pitiful to see the lovely roses that have been trampled upon
being swept up in the streets.

"In the afternoon a band plays in a garden and you drive
in a carriage round and round it. At night you go to a
restaurant—bigger than the Artisan's Institute—and there
another band plays while you eat your dinner—two or three
hundred at once, and all the ladies in low dresses. After
that you go to a Casino, where all is silent and rather dark
and people sit round tables and play cards for money.
Everybody plays cards here because everybody seems to be
always taking a holiday."

"Ah, but the devil never does," said Anna.

"It is shocking to hear, though, how much is sometimes lost in a moment. Last night Oscar pointed out a
pale-faced young man who had gambled away the whole of
his estate—larger and more valuable than the Inn-farm
itself. They say he had not intended to play at all when he
went into the room, but the fever mastered him and he could
not resist it.

"Ay, ay, we don't see the ruts when the snow covers
them," said Anna.

"It made me feel ill and I couldn't stay any longer, but
Helga wished to remain, so Oscar put me in a carriage and
I came back to the hotel and went to bed. I do wish Helga
were not so fond of such places. She is, however, and as a
consequence Oscar is compelled to go with her, although he
does not want to, and sometimes he comes back very depressed. Since we came here his sleep has been much
broken, and his manner very restless. I shall be glad when
we leave this place.

"But we have had such a wonderful time altogether, and
Oscar has been so kind to me and I have been so happy. All

the same, I shall be glad to be home again, to see all the dear old faces—yours and Auntie Margret's and father's and the Governor's. I suppose Magnus does not talk of me now—does he? How is Silvertop? Tell Magnus to rub his ears for me and kiss his rough old nose. What a romp we'll have over the Heath some day! But I suppose I must not romp too much now, must I? It is so strange, Anna—there are hardly any babies about this place! Not like Italy, where you see them everywhere, with their poor little legs wrapped up like a mummy's.

"We are to be back for the first of summer, and I'm counting the days already. Give our love to everybody and if anybody asks after me in particular say I am so well and so happy."

The loom in the hall lay idle on the night when Magnus read this letter. Nobody spoke until Anna lit two candles and gave one of them to Magnus, saying:

"Here! You're tired, and no wonder, being up before daybreak. How many lambs this morning, Magnus?"

"Twenty-two, but one of the best of them is dead."

"That's the way of it always. Good night!"

"Good night!"

At the door of his bedroom Magnus paused, candle in hand.

"Mother!"

"Well?"

"Do you think she is so very happy?"

"Our Thora? God knows, my son!" said Anna.

III

THE snow was gone and the pale ground was green and golden with the raiment and the jewels of spring when the travelers returned to Iceland. Rounding the head of the fiord in the early morning, when the little capital was smoking for breakfast, Captain Zimsen had fired a cannon in honor of their home-coming, and everybody ran out-of-doors in delight, thinking the man-of-war had come from Copenhagen, but there was greater joy still when the "Laura" dropped her anchor and the little boats that had gone out to meet her came back with the news that the wedding party had returned.

Half the men of the town went down to the jetty to welcome the wanderers; among them the Governor in his gala uniform, the Factor in his best scull-cap, smoking his best German pipe, the Sheriff, the Rector, and the Bishop.

The Factor's big white boat had been sent off instantly to fetch the three ashore, and when it was coming back there was a good deal of curiosity as to how they would look after their long journey. Oscar, who was standing in the bow, was seen to be sunburnt, and slightly older-looking, having grown a small, fair mustache, which was curled up at the ends. It was observed by somebody that he wore the latest pattern of waistcoat and carried an Italian cloak over his arm. Helga, who was standing in the middle of the boat, looked a shade more buxom, and wore a new French hat. She had a kodak swung over her shoulder and was looking at the people on the jetty through an ivory-framed field-glass. And Thora, who was sitting in the stern in the costume in which she went away, with Magnus's white bearskin across her knees, looked a thought thinner than before, but her face was bright with smiles, though there were tears in her sparkling eyes.

When the boat came alongside the salutations were lusty and robustious. Such laughter! Such chaff! Such prolonged handshaking and slapping on the back! After the Governor and the Factor had kissed Thora they found their cheeks were wet, but Helga was as bright as the day and Oscar made everybody happy. He shook hands all round and hailed even the fishermen and boatmen by name. "He doesn't forget an old friend, eh?" said an old fellow in bare feet.

Then away they trooped to Government House, where Anna was waiting in apron and hufa at the door of the porch. Thora cried for joy at sight of her, and had to be carried off to her bedroom. And when Aunt Margret came in her oiled ringlets and Oscar would have kissed her she beat him off with a playful pat on the cheek, and saying, "I must see what you've done with my child first," ran straight up-stairs.

Helga went up also to take off her hat, and the Governor and the Factor carried Oscar into the drawing-room, where the Bishop, the Sheriff and the Rector joined them. Maria brought in coffee and chocolate, and the old men charged their pipes and plied Oscar with questions. The Governor asked about English politics, the Factor about custom-house duties, the Bishop about the Vatican, and the Rector about the excavations in the Roman Forum.

Oscar answered all of them with a dash and emphasis that had the look of knowledge and the effect of wit, and then glancing off the heavy ground of fact he went tobog-ganing down the slippery slopes of fiction, with amusing tales of their travels and of the ridiculous things that had and had not happened to them.

All his stories told, every time he pulled the trigger his pistol fired, and the old men laughed until they cried. "What a boy he is!" "He plays with every finger." His high spirits affected them like sunshine after dark days, like a breeze after a calm at sea, like the swing of a boat after the first dip of the oar. He was the same reckless, irrespon-sible, lovable prodigal as before, and it was not until after-ward that anybody remembered there had been a hollow ring in his hilarity, a false note in his joy.

Helga came down to the drawing-room and the men re-ceived her with a shout.

"How plump she has grown!" said the Governor.

"She has certainly filled out on the trip," said the Factor.

"Hasn't she?" said Oscar. "Just what she wanted—all she wanted."

"Nonsense! Let us talk of something serious," said Helga.

Thora came next, with Anna and Aunt Margret buzzing and humming about her like bees. She had changed to her old Iceland dress—just for remembrance—and now that she could be seen without her veil she was undoubtedly thinner, and she had a pinched look about the nostrils and a feverish spot in the middle of her cheeks. But her face was shining with timid smiles and she was overflowing with gratitude.

" Anna has given us such beautiful rooms, Oscar, the big one overlooking the road and the long one behind it, though I don't know what in the world we are going to do with two."

" Oh, don't worry yourself about that, dear—we may find a use for them by and by," said Anna with a knowing nod of the head, and then the color flew up to Thora's eyes like a flag of distress, and the men began to smile.

Anna was smiling also and making signals to the Governor and chuckling to him behind her hand. " Is it so?" " Yes, indeed, I asked her up-stairs and it's just as I expected." Then the Governor in his turn began to chuckle and to whisper to the Factor. " No? Is it a fact?" " So Anna tells me." And then they chuckled together, until everybody laughed at them, whereupon the Factor said:

" And now, Oscar, you've told us all about London and Paris and Rome, but not a word about the place where they make money without working for it."

" Monte Carlo? Haven't I?" said Oscar. " Oh, well— a beautiful place! In fact an absolute paradise."

" An absolute hell if half one hears is true," said the Governor.

" Well, yes—yes, that's so, too," said Oscar.

" I once heard of a man who made ten pounds in a single night—think of that," said the Factor.

" Goodness' sake!" cried Aunt Margret.

" But what's the good of having a chest full of gold if the devil keeps the key?" said the Governor.

Then Helga, who was sitting on the piano-stool, began to play softly, and Oscar swung round to her.

" Ah, 'Addio Napoli!' We must sing you some of the Neapolitan songs, father."

This was received with a chorus of approval, and for the next half-hour Helga played and Oscar sang the gay ditties with which Naples fills the air of Italy with song. And when at one moment the Factor would have come back to the man who made ten pounds in a single night, Helga struck up the tarantella and Oscar danced it.

At length the Governor said, " Everything has a stopping place except Time. It's late, and Thora is looking tired, so I'm going to turn out everybody who doesn't live here."

"Quite right, too," said Aunt Margret, "and I'm going to carry Helga off to her own quarters."

"*I* will take Helga home," said Oscar, and with further handshaking and well-wishing the party began to break up.

"After all I suppose you are glad to be back, Thora?" said the Bishop.

"Very, very glad," replied Thora.

"Ha, ha! It isn't easy to hobble a home-sick pony," laughed the Rector. "And you, Helga?"

"I'm not glad at all, Rector. Who *could* be glad to leave all that loveliness for a wilderness like this."

That chilled everybody for a moment, and thinking to come to Helga's relief, Oscar said:

"There's something in what Helga says, certainly."

"Then you, also, Oscar——"

"No, Rector, no—that is to say—well, I'm glad to be back and I shall be glad to go away again."

And then everybody was as happy as before.

IV

NEXT day Oscar and Helga spent many hours in a round of return visits, while Thora, who was still tired, stayed at home and received some of her old schoolfellows. One of them, who had been the beauty of her day, had married a farmer fifteen miles away and borne him three children. It was all work, work, work with her now and the once-bright girl was a slave.

"Ah, Thora, how lucky you were not to marry Magnus!" she said.

"Do you think so?" said Thora.

"Why, yes, Thora. And then everybody says Oscar is going to be such a distinguished man."

It was the spring caravan time and Magnus himself, who had brought his wool to the Factor's, came late in the afternoon. Thora thought he looked brawnier and bigger than ever, and she could not help seeing that his hands were coarser and his nails chopped off square. But his voice was as soft as it used to be, and he was shy and even nervous.

The light was low when he came into the drawing-room.

and looking closely at her face he asked three times over
if she was well, until she laughed as she gave him the same
answer again and again. Then he laughed, too, and after
that they got on better, and exchanged all the " newses."

Silvertop was in good condition; he had got his summer
coat and looked splendid; in fact, he had been too well fed
and was getting a little over himself and would have to be
taken down a peg or two before Thora rode him again. Ah.
well, she wouldn't want him just yet—not *just* yet—and
Magnus had better keep the rascal at the farm a little longer.

" But what a time you've been away! " said Magnus.

" Haven't we? " said Thora. " Five months, nearly six."

" Six months come Tuesday week," said Magnus.

At that they both became confused, and Thora began to
show some photographs taken by Helga on the journey.

" How beautiful! How wonderful! " said Magnus. " But
I wonder your ship wasn't floating on the pumps, as they say,
before you got back to harbor—it must have cost a good deal
of money to see all those places."

" It must," said Thora, " traveling is so expensive—especially when there is more than one to pay for."

" And then there was Helga," said Magnus.

" Yes, indeed, there was Helga. But the check which
father and the Governor gave to Oscar seems to have been
sufficient for all."

" Still I can not understand how he made it pay for everything."

" No, it isn't easy to understand that, is it? "

" Venice! Rome! Monte Carlo! How you must have
enjoyed your journey! "

" Oscar did—every day of it."

" And you, Thora? "

" I'm not a good traveler—I soon tire of sight-seeing, and
if it hadn't been for Helga——"

" So you are not sorry you took Helga with you? "

Thora faltered a little and then said, " Helga was able to
go sight-seeing with Oscar when I had to stay in the hotel."

" But were you not lonely while they were away? "

" Perhaps—sometimes—just a little—being so much alone,
and among so many strange faces."

Magnus, who seemed to be absorbed in the photographs, said almost unconsciously, "Poor little thing!"

Then the flag of distress ran up to Thora's eyes and she answered hurriedly, "Oh, it was my own fault. Oscar always wanted to stay with me, and if it hadn't been for Helga——"

But a little catch came into her throat, and she had to stop. Whereupon Magnus said:

"And I hoped you were so happy!"

But then Anna brought in the lamp and the lights relieved the tension, yet being able to see the photographs plainly Magnus laid them down and Thora put them away.

He left early, having a long ride before him, and Anna followed him to the door.

"Is Thora quite well?" he asked in a whisper.

"As well as can be expected under the circumstances," said Anna.

"And is Oscar kind to her?"

"Kind? Oscar, kind? Why should you ask that, Magnus?"

"She looks so pale, so depressed."

"Oh, that's often the way with young wives in her condition. Haven't you noticed anything—anything particular? Our Thora will be a mother before long."

"And is that all that's the matter with her?" said Magnus.

V

THE summer session of Parliament was to begin almost immediately and Oscar plunged straightway into preparations for his campaign. He was to move a resolution proposing that the Acts of Althing should henceforward be promulgated on the last day of the session, as in the old times, from the ancient Mount of Laws at Thingvellir. It was to be his maiden speech and much depended upon it. Before he wrote it he went over to the Factor's to discuss with Helga its scheme and argument. After he had written it he went over to the Factor's again to read it to Helga, and obtain

10

the benefit of her suggestions. And when he had committed it to memory he went over to the Factor's a third time to rehearse it before Helga. It was Helga first and last, all day and every day until the day of the opening sitting.

"Helga is a great politician, but you care nothing about politics, do you, Thora?" And Thora would swallow the lump in her throat and answer "No."

Thora and Helga were both present when Oscar took his seat. They occupied the Governor's ante-room that opened off the parliamentary chamber. The galleries were crowded with spectators, and there was much curiosity when Oscar rose to speak. Thora felt a little faint at the first sound of his voice, and she would have fled away if she could have done so, but Helga held her to her chair.

"Hush! For goodness' sake be quiet," she whispered. "You'll make him still more nervous."

The speech was a great success. It was an appeal for the preservation of the old order—for all that made Iceland what it was—the land of Saga and song. Even the party of progress who thought much of its moonshine were carried away by the fervor and enthusiasm, the poetry and passion of the young speaker. When Oscar finished there were vollies of applause; the people in the galleries clapped their hands and Helga stood up and waved her handkerchief, but Thora covered her face and cried into her gloves.

The resolution was passed unanimously, and Oscar was made chairman of a committee to carry out the necessary preparations. This work occupied all his spare time during the six weeks of the parliamentary session. It took him to the Factor's every day, for Helga was full of schemes for the great ceremonial. Being in Parliament every morning and at the Factor's every afternoon Oscar was nearly always from home and Thora saw little of him. Every night he returned with a mouthful of apologies and a torrent of explanations. They had been searching the Sagas for the exact course taken by the procession in the old days, or they had been selecting flags to hang over the rocks, or they had been composing a hymn to celebrate the occasion—Oscar had improvised one in a moment and Helga had written it down.

"And how has my little baby been going on all day long?

Lonely? What a shame! I'm sorry—very, very sorry," he would say.

And then Thora would answer, "Don't think of me, Oscar. You have your work to do, and I only wish I could help you, like Helga."

But in the long hours of loneliness, when her head was on her hands and her feet were in the fender, the poor little soul would sink and the tender heart grow bitter. Only Anna would be with her then, comforting and consoling her, and pretending to be blind to what every eye could see.

"Anna," she said at length, "when Magnus was here he asked me such a strange question."

"What was that, Thora?"

"He asked if I wasn't sorry that Helga had gone with us on our journey."

"And are you?"

"Sometimes—perhaps it is foolish—but sometimes I think I am."

"I know. I think I know. And it isn't foolish of you at all, dear. Oscar is doing wrong. I must speak to him— I must speak to him severely."

"It isn't Oscar's fault. Helga is so selfish."

"Yes, she takes after somebody else in that way, Thora."

"She was always taking Oscar away from me when we were on our journey."

"But your journey is over now, and he must mend his manners."

"Ah, no! That part of our journey isn't over yet, Anna. Sometimes I think it has only begun."

"You don't mean to say that Helga is trying to——"

"Helga has no pity. When she once gets hold of anybody she will never give him up."

"You think she is trying to get hold of Oscar?"

"I think she *has* got hold of him."

"You mustn't say that about your husband, Thora."

"Oh, I don't blame Oscar. Helga is so beautiful, so clever. She has every advantage over me."

"Now that's just where you are wrong. There is one point in which our little Thora has an advantage over Helga and every other woman in the world."

"You mean with Oscar——"

"Yes, with Oscar—you are going to be the mother of his child."

"Will that make any difference?"

"Any difference? I should think it will indeed. My poor mother used to say, 'When people are married it's the children who keep the pot boiling.'"

"You mean that when my baby is born Oscar will come back to me?"

"Certainly I do."

"And that he will never go away from me any more?"

"Never! Oscar has always loved children—wait till he has a child of his own and see."

"Well, you are his mother—you know him best."

"Trust me, Thora! It isn't a good well if water has to be carried to it, but when the child is born Oscar will begin all over again."

"You think that? Really? You think Oscar will love me again for my baby's sake?"

"Any man must if he has a good heart—and Oscar's heart is good whatever his head may be."

"Indeed—indeed it is."

"He must love the mother for the sake of the child, and the child for the sake of the mother."

"How sweet! How beautiful!"

Thora's own eyes were now like the eyes of a child—so full of wonder and love. She fell to counting the weeks that must pass before the fulness of her time.

"Nine weeks—hardly nine—eight—think, mother—only eight. How I wish it were even less! I used to look forward to that time with anxiety and dread, but there is nothing to be afraid of if so much good can come out of a little pain—nothing really—now is there?"

VI

IN this sweet hope Thora comforted herself for four weeks, and then something happened which disturbed all her calculations. It was the eve of the proclamation and the committee of which Oscar was the chief decided to visit Thing-vellir in order to complete their preparations for the ceremony. On this errand Helga was to go with them, and having so many things to attend to they were to sleep one night at the Inn-farm and return the following day. When Oscar announced this program a sudden change came over Thora's patient and submissive spirit.

"Then I must go, too," she said.

"You? You, Thora?" said Oscar. "Why, what can you be thinking of? Thirty-three miles away—in that desolate region—without a doctor or a nurse—and so near your time, too. Impossible! Quite impossible!"

"Then Helga mustn't go either."

"But Helga is so useful, so necessary."

"I don't care. If I can not go with you then Helga shall not do so, either."

"My dear Thora, this is so unlike you. But as you please. I shall be ashamed to tell Helga, and explain to the committee, but still, if you wish it— No, no, you must not cry. You must not disturb yourself. My little woman must keep herself very quiet while I am away—very, very quiet."

Two hours after Oscar had gone Helga came to Government House. Thora was alone, and the sisters faced each other for some instants without speaking. At length Helga said:

"Well, I trust you are satisfied. Now that you have shown your foolish jealousy and made us the talk of the town, I trust you are satisfied."

"Oscar said I was to keep myself quiet, Helga, and you know I ought to do so."

"Oh, you can excite yourself enough it seems, when you wish to express your paltry feelings. Because I have sympathized with Oscar and tried to help and inspire him, you who have never sympathized with him and can never help him, because you cannot understand him, and he is beyond you—you must come with your paltry spite——"

"Helga! You have never been kind to me—never since you came home a year ago—but now you are cruel."

"Am I? Perhaps I am. And perhaps I've gone through enough to make me so."

"You speak as if your disappointment of this morning in not going with Oscar were a great and grievous matter, but you don't seem to remember how often I have been disappointed in the same way."

"Oh, I dare say you think you are much to be pitied."

"I don't say I'm to be pitied, Helga, because I know it was my own fault at the beginning. But I do say I've never known a moment's peace since you came home from Denmark. I persuaded father to send for you because you were my sister, and I wished you to share my happiness, but you have never shown me any sisterly feeling—never. On the contrary, you found me happy and you have made me miserable. You have done your best to render life intolerable to me."

"I thought you said you were not to excite yourself, Thora?"

"It is you that are exciting me, Helga, because you are always inflicting the sharpest tortures upon me and hurting me where you know I can bear it least. From the first you tried to take Oscar away from me—you know you did. You tried to do it before our marriage and you have tried to do it ever since. You were not even ashamed to try during our honeymoon and you are trying now, because you have lost all sense of loyalty or justice or remorse or even shame."

"Oh, yes," said Helga, "you think you have been a great martyr. But would it surprise you to hear that somebody else has gone through a still greater martyrdom? You accuse me of having inflicted tortures upon you—what of the tortures you have inflicted upon me?"

"I, Helga?"

"Yes, you! You speak as if I were the sort of woman who draws a man into her net, who tears him away from the wife he loves and drags him down to his death. You would have been nearer right if you had thought of me as another kind of woman altogether—one who is herself the sufferer—who is shut out and cut off and must remain unmated because the man who loves her is married to somebody else."

"Helga!"

"Oh, I should have had mercy on your condition, but you would not let me. And now if you wish to hear the truth I will tell you."

" And what is the truth, Helga? "

" The truth is that Oscar does not love you at all—perhaps he has never loved you."

" Helga, how dare you! The falseness of what you say is on the face of it. If Oscar has never loved me, why am I his wife? What advantage had he to gain by choosing me instead of you? What compulsion was put upon him? If he did not love me why did he marry me? "

" He married you out of pity—from a mistaken sense of duty—because he had contracted to marry you and thought it honorable to go on with his bargain. But he loved somebody else and so he sacrificed both of them."

" It's false, Helga, it's false, and it's only your vanity that makes you say so."

" Oh, you must not suppose that I am saying this without a certainty. I had it from himself——"

" Himself? He, himself? "

" —— from his own mouth, on the very eve of your marriage."

" On the eve of his marriage to me, he told you—— "

" He told me that he loved me. And since then, if he has not said it in words he has said it in other ways again and again. He loves me still—— "

" No, no, no, it is not true."

" He will always love me."

" It is not true, it is not true."

" And he loves you no more than a man loves his dog or his horse, or the man of the Bible days loved the handmaiden of his wife."

" Helga, for shame! Are you without conscience or truth that you can lie to me like that? If Oscar had never loved me do you think I should not have found it out long ago? And if he loved you do you think I should not know it—I who am bearing his child? "

" Oh, you needn't taunt me with that, Thora. Yes, yours are the lips that kiss him, but it isn't the lips that matter. It is the love behind the lips, and that love is mine, and every time he kisses you the kiss is meant for me."

" You lie, Helga, you lie."

" And the child too, it is not your child, because the love that gave it life was my love."

"You lie, you lie."

"What do I care if you are the bondwoman who bears his child? The child will be my child, and when he is born he will have my face——"

"No, it is not possible."

"It is, it is—you know it is."

Thora gasped for breath. Then an extraordinary change came over her that made her almost unrecognizable. The patient and gentle woman seemed suddenly possessed by a demon. Something strange and horrible seemed in an instant to enter into her soul. The homicidal impulse which takes hold of wild animals appeared to assail and conquer her. One moment she stood facing her sister, convulsed and livid, and then in a voice that was hoarse with rage and shame she said:

"Very well, if that is so, and if my child is not my own, if it has been conceived in the love of another woman, and I am only the bondwoman who bears it, then—then—then—it shall never be born, or if it is born I—I—I will kill it!"

With that she burst into a peal of laughter, and fell on to the floor.

The noise brought Anna into the room panting.

"What have you done to her? What have you said? Thora! Thora!"

"I will kill the child. I will kill it, I will kill it!"

The wild, shrieking laughter continued and increased until the Governor came running from his room. He listened for a moment to the mad cries and then said, "Let us lift her up and carry her to bed. Helga, go for the doctor and for Margret Neilsen. Tell them to come quickly. She's in labor—there's no time to lose."

VII

ALL night Thora tossed about in a strong delirium, which expressed itself in the one wild, homicidal cry. Aunt Margret came and found Anna in the sick-room. The Factor followed, and sat for hours with the Governor in his bureau below.

The Doctor (Doctor Olesen) never left Thora's side. He did not conceal the gravity of her condition. The delirium was due to premature labor. Such homicidal mania was not unknown in the cases of young mothers. It generally originated in some startling event, perhaps a great loss, or a great shock or a grievous disappointment. Doctor Olesen questioned Anna, but she knew nothing to account for Thora's seizure. He asked Helga, but she said little.

Helga was obviously in a state of terror. Her face was deathly pale and her lips quivered. She could not be got to leave the house. When the Factor returned home at ten o'clock, being powerless to do anything, he could not tear Helga away. It was observed by all three attendants on the invalid that Helga did not ask to be admitted to Thora's room. "A sensible girl," thought the Doctor. "She knows better than ask *me*," thought Anna. But Helga seemed anxious to help in any menial way, no matter what.

When there was nothing else to do Helga sat in the drawing-room, still wearing her cloak and hat, and listening in fear to the mad cries from the chamber overhead. In the long dark hours she was a prey to the most agonizing thoughts. She was feeling like one who had committed a murder and asking herself what would happen if Thora died.

Beyond the physical agony of hearing those wild cries from the chamber overhead, beyond the pangs of a troubled conscience and beyond the pain of the sisterly love and pity which overcame her and surprised her in these dark hours, Helga suffered from one overmastering terror—the terror of what Oscar would say to her when he came back. He had been sent for; there would be no need to tell him anything.

Oscar arrived at midnight, covered with dust and sweat. Somebody opened the hall door to him. He did not stop to look who it was—but pushing through the house came first upon Helga in the drawing-room. For a moment they stood face to face, like guilty things. She was trembling from head to foot; he was breathing heavily.

"How is she now?" he asked.

"No better," she answered.

He heard the cries from the room above.

"Is that she?"

"Yes."

"Oh, God!" he muttered, and began to load himself with reproaches. "I should have taken her with me when she asked me. Why didn't I? I ought to have known what would happen."

Helga had expected that he would fly out at her, and she could have borne any insult, but this she could not bear.

"It's all my fault," he said. "I have been a fool—a weak, selfish fool. Oh, Thora, my sweet, innocent, long-suffering Thora, forgive me, forgive me!"

Helga could not endure the house any longer. She felt like a criminal and wanted to escape. Leaving Oscar with his head on his arms over the cushions of the couch, she slipped out and went home through the dark and silent streets alone.

Finding Helga gone, Oscar crept up to the door of Thora's room, but he was not permitted to enter where the mere breath of excitement might quench the glimmer of life within. His mother came out to him in the large room at the back and found him with his face down on the table. She had intended to rate him soundly the moment she set eyes on him, but the sight of his distress silenced her reproaches and she fell to comforting him instead.

"No, no," said Anna, "you couldn't have taken her with you. Things are bad enough as they are, but think how much worse they would have been if all this had happened there."

"Then I should have stayed at home," said Oscar. "I should have given up everything."

"Thora couldn't have wished you to do that, my son. None of us had a right to expect it."

"But you don't know everything, mother. I have behaved shamefully to Thora. I thought I was doing right by her, but I was doing wrong, dreadfully wrong. The poor girl has suffered terribly, and this is the result."

As the first streaks of dawn began to fret the sky above the glaciers of the Eastern fells, the delirium abated, and there came a period of conscious pain. Anna ran in to Oscar to tell him of the change, and then down-stairs on a similar errand to where the Governor lay in his shirt-sleeves on the sofa in his bureau.

"She's herself at last, thank the Lord, and the doctor says she's going along as well as can be expected."

Two hours later, when the sun rose on the little town, and the fiord and the fells were crimson with his glory, the angel of peace came down to the house of pain, bearing a babe in her arms.

With a smile and an outstretched hand, the doctor entered Oscar's room, and said:

"I am happy to congratulate you. A girl—a beautiful child."

"But Thora?"

"She is weak, but quite at ease, and as well as can be expected under the circumstances."

"Thank God!"

"And now go to bed yourself, Oscar, and sleep, if you can, until this time to-morrow."

"I will—I will. Thank you, doctor, thank you a thousand times."

Meanwhile Anna was in the bureau telling the glad news to the Governor, and then running about the house to find some one to carry it to the Factor.

"*I'll* go, mother," said a voice from the kitchen.

"Goodness! Is that you, Magnus? When did you come?"

"About eleven o'clock last night."

"Then you were here before Oscar?"

"Golden Mane gallops fast, mother."

"And what have you been doing in the kitchen?"

"Carrying the wood and boiling the water for Margret Neilsen."

"Then you must go to bed now—you'll be sleepy."

"Not I—I can lie awake six nights, you know, when the lambs are coming."

"Well, a lamb has come to-night, Magnus," said Anna.

"God bless it, and the little mother as well," said Magnus.

VIII

THORA slept until midday under the combined effects of exhaustion and a sleeping draught, and when she awoke the evil spirit which had possessed her had gone, and she was her own sweet simple self once more. But the struggle had been a terrible one, and if the better part of her soul had conquered the frail body which had been its battlefield was a waste of weakness. She was pale and thin and her blue eyes were large and liquid.

Before opening them she heard from the back room (which had been transformed into a nursery) the sweetest, most thrilling sound that ever comes to a woman's ears, a sound which sums up into its joys all the ecstasy that a human soul can know, a sound which no woman in the world has ever heard but once—the first cry of her first-born.

Thora opened her eyes, and saw Anna knitting by her side.

" Is that baby? " she asked.

" Ah, I *thought* you were awake! " said Anna. " Yes, Thora, that is baby. Margret Neilsen is bathing her."

" Bring her to me. Tell Aunt Margret to bring her immediately."

" By and by, dear, by and by."

" No, now! If she doesn't bring baby this instant, I'll get up and go to her."

" Hush! You are to be very quiet, and not to excite yourself. And as for getting up, the doctor says if you stir out of bed within a week goodness knows what will happen."

" Yes, I know. I am very naughty, and you must forgive me. But I've not seen baby yet—not really seen her—and if you will bring her to me I shall be so good. I shall not excite myself at all—not at all. You will see how quiet I shall be."

" Well, if you promise me, faithfully promise me," said Anna.

" Wait! Sit down again, mother. Sit here by the window. I have something to ask you first. Does she—does baby resemble anybody? "

"Resemble anybody? I should think she does, indeed. I have never in all my life seen a child so like its mother."

"Like me? Oh, bring her! Bring her! I can't wait a moment longer."

Anna went into the nursery and told Aunt Margret that Thora was awake and calling impatiently for the child.

"But she'll want to take her," said Aunt Margret.

"Trust her for that, if she's a mother," said Anna

"But will it be safe? Is she quite herself again?"

"We'll chance her," said Anna.

Aunt Margret gathered up the baby in its long clothes and with its feeding-bottle at her breast, and carried it into Thora's room, and stooping by the bed she said, "There! Look at that now!"

"Give her to me, give her to me," cried Thora, stretching out two trembling white arms.

"Carefully then, carefully," said Aunt Margret.

There was no need to fear: Thora gathered her child to her breast with the free and daring but gentle touch that comes to mothers of every species.

"My baby! My baby!" she whispered, and her pale face overflowed with joy. "Yes, she is like me. I can see it myself. But why doesn't she open her eyes? Is she asleep? That can not be, because she is still sucking. Coo-coo! Isn't she beautiful? How foolish of me to say that! And yet it's true. Coo! My baby! My bootiful, bootiful baby!"

Through all this broken jargon—the divine foolishness of motherhood—the two older women stood by, trying to cackle and laugh behind their black silk aprons, but finding it hard to keep back their tears.

"Has Oscar seen her yet?"

"Not yet," said Anna.

"But he has come back, hasn't he? Didn't you tell me he had come back?"

"Yes, but he was quite worn out with watching and I sent him off to bed."

"Poor boy!"

"And Magnus has come, too, but I couldn't get him to go to bed and he still is working away in the kitchen."

"What a deal of trouble I am to everybody!"

"Trouble? We don't call that trouble."

"You've got a baby for it, haven't you?" said Thora, and she looked down at the treasure at her breast as if she had brought them the wealth of the world. All at once she cried, "Oh, oh! Look! Look!"

Aunt Margret, who was at the other side of the room, almost fainted at Thora's sudden cry.

"What has happened?" she gasped.

"Baby has opened her eyes," said Thora.

Aunt Margret dropped to a chair to breathe.

"They're blue like mine. Oscar's are brown, and Helga's —her's are grey. But perhaps baby's eyes will change their color! Do children's eyes change their color, Anna?"

"Sometimes they do," said Anna. "Blue eyes sometimes become brown——"

"Never grey?"

"Not that I know of," said Anna.

"I'm so glad baby is like me," said Thora, and she gazed down at the child with looks of wonder and love. Then her delicious selfishness took another turn and she said:

"Mother, do you not think Oscar has slept long enough now?"

"Doctor Olesen said he was to sleep until to-morrow," replied Anna.

"But couldn't you wake him up for a moment—just for a moment, to come and see us as we are now—baby and me—would it do him much harm?"

"No, but it would do *you* a great deal. You would over-excite yourself, and then, my gracious, I *should* get into trouble."

"Oh, no, I shall be quite calm—I promise you I shall be calm. And Oscar can come in his dressing-gown and then go back to sleep. Do call him—do—please do—Anna, Aunt Margret—mother!"

They could not resist the pleading voice, and Anna went off to Oscar's room. Oscar was awake.

"How is she now?" he asked.

"Still a little weak, but getting stronger every hour," said Anna.

"And the child?"

" She's got it in bed with her, and wishes you to come and see them."

" I'll come at once."

" Dear Thora ! She is happy at last. I have never seen anybody so happy. And nobody ever deserved happiness more. Just now when I left her she had the eyes of a child. But she is still on the brink of life and death. It wouldn't need much to make her take flight from this world. Therefore watch over your words, Oscar, and don't say anything that will agitate her."

Oscar promised, and then followed his mother into Thora's bedroom. At the threshold he heard the soft " Boo-oo— coo-coo " of motherly endearment, and then saw the shining pale face on the pillow with the tiny red one below it.

" My poor Thora," he said, kissing her forehead, " you are not suffering now, are you ? A little pale, perhaps, and a little thin, but better, are you not ? "

" Look ! " she whispered, uncovering the child and having no thoughts to waste on lesser matters. " Who is she like, Oscar ? "

" Like ? Do you ask me who she's like, Thora ? Why, she's like—ridiculously like you ! "

" Kiss me, Oscar. Put your arms around both of us, dearest. That way—so."

But at the next moment the baby was crying and the older women were protesting loudly.

" Come away you great, clumsy creature," said Aunt Margret.

" No, no," cried Thora. " It wasn't Oscar. He never hurts anybody. It was I, auntie," but auntie, making no terms with such heroics, took the child out of bed and proceeded to rock it, face downward, across her knee.

When the baby had been hushed to sleep they fell to the discussion of its name. Oscar was for " Thora," but Thora herself said no, that was her own name, the name Oscar knew her by, and therefore she could not share it even with her child.

" Then what do you say to ' Elin ' ? " said Oscar.

" Beautiful ! Anna, Aunt Margret, listen. Say it again, Oscar."

"'Elin.'"

"Isn't it lovely as Oscar says it?"

So they decided straightway that "Elin" it should be, and next came the question of the godparents. Thora was for Magnus ("Poor Magnus") and Oscar assented. But when Oscar in his turn nominated Helga the sunshine died off Thora's face, whereupon Anna gave him a quick glance, and began to make a noise.

"Then Magnus for godfather and Aunt Margret for godmother," said Oscar, and so it was agreed.

"And let us have the baptism to-day," said Thora.

"To-day?" cried Anna. "Why, Thora, a child is never baptised on the day of its birth except when it is going to die."

It was now Aunt Margret's turn to make a noise, and this she did by wakening baby in rising suddenly, and protesting that Oscar ought to be turned out of the room and Thora left to rest.

"Yes, yes, that's true," said Oscar, and kissing Thora again he followed Aunt Margret and the baby into the nursery. When they were gone, and the door had closed on them, Anna leaned over the bed and whispered:

"There! Didn't I know what o'clock it was striking? Hasn't Oscar come back to you? When he kissed you didn't you feel that all his heart was yours?"

"Yes, it is true," said Thora. "But will it last, think you?"

"Certainly, it will last. Last night he was reproaching himself with all sorts of things, and to-day he is like a man who is beginning over again a new life."

"You think so, Anna? You really think so?"

"Indeed I do. Depend upon it he'll not lose sight of that baby for five minutes in the day. And he'll never look at her but he'll think of you."

"How happy I am! I have never been so happy before—never, never!" She took a deep breath and closed her shining eyes to ease the beating of her heart. There was a moment's silence and then in another voice she said, "Mother?"

"Yes, dear?"

"Last night—when I was so ill—didn't I say——"

"Hush! That's all over. We'll not speak of it any more."

" All the same if I could die now—now when I am so happy—and baby, too——"

And then Anna sank into a chair, trembling from head to foot.

IX

ANNA was right about Oscar and the baby—he could not willingly allow it to be out of his sight for any five minutes of the day or night. When it was to be bathed he felt it necessary to superintend the operation, and when it was fed he was compelled to keep watch and ward. He had a thousand fears of accidents that might happen to it and became dizzy when it lay naked on the edge of Aunt Margret's lap. If it cried while he was in the dining-room he rushed upstairs, and if anything fell on the floor above he turned pale and trembled. Sleeping in the room next to the nursery he kept his door open at night, and if the baby was fretful he walked Aunt Margret to and fro (being afraid to carry the child himself) as if she had taken too much laudanum.

Two days passed in this way and he was never once out-of-doors. Thora overheard him in the adjoining room, coaxing and scolding Aunt Margret, and talking or laughing to the child, and her heart overflowed with happiness. " But *will* it last? " she asked herself.

Meantime Helga, sitting at home, shut out from these joys, was feeling herself neglected. On the third day Oscar had a message from her, saying she wished to see him on an important matter and asking him to come round immediately. He could not resist it. The little scented envelope drew him like a magnet. Going out for a walk, to think of what he should do, every step took him in the direction of the Factor's. Within half an hour he found himself in the little sitting-room overlooking the lake, and Helga was standing before him with head down, more meek and modest, but also more beautiful and irresistible than ever before.

" I have a confession to make to you," she said, " and if you are angry with me I must bear it."

She had been the cause of poor Thora's sudden illness. Stung by the disappointment of some days ago she had gone

11

across to Government House to reproach her sister with the humiliation she had put upon her. Perhaps she had said too much, and more than was true, and she was sorry and ashamed. She could wish to ask Thora's forgiveness, and if Oscar would do it for her——"

"With pleasure, Helga," said Oscar. "But all's well that ends well, and why should we say more on this subject?"

"There is another that I wished to speak of," said Helga, and then came the real burden of her message.

Poor Thora's delirium had been homicidal. She had threatened to take the life of her unborn child. What a frightful thing it would be if out of her weakness and hallucination she should attempt to carry out her threat!

"But that's all over now, Helga," said Oscar. "Since her baby came Thora had been as gentle as a lamb, and running over with tenderness and love."

"So I thought until this morning," said Helga. "But father tells me that your mother sees signs of dementia still."

"Good heavens!" cried Oscar.

"Everybody appears to have heard of it except you. I thought it was wrong to keep you in the dark, and so I've told you."

"Thanks, Helga, it is good of you, and if poor Thora is still suffering in that way——"

"There can't be a doubt of it, Oscar. She told your mother she wished she could die, and baby with her."

"She must be watched—the child, too. There must be nurses night and day."

"Is that enough, Oscar? You know how cunning people are when they are suffering from dementia. And then a child is such a frail thing—it's life might be snuffed out in an instant."

"You mean that baby should be removed?"

"It might be safest—for a time at least. It might come here—I should take the greatest care of it. But it needn't change its nurse—Aunt Margret must come home soon in any case."

"It must be done, Helga. It would be too awful if anything happened to the child. I should go mad."

"And then think of Thora. It would be ten thousand times more terrible for her."

"Poor Thora! It will break her heart," said Oscar. "It seems as if I am doomed to bring grief and pain and death to her."

"We must be cruel only to be kind, Oscar. But don't act on my advice only and for mercy's sake don't say I suggested anything. Ask somebody else."

"I will."

"Ask the Governor."

"The Governor?"

At the mention of that name they paused and looked at each other in silence, as if a ghost had passed between them.

"Any news from Monte Car—I mean Copenhagen?" asked Helga.

"Nothing yet, but I am in daily fear of something happening."

"Whatever happens I shall never forget that you did that for me, Oscar."

She held out her hand to him, and he took it, kept it for a moment, then kissed it passionately and fled from the house.

Later the same day a family conference was held at Government House to consider what ought to be done. The Governor and the Factor were there, as well as Oscar and Anna. Aunt Margret came down last, having left one of the maids in charge of the child.

"Magnus is in the nursery too," she said. "He came up with wood for the stove and Thora heard his voice, so now they are talking through the open door."

Doctor Olesen had been called into consultation and he gave a guarded opinion. Such forms of homicidal mania were due to weakness and were usually transient. Since the night of the confinement he had seen no signs of it himself, but if Anna had seen them he would not take the responsibility of opposing the step that was suggested.

Anna rocked herself and moaned and said that after all she could not be certain. She might have mistaken what had fallen from Thora. Perhaps the poor child had been thinking of something quite different.

Aunt Margret was now of the same mind, but much more

emphatic. "I don't believe a word of it," she said, "and I'm sorry I ever doubted her. Thora is a Neilsen, and she wouldn't hurt a hair of the child's head."

"This is no time to indulge sentimental feelings," said the Governor. "If Thora is suffering from dementia, however transient, we must protect her from the dangers of her weakness."

"I agree, Stephen," said the Factor. "I'm sorry—I'm sorry for my daughter—but I agree, I agree."

"That is our duty—our plain duty," continued the Governor, "first to the child who is the offspring—at present the only probable offspring—of two families, and next to the poor young mother herself, than whom no one would have more right to reproach us if we failed to do it and a disaster occurred."

"No one, Stephen, no one," said the Factor.

"It seems so cruel, so dreadfully cruel," said Anna.

"But it's all for Thora's own good, mother," said Oscar.

"I know, Oscar, I know, yet it's cruel for all that."

"But I should like to know who's going to do it," said Aunt Margret. "I'm not, I tell you flat."

"Then Anna must do it herself," said the Governor.

"No, no, don't ask me," said Anna.

"Why not? Who so proper to do such an act of mercy and love? And Oscar, too—Oscar himself if need be must carry the child over to the Factor's."

Oscar's lips whitened and quivered and his heart clutched at his ribs.

It was decided that the child should be taken from the mother that night, as soon as she was asleep and the house was quiet.

"But she goes to sleep with the child at her breast and always awakes when it wants the bottle," said Anna. "I'll give her a draught—she'll sleep until morning," said the Doctor.

"Oh, dear me! Oh, dear me! I shall feel like a thief," said Anna.

"Or like a murderer," said Aunt Margret.

X

MEANTIME Magnus in the nursery was looking down at the little face in the cot, sometimes blinking at the light, sometimes digging its little fist into its face, sometimes gripping with its tiny soft hand his own coarse finger. Through the open door to the adjoining room there came the voice that he knew so well, a little weaker, a little thinner, but more joyous and silvery than before.

"Is that you, Magnus?"

"Yes, Thora."

"Have you seen my little Elin?"

"I'm looking at her now, Thora."

"Isn't she beautiful? Isn't she a darling?"

"She's like a little angel, Thora."

A joyous thrill came from the other room, and then the silvery voice began again: "She's awake, isn't she? Can't I hear her laughing? She laughs already, the little rogue! Do you know you are to be her godfather, Magnus?"

"I am?"

"Yes, Oscar agreed to it immediately, and the baptism is to take place soon."

"It will be the happiest moment of my life, Thora."

"Oh, she'll give you lots of trouble. She's going to be such a little mischief. Can't you see her growing up, Magnus?"

"I see her just like her mother when she was a child, Thora."

Another joyous trill came through the open door and then the silvery voice once more: "She'll be going to stay with you at the farm some day, and then she'll pull up all the flowers in your garden."

"She shall do whatever she likes, Thora."

"But there are chasms and caves and rifts in the earth there, aren't there?"

"I'll keep watch on her, Thora."

"If she should slip anywhere——"

"I'll keep watch on her all her life, Thora."

The joyous trill came again, but with a slightly different note: Then: " Magnus ? "

" Yes, Thora ? "

" Why don't you marry and have a little Elin of your own, you know ? "

" I ? Oh, no." And then a gruff laugh and something about " a poor farmer."

" Don't say that, Magnus."

Then the silvery voice that came to him through the open door became serious and sweetly patronizing, hoping he would be happy and prosperous at Thingvellir. It wasn't a great life, certainly, not a distinguished career like Oscar's— that is to say what Oscar was to be—and it wanted hard work early and late, yet still——

" But, Magnus, you've been here three days, haven't you ? How have you been able to spare them ? "

" I'll make up for them when I get home, Thora."

" But Anna says you haven't been to bed since you came, and now the Proclamation is near and you'll be kept busy at the Inn with that. "

" I'm strong, Thora—fearfully strong," said Magnus.

Thora lay back in her bed and with a blush there was none to see said :

" Magnus, I think—I really think you would do anything in the world for me."

A gruff laugh came back to her, half smothered as in a man's beard, and then a choking voice said, " I believe I would, Thora."

" And if I wanted you—or baby wanted you—I think you would follow us to the ends of the earth."

" Only say ' Come ' and I'll come, Thora."

There was a moment's silence, and then a merry laugh came rippling out to him, and he felt hot to the roots of the hair.

" But of course that can not happen, Magnus. We have Oscar, so we can never need you."

" No, you can never need me, Thora."

At that moment Anna and Aunt Margret came back, heated and nervous after the conference, and bundled Magnus out of the room. Then while baby was being bathed for bed, behind closed doors, to the customary chorus of screams, Anna combed out Thora's hair for the night, and Thora talked of Magnus.

"People think him heavy and stupid, but he'll startle them some day," she said.

"Is it to be plaited as usual?" asked Anna.

"Just as usual. But how your hands tremble to-night, mother! That's nursing, you know. Poor Magnus! He hasn't a selfish thought in his heart. Any girl might love him, and perhaps if I had never known Oscar——"

"Doctor Olesen says you are to take a powder to-night, child. It will make you sleep until morning."

"It's you that should take the powder—you and Aunt Margret."

"Ah, if I could take it for you I would, dear," said Anna. "But here it is—take it quickly or I may."

Thora drank from the glass Anna gave her and said, "There! It's gone! Now bring me baby."

Aunt Margret came with the child, hushing it to sleep, and put it gently down into the mother's arms.

"The darling! *She* needs no sleeping draught. My precious, precious pet! But I declare—Aunt Margret's hands are trembling, too! I've worn you out, both of you."

"Nonsense! Go to sleep. I'm going to put down the light," said Aunt Margret, and she lowered the lamp and put it to stand on a table behind the bed-curtains.

"How good you are to me! Everybody is good to me," came in a fainter voice from the shadow of the bed.

"That is because everybody loves you, Thora," said Anna in a husky murmur. "You must always believe that, whatever happens."

"How sweet it is to be loved! If I could only think that it would last——"

The baby became fretful, and Thora began to sing it to sleep.

> "Sleep, baby, sleep,
> Angels bright thy slumbers keep,
> Sleep, baby, sleep."

Her drowsy voice ran a line and stopped; then ran another line and stopped again, and then the faint voice said:

"How sweet it would be to fall asleep like this some day—baby and I—and awake in heaven!"

"Hush!"

"I should be sorry for Oscar, but still——"

The faint voice lisped, the soft breathing lengthened, the blue eyelids closed, the pale lips parted, the white arms slackened, and then the two children, mother and babe, lay together in the lap of sleep.

There was silence for some minutes, wherein the two older women who sat in the gloom like guilty things heard nothing but the ticking of a clock. Then Aunt Margret crept over to where Anna sat with her head covered by her black silk apron and whispered:

"Oscar is waiting at the door. If it has to be done at all let it be done now."

Anna uncovered her face and saw Oscar on the threshold in his cloak and hat. She rose on trembling limbs and felt her way to the bedside. There she stood listening for a moment to Thora's measured breathing. Then she drew the mother's white arms apart and lifted the baby out of them.

Aunt Margret wrapped a shawl about the sleeping child and Oscar covered it with his cloak.

"The night is warm, she will take no harm," he faltered. At the next moment he had gone and Aunt Margret had followed him. Then Anna tottered into the outer room and sank into a chair and covered her head again. "Oh, God forgive me! God forgive me! God forgive me!" she said.

XI

THE sun was shining into the bedroom when Thora awoke, with a slight flush on her pale cheeks and a look of happiness in her eyes, and saw Anna rocking herself sadly by the bedside.

"Where is baby?" asked Thora.

"Presently, dear, presently," said Anna.

"Where is she?"

"Lie quiet, Thora. You shall hear everything by and by."

"But tell me where is my little Elin, Anna?"

"Promise me not to excite yourself, Thora, and I will tell you all about her."

Thora raised herself on her elbow and said with quick-coming breath, "You don't mean that you have taken her away?"

"There now, you are exciting yourself already, Thora."

"Have you stolen my child away from me?" cried Thora.

"Oh, dear! Oh, dear! What things you are saying, Thora."

Thora thought a moment and then she said, "I am sorry I said that, Anna. It was very, very wrong of me. I know you wouldn't hurt me for worlds. But why don't you tell me where my little girl is? She's in the nursery, isn't she? You took her away from me in the night, and now she's asleep in her cot—isn't that so? Or perhaps Aunt Margret has taken her down to the door? There! Isn't that she?—that child crying in the home-field? Or was it somebody else's baby in the road? Speak, Anna! You are only teasing me, I know. But I'm so weak, so foolish, and my heart is beating like a drum."

Anna continued to rock herself and to moan, "Oh, dear! Oh, dear!"

Thora watched her for a moment with eyes that filled with fear, and then called in a shrill voice, "Aunt Margret! Aunt Margret! Aunt Margret!"

"Aunt Margret has gone, Thora," said Anna.

"Gone! And my baby—has she gone too?"

Anna only rocked herself and moaned, "Oh, dear! Oh, dear!"

Thora struggled to raise herself in bed, but her cheeks whitened and her eyes rolled and with a loud scream she fell back fainting.

The maids came running into the bedroom and opened Thora's clinched hands while Anna bathed her forehead.

"What have I done? Oh, those doctors! Little they know of a mother's feelings! It will kill her in any case. My poor child! My poor child! Come, then; come, then!"

Thora recovered consciousness after a moment, and looked about her with dazed eyes.

"Oscar!" she said. "I want to see Oscar."

"And so you shall, dear," said Anna, and she sent one of the maids across to the Factor's to fetch him instantly. Oscar came up-stairs four steps at a stride and entered the room like a rush of wind.

"My poor Thora!" he said with panting breath, and he leaned over the bed to kiss her.

Thora's eyes, which had been dry and hard, now melted and grew wet. "Oscar," she said, "your mother has sent our little Elin away—stolen her from me in the night—and I am so weak and faint I can not get up to follow her."

"Ah, no, dear, not mother," said Oscar. "Lie quiet and I will explain."

"Fetch her back to me, Oscar. I love my baby. I can not live without her."

"I know you love her, Thora, and I promise you that you shall have her back in due time."

"No, no, dear, now."

"Not just yet, Thora, but I give you my word for it that baby is safe. They are taking every care of her."

"What *right* have they to take care of my baby?" cried Thora. "I must have her back. I *will* have her back."

In Thora's flashing eyes, which changed the character of her countenance, and in her voice, which was husky with rage and hatred, there was something of the fierce animal which has been robbed of its young. Oscar shuddered at sight of the convulsed and livid face, but he answered quietly:

"Thora, if you give way to feelings like those you will make yourself ill again, and then baby will never come back to you. If you will only listen, I will tell you everything. You were very bad before baby came, and doctor feared you might even do some harm to her. Therefore to save you from pain and shame I took her away from you for a little while—only for a little while—until you were better and more sure of yourself, Thora."

Then a great silence fell on Thora's bewailing and she said in a husky whisper:

"So it was you, Oscar?"

"Well—yes, dear, it was I—but what I did was for your own good—yours and our little Elin's. And if you will only wait, only be patient, your baby shall be brought back to you and we shall be happy."

Thora's wet eyes dried of themselves, but it was a glassy and smileless light that came into them.

"Where is my baby now?" she asked.

"Not far away. In fact, only at your father's. Aunt Margret wrapped her in a shawl and I took her across myself."

"Then you gave my child to Helga?" said Thora.

"Well—yes, I gave her to Helga. But Aunt Margret is there now. And besides, I intend to go over myself off and on all day long, so you are not to worry or be ånxious about anything—not about any single thing. You understand everything now, dear, do you not?"

"Yes, I understand everything now," said Thora.

The glassy, smileless eyes continued to look up at him, but he mistook the light that shone in them.

"That's a dear, good girl," he said. "Everybody will be delighted to hear you are so reasonable and resigned, because everybody thought you would be inconsolable—everybody except Helga."

"Helga?"

"Helga said you would be yourself within an hour, and she was right. Helga knew you better than any of us."

"Yes, Helga knew me better than any of you," said Thora.

Then he sat on the end of the bed and chatted gaily on many subjects, while Anna, crying for joy of the change in Thora's spirits, called for her breakfast and coaxed her to swallow some of it. He talked of his work—of the work he was going to do when he began, which would be soon, very soon now. Then of his ambitions in Parliament, and finally of the Proclamation. It was fixed for the day after to-morrow, everybody was going to it and the town would be empty. As for himself, he had made up his mind to stay at home with Thora, but seeing that the celebration at Thingvellir had been his idea and that he had taken such a prominent part in it, people were saying that it would be a thousand pities if he could not be present.

"Then there's the hymn, you know," said Oscar. "I've been rehearsing the choir and they are very shaky, but if I thought the organist could hold them together I shouldn't go in any case."

"What does Helga say?" asked Thora.

"Helga? Oh, Helga? Helga says I *must* go," replied Oscar.

"So do I," said Thora.

"You do? Really? What a sweet, unselfish soul it is, to be sure," said Oscar, and kissing Thora on the forehead he ran back to see Elin.

The glassy, smileless eyes on the pillow followed him out of the room, but their light was the light of despair.

XII

Going out of Government House Oscar came upon Magnus, who was standing at the foot of the staircase, riding-whip in hand, and with Golden Mane at the door of the porch. By the dark cloud on Magnus's face Oscar could see that his brother was in a sullen and rebellious mood, and to avoid further hostilities he saluted him and tried to run on.

"Wait," said Magnus.

"Another time," said Oscar.

"Now," said Magnus, and laying his big hand on Oscar's arm, he drew him back into the hall.

Oscar flushed up at the indignity and said sharply, "Well, what is it?"

"Oscar," said Magnus, "I heard what passed in the bedroom."

"Then you were listening?"

"I was."

"You are not ashamed to say you were listening on the stairs—on your hands and knees perhaps—to my conversation with my wife?"

"I would have listened on my belly if need be," said Magnus, and his face darkened more and more.

"May I ask why you listened?" said Oscar.

"Because I could not do otherwise."

"How so?"

"I had given my word to be here when wanted."

"To my wife?"

"Yes."

"You will excuse my saying, Magnus, that it would be much better if you attended to your own business."

"This is my own business. Oscar, you must give the child back to Thora."

"Really, Magnus, you are taking a most unwarrantable liberty. If you were not my brother——"

"Shah! Give the mother her child."

"Good Lord, man," said Oscar, breathing hard as if he had been running, "do you really think that I am going to allow an outsider, even if he *is* my brother, to dictate to me what I shall do with my family difficulties and to travel all the way from Thingvellir to conduct my domestic affairs? What right have you to mix yourself in my business—the business of my wife and me?"

The cloud that contracted Magnus's face grew darker every moment, and he said:

"You ask me what right?"

"I do."

"I loved Thora Neilsen."

"You think it necessary to tell me that?" said Oscar. "To remind me that she threw you up for me?"

"That's a lie, Oscar Stephenson."

"Strong!" said Oscar, with a laugh, but he was trembling visibly.

"I gave her up when I could have kept her to her word. I decided in favor of the girl's happiness against my own. I gave her up to you that you might make her happy. Those were the terms on which I gave her up to you, and what is the result? What is the result, I ask you? You have allowed another woman to take her place."

"Another woman?" said Oscar. "Is that the way you talk of her own sister—of Helga?"

"Sister or not, she has tortured Thora by every art her selfish soul could think of," said Magnus. "That's what she has done, and you have helped her, and the treasure I valued more than my life you have flung away."

Oscar made a cry of protest, but Magnus bore him down

with a torrent of words such as never came from his silent lips before.

"Do you think I don't know what kind of life you led that poor unhappy child while you were away—you and the girl together? And now that her baby comes and her husband returns to her, as he must if he is a man, you let her sister's scheming heart rob her of her only happiness."

Again Oscar with his whitening lips did his best to laugh. "Magnus," he said, "it is impossible to be angry with you. Apparently you do not know that it was with the consent of the family and by the advice of the doctor that the child was taken from its mother."

"Bah! Do you think I don't know who suggested it? . . . . Do you think that I don't see her object? Do you think I don't hear her pitiful pleas—the same as if I had listened to them! The little innocent is in danger of its life! It must come to her—*she* must take charge of it. Why? To bring you back to her feet—to attach you to her at any cost. And you like a fool fall into her plans—because you want to—because you don't know yourself or your wife or the woman that isn't worthy to tie her shoes."

Oscar winced under Magnus's words, for they cut him to the bone.

"Oscar," said Magnus again, "you will give the child back to the mother—it will be best, I promise you."

"I have my own opinion of what is best," said Oscar, bridling, "and if I think that for the time being mother and child are best apart——"

"Oscar Stephenson," interrupted Magnus, "you will give the child back to the mother."

"And if I refuse, by what right will you command me?" said Oscar.

"By the right I acquired when I gave Thora up to you," replied Magnus.

"And by the right *I* acquired when she became my wife I will do with her child as I think proper," said Oscar.

At that Magnus lost all control of himself.

"Is she a dog that you can take her whelps?" he cried.

"The law gives me the right to dispose of her offspring as I think proper," said Oscar.

"Then damn the law," cried Magnus. "And if you are deaf to my entreaties I—I will——"

"Go on," said Oscar. "It will not be the first time that you have threatened to break the law."

"*You* are breaking that poor girl's heart, yet you talk to me about breaking the law. But I'll do more than that. If you will not give the child to its mother I will take it by force and give it back to her myself. And if any man tries to prevent me, no matter who he is or what he is, by God I'll break his teeth down his throat."

Flinging down his riding-whip Magnus had taken a step forward and lifted his clinched fist into Oscar's quivering face when a cry came from the head of the staircase: "Magnus! Oscar! Magnus! Magnus!"

It was Anna. She ran down and put herself between the two men—the slight, lithe figure and fair head of Oscar, and the burly form and swarthy face of Magnus, both panting hard and livid with rage and hate.

"My sons! My sons! For shame! For shame!" she cried. "Every word could be heard in the bedroom and Thora is crying her eyes out."

Magnus dropped his arm and fell aside a pace or two, rebuked and ashamed, but Oscar stood with an unflinching front where his mother had found him.

"Magnus—Oscar," continued Anna, "if you both love the poor girl who is lying helpless up-stairs, isn't that a reason why you should be friends and not enemies? And then think of me, my sons. I am your mother. Surely the sons of one mother can live at peace. I nursed you both when you were little ones and if there should be strife between you now, and blows and perhaps bloodshed, it would kill me—I could never survive it."

Then she turned toward Magnus and said, as well as she could for the tears that choked her:

"Magnus, you mustn't be angry with Oscar. He is your younger brother, remember. You and he slept in the same bed when you were children. And when he was a boy you used to carry him on your back and fight all his battles."

Magnus groaned and turned again until he stood sideways to his mother, and thinking he was not to be moved, she faced about to Oscar.

"Oscar," she said, "you must make peace with Magnus. You must, if only for Thora's sake. Remember, *you* have got her, Oscar, and if it is true that Magnus gave her up to you, although he loved her himself, think of the sacrifice he must have made for both of you! Perhaps he loves her still, and has condemned himself to life-long loneliness because he has lost her. And perhaps he weeps his heart out for her the long nights through. Love that suffers like that has a great excuse, Oscar. Doesn't it give him a right to look to Thora's happiness? And if he thinks she is suffering for want of her little Elin——"

Oscar's throat was hurting him, and in a husky voice he said, "She shall have the child back, mother. If the doctor says it is safe she shall have the child back immediately."

"There!" said Anna. "That's fair—nothing could be fairer than that, Magnus. Come, now, you must shake hands with Oscar."

She put her hand on Magnus's arm, but he did not move.

"Magnus," she said, "your mother's love may be all that is left to you now, but it will last long, my son. You need not give it up to any one, and no one can take it away. After all a mother's love is best. It will cling to you and comfort you whatever you do and whatever the world may do to you. Magnus, you must make friends with your brother—for your mother's sake, Magnus——"

Magnus turned about and saw Oscar before him with broken face and outstretched hand. Then his own hand swung out, drew back, swung out again, and at the next moment the big, burly fellow had flung his arms about Oscar's neck and was sobbing over him like a child.

Two minutes later Magnus was on his way home, cracking his long whip over Golden Mane's flying head and whooping and galloping like a madman.

PART IV

" For some we loved, the loveliest and the best
That from his vintage rolling time hath prest,
Have drunk their cup a round or two before,
And one by one crept silently to rest."

I

THE day of the Proclamation of the Laws was to be kept as a general holiday. A hundred pack horses, carrying tents and provisions, had left the little capital for Thingvellir the day before. The Danish man-of-war anchored in the fiord had lent half its flags and the Order of Good Templars had sent all their insignia. It was to be a great and gorgeous spectacle.

Before daybreak the town was astir, and elderly people on slow ponies were setting out on their journey. Everybody was on horseback, for the way was long and Iceland had few roads and no coaches. Soon after dawn the Governor started off in his cocked hat, and with his inverness belted over the bright gold of his official uniform. Factor Neilsen rode beside him, and the Bishop, the Chief Justice and most of the Thingmen followed in his train. The idea of reviving a great ceremony of ancient days, and clasping hands with the mighty dead over a gulf of a thousand years, had taken hold of everybody's imagination.

Oscar Stephenson, who had been the first to think of it, was among the last to go. He had been round to the Factor's house to see the child and to fetch Helga. The sun was reddening the sky over the eastern hills when they mounted their fleet young ponies. It was a quiet morning, with the promise of a radiant day.

Helga wore her woolen helmet and a fur cape over a white jersey. Oscar was in riding dress, with his new Italian

12   169

cloak hung loose from his shoulders. Their way out of the
town lay past the end of Government House, under the windows of Thora's bedroom, and Oscar stopped and called up
to it.

"Helloa! Helloa!" cried Oscar.

"Is it worth while to waken her?" said Helga.

But the window opened and Anna's face appeared at it.

"It's Oscar," she said, facing back into the room.

"Good-by, Thora! We'll be back this evening."

There was an indistinct murmur from within, and then
Anna said, " Thora says ' Good-by ' and you are not to hurry
home on her account."

Oscar laughed and answered, "We'll see, we'll see." And
then the riders put their heels to their ponies and bounded
away. Helga was in high spirits, but the clouds hung on
Oscar and he tried in vain to banish them.

"All goes well, doesn't it?" asked Helga.

"God knows," said Oscar. "She's quiet certainly, and apparently resigned. Yet her eyes are so dry, her lips so pale,
and her cheeks so white and thin——"

"But what else can you expect four days after her confinement?" said Helga.

"True! But I've never seen her quite like this before.
It is almost as if a wall of ice had frozen about her soul."

"You took my advice, didn't you?"

"I did."

"And what did the Governor say?"

"He said Magnus's interference was an impertinence,
and he wouldn't hear of it for a moment."

"So things are to remain as they are?"

"As they are," said Oscar.

"And what about Magnus himself?" asked Helga.

"Magnus is at the farm."

"But if he should come back while everybody is away?"

"He can not come back to-day—his guests will keep him
busy."

"But if he should in spite of everything?"

"In that case," said Oscar, dropping his voice and turning
his head, "the Sheriff has orders to deal with him."

By this time they had come to the tail of the train which

had started before them, and the dust and the noise of the clattering caravan were too much for Helga.

"Let us go round by the hot springs and come out ahead of them," she said, and they went cantering down a lane to the left where vapor floated over a flowing stream. Half an hour later they returned to the main road, forded a river and toited up a hill beyond it. The cavalcade was now far behind them, and the little wooden capital was a long way off, with its feet in the grey fiord and the white encircling arms of the snow-covered hills stretching out to the brightening line of the sea and sky.

"There!" said Helga, drawing rein and looking at Oscar with a sparkle in her eyes.

"Poor little Thora! I was sorry to leave her. But I dare say everything will be well," said Oscar.

"Sure to be," said Helga.

"Is that a steamer out there—out by the head?" asked Oscar.

"Undoubtedly it is a steamer," replied Helga.

"The 'Laura' is a day late—she was due to arrive yesterday."

"Then it's the 'Laura' to a certainty."

The sun had now risen, but Oscar shivered as with cold. "I must be a miserable coward, Helga, for the sight of a mail-ship frightens me," he said.

But Helga only laughed and held up a warning hand. "We'll not talk of that to-day, Oscar—not to-day at all events. Look!" she cried, pointing to the line of moving forms on the brown streak of road that ran through the plain of black lava. "Look at your tribe down yonder. Don't you feel like Mahomet going back to Mecca? Or like Jacob going up to the Mount of Gilead with his flocks and his herds and——"

"And his wives?" said Oscar.

"Yes, and his wives," laughed Helga, and then both laughed together.

They put heels to their ponies again and Helga sang to herself as they swung along.

"What a fool I am," thought Oscar. "Why should I meet misfortune before it comes? And why should I trouble so much about Thora? Isn't Helga as greatly to be pitied? In the wretched tangle of our fate hers is the knot that can never be untied. Yet how happy she looks! Why shouldn't *I* be happy?"

"Helga!" said Oscar, when they slowed down again, "you wouldn't like to have lived in those old days I suppose?"

"Certainly I should," said Helga.

"What? And share your husband with another woman?"

"That's nothing. Women do the same in these days, you know."

And then they laughed again, though with a dubious gaiety, and broke into a canter once more.

"I'm a brute," thought Oscar. "And badly as I have injured Thora the wrong I have done to Helga is still more terrible. For her there is no outlook, no prospect, no future. She must go back to Denmark and I must go on with my duty. But why shouldn't we have one day of happiness first? One day of delight before the dream is over?"

They drew up at a river that ran by the road to water their ponies and to take off their cloaks and pack them behind their saddles, for the sun was now bright and the air was warm.

"There's one curious point about the patriarchs," said Oscar.

"And what's that?" asked Helga.

"Clearly they thought it possible for a man to love more than one woman."

"And can't he?" said Helga.

"I ask *you*," said Oscar—"can't a man love more than one woman?"

"Why not? Aren't we *all* told to love one another?" laughed Helga, and then Oscar lifted her in his arms and swung her back to her saddle and they started on their journey afresh.

Their road lay through a bleak and barren country, past red hills of volcanic sand and jagged mouths of extinct volcanoes, over a deep dale of lava rocks, rutted with paths and scored with fissures, but brightened by a farmstead here and there with its little green-roofed elt house smoking for breakfast and its hummocked home-field gleaming like a gem in a wilderness of waste. At the last of these farms they stopped to rest their ponies and to refresh themselves, being now half-way to Thingvellir, with the caravan far behind them.

An untidy man in his shirt-sleeves took possession of their ponies and a slatternly housewife in a soiled apron brought them milk and skyr. She was still young, but already she had three children. One of them was whimpering at her breast, another was dragging at her skirts and the third was bellowing for her from the floor above. She belonged to the capital and had once been considered a beauty, but she was seven years married and it was six since she had seen the town.

"There!" said Oscar, when they returned to the road. "That's the patriarchal life, if you please."

"Then I'm done with it," said Helga. "Ugh! To think of being buried in a place like that, year in year out, with three children and only one man! It might do for Thora, but give me life, life, life!"

"And the man who gives you that may have you body and soul, perhaps?" said Oscar.

"Body and soul," laughed Helga.

For the next hour their course lay across an almost trackless heath, bare as a desert and flat as an inland sea. The mountains that bounded it were stark and cold and far away —on the one side steep with running screes and on the other side clouded with steaming vapor, which rose out of the glistening snow. Not a house was to be seen on any side, not a tree or a bush or a flower or a plant, and hardly a blade of grass, but only a broad stretch of silver moss, leaden and dull, like the mold on a dead man's face. No birds sang in that solitude, but sometimes the wimbrel sent its long love cry across the waste; sometimes the wild swan sped far overhead and uttered its eerie ululation, and sometimes the raven perched on a stone and croaked out its melancholy note. A line of beacons, broken and old, each with a projecting stone like an amputated arm, showed the course of the road, going on and on like soldiers in single file tramping back after a lost battle. Midway on the Heath there was a House of Rest for travelers overtaken by the storms of winter—a little hut, half cubicle and half stable, with nothing but a plank bed and a truss of hay.

"Gracious heavens, what a place to be lost in in a snowstorm," said Helga.

"But what a country for Saga and song," said Oscar, "and if some one could set it to music, grim as its glaciers and fierce as its fires, it would take the world by storm."

"Do it, Oscar, do it, and I'll love you," cried Helga.

"As we are commanded to love one another?" asked Oscar.

"Perhaps," laughed Helga, and when he swung her to the saddle again her hand slipped from his shoulder and his lips touched her cheek.

After that they both sang as they cantered along, for the clouds that had hung over Oscar had gone by this time, and if the ground was grey the sky was blue and their blood was red and warm.

But suddenly a new scene opened at their feet—a deep plain with a shining blue lake in the midst of it, splashed with islands like spots on an eagle's egg and fenced by soft green fells. It was a dream in a desolate land, a cistern of sunshine encircled by countless peaks which stood round it clothed in white, like a surpliced choir that were singing their hymns to God. The black lava was there as elsewhere, and the valley was blistered with mounds and wrinkled with ruts and scored with fissures; but the blood-root grew in the clefts of the jagged rocks and the blueberry hung over the face of the gaping chasms, and it was almost as if an angel had passed over the surface torn by earthquakes and brushed it with the bloom of his wings.

This was Thingvellir, the place of the Proclamation, the Thing-place of the Northlands, the scene of a hundred Sagas, the subject of a thousand songs.

Oscar and Helga were now near the end of their journey and they watched for the townspeople to overtake them. Half an hour later the caravan came up in a cloud of dust, all noisy, but good-natured and ravenous for breakfast. There were some shouts at the pioneers, and certain dubious compliments, but Oscar did not hear and Helga did not heed. They took their places behind the Governor, and went down to the law-plain in his train.

The way to it was through a wide chasm whose parallel walls stood up on either side of the steep causeway like the ruined street of some prehistoric city, but thrice grander and more awesome than any work of the hand of man, because straight from the loins of nature and rent from the womb of the earth. There were great openings as of arches, empty spaces as of windows, broken peaks as of pediments and curious stones as of carvings, all shaken from their foundations and toppling as if to fall; while over them, from beetling side to side, hung the gay flags of the Danish man-of-war, and through them came the bright shafts of the morning sun.

Half-way down the gorge there was a mound like a plat-form (the "Law-mount" explained Oscar to Helga) and at the foot of it there was a pool whose clear green depths looked cold and chill in the palm of the cliffs that darkened it.

"That's the drowning pool," said Oscar. "When a woman was unfaithful to her husband they hurled her from the rocks into the water."

"And what did they do with the unfaithful men?" laughed Helga.

From the edge of the pool a frothy river fell with a thunderous clamor over a precipice to the valley below, where it forked into many fingers and ran off to the margin of the lake. Beyond these rivulets there was the rutted plain, now dotted over with tents, but having only two houses within sight—the little wooden parsonage with its tiny church built of stone and shingles and the Inn-farm of Magnus Stephenson.

Magnus himself stood waiting there, washed and dressed, after working the whole night through with his man John Vidalin, to prepare for his expected guests. And when Oscar rode up, a little excited and confused, he received him with the cheerful face of one who had made his peace with his brother and meant to keep it.

"How's Thora to-day?" asked Magnus, as he loosened the girths of Oscar's saddle; and Oscar answered nervously:

"Better—that is to say—well, perhaps not so very well to-day, Magnus."

"Her child has been given back to her?" said Magnus.

"Not yet," said Oscar. "To tell you the truth, the Governor—," and then he faltered out the sequel to his broken promise. Magnus's face darkened, and he said:

"So the doctor has not been consulted at all?"

"No. In the teeth of the Governor's orders it was plainly impossible——"

"And Thora is still at Government House and her child is still at the Factor's?"

"That is so."

Magnus looked from Oscar to Helga, who now stood beside him, and his face darkened more and more.

"John Vidalin," he cried in a thick voice over his shoulder to a man behind him, "saddle my horse—I am going to Reykjavik."

"But Magnus," said the servant-man, "with all this work to do to-day and all this money coming——"

"Saddle it quick," cried Magnus, like a man who was choking.

"Magnus," said Oscar, "for your own sake I think it only right to tell you——"

But Magnus cut him short by turning on his heel.

"Let him go," said Helga, and before the people in the tents and the Inn-farm had settled down to breakfast Magnus was riding back to town.

II

MEANTIME Thora at home was in the throes of a great temptation. She had heard the peace-making between Magnus and her husband and had said to herself, "Oscar will go to see Dr. Olesen at once, and the dear doctor will say: 'Certainly, the little mother is quite well enough now to take care of her baby—give the child back to her immediately.'" Then Oscar would come rushing up-stairs, and her room would be the same as if a window had blown open, and he would cry, "Hip-hip-hurrah! Doctor says baby may come back!" and then Anna would take him by the shoulders and turn him out and everybody would laugh.

But Oscar was long in coming, and when he came he said nothing about the doctor. He only talked about their little Elin, and said he had just returned from seeing her. She was so rosy and well, and she was beginning to "notice." If you held out your finger she looked at it as if it were the bough of a great tree, and then held it tight as if her little body hung by it.

"I couldn't tear myself away from her, Thora," he said. "It's wonderful what a lot of pleasure you can get out of a baby."

It was strange that Oscar did not see that he was hurting her every minute, but she only thought, "I know what it is— he is going to take me by surprise. He doesn't want to tell me that baby is coming until she comes. He will bring her back as he took her away, in the night, while I am asleep; and when I awake in the morning she will be there."

In this sweet hope Thora closed her eyes early that evening, before the red glow of the sunset had quite gone from the walls of her room, saying a little prayer for Oscar, and another little prayer for Elin, that she might be as lovely as ever when she saw her in the morning; and then she fell asleep.

When she awoke next day she listened for the baby's breathing, and thinking she heard it she stretched out a gentle hand to the place where the child should lie, and then with a smile she opened her eyes. But her baby was not there, and the sun in the room died out.

When the doctor came to see her that morning he looked grave and anxious. "I'm afraid my little patient is worrying overmuch," he said. "The head is hot and there is some fever. She must lie quiet, perfectly quiet for the next few days, or I won't answer for what may happen."

Only this, not a word about baby, and even when the doctor took Anna into the nursery to give the usual instructions Thora listened intently, but there was not a syllable about the child.

The Governor came next, with the odor of snuff on his gold-laced coat, and he stroked Thora's arm as it lay on the counterpane, and said she was not to worry about anything.

"My dear little daughter must get better as fast as ever

she can," he said. " She must eat more and if she wants anything she must ask for it and she shall have it, whatever it is."

She tried to say that all she wanted was her little baby,
and if they would give her that she would soon be well, but
her throat was hurting and she could not speak.

Her own father came last, smelling of breakfast and
strong tobacco, and he rallied her in a loud voice.

" Tut, tut! This will never do! We'll have to send you
away again, with Helga to look after you. And look here,
young lady, you've got to get better soon and come and carry
away that baby. She's turning our house upside down. Nobody over there can see the sun for that little mite, and Aunt
Margret and Auntie Helga haven't a thought for anybody
else."

By this time the conviction had forced itself upon Thora's
mind that the family had agreed that the child was not to
be returned to her, and that Helga was responsible for this
cruel resolution. Then a fierce passion took possession of
her, such as she had never known before. She hated her sister with a terrible hatred. Helga, who had first robbed her
of her husband, had now robbed her of her child, and throwing dust in her people's eyes had used her weakness as an
excuse and a blind. But she would defeat her, she would
defeat everybody, she would get back her child whatever the
consequences, and not all the powers of earth or heaven or
hell should take it away from her again.

The intensity of her feeling, if it could have been realized
by those about her, would have made her sweet and gentle
soul unrecognizable. She was like a feline animal robbed of
its young and going out to recover it. All the other passions
and emotions that had ever possessed her—love of her husband, affection for Anna and Aunt Margret and her father
and the Governor, pity for Magnus and tenderness toward
all living things—were burnt up by the one consuming desire—the desire for her child. It made her terrible, it made
her cruel, it made her cunning.

Thora determined to steal back her own child.

The following day—the day of the Proclamation—would
give her an opportunity of doing so. Nearly everybody
would then be at Thingvellir, therefore her path would be

more clear. Only Anna would stay at home to attend to herself, and Aunt Margret to attend to the child. Her one feverish anxiety was that Oscar should not stay behind as well, for if Oscar were to remain Helga would remain also and then her scheme would come to naught.

Thora lay awake the whole night through. Before daybreak she heard the people shouting in the darkness; at dawn she heard the departure of the Governor, and when Oscar called up at her window she knew that Helga was with him, for she heard the hoofs of two horses.

When everybody had gone she lay back on her pillow with a sigh of immense relief.

"How soon will they be back, mother?" she asked.

"Not much before midnight, I'm afraid. But you must not fret after anybody, my child, for everything shall be done for you," said Anna.

Then the transparent young soul, in the fierce fire of its temptation, began to lay plans for deceiving Anna and for getting her out of the way. At one moment she said:

"Haven't you any errands to do this morning, dear—in the town, I mean—being left alone, you know, and even the servants gone?"

"Errands? Bless your dear heart, it's like Sunday in town to-day and not a shop open anywhere," said Anna.

At another moment Thora said:

"Mother, if you wish to go down into the kitchen to cook you needn't think of me?"

"The cooking is all done, dear," said Anna. "Maria did it yesterday, and I've nothing to do now but warm up the dishes on the nursery stove. So I needn't leave you for a minute, you see."

Thora was beginning to be restless in her perplexity, but presently she thought, "I know! I'll tell her to lie down after dinner, and then I'll get up and dress and go."

That suggested thoughts about her clothes, which had been taken off on the night of her attack and packed away somewhere. There would be drawers to open and search, and that would take time and make noises. So she said:

"Mother, dear, don't you think my clothes must be getting damp lying so long unused?"

"Damp? In five days and the middle of summer, too!" cried Anna.

"Still, it would be nice to see them airing—it would make me tnink of getting up, you know."

"Then you shall, sweetheart, certainly you shall," said Anna, and with the playfulness of one who indulges a child the good soul took Thora's clothes out of a wardrobe, held them up to her one by one, and then hung them on the chairs in front of the stove in the nursery, clucking and crowing of the day when Thora would put them on and go down-stairs, with wraps and scarves, and Oscar helping her.

Thora watched intently and then said:

"I haven't seen my cloak yet, mother."

"Your cloak! Your outdoor cloak! Bless me, what a heart she has to be sure! But no, no! We'll all be dancing with delight if you need that for the next three weeks, Thora."

The hours lagged cruelly before dinner, and after it the sun's line on the wall was long in leaving the bed; but at last three o'clock struck on the Bornholme clock below stairs and then Thora said:

"Mother, I'm sure you are very tired—I wish you would go to your room and rest."

"And leave my honey alone? Not I," said Anna.

"But I want to rest myself and I can't rest unless you are resting."

"If you really think you'll sleep better——"

"I'm sure I shall," said Thora.

"Well—seeing you slept so little last night," said Anna, and Thora began to yawn and sigh.

"I'll leave both doors open then. And see, Thora—I'll put this little handbell on the table, and if you awake and want me—I sleep like a cat, you know, the least noise wakens me——"

"Good night, mother," said Thora in a drowsy tone, and Anna, smiling and nodding to herself over Thora's "error," stole on tiptoe out of the room.

Thora listened for the last footfall in the corridor and then raised herself in bed. She was alone at last, and the time had come to defeat the conspiracy of love and kindness, prompted by jealousy and envy, that had robbed her of her child. Her child, her child! She must get back her child, whatever it might cost her!

She dropped to the floor and in doing so she brushed the hand-bell off the table. It fell to the carpet with a deadened clang, and for a moment she held her breath and listened. But there was no sound from Anna's room, so she clutched at the bedclothes and stood erect. Then the walls went round, and she knew for the first time how weak she was. But her heart was strong if her limbs were feeble, and she found her way to the nursery, where her clothes still hung over the backs of chairs. It was a weary task to put them on, but her purpose never flagged. At last she was dressed and looking at herself in the glass. Her eyes were red, her lips were pale, and her cheeks were sucked in and white. Nobody would know her who met her in the street, yet still if she could find her cloak——

The Bornholme clock chimed half past three, and Thora began to steal down the corridor. She had to go by Anna's bedroom and the door was standing open. Anna's shawl lay on a chair within and she snatched it up and wrapped it over her shoulders and her head. Then she went down-stairs. Her limbs trembled under her, but not from fear, and if anybody had tried to stop her now she would have fought like a fiend.

"My child is mine!" she thought. "What *right* have they to keep her from me?"

The next moment she was in the street.

III

THE Bornholme clock struck four. Anna awoke and hearing no sound from Thora's room she went back to the nursery and busied herself noiselessly at the stove.

Presently the lace curtains in the bedroom were rustled by the wind from an open window and Anna cried through the door:

"Lie quiet, Thora—I'm making tea," and then she began to sing to herself in the voice of her youth.

A few minutes later she said, " That sleep must have made me stupid—I've actually put in the hot water before the tea-leaves."

Soon afterwards she sailed into Thora's room with the tea tray in both hands and a smile on her face, saying, " Here it is, but you'll thank your stars when Maria comes back in the morning."

She was setting down the tray on the round table by the beside where the hand-bell should have been, when her eyes fell on the empty bed. Her breath jumped in her throat, and she turned her head slowly over her shoulder, calling, " Thora!"

There was no answer; the room was empty. Anna remembered the clothes which she had laid out on the chairs in the nursery. They were gone. " Thora! Thora!" she cried, in an agitated whisper.

Then the smile came back to her face. " I know," she thought. " Thora has dressed herself and gone down to the drawing-room, just to show me what she can do."

At that thought the smile was chased away by a mighty frown. " But I'll give it her," she thought, and downstairs she went with a determined step and banged the drawing-room door back saying, " Really, Thora, it is very naughty——"

But the protest died in her throat, for Thora was not there. Then her heart shook like a leaf stiffened by hoar frost and she ran through the house, from room to room, crying in a voice shrill with fear and thickened by sobs, " Thora, where are you? Thora! Honey! Don't hide yourself from me! Thora! Thora!"

At that moment Golden Mane came tolting up to the green and Magnus entered the house. Hearing his mother's voice he ran up-stairs, and came face to face with Anna in the corridor.

" What has happened?" he asked.

" Thora's lost," said Anna.

" Lost?"

" She coaxed me to lie down this afternoon, and while I was asleep she got up and dressed herself, and she is gone."

" Let us be sure first," said Magnus, and the slow fellow

shot through the house like a torpedo, while Anna sat on the chair by the door of her own room and wrung her hands and reproached herself.

"Oh, dear! Oh, dear! What have I done? How can I ever forgive myself? The poor child was not herself—she didn't know what she was doing."

Magnus returned with a slow step, saying, "Be quiet, mother! Can't you see what has happened? Thora has gone to the child."

"The child? The Factor's? God grant you may be right, Magnus. But she hasn't mentioned the baby for two days."

"Nevertheless," said Magnus, "her poor heart has been torn to pieces by this accursed scheme of separating her from her child, and she has gone to join it."

"Let us go and see," said Anna. "But, oh dear, what a thing to do! And she so ill and weak! It will kill her! Oh, why did I leave her for an instant? What will Oscar say?"

"If Oscar's wise he will say nothing," said Magnus. "And if anything happens, and he has any conscience, he'll damn himself to the last day of his life."

"Don't say that, Magnus," said Anna. "If there was anything wrong we were all to blame for it. It wasn't Oscar's fault——"

"Certainly, it was Oscar's fault," said Magnus. "It was Oscar's fault that he allowed Helga to twist him round her finger and make you all her miserable slaves."

"Where is my shawl? I laid it down somewhere, and now I can not find it. But let us go. And don't be hard on your mother, Magnus. She was trying to do her best——"

"It's not you I'm blaming, mother," said Magnus, "but if," he added, and his words came through his clinched teeth, "if there were a law in this infernal land to punish people like Oscar, as sure as I live I should be the first to use it."

They were going out of the house when three men came up to the door—the Sheriff and two strangers.

"Good evening, Mrs. Anna," said the Sheriff. "These gentlemen are officials from Copenhagen, just arrived by the 'Laura.' They wish to see the Governor on an important matter, and I thought perhaps you could tell them when he will be back from Thingvellir."

"I can't say—I don't know—I am in a great hurry," said Anna.

"This young man," said the Sheriff to the strangers, "is the *elder* son of the Governor, and if you would like to speak to him——"

"We should," answered the men.

"Is it so very important? My son is going out with me. Can't the matter wait until to-morrow?" said Anna.

"Go on ahead, mother—I'll follow you presently," said Magnus, and while Anna hurried away, he led the strangers into the Governor's office. One of the two men took a paper from an inner breast pocket and said:

"Naturally, you know your father's handwriting?"

"I do," said Magnus.

"And of course you are familiar with his signature."

"I am."

"Will you be good enough to say if *this* is your father's signature?" said the man, opening his paper and handing it to Magnus.

It was a note of hand in favor of Oscar Stephenson for an advance of one hundred thousand crowns, signed in the name of the Governor and witnessed by the Factor.

The world reeled round Magnus, for he saw in a moment what the paper meant. It was almost as if his prayer to punish Oscar had been answered on the instant. The paper rustled in his hand and for some seconds he did not speak. Then he lifted his face and said:

"You ask me if this is my father's signature. Don't you think it would be more proper to ask my father himself?"

"No doubt—certainly—you are right," said the stranger, "but to protect your father—not to say yourself per- haps——"

"Perhaps," said Magnus, and he handed the paper back.

"Magnus," said the Sheriff, "I was told to watch you if you came to town to-day, but it seems to me that somebody else in your family needs watching a good deal more. Will you not give us your assistance?"

Magnus shuddered in the toils of his temptation. A voice

within cried, "Speak! Denounce him! Now's your time!"
His lower lip quivered, his eyelids trembled, and he
answered in a hoarse voice:

"The Governor will not be back until midnight—let me
come to you to-morrow morning."

"Good!" said the Sheriff, whereupon Magnus showed
them out of the house and then fled away to the Factor's.

"That big fellow will speak when he wants to," said one
of the strangers as the three men walked down the street,
"and when he doesn't the devil himself won't make him
do so."

IV

OF two ways to the Factor's Thora had taken the shortest
and most frequented, yet she had gone through the streets
unobserved. Coming near the house she had passed the
Sheriff and the two strangers, but they were immersed in
their conversation and did not see her as she stumbled by
them with her head covered up in Anna's shawl.

Twice she had stopped to take breath, and once she had
steadied herself by a lamp-post, for she was dizzy and her
ankles ached. The little distance which had hitherto seemed
so short was now a great journey, but it came to an end at
length, and she approached her father's house from the front.

She had intended to creep up softly, enter by stealth, listen
until she learned where the child was kept, watch until Aunt
Margret left the little one alone for a moment and then
steal into the room and take it.

With this purpose she ascended the stone steps to the front
entrance and gently turned the handle, but as soon as she
had given the door a noiseless push, there was the loud ringing of a bell which had not been there before.

At the next moment there was a sound of slippered feet
coming hurriedly down-stairs and before her dizzy brain
could tell what to do Aunt Margret was peering into her
face.

"Mercy me, is it you?" cried Aunt Margret, and she
looked as if she were ready to drop.

13

With a crushing sense of failure Thora stood silent and her heart fluttered like a captured bird.

"Good Lord! How did you get here alone? And what on earth was Anna doing to let you come?" said Aunt Margret.

Then with a convulsive little burst Thora said, "Anna knew nothing about it, Aunt Margret—she was asleep—I came to see baby." And then she broke down utterly, leaned against the doorpost and cried like a child.

The kind soul with the sharp tongue could bear no more. "And so you shall, dear. Certainly you shall, my pretty poppet," she said with infinite compassion. "As sure as my name is Margret Neilsen you shall," she said again, with stern determination. "They have left me here as a watch-dog with an order that nobody is to come near the child, but that was meant for somebody else—somebody who was going to steal it—so they said—though what a grown man can want with a suckling infant it baffles my stupid old head to see. But what a silly I am to keep you at the door! Come up-stairs, my precious. Go before me, Thora, dear! That's right—but not so quick—you shall see your baby soon enough. And Thora, darling, if I haven't exactly tried to take it back to you it wasn't because I didn't love you, and feel for you, and suffer with you, my poor child, but because your father and Helga and even Oscar—no, the other way, Thora—baby is in the front bedroom."

"Is she well?" said Thora, breathing quickly as she reached the landing.

"She's as well as well, and so rosy and bonny—look!" said Aunt Margret, pushing ahead of Thora and opening the bedroom door.

But having climbed the stairs so much too rapidly, Thora paused at the threshold of the room and held her left hand hard against her side. "Wait! I can't go in yet," she said. "Not just yet, Aunt Margret. Is she asleep?"

"Yes, she's fast asleep, bless her!"

"Is that her breathing?"

"No, that's the cat. Yes, it is the baby. But come, my own, come," said Aunt Margret, and then, holding her breath, the young mother entered the room.

The child was sleeping in a cradle with a hood covered with light blue lace, and its little head, streaked with yellow hair, lay red against the white pillow. A cat purred on the floor in a warm shaft from the setting sun, and all was sweet and peaceful.

"My baby! My baby!" cried Thora, and she sank down on her knees by the cot and stretched her arms over it like a bird covering its nest with her sheltering wings.

The child was awakened by the soft gale of its mother's breath on its sleeping face and it began to cry, whereupon Thora gathered it in her arms and lifted it out of the cot and nursed it lovingly, holding its little plunging hand in her own hand, so thin and white and delicate.

"It's her bottle she wants, Thora," said Aunt Margret, "and here it is ready and waiting—I keep it warm on the top of the stove."

"Let me give it her, let me give it her," cried Thora.

"Do you think you can, my pretty? But of course you can! My goodness, it's wonderful—when a person is a mother she can do anything with a baby. An angel seems to whisper, 'Do that,' and she does it, and it's just right for the child."

The little creature was now sucking vigorously with its tiny face toward the mother's breast and its plump red hand on her pallid cheek.

"But it's you that wants milk, my child," said Aunt Margret. "Yes, and some spirits too, and you shall have both in a minute. Lay your poor head against this pillow, my precious, and wait while I get the decanter."

The child was now dropping off to sleep and Thora looked lovingly down at it and said:

"God bless my motherless baby!"

"Motherless, indeed! Who says she's motherless? She has too many mothers, it seems to me," said Aunt Margret.

The tit slipped from the child's slackening lips, and Thora leaned down and kissed away the drops that trickled from the little mouth.

"I wish I could die," she said. "I wish I could die now, Aunt Margret."

And Aunt Margret, who was snuffling audibly, said, "Die,

indeed! Just drink off this drop of brandy and water and don't talk such nonsense."

Thora drank the brandy and straightway her weakness left her, and with the return of her strength the secret purpose which had brought her to the house revived.

"I must be quick," she thought. "Anna will follow me."

The innocent selfishness of her starved and injured motherhood knew no conscience, and she set herself to consider how she could get rid of Aunt Margret and so carry away the child. That was a perplexing problem, and she sat long to think it out, but accident solved it at last.

"Goodness me," Aunt Margret was saying, "how lovely you look, sitting there with the child! But what a fit some people would have if they could drop in and see you! They can't, thank goodness! They're thirty miles away, and before they get back you'll be gone, and nobody a penny the wiser. When the cat's away the mice will play! But mercy me, what a storm there would be if they ever came to know that I had let you touch the little angel! I don't know which is the worst on that subject—your father, or Oscar, or Helga. I think Helga is the worst if you ask me. You're a Neilsen, Thora, but Helga—she's a sheep from another sheepfold. She's so cute, and she has such ways with her. It was Helga who put those bells on the door, and when I heard you coming in I thought, 'It's that Sheriff again,' but you could have knocked me down with a feather— Good gracious!"

Aunt Margret, who was looking out of the window, suddenly threw up her hands.

"What is it?" said Thora.

"It is—no—yes, it's Anna! And the Sheriff and two officers are coming behind her!"

"They're coming for me," cried Thora. "They want to tear me away from my baby. Go down and stop them, Aunt Margret. Say I'm not here—say I'm gone—say anything——"

"Hush, dear, don't excite yourself. Leave Margret Neilsen to manage this little matter. I'll take Anna and the Sheriff into the back parlor and tell them something. Then you'll slip out by the front and get back home and nobody will know."

"Yes, yes, that will do," said Thora.

"You'll be as quiet as a mouse, and I'll make lots of noises."

"Yes, yes, yes."

There was the clang of a bell from below, and Aunt Margret whispered, "There they are! Now put baby back in the cot, my own, and cover her up with the blanket."

"Not yet, let me kiss her again, just for the last time," said Thora.

An agitated voice came from the bottom of the stairs, "Margret! Margret Neilsen!"

"I must go—be quick," whispered Aunt Margret, and scuttling down-stairs, she cried, "I'm coming," and then there was a rumble of confused voices, followed by the closing of a door.

Thora was alone once more, and the feverish strength of outraged motherhood possessed her like a madness. "They've come to take my child again," she thought.

In a moment she had slipped off her slippers, snatched up the blanket and wrapped it about the sleeping infant, crept down the stairs in stocking feet and out of the house by a back passage.

V

MEANTIME a little tragi-comedy was being acted in the back parlor. Anna was white and trembling, while Aunt Margret was looking wondrous wise and subtle.

"Thora?" gasped Anna. "Have you seen anything of Thora?"

"Have I seen anything of Thora? You must be dreaming, Anna dear."

"Then she has gone, and I was right after all," said Anna.

"Can it be possible?" said Aunt Margret.

"Magnus would have it that she had gone to see the baby, but she has gone farther than that, poor child, and we shall never see her again."

"What a pity!" said Aunt Margret, and then Anna flew out at her.

"Margret Neilsen, don't you understand what I am saying? The poor child was demented, and she stole out while I was asleep and goodness knows what she has done with herself."

"Hush! Hold your tongue, Anna, and come into this room and I'll tell you something. Magnus was right after all."

"Then she *has* been here?"

"She's here now—she's up-stairs this very minute."

"Oh, thank the Lord——"

"Don't speak, or the poor thing will hear you. And don't be angry with her either, and if you brought the Sheriff to take her back——"

"*I* brought the Sheriff! What are you saying, you crazy woman?"

"Then can't we let her stay a little longer? It isn't every day she has the chance——"

"She can stay all night for me, Margret."

"That is impossible—the Factor is so frightened. And then there's the Governor——"

"That's true," said Anna.

"But she can safely stay an hour more with her child, can't she?" said Aunt Margret.

"Just one hour more," said Anna.

"Poor thing, she was to steal out while we were talking, but we'll go up and surprise her. And when you see her with the little mite at her breast, looking down at it and kissing it, with such a pitiful smile, the dear, it will fill your heart brimful But for goodness' sake wipe your eyes and blow your nose, Anna, and do for mercy's sake look more cheerful. Quietly now, quietly, or she'll think the Sheriff is behind us."

With that the two old things, snuffling as if they had colds in the head, but struggling to smile and seem happy, went creeping up to the bedroom.

By that time the room was empty and Thora was gone.

The women looked at each other for an instant, and then Aunt Margret ran to the cradle. The child was gone, too.

At that moment the bell of the front door rang again. Aunt Margret cried, "There she is," and the two women raced down-stairs to see.

It was Magnus coming in.

"Thora *has* been here, but she has gone—gone this very minute," cried Anna.

"And she has taken the child along with her," cried Aunt Margret.

Without a word Magnus turned about and leapt back to the street. There he met the Sheriff and told him what had happened. At the next minute the two women were running hither and thither and the two men were gone different ways.

Half an hour afterward they met at the Factor's house again. Thora and the child had not been found. They had disappeared as utterly as if a lava stream had swallowed them.

The women were sitting side by side with blanched faces and startled eyes, twisting their handkerchiefs into knots.

"The doctor was quite right after all," said Anna. "They were all right, though we thought them so hard and cruel. The poor thing wanted to die—she told me so herself."

"She told me too—she told me this very day," said Aunt Margret.

"Is there no house in town she was accustomed to go to?" asked the Sheriff.

"None," said Anna, and Aunt Margret said, "Thora was not like that—she would never drink coffee or talk scandal with any one."

"Let us try again," said Magnus to the Sheriff.

The sun had set over the fiord and the black rocks of the plain were dying out in the dusky haze of evening when the two men returned to the Factor's for the second time. Their search had been fruitless and Magnus's face was white and haggard.

Anna and Aunt Margret sat in the parlor window stricken with grief, but finding a certain satisfaction in their affliction from the melancholy glances of groups of other women who had gathered in the street.

"I knew it would be useless," said Anna. "She's gone, poor dear—I'm afraid she's gone to heaven, poor darling."

"And taken the little innocent infant along with her," said Aunt Margret.

"Has anybody thought of going back to Government House?" asked the Sheriff.

"I went there first," said Magnus.

"And to the lake?"

"I went there next."

"And the jetty?"

"I went to the jetty also. But I don't believe Thora has destroyed herself," said Magnus.

"Then she has died of exhaustion by this time and it's all the same in any case," said Anna.

"She's in her stocking feet too—see," said Aunt Margret, showing the slippers which Thora had left up-stairs, and falling to kissing and weeping over them.

"There's one chance left—she may have tried to follow her husband," said Magnus.

"So far, and without a horse?" said the Sheriff.

"It's the last hope—I'm going to follow it up," said Magnus. "Mother," he added, "you had better go back home."

"I can't—I daren't—and if anything happens I'll never be able to go into the poor girl's room again," said Anna.

Outside, in the fading light, Magnus stood for a moment wiping the flanks of Golden Mane and patting his drooping neck.

"I suppose there isn't another horse left in the town," said the Sheriff, "but you'll kill your splendid pony."

"Then he'll die well," said Magnus.

"Magnus," the Sheriff continued, "I intend to search every house in Reykjavik, and if I succeed to-night I'll expect you to help us in the morning."

"If you *don't* succeed I'll help you," said Magnus, with a hoarse laugh, and at the next moment he was lost in the darkness.

VI

THORA had done the most natural and therefore the most unexpected thing. Only thinking of getting back to her bed in Government House, and of carrying the child along with her, she had taken the simplest means toward doing so. In order to escape the Sheriff she had left her father's house by

the back, and to avoid observation from people in the frequented thoroughfare she had taken the longer and quieter
of the two roads home.

This road led her past the lake, but she had no desire to
destroy herself. Often before she had longed for death from
the depths of her heart, but love for her child conquered
all such feelings now. The way was very long, but she did
not know that she was tired; the roads were rough, but she
did not feel that they were cutting her feet; she was going
fast, but she did not realize that she was breathless. She
had only one fear—the fear of being overtaken; only one
dread—the dread of the child being torn away from her.

Clinging to the little one with feverish arms she hastened
along, weeping to herself, laughing to herself, full of a wild
joy that had no remorse, no qualms of any kind, and neither
looked before nor after. It was motherhood—the most
divine, the most devilish, the most tender, the most terrible,
the most sweet, the most sublime, the most savage of all the
passions of the heart.

Reaching home at last she found the house silent, but
every room wide open, as if lately ringing with the noise of
hurrying feet. Creeping up-stairs with her precious burden
she got safely back to her room, and instantly locked the
door behind her. She laughed as she did so, thinking how
Anna and Aunt Margret would follow her and find themselves defeated.

Then she undressed and got back into bed and for one
long, heavenly hour she gave herself up to the delight of
having her child—to hold it, to nurse it, to fondle it, to kiss
it, and to devour it with all her senses. The little creature
had slept during its journey through the town, but now it
awoke, and lay quiet by its mother's side while she ran her
hungry hands over its tiny body and put its clinched fists
and its feet one by one into her mouth.

After a while the child tired and began to cry, whereupon Thora remembered for the first time that she had left
its feeding-bottle behind her. She tried to hush it, but it
would not be hushed, and then a sudden thought, a blind impulse of maternity, came to her, and she put the little one
to her breast. The child clung to it and was quiet, and the

milk, which had never come until now, instantly began to flow.

It was the crowning miracle of that joyous hour, a physical rapture such as Thora had never known before.

After that a more tender spirit stole over her, and she looked lovingly down at the child in her bosom and kissed it again and again, and said, " God bless my baby."

Then in a voice so weak and silvery that it was like a voice descending from the sky, she began to sing the child to sleep:

> "Sleep, baby, sleep,
> Angels bright thy slumbers keep,
> Sleep, baby, sleep "

The child slept, and even while she sang Thora became aware of alternate waves of heat and cold going over her. A vague, broken, delirious consciousness came and went, and people seemed to be entering and leaving the room. First it was Helga, then it was Oscar, and finally it was Magnus. Helga was taking the child out of the bed and Oscar was helping her, and she was trying to cry out and could not, when Magnus appeared in the doorway.

At one moment she thought she was dead, and people were talking around her. They were all strangers, chiefly women whom she had seen going into the Salvation Shelter. "She's gone, poor girl," said some one, and somebody else said, "So much the better—the poor thing's troubles are over." "They say she tried to make away with herself," said one. "And what wonder?" said another. "There was no place left for her in this world." "Nobody can say she didn't love her husband," said a voice at her feet. "That was the pity—he loved her sister," said a voice above her. "Perhaps that was why she thought of taking her life—to leave him free—perhaps to make him happy?" "Well, she did wrong by Magnus, but we all know who killed her." And then everybody said in chorus, "He'll get his reward, he'll get his reward," and she was sorry for Oscar.

At another moment she thought she was a blessed saint in paradise, with lilies and roses around her head, but there was a thorn in her heart for all that, and even among the joys of heaven she had a dull pain there was no ease for, because she could not help thinking about her baby. So she asked the dear God to let her go down to earth to see her little Elin, and He suffered her to come and she came. Oscar and Helga were together now, in a country that was sweet with smiling gardens and a house that was full of gilded furniture. But she could not see her Elin anywhere, until at length she found her in an upper room, neglected and lonely. Then the burning tears ran down her face and she sat by her child and comforted her, and Elin was not afraid. "Stay with me a little longer," said the child, and she stayed with her and sang to her, and no one heard but little Elin:

> "Sleep, baby, sleep,
> Angels bright thy slumbers keep
> Sleep, baby, sleep."

When she came to herself again it was dark in the bedroom, yet she was still singing. The baby began to cry and she wished to comfort it, but she found she could not speak. It's little body felt cold against her breast and she wanted to cover it up in the blanket, but her arms were heavy and she could not lift them.

There was a moment of agonized consciousness, but the good Father sealed the senses of His suffering child again. She thought a majestic figure entered the room, clothed all in white, and lifted the baby out of her bosom, saying, "Suffer little children to come unto Me." She knew quite well who It was, but when she looked a second time the figure had the face of Magnus.

Then it seemed to her that it was she herself and not the baby that had been lifted up, yet she felt no fear at all, nor any pain, nor any heartache.

At that moment the women who had stood about the bed came back and they began to sing, "Safe in the arms of Jesus"—just as she had heard them singing it when she listened at the door of the Shelter.

She smiled and drew a deep sigh; a sweet, long breath of joy and rapture; and then the darkness lifted and—it was day.

VII

THAT day had been a prolonged triumph for Oscar. The
festival of the Proclamation began with service in the parish
church, and though the Governor and the Thingmen only
had been able to pack into the little place, the churchyard
outside and the home-field of the parsonage had been
thronged.

After the service there was a procession from the church
door to the ancient place of proclamation, and Oscar had
ordered and marshaled every one. First the town band,
then the Governor and his executive in their gold-braided
uniforms, the Bishop in his robes, the Thingmen in their
scarfs, the clergy in their black cassocks and white ruffs,
and finally a vast following of the people. It was a gorgeous
spectacle, such as no man could remember to have seen on
that spot before.

The Proclamation itself was an imposing ceremony. Sitting on the law-mount as on a natural platform of lava rock,
with his face to the east and the Cross of Dannebrog on his
breast, the Governor read out one by one the titles and
descriptions of the Acts which had been passed by Parliament; and after each of them he lifted his head and cried to
the people on the plains below, "Is it Yea or Nay?" And
then the people, led by Oscar, shouted "Yea."

When the reading was finished the Governor cried, "Long
live the King," whereupon Oscar led the cheering, three
times three, and when the band struck up the national hymn
he started the words of the chorus.

But the last feature of the function was the best, and
that was the singing of the hymn composed by Oscar himself. It was a hymn to Iceland, the cradle of the Vikings, the
scene of the Sagas, the parent of parliaments, the mother of
the mighty Northlands.

Standing under the brant face of the law-mount with his
choir of one hundred and fifty on the sloping ground in
front, Oscar conducted with great vigor. His prelude pleased
the people, but when he rose to the height of his argument

and struck the patriotic note, his love for the stern old
Northland—

"Isafold! My Isafold! Great land of frost and fire,"

his hearers were carried away and some of them shouted and
wept.

After the hymn was over the Thingmen crowded about
Oscar to congratulate him and some of the country-people
fell upon his neck. The Governor, too, sitting above, was the
object of many congratulations. "But this is genius," said
one. "An inspiration," said another. "Our Oscar will be
a great musician some day," said a third. And the old man
took the tributes quietly, almost silently, but with the shining face of a father proud of his favorite son.

When the ceremonies ended only one name was on everybody's lips, and that was the name of Oscar Stephenson,
and hundreds hummed the strains of "Isafold! My Isafold!" as they trooped off to dinner.

Oscar and Helga dined together at the Inn-farm in a corner of the hall which was thronged with guests. But they
were both too much excited to remain in mixed company,
and after dinner they escaped to the margin of the lake and
to the solitary parts of the plain. There they gathered
blueberries and, partly to restrain their excitement and
partly to nourish it, they talked of nothing but the wild
flowers.

When the sun began to sink they returned by way of the
parsonage, where the Governor, with the Factor, the Bishop
and certain other officials had taken their dinner apart. The
little guest room was dense with smoke, like the mouth of
a geyser, and the faces that came and went in it were dis-
cussing the merits and defects of the old order and the new.
Both Governor and Factor were for the old, as exemplified by
the day's ceremony and Oscar's hymn, but others held that
changing times brought changing needs and that Iceland
would be the better for a new constitution, with Free Trade
and modern methods.

"They'll go on till midnight and never get home to-
night," whispered Helga, as she slipped out with Oscar.

On returning to the farm they found people striking tents

and leading horses from the crowded horsefold to prepare for the return journey.

"I'm afraid I'm too tired to go back to-night," said Helga.

"Then stay—stay by all means," said Oscar.

"And you?" asked Helga.

"I must go home in any case—there's Thora," said Oscar.

"Your mother will look after her," said Helga.

But Oscar shook his head, and ordered Gudrun, the housekeeper, to make one of the two guest-rooms ready for Helga.

At that moment some young townspeople were clearing the floor for a dance and they called on Oscar and Helga to lead off with a waltz. They did so with great delight, and when the waltz was finished they joined the round dance which followed it, and then they danced a second and a third waltz, until they were flushed and hot and had to go out to cool.

By this time it was dark, and the people who meant to encamp for the night had lighted fires at the mouths of their tents and were beguiling the hours with various pleasures. One of these was fortune-telling. An old woman, not thought to be overwise, was going from tent to tent, making random shots amid shrieks of laughter.

"And what do you see here?" said Helga, holding out her hand.

"Ah, this is a good hand," said the witch. "You are going to be a great lady and eat mutton and beef every day and drink golden wine and ginger."

"And what do you see in this?" asked Oscar.

"This? Oh, dear! Oh, dear!" said the witch.

"What's amiss, mother?"

"Cold water runs between my skin and my flesh."

"Is it as bad as that, old lady?"

"Don't ask me—don't ask me! You have a brother, haven't you?"

"And if I have, what about him?"

"Beware—beware!" said the witch, and Oscar and Helga turned away laughing.

The moon rose and they wandered into the great chasm, and walked among the shadows of the toppling stones, until they came under a huge stone called Stoker, which stands like a mighty gravestone over a deep pit that is like a tomb. There they sat, with the white moon above and the red camp fires below them, and then the boiling, bubbling geyser of excitement in their breasts could be kept down no longer.

"You have had a great success to-day, Oscar," said Helga.

"So have you, Helga, so have you, for without your presence to prompt and inspire me I should have done nothing."

"I am happy if I have helped you, Oscar, but you must go on now, and never look back—never."

"You are right, Helga, you are right—to stop would be a sin—an unpardonable sin—almost like a sin against the Holy Ghost."

"Exactly like it, Oscar, for if any one has a gift he gets it from God, and to bury it, like the man in the parable——"

"There would be no fear of that if I could have you beside me always, Helga."

"And can't you, Oscar?"

A fragrance seemed to envelop him. He felt Helga's breath upon his face. It made him tremble all over.

"Would to God I could, but it is impossible. You will return to Denmark——"

"Not I, indeed! I am not without my own ambitions also. I must go back to England, to France, to Germany, to Italy. And so must you, Oscar—you must, if you are to be true to your talents and to yourself and to the great future——"

"I know it, Helga, I feel it, and if I could write even one song that would stir the souls of millions it would be better than making a fortune or passing an act of parliament. But when a man has given hostages to fortune, and they are dragging him down—with silken threads, perhaps—but still down, down, down——"

He was speaking out of a dry and husky throat, but she answered softly and sweetly, "Are things so absolutely irretrievable, Oscar?"

"Absolutely, Helga, absolutely; and henceforth and all my life long I must learn to go without your comradeship——"

"And what must I do?"

The compulsion of passion was driving him on, but he was struggling to hold back. "Helga," he cried, "do you know what is the deadliest thing in life? It is Love. The painters paint Love as a harmless little Cupid, with a handkerchief about his eyes and a tiny bow and arrow in his hands. But Love is a great, blind, blundering monster with a two-edged sword, dealing destruction on every side."

His words were as nothing, but his quivering voice sang like music in Helga's ears, and she said, "Is it Love or man that does that, Oscar—man with the false sense of right and wrong, his foolish ideals of honor?"

"God knows! Perhaps if I could have thought so a year ago, before I added injury to injury and brought unhappiness on others—but now—now——"

A sensation of triumph came to her and she said, "Isn't it cowardly to talk like that, Oscar?"

"I *am* a coward, Helga," he answered, trembling from head to foot; "to you I can speak the truth—I am a coward, a moral coward, and I can not face the certainty——"

"But if," said Helga excitedly, getting closer, "you had some one beside you who had the courage of life, the defiance of life——"

"Helga!" cried Oscar, breathing heavily—the earth seemed to be slipping under him like an avalanche.

"Some one who would go on helping you, and ask nothing but your comradeship——"

"Helga! Helga!" He was gasping as for breath in the intoxication of his emotion.

"Nothing but to work with you and to conquer the world with you——"

"Helga! Helga! Helga!"

"Oscar!"

There was a breathless cry from both, and then an almost inaudible whisper, "I shall not go back to-night, Helga."

. . . .

When they came to themselves again they were returning —more flushed and excited than before—out of the white moonlight into the yellow mist of the smoking lamp that hung over the dancers in the hall. The young townspeople received them with a shout and called on them to join the dance they were dancing. It was called "Weaving the Cloth," and the figures were intended to represent the spinning and carding, the weaving, stretching, hammering and rolling of the thick Icelandic Vadmal.

The dancers crossed and recrossed, twisted each other about, beat each other breast against breast, and finally rolled each other round and round.

The music was going fast, and the dancers were singing loud and laughing louder, when there came from outside the sudden barking of dogs, followed by the clatter of the hoofs of a galloping horse. Immediately afterward there was the rattle of the metal end of a riding-whip against a window-pane, and a voice crying, "God be with you!"

The newcomer did not wait for the customary answer to his salutation, but pushed the door open and entered hurriedly. It was Magnus, dusty and dirty, with a white face and wild eyes.

At that moment Oscar and Helga, blushing and smiling, were in the middle of the floor, locked in each other's arms, performing the last figure of the dance, and it was thus that Magnus came face to face with them.

"Is she here?" he cried.

"She?"

"Thora! She is lost—I thought she might have found a horse and followed you."

Then the shuffling feet stopped, and the fiddles tailed off into silence as Magnus, in broken sentences, told the story of Thora's flight to the Factor's, her disappearance with the child, and the vain search that had been made for her.

"But surely she would go back to Government House eventually," said Oscar. "The poor girl would go the long way round to escape observation and home by way of the lake. Did nobody think of that, and stay in the house to see?"

Magnus looked like a man whose eyes, dulled by groping in a dark tunnel, had been stunned by sudden light. Before the others had recovered themselves he had turned about and was gone.

At the next moment Oscar was tramping to and fro on the floor, with his clinched fists to his forehead, moaning, "My God! My God!" Helga was combing her hair and putting on her wraps.

14

VIII

JOHN, the servant at the farm, was sent over to the parsonage to tell the Governor and the Factor. He found the gentlemen settling themselves for the night, having talked so long that they had decided to remain until morning. But the news of Thora's disappearance altered everything.

"We must go back immediately," said the Governor.

"Bring the horses round instantly," said the Factor.

Less than half an hour afterward a silent and gloomy company were going home—the Governor, the Factor, Oscar, Helga, and a various following of the sympathetic and the inquisitive.

The two old friends were morose and ill-tempered, and for the first time in fifty years disposed to nag and quarrel. The Governor blamed Aunt Margret, the Factor blamed Anna; the Governor blamed Helga, the Factor blamed Oscar; the Governor blamed the Factor, and the Factor blamed the Governor. In the half light of uncertainty and suspense their friendship fell before fear, and blood was thicker than water.

It was a miserable home-going to Oscar. The explanation of Thora's movements with which he had surprised Magnus soon ceased to satisfy himself and he thought of a hundred fatal consequences. Helga tried to comfort him with various plausible arguments. He had acted for the best—the best for Thora, the best for the child, the best for himself, the best for everybody—and if accident had intervened or the dreadful freaks of dementia had followed, he was not responsible and could not be blamed.

But Oscar's worst sufferings were from a secret purgatory which Helga's pleadings did not touch, for the cruelest part of his remorse concerned Helga herself.

The journey was long and tiresome and every step had its own peculiar misery. During the first hour the moon was shining—a brilliant moon that bathed everything in loveliness—and Oscar remembered the scene in the chasm and reflected that in the very hour of his delirious happiness Thora, perhaps, was lying dead.

Then the moon died out and darkness fell—a murky darkness, blacker than the lava—and as Oscar pushed and plunged along over the stumbles of his pony, the thought came to him that if Thora were dead perhaps it was the best that could have happened to her—the best under the circumstances—saving her from the bitterness of a future which must surely come when Helga and he, struggle as they might, would have to break the bonds that bound them.

And then in that dark and treacherous hour, with no face to look into his face, he felt an immense relief, remembering that if Thora was gone, the consequences of his life's error were at an end and he was free.

But the dawn came—a bleared, rainy dawn, with scarfs of vapor stretching across the sun like a cataract over a blood-shot eye—and Oscar's remorse was doubled by the wounds he had inflicted upon his conscience in the darkness, and he dare not look at Helga as she rode, muffled up and silent, by his side.

They were crossing the Moss Fell Heath by this time, and everything around was dark and drear. A solitary raven kept them cheerless company for a while, flying from beacon to beacon and uttering its husky cry. Oscar remembered the scenes of yesterday when the sky was blue, and their blood was warm, and then the thought came to him—like the shooting of the bolt on a man buried in a tomb—that if he was not to be henceforward the most miserable of men he must pray with all his soul and strength that when they reached the end of their journey Thora should be alive.

On reaching the more inhabited districts Oscar allowed the Governor and the Factor to forge on ahead, and Helga to wait for him in the road, while he glanced off to the farmhouses and shouted up at the bedroom windows. But the result was always the same—Thora had not been seen and Magnus had been there before him.

When they came to the top of the hill from which they had looked back on Reykjavik and on the Danish mail-steamer entering the fiord, the little capital floated in the mist of morning like a city in a woolly sea, and the " Laura "

lay anchored outside of it; but the apprehensions of yesterday were consumed by the fears of to-day, and Oscar thought
of one thing alone.

They met farmers trotting out of the town on their little
caravans of ponies, yet Oscar did not question them, lest he
should hear the news he dare not listen to, and coming at
length to the long street of the little capital, he did not
raise his face to the eyes that peered at him through the curtains of upper windows, lest they should reveal the truth he
dared not learn.

The fear of disaster had by this time swallowed up any
flicker of hope in Oscar, and when, coming up to Government House, he found a crowd of people standing in front
of it, he knew too well that all was over. From that moment
onward fact after fact led up to the fatal certainty.

The window of Thora's bedroom—the window at which
Oscar had shouted his adieus the day before—stood open,
and a ladder had been raised against it. By the gate to the
green a horse lay dead on the gravel—it was Magnus's horse,
his magnificent Golden Mane—covered with dust and sweat,
as it fell under its rider at the last step of his fearful
journey.

In the middle of the hall Anna and Aunt Margret stood
with the Governor and the Factor, sobbing out their pitiful
explanations. Afraid to return to the empty house which
had been the scene of a painful memory, Anna had sat the
night through with Margret at the Factor's, waiting hour
after hour for the reports of the Sheriff and his constables.
Nothing had been heard of Thora, but in the early morning
Magnus had returned and found the door of her room
locked on the inside. Then he had run for them and they
had called to Thora, but received no answer, though sometimes they heard the baby crying. And now Magnus, having
failed to force the door, had gone for a ladder, and he intended to climb into the room from the outside.

Oscar was conscious of no more until he found himself
knocking at Thora's door and calling in his agony:

" Thora! Thora! Thora! "

There was a heavy, staggering step inside the room; the
lock was thrust back and the door thrown open.

"Thora!" cried Oscar again, but it was Magnus who stood before him—Magnus with a face white and set and full of anger and hatred.

"You were right," he said, pointing to the bed. "There she is with God—and you!"

Thora lay high on the pillow, with her eyes open and her parted lips smiling, as if she had just awakened from a beautiful dream. She was dead, but her baby was alive, and it was rolling its little round head and digging its red hand into her cold, white breast.

With a low, choking cry, Oscar fell to his knees at the bedside and buried his face in the bedclothes. Magnus left the room, the others entered it, and Aunt Margret lifted the living child out of the mother's breast over the father's kneeling form.

IX

DURING the few days before the funeral the Government House felt motionless and empty, like a room when the clock has stopped in it. Behind the drawn blinds everybody talked in whispers, as if the dead were asleep and must not be wakened. The stillness of the house centered in the room where Thora lay, and that was white and fresh with the odor of clean linen and wild flowers. In the deadened sunshine, as it filtered through the yellow blinds, there was a halo about the waxen face on the bed, and it seemed to diffuse solemnity on all around it.

Anna never allowed herself to be long away from this chamber. Her fear of the room had gone, now that death had entered it. Early and late, in daylight and dark, she went to and fro in the silent place, walking softly and seeming to count the hours during which her dear girl would be above ground.

The Governor did nothing from the day of Thora's death until the day of her burial. Dressed always in his official uniform he sat in his bureau, but received no one. He wrote no letters and read no books and seldom spoke at his meals. For hours together he would sit with folded arms looking fixedly at the pattern on the carpet. A shadow had fallen on him—a shadow of shame—and in the sealed chamber of his proud soul he was struggling to reconcile his conduct to himself and finding it difficult to do so.

The Factor went on with his work as usual, for in the decalogue of his duty there was no maxim that forbade business, but sometimes as he turned the leaves of his ledger he looked long and saw nothing, and once, as he counted up the figures in his bank-book, the thought smote him with the force of a blow on the brain that perhaps Nature was beginning to strike a balance with him against the sum of his successors, and that the cruel bereavement which had just befallen him was the first stroke of the Nemesis which was to follow in the wake of his wealth.

Aunt Margret and Helga were always at home, the one busy with the baby, which had been taken back to the Factor's, and the other with the "black" which had to be ordered for everybody.

Little was known of Magnus, except that he was still in town, that he had been seen with the Sheriff and two strangers, that in spite of the trouble which had overtaken his family he was spending most of his time in the dark smoking-room of the Hotel, and that he was said to be drinking heavily.

But the grief of Oscar touched and satisfied everybody. He had eaten little and had never been known to sleep. Sometimes he was seen to be sitting apart and weeping silently; sometimes he was moving from room to room, as if every spot on which his eye could rest was charged with the memory of happy days that were dead; sometimes he was heard in the white room in which Thora lay—the room in which she had been so merry and so sad, so wild with delirium and so happy with her baby—and there he was sobbing out his wild regrets in muffled cries of " Forgive me! Forgive me! " Once in the middle of the night he was heard at the harmonium in the room below the death chamber, playing softly a pitiful lament which awakened his father and mother and brought the salt tears to their eyes.

The desolate soul in these ghastly hours was prostrating itself in the dust. Death strikes sternly, and Oscar in his penitence was accusing himself of every crime. He had killed Thora—not her body only, but her heart, that faithful heart which had loved him so deeply, so tenderly, so passionately.

In this conscience-stricken condition he looked back on the path of his life with Thora, and every step as he now saw it seemed to be thick set with the stubble of sin and rank with the weeds of self-deception. When he returned from England he had taken Thora from Magnus, although he did not love her. It was true he had thought he loved her, but the brotherly thing would have been to stand back in silence, and if he had only done so Time itself would have undeceived him.

That was the first of his offenses, and the next was no less hideous. When, being betrothed to Thora, he awoke to the certainty that his heart was with Helga, he had gone on with his bargain and led the girl who loved him into a loveless marriage. It was true he thought he was doing his duty, but behind duty was fear, fear of the world and fear of Magnus, while the courageous thing, the manly thing, even the merciful thing would have been to stop at the church door, if need be, and face the facts and take the consequences.

But having cheated Thora of her love and lied to her at the altar, he had crowned the sum of his sins by exposing himself to the temptation of infidelity. It was true that Thora herself, in her innocent affection, had paved the way to this temptation; true, too, that his marriage had been an imperfect partnership; but all the same his course had been clear and he should have cut himself off from Helga at once and for ever. That he had not done so, that he had paltered with temptation was the last cause of this terrible calamity. Thora had died because her heart was dead, and he himself had killed it.

Thus the desolate soul of the unhappy man laid down its faults at the feet of God, hiding nothing, palliating nothing, and seeing everything in naked light. If to be sorry for having sinned is to be innocent, Oscar had ceased to be guilty in his pitiful, but useless, sorrow. In the dizzy hours of pain and shame, when the wheel of life goes rapidly, Oscar asked himself how it had come to pass that Thora was dead,

and something whispered " Helga," and again and yet again
something whispered "Helga," but his heart would not
listen to that excuse. Helga had not been to blame. He
alone had been at fault. He had sacrificed Thora to his am-
bitious dreams—his dreams of greatness, of glory. Helga
had been merely the symbol of those dreams, and Thora was
dead because he had tried to become a great musician.

But the past was past, and when Oscar asked himself
what punishment he could impose upon himself for the future, he heard but one answer. If his ambitions had been the
cause of his sin, to bury them would be the true expression
of his repentance. He *would* bury them. He would bury
his genius and the expectation of becoming a composer in
the grave of the sweet girl he had destroyed, and go through
the rest of his life in the drudgery of the nearest duty, eating
the bread of affliction in obscurity and remorse.

When Oscar first attempted to carry out this resolution, it
was in a scene of such tragic beauty that no one who witnessed it could ever afterward wipe it out of mind. The
family had gathered for that last office of love, which makes
perhaps the saddest moment of human experience—sadder
than the moment of turning away from the newly covered
grave, sadder even that the moment of returning to the
void and empty home—the moment when the coffin-lid is
closed down and the beloved face disappears for ever.

The death chamber was the same that in a better time had
been the bridal chamber, but the air which had tingled with
all exquisite thoughts of life was now heavy with the hush
of death. It was night-time and the same lamp burned under
the same shade, while a gilt-edged prayer-book lay in a
circle of lighted candles on the little table that stood by the
bed. Besides the members of the family, only two persons
were present—one of the sewing-maids, who had made the
wedding-dress for the cathedral, and had just put the last
stitch to the garment intended for a darker house, and a
joiner in his shirt-sleeves.

One by one the family approached the bed to take their
last look at the burden that lay on it—the Governor with a
solemn tread, as if he had been approaching the presence
of a king, the Factor with rigid strides and a bewildered

stare, and Helga with a nervous step and a furtive glance, as if duty had called her and she wished herself away. But Anna and Aunt Margret moved about the body without dread or ceremony, laying flowers on the bosom and smoothing the soft hair that was dressed down the cheek, as if the dear dead belonged to them by right of nature, and they would give it up to no one until Earth herself, the mother of us all, should claim it for her own.

The man in the shirt-sleeves had stepped forward to finish his task when the Governor held up his hand.

"Wait! Where is Oscar?" he asked, and then Maria, the old housemaid, who had been weeping noiselessly outside the door, was sent to fetch him.

While Maria was away, Aunt Margret went up to Thora and whispered over her:

"My precious, precious pet! You never changed to your stupid old auntie, did you?—not even when she kept your dear baby away from you and your sweet heart was broken! Don't think she didn't love you for all that, my precious. She loved you every minute, my own. And now that she has got your baby she intends to keep it. She *will* keep it as long as she lives, so don't you ever be troubled about that, Thora. Aunt Margret is going to be a mother to your little girl, and nobody in the world shall ever touch a hair of your darling's head."

It was at this moment that Oscar entered the room, with old Maria creeping up behind him. His pale cheeks and sunken eyes testified to the strength of his remorse, but his step was firm and his whole figure showed intense vitality of will. He carried a bundle of papers in one hand, and they were loose and irregular, as if they had been snatched up hurriedly at the moment he was called. In the utter absorption of his mood he seemed to be unconscious of anybody or anything in the room except one thing—the thing that lay upon the bed—and walking up to it he looked down at the white face and spoke to it as if the dead—and the dead alone—could hear.

"Thora," he said in a calm voice, "these are the only copies of my compositions, and I wish you to take them with you. They were written in hours when your faithful heart was suffering through my fault—when I neglected you and deserted you for the sake of my foolish visions of art and greatness. That was the real cause of your death, Thora, and in punishment of myself for sacrificing your sweet life to my selfish dreams, I wish to bury the fruits of them in your grave. Take them, then, and let them lie with you and fade with you and be forgotten. I will never write another note of music as long as I live, and from this hour onward my ambitions are at an end."

Saying this he put the papers beside the body of Thora and wrapped them in the long plaits of her beautiful hair.

"Oscar! Oscar!" cried Helga in breathless horror.

The others listened and looked on, hardly realizing what Oscar had resigned, but Helga realized it, and she was trying to warn him against the life-long sacrifice. But he did not seem to hear her, and at such a moment further remonstrance was impossible.

"My sweet girl," said Oscar, stretching both arms over the bed, "forgive me for all my failures of duty. Oh, what I would give to forget them now; but I can't, I can't! You are gone, and I can never make amends."

Thinking to put an end to a scene which was touching everybody too deeply, the Governor signed to the man in the shirt-sleeves, but when the man stepped forward Oscar's grief broke out afresh, and in the vehemence of his sorrow his tongue lost all control of itself.

"Not yet!" he cried. "Oh, God! Thora! My wife! My sweet young wife! Let me look at her face again! How bright and happy it used to be, and now it is leaving me like this! Forgive me, my angel! Say you forgive me before you go! I can not live without your forgiveness! I wronged you and sinned against you, but you were good and your childlike heart was from God!"

The desolate cry rang through the room, and each of those who heard the revelation of the naked soul read it by the light of his own. Helga trembled and turned to the window, the Governor and the Factor dropped their heads, but Aunt Margret cried openly in innocent sympathy, and Anna touched Oscar's arm and tried to comfort him.

After a moment Oscar became more calm and even signed

to the man himself, and when all was over he walked firmly and courageously out of the room.

X

On the day of the funeral Oscar was weak and ill, and more fit for his bed than for a journey to the cemetery, but no one could prevail on him not to go. The morning was dull and drear, with black clouds from the mountains and some sprinklings of rain, and when the dread hour struck, and Oscar came down among the mourners, his face looked ghastly in the void and heavy air.

The bell in the cathedral tower began to toll, the solemn burden was borne slowly down the stairs, and then Oscar's white face became yet more white and he would have fallen but for his father's arm which held him up.

The body was first rested on the green outside the door, and while the mourners grouped themselves round in a wide half-circle to sing a parting hymn, Oscar stood bareheaded in the drizzling rain which had begun to fall.

John, the servant, stood at the gate, holding Silvertop, Thora's pony, which he had brought from the farm to carry her on her last journey, and the sight of this horse seemed to be more than Oscar could bear. The coffin was laid cross-wise on the panniers and the procession began to form. It passed through deep lines of the townspeople, Oscar walking first after the body, alone, bareheaded and conscious of nothing but his grief. The bell was still tolling and a Sabbath quiet had fallen over the town.

The cathedral was crowded with the same faces that had looked on at Thora's wedding, when she came down from the altar in her bloom and beauty, happy and smiling on her husband's arm; and now that she was being carried up to it, while the organ played the funeral march, and Oscar walked with drooping head behind, the people nearest the aisle said he was weeping audibly.

The coffin in its pall was set down on the steps to the communion rail—the spot where Thora had knelt as a young girl to be confirmed and as a bride to be married—and then the Bishop who had been waiting to receive it delivered a consolatory address.

They should not ask themselves why this sweet and lovely life had been so ruthlessly cut off. The ways of Providence were inscrutable, but God was in heaven and the Judge of all the earth did right. Neither should the family who were there to mourn take blame to themselves for what had occurred, for if it had pleased the Almighty to lay His hand on the afflicted brain of their dear departed sister. He knew best why He did so, and to what end it was done. Rather let them kneel in gratitude to God that in His mercy He had not suffered her to lift her hand against herself, and so rob them of the blessed hope of eternal life.

"To the young husband who is here plunged in sorrow," said the Bishop, "what can we say but that all our hearts go out to him? It seems only yesterday that he stood on this spot to make his vows before heaven and before men to love and cherish the dear girl who has been so suddenly taken away. If she had lived he would have kept his promises, and though she is gone, he will preserve the spirit of them still. The pure and innocent soul who linked her life with his life will be an abiding memory, a perpetual inspiration against sin, and when the first pangs of grief are over, a constant solace and a lasting joy."

If it was possible for Oscar to look more wan and weak than when he went into the cathedral, he did so when he came out of it. The rain was now falling heavily, but when the procession was formed again for the last stage of the journey, he walked bareheaded as before.

The Factor, who was behind Oscar (with Helga quivering on his arm), begged him to put on his hat, but he refused, and when the Governor, who came next with Anna, passed up an umbrella, he shook his head and sent it back. The bell tolled again, the little town sat quiet, and the townspeople who wept floods of tears for Thora, wept for Oscar even more.

When the procession reached the cemetery the rain was coming down in torrents and even the priest put an overcoat over his cassock, but Oscar stood uncovered by the open grave. During the short prayer—"dust to dust"—he suffered visibly, and during the long hymn that is always sung at an Icelandic funeral, while the grave is being filled in, the hollow thuds of the falling earth seemed to beat upon his twitching face.

When all was at an end he could not be drawn away until his father took him by the arm and said in a firm voice, "Come." Then with a stronger step he walked with a remnant of the broken procession across the little cemetery—the hummocked home-field of the dead—through the gate to the road—where Hans, the water-carrier in the sleeveless waistcoat Thora had made for him, was giving water to her horse—past the Factor's house—where Aunt Margret watched at a window with the baby in her arms—and thus back to his empty home.

At the foot of the stairs he excused himself when the mourners went in to their meal, and he was seen no more that day.

The dinner was a cheerless thing, being served in the room that had witnessed the home-coming, and so chilled with memories of that happier event. Silently, or in whispers, the mourners bade their adieus and crept away one by one, leaving the few remaining members of the two families with wide spaces between them at the table like gaps in a toothless skull.

The Governor and the Factor had not spoken since their return from the Proclamation, and the interval of silence had made the rift between the two old friends grow wide.

"Ah, well!" yawned the Factor, "it's all over, I suppose."

Then he turned to the Governor and asked sharply, "Where is Magnus? I've seen nothing of him to-day."

The Governor did not answer and Anna dropped her head, and then Helga, who was the only other person present, said quietly:

"Somebody saw him at the Hotel—he did right not to come to the funeral—they say he was not quite sober."

"Just like him," said the Factor. "A yell is all you hear of a wolf, and but for his last drinking bout, perhaps nothing of this would have happened."

The Governor's proud face quivered, but he did not speak, and soon afterward the Factor and Helga went away.

XI

EARLY next morning, before the household was astir, the Governor was in his bureau, ready to begin on the arrears of business, when somebody knocked at the door. It was Magnus, white and worn, but sober and serious as a judge.

"May I speak to you, sir?" said Magnus.

"Well—perhaps for a moment—come in," said the Governor.

It occurred to the Governor as Magnus entered the bureau that he had come for money to help him with the farm, and he said immediately:

"If you have come for financial assistance toward stock and seed and what not, I ought to tell you at once, Magnus, that I have nothing to give you. I have already spent as much on the farm as I am justified in spending—more perhaps than I ought to have spent on the inheritance of one of my sons in justice to the claims of the other one—and if it is money—ready money——"

"I do not come to ask for money," said Magnus. "But I come to speak about it," he added, and then he sat on a low seat and twisted his felt hat between his knees, while the Governor leaned back in his desk-chair and fingered a pen.

"I wish to ask," said Magnus, "whether you drew, about six months ago, a bill on the Bank of Denmark for one hundred thousand crowns."

The Governor uttered a contemptuous snort and said, "Certainly not; I have never drawn a bill in my life and never shall do so. Why do you ask?"

"Because a bill for that amount is in town at this moment," said Magnus.

"Then it is a forgery—an impudent forgery—and the forger must be found and promptly punished."

The Governor had risen in his chair when he looked at Magnus's drooping head and a thought occurred to him.

"But are you sure of what you say? Is this story true?" he asked.

"I have seen the paper myself," replied Magnus.

" And it is signed in my name?"

" It is signed in your name, sir, and witnessed in the name of the Factor."

" That, too," said the Governor, while a painful smile came into his face. " And pray whom is this extraordinary document drawn in favor of?"

Magnus did not reply immediately—he continued to twist his hat between his knees.

" That may help us to find the motive, and therefore the forger—who is it?"

" Oscar Stephenson," said Magnus.

" Oscar? Your brother?"

" Yes, sir—and the money was paid to him in Paris."

" What?" cried the Governor, crossing the floor. " You tell me that Oscar—your brother Oscar—has committed a forgery? Oh, that's what you mean—don't deny it—you mean that my son is a forger?"

Magnus made no answer, and after a moment the painful smile about the Governor's face broke into a more painful laugh. " But why do I trouble myself with such a trumpery story? I see how it is, Magnus—strong drink is a strong tongue—you have been drinking."

" I *have* been drinking, sir—I was ill and I couldn't help it—but I'm sober now, and what I tell you is God's truth."

Magnus rose as he said this and father and son stood face to face—the little Governor in his uniform with flushed cheeks and pigeon-breast distended, and Magnus big, black, clumsy, unkempt, and with lines of suffering in his face.

" And this document, you tell me, is at present in Iceland?"

" It is, sir—two officers of the law brought it here from Copenhagen."

" Officers of the law, you say?"

" The bank found reasons to suspect the signatures, so they sent across to verify them."

" You have talked with these men yourself, no doubt?"

" The Sheriff brought them to see me," said Magnus.

" The Sheriff, too! The Sheriff of all men!"

" He is to bring the two men here to-morrow morning."

" So he is to bring them here to-morrow morning!"

The Governor, though heated and agitated, laughed once more, and said with a sneer:

"Of course, in the interests of the family, you felt it necessary to examine the signatures they showed you?"

"I did," said Magnus simply.

"And without consulting me to denounce the forger?"

Magnus made no reply.

"And even to hint—only to hint—that perhaps you could point to the forger?"

Still Magnus made no answer, and dropping his cynical tone, the Governor burst out in choking anger:

"Out on you, man, out on you! I thought you were drunk, or suffering from the delusions of drink, but you are worse—you are sweltering in hatred—and it is an unnatural hatred, too—the hatred of your own flesh and blood."

Magnus flinched as if a lash had cut him through the skin.

"You are jealous of your brother—always have been, always will be—because he is clever and successful and amiable and because everybody loves him—you are as jealous of your brother as Cain was of Abel, and this is your way of destroying him."

Magnus stood with drooping head while the Governor's lash fell over him.

"Aren't you ashamed to stand before your father and parade the whole diabolical catalogue of your unnatural passions? You allow yourself to consort with my enemies, with Oscar's enemies, with your own enemies, if you had the sense to see it, while they try to bring him down at the highest moment of his success."

The Governor was walking to and fro and lashing himself into a fury.

"At the deepest moment of his distress, too! Just when the poor boy is unmanned by the loss of his wife—the dear girl he loved and you insulted. But I don't believe one word of this cock-and-bull story. That accursed document is nothing but a trick to dishonor my son and to discredit me at the very time when a pack of rascals who call themselves reformers are trying to abolish the Governorship. Let them do it if they can, but while I am Governor here I'm master in this house, and Mr. Sheriff shall be suspended and those men sent back to Copenhagen."

"Hadn't you better speak to Oscar first, sir?" said Magnus.

"Certainly, I shall, and if I find as I expect—as I am sure—that your story is a pack of falsehoods—let me never see your face again."

Without a word of defense or explanation, Magnus left the room, and a few minutes afterward Oscar, at the call of the Governor, entered it.

Oscar's face was as pale as yesterday, but with a different pallor, a different expression—an expression not of grief and regret, but of fear and shame.

"Oscar," said the Governor, "I am sorry to trouble you about business so soon after your great sorrow, but an ugly story is being told about you in town, and as every lie has its tail, it is only right that you should hear of this one immediately, so that it may be quashed without delay."

Oscar's lower lip trembled—he felt the blow before it fell.

"Magnus—your brother Magnus—I am aware he has not been on brotherly terms with you—your mother has told me something about that—and let me say I do not sympathize with his protests and pretensions—I think them nothing but an excuse for his own selfishness—Magnus has just been here, and he tells me that a note of hand drawn in your favor for no less a sum than one hundred thousand crowns has been forged in my name. I do not believe the story and I do not want you to discuss it. I only ask you to contradict it—to contradict it flatly—or to leave me to deal with the real offender as I think best."

Oscar, standing by the Governor's desk, remained for a moment quite still. Then in a voice so low that it hardly seemed to come from him, he said:

"I can not contradict it, father. What Magnus has told you is true."

"True? You say it is *true?*"

Father and son stood facing each other for some moments without a word more being spoken. Then in hot words, broken by breathless pauses, the Governor poured out question after question, to which Oscar made no answer.

"You received that sum and signed for it in your father's name?—in the name of your father-in-law also? One hundred thousand crowns? What has become of the money?"

15.

"It is lost," said Oscar.

"Lost?"

"It was to pay the debts I had already contracted."

"Was that at Monte Carlo?"

"Yes."

There was another long silence, in which Oscar stood with quivering lips and the Governor with contracted brows.

"But this document—how did it come about?"

"I ask myself that question over and over again, father, and I fail to find an answer. I can not understand myself— I try and I can not."

"Were you mad?"

"Sometimes I think I was—I must have been."

"Did somebody tempt you—put the idea into your head? —somebody, perhaps, who helped you to lose and promised to help you to repay? If so, who was it?"

"I do not wish to accuse anybody, father—I suppose I have no right to do so."

"Right? Don't talk to me about rights. Think about your duties—and the first of your duties is to me, not to the person, whoever it may be, who has helped to destroy you. You have pledged my credit and my honor, but I don't want to think you altogether bad, and if anybody suggested this devilish device to pay your debts, I ought to be told who it was. Was it Helga?"

At the mention of that name Oscar's drooping head drooped lower still; the Governor saw this and then he understood everything.

"Lord God forgive us," he said, in a breathless whisper. "Then Magnus was right, after all! And the death of the poor child we buried yesterday was perhaps a part of the diabolical harvest we are reaping to-day! You needn't wince, sir—I see it's true without that."

Oscar did not attempt to excuse himself, and after some moments of silence the Governor spoke again.

"You have deceived and disappointed me, Oscar. I thought I had one son who was an intelligent man and a gentleman, not a forger and a fool. But it is of no use to prolong a painful interview. You may go."

Oscar staggered out of the room and the Governor sank into his chair.

XII

THE proud man was abased. For the first time in his life he was degraded in his own eyes. His own son had committed a vulgar crime and exposed himself to a vulgar punishment.

In the first pain of surprise and humiliation he saw himself covering up the whole wretched episode. But he was too proud to be proud, and at the next moment he began to count with his conscience. Thus far he had tried to do what was right in Iceland, and he would do what was right to the end, whatever it might cost him.

Oscar had offended against the law and he must bear its righteous punishment. It might be eight years' imprisonment, with the ruin of all his prospects, the waste of all his talents, and the wreck of all his happiness, but he must go through with it to the last hour, the last penalty, the last pang.

So felt the Governor as Judge, and if as the father he felt differently it was only with a different intensity. His favorite son—the son whom he had indulged and pampered in the past—for whom he had planned and prepared so many things in the future—had committed a crime against his country and against himself, relying upon his father's love and pride to save him from the painful consequences, no matter what sacrifice it might cost him in hard-earned money or in money still to earn; no matter how much it might put him at the mercy of a scheming crew who were striving to pull him from his place! It was selfish. it was heartless, it was shameful, it was infamous, and it deserved a double punishment.

Feeling more bitterly against his son than he had ever felt before against any human creature, the Governor passed the day in torment, and he was sitting alone in his room late at night, with no light but the sleepy glow from the open stove, when the door opened noiselessly and Anna entered. She looked as if she had been crying, although her eyes were dry, and the Governor reproached himself that in all his sorry summary of the consequences of his son's crime he had never once thought of his son's mother.

But neither did she think of herself, and now sitting by the stove and stirring it, she began to talk of Oscar.

"He has fallen asleep at last," she said, "and his troubles are over for a little while anyway. He went up to his old bedroom to-night, Stephen, the one he slept in when he was a boy—when Magnus and he were boys together. I sat with him until he dropped off, and he held my hand all the time, just as he used to do after he had been naughty and you had sent him to bed without his supper. He looks quite like himself now, poor boy, and if you could see him lying there on the pillow, you would think the old days had come back, when you used to go up with the candle to look at him, and wipe the tears from his little face while he lay asleep, and stroke his curly hair. Ah, dear, how easily he could throw off his troubles in those old days, Stephen! Next morning you would hear him romping about overhead, and singing like a lark."

"A shallow nature, Anna," said the Governor, "a shallow nature, on which nothing makes a serious impression—always has been, always will be."

"Oh, but this will, Stephen, this will make a deep impression, and if the poor boy could only have another chance he would turn over a new leaf and set to work in good earnest, and realize all your expectations. And then think—only think, father, what a dreadful thing it would be if one brother were to drag the other into the dock—dreadful for us, I mean. We should lose both our children, for Oscar would be lost to us one way and we should never be able to look on Magnus again."

"Our children have always been at war, Anna, ever since their earliest infancy."

"Don't say that, Stephen. When they were little they loved each other dearly. It was not until they grew up that they were different. And then others came between them—one other anyway, and—who knows?—perhaps she has been the cause of all this trouble."

"Has Oscar said so?" asked the Governor.

"He will say nothing against anybody," replied Anna. "That was always the way with Oscar. But if somebody tempted him and he was weak, and if our poor boy must go to prison while she——"

"There is a weakness that is wickedness, Anna, and must bear its pains and penalties."

"Yes, I know," said Anna. "I remember you said the same words long ago when the sailor lad killed his sweetheart in a fit of drunken passion. The mother was a widow and she came to ask me to plead with you for her son. He was a good boy, she said, and if it had not been for the drink he would never have hurt any one. You spared his life, you know, and he was sent to prison. And dear me, how the poor woman kissed me and wept on my face for joy! But she came to think that for her part it might have been better if her boy had died instead of being locked up for ever. She could never forget it, and when her eldest daughter was married and her house was full of people, and everybody was happy, she suddenly remembered and ran up-stairs to cry. And then on wintry nights, when the wind was moaning over the sea and she was putting the little boys to bed, she always thought of their brother lying alone in the big brown house up the road and round the corner. It wouldn't have been so bad if he had been sent away, she thought. And she was only a poor widow who washed at the hot springs."

The night wind was moaning over the sea at that moment, and the Governor, who had been walking to and fro, struggling to be righteous and severe, was feeling a pain in his parched throat.

He stood for some moments by the window, with his hands interlaced behind him, looking out through the dark pane on the flying moon, and then with an obvious inward effort he said:

"Anna, if I acknowledge this signature we shall have nothing left—nothing but my salary. Even my salary is threatened, and if it goes we shall be without anything in the world."

"Why should we think of that, Stephen?" said Anna. "We had nothing when we married, and yet we were very happy. It is true we were young then, and now we are old, but if poverty comes again we shall know better how to bear it. And if we have nothing else we will have each other—and our boys, too—both our boys—wherever they may be by that time—and neither of them will love us the less because we have given up everything—everything we had in the world—that they might still be honored and respected."

The clock struck twelve in the tower of the cathedral, with a reverberant ring that passed over the sleepy town, and the Governor stopped in his restless perambulation.

"It is late, mother," he said, in a husky voice, "let us go to bed."

XIII

NEXT morning the Governor was in his bureau again. He was now firm and composed and waiting calmly for the officers from Copenhagen. They came early, headed by the Sheriff, and bore themselves largely, like men who were conscious that they were about to administer a painful shock.

After the formal introductions the Sheriff leaned above the Governor's desk and said suavely, almost condescendingly:

"These gentlemen have been anxious to show every consideration. They came on an urgent matter—I may say a *most* urgent matter—but they have waited five days, rather than break in upon you at a time of domestic tribulation."

"I am busy this morning, Mr. Sheriff," said the Governor. "Be so good as to waste no more time than is necessary."

The Sheriff gasped and fell back from the desk, whereupon the strangers stepped up to it, and one of them opening a large envelope, said in a tone of indulgent courtesy:

"We have a document here, your Excellency, which claims to be drawn by your authority. Will you be good enough to see if this is your Excellency's signature?"

The Governor fixed his eye-glasses leisurely, and glancing hastily, almost casually, at the paper put before him, replied promptly:

"It is."

The strangers looked at each other in silence before they spoke again.

"In that case we presume your Excellency will be prepared to honor it?"

"Certainly," said the Governor.

" Then your Excellency will be aware that the bill is already overdue and that two applications have been made for payment ? "

The Governor flinched at that question, but recovering himself in a moment, he said, shortly:

" The bill shall be met immediately."

" How soon, your Excellency—a week, a fortnight ? "

" Three days," said the Governor. " Good-morning, gentlemen," and without more ceremony he took up his pen and began to write a letter.

The Sheriff, who was perspiring visibly by this time, had edged round to the door, and after a short silence, in which nothing was heard but the scratching of the Governor's quill, the strangers bowed to his stooping forehead and backed themselves out of the room.

The Governor's letter was to the Factor, asking him to come immediately. He came, looking sullen and suspicious, with the air of one who knew something already of the business for which he had been summoned.

" Old friend," said the Governor, " we have known each other for fifty years, and I have never yet asked you to do me a favor, but I am going to ask you now."

" H'm! " said the Factor, with a cold smile.

" It is not for my own needs I ask it, but for one who is nearer to me than myself. We who are fathers know what that means; and we also know that a favor done once to our children is done twice to ourselves."

" H'm, h'm! " said the Factor, with the same cold smile.

" It is a private matter—strictly private—but to you, old friend, I can reveal the secret—your godson has got himself into trouble."

And then, excusing and extenuating nothing, the Governor told the story of Oscar's downfall, and the Factor listened with the impatience of one who had heard the sorry tale before.

" He signed my name also, you say ? " said the Factor.

" That, too, unhappily," answered the Governor, " but you were merely made witness to the deed, and I am responsible for the money."

" What are you going to do about it ? " asked the Factor in a hard tone.

"Pay it and give the lad another chance in life," replied the Governor. "And that's why I sent for you this morning. I can find fifty thousand crowns and I want you to lend me the other fifty thousand."

"Not fifty thousand cents," said the Factor. "Not fifty— to shield a criminal and to cheat the law."

The Governor's face whitened, but he answered quietly, "Don't speak so fast, old friend. Remember that the offense against the law is only an offense against myself, and if I choose to forgive it the law can have nothing to say."

"What about the offense against me?" said the Factor.

"Remember, too," continued the Governor, "that if Oscar has made free with your name he has certain claims upon your purse—there is the marriage contract."

"The marriage contract was made for Thora, and Thora is dead," said the Factor.

"There is the child," said the Governor.

"I hold the child now and I am prepared to provide for it in the future," said the Factor, "but I will have nothing more to do with a man who has forged my name, and if any further claim is made—on my business or estate or what not—I will protest against it and publish my reasons for doing so."

"Oscar Neilsen," said the Governor, "there is something I have not told you, something I did not intend to tell you, but I must tell it to you now. I have reason to believe—to be confident—that for the trouble in which Oscar finds himself Helga is partly responsible."

"Can you prove that, Stephen Magnusson?" said the Factor.

"If I can not prove it," replied the Governor, "it is because my son—whatever his faults and follies—is still a gentleman; and if you do not know it by this time it is because your daughter is not a lady."

"Speak for your own, Stephen Magnusson, and leave mine to me," said the Factor.

"Therefore," continued the Governor, "when I pay this money—and I shall pay it—you will have the satisfaction to know that though I am a poor man and you are a rich one, I am discharging your debt as well as mine."

With that, red and angry, the Governor walked to the door and opened it. The Factor looked at him in blank amazement, and for one swift instant his better nature conquered his greed and he saw what a pitiful thing it was that after fifty years of friendship they should quarrel thus about their children. But one sword draws another from its sheath, and he snapped his fingers contemptuously and strode out of the room.

Then the Governor sent for the manager of the Bank of Iceland.

"Manager," he said, "I wish you to arrange a loan of one hundred thousand crowns on the security of my farm at Thingvellir."

"The farm is hardly worth so much, sir—I say it is hardly worth so much," said the manager. "But in your case there can be little difficulty—none whatever if you are willing to pay the higher interest—I say none whatever if you are willing to pay the higher interest."

"I agree," said the Governor, "and let the deed be drawn without delay."

XIV

HAVING gone through the material part of his preparations the Governor had now a spiritual and more trying ordeal before him, and he went out into the home-field to think over it. Leaving the town behind he walked, with hands, as usual, interlaced behind him, as far as to the margin of the fiord.

It was a beautiful morning. The light was wonderful, a silvery light that made the light of other days seem dull and leaden, full of innumerable sparkles like the stars that are sown in snow. The waters of the fiord were heaving slowly under a quivering haze, and on the sea outside—wide, vast, stretching far away—a number of fishing-boats, with their white sails bellied to a breeze that could not be felt on shore, were going on and on as if sailing into the sky. The mail-steamer was lying at anchor in the bay, getting up steam for her voyage back to England, and a flock of lighters, painted white, were floating about her black hull, like sea-fowl at the foot of a lava rock. The gulls were calling high up in the air, and from the sheltered side of a little island the last of the year's eider-duck were coaxing or driving their young ones into the sea to prepare them for their flight to far-off lands.

It was a cruelly beautiful morning, one of those radiant days when Nature in her indifference to man and his suf-ferings, seems to conjure up every joyous sound and sight that can trouble the bitterest waters of memory—when the very sunshine seems to break one's heart.

At length the proud man who was walking through the hummocked home-field, with head bent low by the sorrow of a wrecked and shattered hope, saw plainly what he had to do. In love no less than anger, in justice no less than duty, he had to cast off forever his favorite son, the pride of his heart and the hope of his life.

As soon as he returned to the house he sent up-stairs for Oscar. After some moments Oscar came down slowly, look-ing more ill and weak than ever, and stood by the stove with drooping head like a prisoner about to receive his sentence. The Governor glanced up at his son from over the rims of his eye-glasses, and at first his heart failed him, but after a moment he steeled himself to his task and began to speak in a steady voice.

"I have sent for you to tell you," he said, "that for your mother's sake—I prefer to put it so—I have acknowledged that signature and am preparing to pay the money you have wasted. To do so I am compelled to mortgage every penny-worth of property we possess, so that apart from my official salary I shall soon have nothing. Worse than that I have had to eat up your brother's inheritance in order to purchase your liberty, and whether I had a right to do so God alone can say."

Oscar shivered as from cold; the Governor saw this, waited a moment, and then went on.

"The condition on which I make this sacrifice is that you leave Iceland immediately. You will sail by the 'Laura,' which goes back this evening, and, as your honor is my honor, I will give it out that your health is broken after the death of your wife, and that you have gone away to recruit."

The Governor paused a second time, and when he spoke again his voice was thick and hoarse.

" I shall not expect you to come back soon—I shall not expect you to come back at all. Inasmuch as you have done your best—or worst—to wreck my happiness I will ask you to consider that henceforth our lives are to run in different courses, and that for my own part I wish to see you no more."

The Governor's voice was now husky and indistinct, but still he struggled on.

" You will look to yourself for your livelihood in the future, but that—with your talents, little as you have made of them hitherto—should not be difficult. Whatever happens here I shall never expect you to do anything for me, or for your mother, but if fortune should favor you, and you are able to repay your brother, your conscience may be the easier and—though I do not pity him, for his heart was hard—the earth on my grave the lighter."

The Governor paused for the last time, cleared his throat, and then said in a firmer tone:

" Only one word more. I thought perhaps your father-in-law might have done something for you, but apart from a promise to provide for the child, he will do nothing. Therefore, as I have reason to fear that his daughter Helga was at the root of the trouble which has so nearly wrecked us all, and perhaps a first cause of the death of our dear Thora, I will ask you to promise me—for your own sake more than mine—to hold no further intercourse with him or his—do you promise? "

There was silence for some moments and then a muffled sob came as from the stove itself:

" I promise."

After that there was silence again for a perceptible period, and then a voice—a strange voice that was like a cry—said:

" That is all. And now—good-by and—and God help you! "

Choking with emotion and blind with tears, Oscar turned

about to acknowledge the justice of his punishment—to say
that he deserved everything—everything and more—a hun-
dred-fold more—but he found himself alone. His father had
fled from the room.

XV

WHEN Magnus heard of what his father had done, his
wrath knew no measure. On the day when he found Thora
dead in her bed he had said to himself, " Oscar has done this
and he must be made to suffer." But there was no legal way
to punish a man who had tortured his wife to death by every
refinement of hypocrisy and pretense, and it was at the
height of his anger that the offense against his father's
property had come to him with its diabolical temptation.
" Use me," it whispered, " the damnable spirit of the world
understands me better," and after a struggle in which the
devils seemed to fight for his soul, he yielded.

He thought he knew the price he would have to pay and
that was the reason he did not join his family at the funeral.
Everybody would loathe him for giving up his brother to the
punishment he deserved. His own mother would turn from
him, and after his father, being confronted by poverty, had
allowed the law to take its course, he would hate and despise
the son who had saved him from beggary.

But no matter! When he stood up in court and said,
" This is Oscar Stephenson's handwriting, for he is a forger
and a thief," and a thrill of horror ran through the crowded
room, and every eye turned on him with contempt, he would
say to his secret heart, " He killed her, and he had to suffer,
and there was no other way than this! "

Yet that was not what had happened. His father had
saved Oscar from the just punishment of his infamous offense. And how had he saved him? By making him—Magnus—pay the price of Oscar's riotous living abroad. Thus
the vengeance which he had vowed upon his brother had re-
coiled upon himself, and while his rightful inheritance was
wiped out, while the farm on which he had built his last
hopes was embarrassed beyond the possibility of redemption,

and he was ruined for the rest of his life, the man for whom and by whom he was ruined—ruined in his affections as well as his fortunes—was to be allowed to steal away amid a croaking chorus of sympathy and pity under the cloak of broken health and a broken heart!

What a devil's world it was in which infamy could masquerade as honor and hypocrisy as grief! When Magnus thought in this way his eyesight grew dull and his hearing dense and he felt a cold pain at the back of his neck. Then he began to use again the only remedy he had recourse to when his head was bad—he began to drink.

But sitting in the darkest corner of the smoking-room of the hotel, every word he heard—every conversation that filtered through the smoke and noise and his deadened senses —seemed to stimulate the idea which had taken possession of him—it was the devil's own world and God had nothing whatever to do with it!

At one moment a student ran into the room and shouted, above the laughter and singing of his fellow-students, " Boys, what do you think? Oscar Stephenson is sailing by the ' Laura' to-night!" And thereupon a babel of voices cried, "Really!" " Never!" "You don't say so!" " True enough —smashed up for good and going abroad for an indefinite period!" " Not a bit of it! Oscar isn't the sort to be broken up like that. Six months abroad and he'll be home again as bright and fresh as ever."

" So he will," thought Magnus, but his heart was fierce and bitter.

At another moment the chairman of the Town Board came in panting and cried, " News, gentlemen, news! Oscar Stephenson has resigned his seat in Parliament!" " Impossible!" " Listen!" and the little fat man read, out of his rasping, asthmatical throat, from a sheet smelling of damp paper and printer's ink a letter from Oscar to his constituents. Broken in health and happiness—compelled to go abroad—impossible to fix date of return—consequently forced to tender resignation—deeply grieved and disappointed—but set the duties too high to ask his constituents to wait, etc.— " That means he's not coming back!" " But, good heavens, does he know what he's giving up? Why, there's nothing that's not within the man's reach—absolutely nothing!" "I wonder the Governor has allowed him to do it!"

And then Magnus laughed out loud in the fierce bitterness of his heart.

After that the voices were lower for a little while, and when Magnus heard them again somebody was saying, "But a man can love a woman too much altogether. Breaking your life to pieces because you've lost your wife isn't brave, it isn't manly." "Perhaps not, but it's human," said somebody else, "and if Oscar Stephenson is smashed up by the death of Thora Neilsen, he's in the right of it, I say."

"So do I," cried Magnus, and laughing wildly, he dropped his head over his arms on the table. What a devil's own world it was to be sure!

There was some whispering and then two louder voices: "Poor fellow! So unlike his brother! Going it fast, they say!" "His father was pretty hard on him, though!" "Not harder than he deserved, poor devil!"

The poison in the soul of Magnus was fermenting every moment. Hearing the contemptuous pity with which he was contrasted with his brother—his brother who had wrought all the evil—his temples beat furiously and one wild thought expelled all other thoughts from his brain. If there was no law to punish Oscar, if his father had conspired to help Oscar to escape and if the hypocritical community agreed to cover up his fault, one thing at least remained— before Oscar left Iceland he must meet with him! Then if this was the devil's own world let the devil look after his elect!

Magnus's mind was weltering in this thought as in a boiling sulphur pit when the captain of the "Laura" came into the smoking-room with the agent of the steamship company, and seating themselves near to him, began to converse apart. "Then he will have to put up with a bed in the hold, for all the berths are gone," said the captain. "But why can't he wait for the next steamer?" "I'll tell you why," whispered the agent, "because the Factor's daughter is to sail by the Vesta and there seem to be reasons why they should not meet." "So that's it, is it? But their fathers are fools not to know that they'll meet on the other side if they want to."

Overhearing this conversation, Magnus lifted his head from his arms, drank a large tumbler of brandy and water to the last drop, and walked heavily out of the house. He had not been conscious of the passing of time, but the darkness was now closing in, porters were hurrying with luggage toward the pier and the first of the " Laura's " three bells was ringing.

Magnus was like a man who could not see or hear properly. More than once he collided with people on the parapet, and being big and strong he brushed them out of the way. Some of them cursed him, but he did not stop. His clouded faculties were conscious of one idea only—that he must go to Government House and meet Oscar face to face before he sailed.

Reaching his former home he found the door open, as usual on an autumn evening, and nobody in porch or hall. Avoiding his father's door, he walked up-stairs and turned mechanically toward the apartments which had lately been occupied by Oscar. But that was a part of the house sacred to his memory of Thora, and even in this hour of passion and pain something whispered to his tortured conscience, and he turned away. A moment later he was in Oscar's bedroom on the upper floor.

The furniture was in disorder, the carpet was awry, and articles of apparel were scattered about as if somebody had been packing trunks, but the trunks were gone and there was nobody in the room. Magnus was about to go when his eyes were arrested by papers on a desk. Among sheets of music and scraps from newspapers there were the remains of a letter doubled up and torn across.

Magnus knew the handwriting—it was Helga's—and without any compunction he put the pieces together and read the letter:

"Oscar:—As soon as I heard that the Governor had spoken to you on the fatal subject, I confessed everything to my father and took my own share of the transaction. Of course, he was furious, and now he vows that I must go back immediately to my mother in Copenhagen. That does not trouble me, seeing that you are leaving Iceland, but I must see you before you go. In spite of all you say, and notwithstanding any promise you may have given to anybody, it is impossible that we can part like this. It would be too selfish and too cowardly not to give me the chance of seeing you for the last time. Your steamer sails at nine o'clock—come to me at half-past eight. If you do not come I may even follow you to London—I *will* do so if——"

Magnus read no more, but ramming the pieces into his pocket he plunged down the stairs and out into the street. If anybody could have seen him at that moment his appearance must have seemed terrible, for his eyes were bloodshot, and the veins on his forehead were swollen and dark. It was now night and the second bell was ringing in the bay.

He was lunging along in the direction of the Factor's, when somebody crossed in front of him in the thoroughfare. It was Oscar himself and he was going in another direction. Magnus was like a man whose reason is clogged, but he saw everything in the light of his own making. His brother was returning from the pier after taking his baggage aboard, and he had come ashore on a last errand. Magnus knew what errand that was—it was to see Helga, and they were going to meet where they could be unobserved.

The moon had risen by this time and Magnus could keep his brother in view while he followed like a hound behind him. He saw nothing else and was not even conscious of what streets they passed through, save that they were going toward the upper part of the town, near to the lake, and down the road that runs beside it.

He tried to walk softly and to make no noise, but sometimes a hard laugh broke from his dry throat and once or twice a great sob came behind it. He was thinking of Thora, and telling himself what he would say when Oscar met Helga and he came face to face with them. He would say, " I loved your wife—I'm not ashamed to say so—I loved her and gave her up to you and you promised to cherish her, but you neglected her and allowed her child to be stolen away. I would have given my heart's blood to make her happy, but you made her miserable and now she is dead, and you are here with this woman who helped to torture her. You are a perjurer and a forger and a scoundrel and you may take that—and that—and that—and carry the mark of my hand on your face when you go where this wanton means to follow you!"

He was now outside the town, but he could not see or hear or think like a Christian man, and was merely ranging along the road like a beast. Then all at once, in the still air and the silence of all around him, he heard the voice of some one who was saying in low, quivering, pleading tones:

"My darling! My darling!"

Magnus knew whose voice it was! He thought he also knew what sight he should see a moment later. It would be Oscar and Helga locked in each other's arms as they had been when he saw them last in the dance at the farm—flushed, hot and excited.

With his fists clinched and his teeth set hard, he plunged through a gate that was like the gate to a garden, and then ran forward a few paces. But he drew up suddenly, as if an unseen hand had seized his arm. He saw where he was, and his breath seemed to leave him—he was in the cemetery, and some twenty yards farther down the path his brother Oscar was kneeling by the side of a grave and sobbing as if his heart would break.

Magnus stumbled back to the road, sobered, ashamed and broken into utter helplessness.

It might be the devil's own world, but God was in it also.

XVI

WHEN the last of the "Laura's" three bells were ringing, Magnus stood alone on the little wooden jetty going down to the bay. The whistle screamed in the steam-pipe, the anchor-chain rattled in the hawse-holes, and the steamer turned her head to the sea.

Then a row-boat came back from the vessel's side, bringing an elderly lady who was trying to hide her tear-stained face from the gaze of the boatmen and even the eyes of the night, behind the folds of a little lace shawl which she wore over her hufa. It was Anna, and as Magnus helped her ashore, she said:

"Give me your arm and take me home—I'm not feeling well to-night, Magnus."

16

But before they had gone many paces she stopped and looked back lovingly at the ship that was now steaming down the fiord, and said in a pitiful voice:

"He is gone and I have lost him! My poor boy! My poor Oscar! I had him for six and twenty years and to think it should come to this!"

She walked a few more paces and then looked back again, and said:

"I have never seen anybody so deeply affected. 'Oh, mother, mother!' he cried at last—just like a child. I could have fancied the years had rolled back and he was still a boy —feeling ill and helpless and wanting to lie in his mother's lap."

Again she walked a few steps and looked back as before.

"There was nobody to see him off—nobody at all. The story must have leaked out somewhere, and of all the people he used to call his friends there was not one to say farewell. My poor boy! My poor Oscar! He did wrong—very wrong —but God knows how he is suffering. We think we punish people when we put them in prison, but what punishment is like the pain of an awakened conscience? And Oscar is leaving everything behind him—everything and everybody— and going away in disgrace."

Once more she walked a few steps and then she said in the voice of a crying child:

"I shall never see him again. I pretended I should, but I know quite well I shall not. 'Some day you will come back,' I said, 'and make amends and wipe out everything.' And he said 'Yes' and 'Yes,' but we both knew well it wasn't true. When the bell rang and I had to come away he said, 'Mother, you've been the best mother a man ever had,' and I knew it was the last word I shall ever hear from him."

After that she could not speak for some minutes and then she said, as if trying to comfort herself:

"Perhaps God will give my boy another chance where he is going to. If so I think he will do better, but if not——"

She could not finish what she intended to say—that God's mercy was more terrible than the vengeance of man, and he who renounced it would surely be destroyed.

They walked on in silence until they came to the gate of

Government House, and then Anna took her last look at the dark ship that was dying away to an indistinguishable mass in the shades of night and the mists of her blinding tears, and said in a brave voice:

"We must be very good to each other in future, Magnus. You are the only son left to me now, and if you have to suffer for the sin of somebody else you must let me help you to bear it. I will always do so as long as I live, Magnus, and when I am gone from you God will not forget. Good-night, Magnus! And God bless you!"

Magnus stood for some time where his mother had left him, for the breakers of passion were still surging in his throat. Then he returned to the jetty and dropped the remains of Helga's letter into the sea, and they went out with the ebbing tide.

PART V

" *Indeed, indeed, repentance oft before*
I swore—but was I sober when I swore?
And then, and then came Spring, and rose-in-hand
My threadbare penitence apieces tore."

I

ABOVE all other cities of the world, London is the home of the outcast, the refuge of the disgraced and rejected, the asylum of the moral leper, the grave of the moral suicide. She offers him obscurity and a kind of cleansing if he will cast himself into the rolling billows of her six millions of people, and she keeps her word but exacts her penalties. Her penalties are homelessness, friendlessness, and loneliness, but above all loneliness. There is no loneliness like that of London. The loneliness of an open boat on an open sea in an impenetrable fog, or the loneliness of a trackless heath in a blinding snowstorm, is not so desolating to the human soul as the loneliness of London's crowded thoroughfares, with their lines of unknown faces filing on and on.

Within a year Oscar Stephenson knew the loneliness of London to its last pang, its utmost bitterness.

When he parted from his mother on the deck of the "Laura" she slipped a purse into his pocket, just as she used to do when he was a boy going to college or going away for his holiday. The purse contained gold and notes to the value of fifty pounds, and this, with the little he had of his own, was the whole sum of his fortune and all he had to face the future with. He was not so young as to think it inexhaustible, or so sanguine as to expect the world to fall at the feet of a fallen man, so he tried to be frugal and to spend his substance prudently.

He spent his first night in London at the hotel in Trafalgar Square at which he had stayed with Thora and Helga on their way to Italy, but besides being too expensive for his present means the place was too full of tragic memories, and next day he removed to a house in one of the first of the side streets going down to the river from the Strand. His lodging was a single room on an upper floor, having a stuffy odor of carpets and curtains and a prospect of the neighboring roofs with various causeways of red chimney-pots.

In this apartment Oscar Stephenson had his first experience of the loneliness of London. He lived there six months without seeing any face belonging to the house except the face of his landlady, and without knowing more about his fellow-lodgers than that his neighbor in the adjoining room never returned home at night until after the great clock at Westminster had struck twelve, and that he whistled " Onward, Christian Soldiers " in varying degrees of alcoholic uncertainty while he put himself to bed.

Before the end of those six months Oscar was in debt to his landlady, he had no regular employment and no prospect except the imminent one of being homeless and penniless.

By what stages of quick descent he came down to this condition it would be a needless task to tell. His story is that of the great army of the disgraced and the castaway who fly to London as to a sanctuary and are allowed to live only by lying at its doors. He had struggled and failed. He was young and active, but nobody needed him. In some places his want of references was a difficulty. In others his superior education was a cause of suspicion. He was too good for one post and not good enough for another. In a world full of work there was no work for him to do.

The slow agony of those first six months kept alive the shame and misery of his breakdown and nearly sapped his moral courage. As day followed day and the feeling of uselessness deepened, he felt like a boy, a friendless, abandoned boy. He had done wrong and he was ready to bear his punishment, but the great, irresistible, unanswerable world was using him cruelly. It would not make peace with him on any terms. It was leaving him without hope, or counsel or encouragement or consolation—it was leaving him alone. This sense of being of no account, of being nothing and nobody in the world, with the terror of sinking out of sight some day and nobody knowing or caring, was harder to bear than poverty or even shame itself.

When the clouds looked blackest he swallowed the last remnant of his pride and appealed to the few friends of his father in England who had been so good to him in the careless days of his college life and so boundlessly hospitable in the happy time of his honeymoon. He appealed to the professor at Oxford, making a clean breast of his misdoings and no concealment of his sufferings and asking for influence and assistance in obtaining a sub-librarianship or such other employment as might provide him with bread and butter, and the answer that came back was prompt and courteous but as cold as the breath of an iceberg.

He appealed to the banker in London, asking for a junior clerkship, or a position as messenger or even porter, and the reply he received was as smooth as a dog's tongue and as useless for help and healing. And then he knew by bitter knowledge that the kindness which had been shown to him in the better time was kindness to his father's son, and that he had wasted that heritage and was his father's son no more.

Meantime he spent his days, and a great part of his nights also, in the streets. There he was like a piece of helpless driftwood in the roaring current of life, always going on yet never going anywhere, always floating along yet never making headway. The ceaseless stream in the busy thoroughfares tormented him terribly, but the emptiness of the obscurer streets tortured him still more, and the blankness of Sunday morning in the Strand afflicted him most keenly of all, for it was full of memories of Sunday morning in Iceland with its atmosphere of peace and rest and the sound of church bells.

When he was at his lowest depths of hopelessness he sent his first letter home.

"Dearest Mother," he wrote, sitting in his stuffy back room overlooking the roof-tops, "You would naturally have expected to hear from me before this, and I certainly should have written earlier, only that I have been waiting for a long, quiet hour in which I could tell you all the news, everything that has happened to me since we parted on the steamer and I saw your dear face disappearing in the boat. That hour seems never to come, so I must snatch a few moments without any more delay to say that all is well and everything goes swimmingly."

"The dear old soul, why should I make her miserable?" he thought.

"You will easily understand that in a great city like London, especially when one is beginning again and one has so much to do and so many people to see, there is not an hour left for oneself and hardly a moment to write a letter. But this does not prevent my thinking of you at all events, and I do so every day and always."

"That's true at least," he told himself, and he went on boldly with his affectionate fictions.

"I know that my dear little mamma will want to know first the condition of my creature comforts and I hasten to tell her that these are as right as can be. This is a large and handsome house just off the tide of greatest traffic where splendid horse wagons (called omnibuses) and upholstered sleighs on wheels (called hansoms) roll about in countless numbers day and night, making a roar like that of the Ellida river where it falls into the fiord. But my bedroom, in which I am writing this letter, is quiet and cozy and homelike, and my landlady is a good little creature who visits me daily and is always most kind and motherly."

As he went on his pen flowed freely and his handwriting became big and reckless.

"I am making new and influential acquaintances every day, and seeing in the flesh the faces we are all familiar with in prints. Walking in the Park yesterday I passed the Queen, who is one of our own princesses, you know, so I felt myself entitled to bow to her and she bowed back with the sweetest courtesy. I see the Prime Minister frequently, for he lives in a house that is only down the street and round the corner, and the homes and offices of nearly all the Ministers of State are within a stone's throw of this place. In fact one way or another I am certainly coming in touch with the leading men in England, and when I open my window at night I can see the light that burns in the clock-tower above the Houses of Parliament.

"So you see that I am finding life wonderfully interesting in this mighty maelstrom of human activity, and if I do not write as often as I ought, my anxious little mamma is not to imagine there is anything amiss with me, but merely to tell herself that no news is good news and that I am immersed in many occupations.

"Perhaps if I have a lonely hour occasionally"—the pen trembled in his fingers and the handwriting became loose and shaky—"it is when I think about home and wonder what is happening there and what people are saying about me now. I suppose I have no right to complain whatever it may be, but sometimes when I am coming back to my lodging on a starry night after a tiring day and I look up to the Milky Way and think, 'That is the road to my country,' the thought goes to my heart like a stab that when I left it last my father's door was closed against me, and I saw nothing of Magnus at the end.

"How are they both, and how are you, and how are the Factor and Aunt Margret, and how—oh! how is our dear little Elin? My sweet, sweet child! What I would give to see her again! Has she grown? Is she still as much like her poor mother? Does she 'notice?' She will begin to babble and talk by and by. Will they bring her up to know nothing about her father? Or perhaps to think ill of him? If I return to Iceland some day (and I shall) to take up the broken threads of my life again, and find that the mind of my own child has been poisoned against me, I don't know what will happen; I believe I shall go back instantly and wipe myself out for ever.

"But I will not think of that even as a remote possibility, and, meantime, I am working day and night to build up a new career, and, as you see, I am getting on splendidly. So good-by, dearest, and God bless you, and God bless everybody at home, for we shall all be good friends yet.—Oscar.

"P. S.—Is Helga still in Iceland, or has the Factor carried out his threat of sending her back to Denmark? I suppose I ought not to think of her, having given that promise to the Governor, yet I can not help doing so, and I can not help asking."

II

IT was the time when a young English composer was creating some sensation by writing an opera on the subject of "King Olaf." The theme was one which Oscar had often proposed to himself, and raised his fancy and emulation upon, in the delirious days when he had hoped to become a musician, and the dazzling dreams of glory were not yet so dead that he could restrain himself from rambling up to Covent Garden on the night of the first performance.

He knew he was penniless and he was conscious that his clothes were shabby and his shoes in a woful condition as he lounged by the arches and watched the audience assemble. The carriages were rolling up and discharging their occupants—the Queen and her ladies, the Prime Minister and finally the King—and he was turning away feeling more miserable and destitute than ever, when a hand touched him on the shoulder and a familiar voice at his side said cheerily,

"Helloa! Can it be possible?"

It was Neils Finsen, his former schoolfellow and companion, fresh and bright in evening dress under a handsome fur-lined overcoat.

"Heard you were in London, but didn't know where to find you. Want to see you immediately, old fellow. Where do you stay?"

As soon as he had got rid of a stifling sensation in the throat Oscar answered him, and then Finsen said,

"Should I call upon you there, or would you prefer to come here to me?"

"I will come to you," said Oscar.

"Good! When shall it be? Will to-morrow at twelve be convenient?"

"Any time will be convenient to me."

"Happy man! Twelve to-morrow in my office, then. Glad to have found you at last. Thought you might have looked me up and wondered what on earth had become of you. Good-by! Busy to-night and enough work for a regiment. By the way, if you would like to see the performance—can't promise you a seat, but if you would care to stand at the back of the balcony— You would? Come this way— Johnson! Take this gentleman in front and give him anything you have left. By-by!"

Before Oscar had quite recovered his breath, he was sitting in the half-light at the back of the upper circle, feeling miserably humiliated and ashamed, yet tingling with a strange excitement. He never quite knew what happened thereafter. He forgot that his money was all gone, that he had not eaten since morning, that his trousers were frayed at the bottom and his shoes down at the heels. He only felt that out of the sordid conditions of the past six months he had suddenly emerged into an atmosphere that was as the vivid breath of his soul.

When the conductor entered—it was the young composer himself—Oscar craned forward to catch a glimpse of the man who was on the eve of snatching the triumph which but for the hard buffetings of fate might perhaps have been his own, and when the opera began he listened with every faculty. It was good, it was human, it was modern, its harmony was exquisite, its orchestration sure, its form showed mastery of the mystery of music, and yet it lacked something. What did it lack? It lacked the life-blood of the stern old Northland. The Englishman could not give it that, for the root of the matter was not in him. But *he* could have done so, for his blood was the blood of the Vikings, the blood of Flosi and Snorri and Eric and Olaf and all the mighty men of old.

Oscar did not hear his fellow-lodger go to bed that night, with his lunging step on the stairs and his drunken whistling of "Onward, Christian Soldiers," and next morning when his landlady came up to speak to him, according to her wont, he was hardly conscious of what she said except that it was some protest, some threat, and that he did not feel it worth while to soften and sweeten her with such promises as he had made before.

The intoxication of last night was still upon him when he set out to keep his appointment. Music was calling to him again, calling him like a siren, out of his friendlessness and loneliness, his humiliation and obscurity, his poverty and shame, out of the pitiless cruelty of crowded thoroughfares and the grimy sordidness of obscure streets, into the glory of success and fame.

"Come in, old fellow," cried the familiar voice of yesterday, and Oscar found himself in Finsen's office.

"Let me see," said Finsen, removing a pair of pince-nez, "how long have you been in London?"

"Six months—nearly seven," said Oscar.

"And what have you been doing?"

"Nothing."

"Lucky chap! Nothing at all?"

"Yes, there is one thing I've been doing—I've been doing it rather industriously."

"What's that?"

"Starving."

Finsen laughed loud, but Oscar laughed louder—he had not yet broken his fast.

"We all go through it at some time," said Finsen, "and it's best to get it over at the beginning. So I congratulate you, old fellow, and now to business. I'm managing here—managing for a syndicate. Under four eyes, as we say in Iceland, I intend to give a series of concerts and I'm looking out for fresh material. You compose?"

"Used to do," said Oscar.

"I understand," said Finsen. "Your life has been off the tracks lately and you'll not write much more that's worth anything until you get back into the groove. But I know what you used to do and that's good enough for me. I heard some of your songs from the Sagas, you remember, and I don't mind saying that as the work of a man who was nearly self-taught in the matter of harmony I thought them wonderful. But Helga tells me—Helga Neilsen, I mean, I hear from her occasionally——"

Oscar flinched as if a lash had cut him.

"Helga tells me," continued Finsen, "that you did some things in Iceland last year that beat your Saga songs to little bits, and if you think we can try them here——"

"They're gone," said Oscar.

"I know," said Finsen. "I've heard what has become of them. But perhaps you have copies?"

"Not a copy," said Oscar.

" Or perhaps you can remember some of them?"

" Not one."

" Even so, the case is not quite hopeless. You are a person of some influence in Iceland?"

" Used to be," said Oscar.

" Well, I presume to think I am—my father is Sheriff and likely to be something better—so if you care to give your consent we may recover the things still."

A mist arose between Oscar's eyes and Finsen's face. " You surely do not mean——?"

" Certainly I do. If the things are half as good as Helga says, they're worth all the trouble. Anyhow, I'm willing to gamble on her judgment, to give you something to go on with, and when the stuff comes to devote a morning to trying it with the orchestra, and ask you to conduct the rehearsal."

Finsen's figure was floating in the mist that was between it and Oscar's eyes.

" You wish me to authorize you to exhume——"

" Why not? It's not an unheard of proceeding. And if ever there was a moment that justified it it's now. If compositions that might give pleasure to the world and make pots of money are lying buried in a grave——"

" I'll starve first," said Oscar, rising from his seat.

" My dear chap," said Finsen, putting back his pince-nez, " you tell me you're doing that already. But here's your chance of doing it no more, and if——"

" I'll starve to death first," said Oscar, turning to the door.

" Nonsense, old fellow! If the things were doing any good where they are I could respect your feelings. But they're not. They are merely rotting away and they will soon disappear altogether. What your object was in burying them you know best—I confess I thought it very quixotic —but whatever it was it has served its purpose. And now there they lie—works of genius, as I'm willing to believe— that might possibly make your name and begin to make your fortune, while you——"

" I'll die in a ditch rather than touch them," said Oscar, and without a word of farewell he flung out of the room.

No words could describe the agony he endured during the remaining hours of that day. The intoxication of the night before was gone by this time and he suffered the pains of the spirit that has buoyed itself up on a bankrupt hope. If he had ever had any uncertainty about the meaning of the blind impulse of remorse which had prompted him to bury his compositions in his wife's grave he had none now. It was God's own punishment to shut up the only channel to fame and success, nay to livelihood itself, as by the door of a tomb.

Hour after hour he walked the streets, feeling that escape from the way of life he had been living was now utterly hopeless. He would go down and down, day by day, little by little, until he was submerged beneath the flood, or became, but for the mercy of God, a vagabond and a castaway.

It was long before he could bring himself to go back to his lodging and when he did so he found that the street door would not open to the key he carried in his pocket. He rang the bell and a little maid-of-all-work came up as from her bedroom below stairs with curl papers in her hair and some loose clothes about her body.

"Why did you bolt the door, my child?" he said. "Didn't you know that I had not come home?"

"Yes, sir, but mistress told me to tell you as how your room has been let and you can have your trunks when you pay what you owes her."

"Do you mean that I am to be turned out?"

"It ain't my fault, sir, and I'm very sorry."

Oscar and the girl stood looking vacantly at each other for a moment, and then he turned away and walked up the street with a new sensation—the blank, desolating sensation of not having a roof over his head. No one knows what it means to be one night homeless in a great city except those who have gone through it. It is not so much the poverty of privation that is hard to bear as the sense of utter worthlessness, of being less to the world than its dogs, for they are cared for, or its horses for they are housed.

His money was gone, and he had no luggage in his hands to make shift to find another lodging with, so he walked on and on, up Lower Regent Street and across Piccadilly, through noisy throngs of people—young women smoking cigarettes, young men laughing and singing and a bedraggled girl being lugged along by a policeman—on and on until he came to a wide and quiet thoroughfare where a line of broughams waited outside a house that was brilliantly lighted up, and there he paused in his aimless perambulation to listen to the music that was coming through the open windows.

He had been asking himself for the hundredth time how it had come to pass that he, so lately the pampered son of his father—who was the Governor of his people and their upright judge—was tramping the streets of London without a penny in his pocket or a roof to cover him, when the door opened and an elderly gentleman came out bare-headed to escort some ladies to their carriage. Then his stunned faculties awoke and he saw where he was standing. He was outside the house of his father's friend, the banker. The deep remembrance came back to him of the time, so near yet so far away, when he himself, with Thora and Helga, had been honored guests in that house, and lest the banker should see him, the wayfarer he then was, skulking there at that untimely hour, he turned about and walked quickly away.

Nothing that had happened on that evil night had wounded his feelings so acutely, or made him feel so surely that rescue from his accursed condition there could be none. Was it to be a part of his punishment that even when his senses slept he was to be constantly brought up against himself and reminded of the days that were dead? If so, life would be unendurable, and existence an everlasting hell. Did Nature never forget? Did God never forgive?

Half an hour afterward he was walking along the Embankment, past the crouching and sleeping forms of the sordid things whom the city casts out on to the river's bank by night; and looking wildly at the waters of the Thames, glistening and glimmering under the electric light, he asked himself why he should not end it all and have done with further torture.

What was the thought that restrained him? Was it the thought of his dead wife whose memory was to be a safeguard against sin and a perpetual inspiration? No!

By the inscrutable will of fate it was the thought of the

one being whose love had wrecked him—it was the thought of Helga. In spite of the pledge he had given to the Governor, he could not help thinking of her. No day had been so dark but he had thought of her on going to bed at night and on awakening in the morning. She was gone, they might never meet again, their love was a page of his life which he had crossed out and turned down for ever, yet her eyes were in his eyes and her smile was the only sunshine that shone upon his face.

The thought of Thora was a sweet and sacred thing which he had wrapped up and laid by in the lavender of memory, but the thought of Helga was warm and alive and always with him. It was with him now, and it saved his soul from despair and his body from death.

III

BEFORE Oscar's letter reached Iceland many changes had taken place there. The estrangement of the Governor and the Factor had developed into open antagonism. Everybody knew of it and the enemies of each had been playing upon his hatred of the other.

The Factor was the first to suffer. The downfall of the barter trade, which Magnus predicted, had already come to pass, and the Factor's business had tumbled to pieces like an unbound faggot. There is always a good reason to kill a fat ox, and while people said, " The Factor gives the farmers what he likes for his wool and charges them what he pleases for foreign produce," the true ground of the attack upon his business had been his intimidation of the town at the time of Oscar's election.

Oddsson, the defeated candidate of that day, never rested until he had established a company on the cash principle. Even then the Factor would have borne down all opposition, for the Factor was rich while the farmers were poor, but Oddsson had secured an ally in the most powerful person. As the smith uses the tongs to spare his fingers, so Oddsson had used the Governor to save his company.

The Governor knew full well that Oddsson was his enemy,

and that if his party got the upper hand they would upset
the old order, but he could not resist the temptation to join
him when he was trying to destroy the Factor. By his help
the preferential tariff with Denmark was broken down and
the Iceland markets were opened to English produce, and that
was the death-blow to the barter business.

For three months the Factor kept his doors open by selling at less than cost price and buying at more than market
value, but the end was sure. It was whispered at the bank
that he was parting with his securities in stocks and shares
and his estate in land and loose property, and that sooner
or later he would come down with a crash. Nobody pitied
him, and at the bottom of his tortured heart one man
rejoiced.

But the smiter has often short joy of his stroke, and when
Oddsson and his party, having done with trade, turned their
attention to constitutional subjects the Factor, though he
hated them, joined their agitation. The winter had been severe, there had been many deaths among the older members of
Parliament and as often as a by-election had occurred the
Factor had thrown the weight of his remaining influence
and the force of his diminishing fortunes into the scale of
reform. By the end of the spring it had become certain that
the next session of Althing would witness the passing of a
bill for the reconstruction of the Constitution and the abolition of the Governorship.

Thus each of the two men who had stood shoulder to shoulder for fifty years destroyed himself in destroying the other,
and the prophecy of long ago was fulfilled that if the Governor and the Factor ever ceased to be friends they would
become the bitterest of enemies.

Meantime Anna had tried to make peace and failed. When
the quarrel was young, and chiefly about the children, she
had attempted a tone of sympathetic protest. " Come, come,
Stephen, pardon is the best punishment—you must make
peace with the Factor."

" He might have saved my son by the lifting of his hand
and he would not do so—I shall never make peace with him,"
said the Governor.

" Oscar Neilsen," said Anna, meeting the Factor in the

street, "when are you coming to see Stephen? If you stay away much longer the house-dog will fly at you."

"The house-dog flew at me when I was there last, Anna— I shall never trust him again," said the Factor.

When the quarrel grew old and ugly and personal to the men themselves, Anna thought of another means of reconciliation. The child was the last remaining link between the Governor and the Factor—it should bring them together again. "God has always a use for these little angels," she said.

Aunt Margret joined in the conspiracy and the two old things concocted many schemes—all simple and transparent but womanly and good—to get the men into the same room. They never succeeded, but a thousand beams of sunshine shone out of the baby's cradle, and little by little the ice that had frozen about the men's souls was seen to melt.

When the child was "shortened" it was taken over to Government House and wheeled in its perambulator into the Governor's bureau.

"Isn't she a beauty, Stephen?" said Anna; and Aunt Margret said,

"The precious pet couldn't possibly be more like her father if she were not so wonderfully like her mother, too."

The Governor looked down at the little face without saying a word, and when the child blinked up at him with the eyes of Thora and the smile of Oscar he went up-stairs to his bedroom, and Anna heard him lock the door.

When the child cut her first tooth, and everybody according to custom ought to have given her a "tooth-fee," the Factor, coming home at night, found no presents on the nursery table, but the little one was propped up under the blue lace of her hooded cradle and making the air hideous with the divine discord of a baby's silver-mounted rattle.

"That's Stephen's present and it must have cost him a fortune," said Aunt Margret, whereupon the Factor, weary as he was, walked out into the road where he could hear nothing but the cold lapping of the lake.

Yet love of the little one was not bringing the two men together—it was thrusting them still farther apart. "That man is scheming to get hold of the child," thought the Fac-

17

tor. "He and his have robbed me of my daughters and now they're trying to rob me of my granddaughter also."

"She's my son's child," thought the Governor, "and my son's child is my child—why did I allow that man to have her?"

"No use, woman!" said Aunt Margret. "It's late to withdraw the sword when it is thrust to the heart."

But then came Oscar's letter and Anna's hopes went up with a bound. She was like a child herself in her joy over it. Her happiness was too great to permit her to see holes in its picture of prosperity. Oscar was well, he was getting on splendidly and he sent his love to everybody.

She read the letter first to the Governor, and after he had heard it he walked out into the home-field where the eider-ducks were building their nests afresh on the edge of the fiord, and the fishing-smacks were coming back to harbor. Then she took it over to the Factor's, rolled it up in the baby's hand like another rattle, and left it with Aunt Margret to be shown to her brother.

But that day had been a bad day with the Factor and when Oscar's letter came back to Anna it was torn across the middle and enclosed in an empty envelope. Anna was nearly broken-hearted at the treatment of her treasure, for no girl of sixteen had ever so loved her first love-letter, and she had intended to show it to everybody—to the Bishop, the Rector, the Sheriff, and above all to Magnus.

Magnus had been coming and going at intervals throughout the winter. It had been a hard one for him as for others, and he had begun to realize what it would be when his father was gone and he had to bear the burden of the monstrous mortgage. But harder to bear than any winter had been the sight of his mother's sufferings during Oscar's silence.

"Any news yet?" he would ask, and Anna would say No and No, with countless explanations and excuses.

So it was through the dark days, and his feeling against Oscar grew hard as the ground he trod upon. But when the snow had gone and he went up with the spring caravan there was Anna with a face like the rising sun, and by that he knew that a letter must have come at last. Sure enough in less than a minute out it came from the bosom of her embroidered treya, torn across as the Factor had left it and she was calling on him to write an answer to her dictation. This is what he wrote:

"MY DEAR SON: Your letter arrived safely by the last steamer and made up by its welcome news for the long time we had to wait for it. It is so good to hear that you are well and prosperous and enjoying your life in the great English city. Many a time I feared it might be otherwise, but now I have your letter and I am happy and contented.

"I am proud that my son is rising into such high and good company, and though your father speaks little I am sure that he feels the same. He always said that you would do great things some day, and it is not the way of God's goodness to disappoint such expectations where they are built on a good foundation.

"And now I have to tell you that your father is well in bodily health, though a little oppressed by worldly anxieties, but I tell him our home in this life is always on a steep mountain and if we trust in God there is no reason to be afraid. As for myself, I am as well as can be expected at my age, though my left ear troubles sometimes and my eyes are not what they used to be for knitting and small print. But I must not allow myself to complain, for perhaps it is a part of God's mercy to us old people that our senses should die by degrees so that when they come to die altogether we may not be taken unawares.

"Magnus is writing this letter and he is strong and hearty. The snow was deep at the farm this year and he lost six of his best beasts, but his lambs came beautifully and now they are on the mountains and his ewes are milking well and the home-field is closed for the hay.

"I have to tell you that the one you ask about has gone back to her mother at Copenhagen and that there are those who can not be very sorry. Sometimes to silence the evil tongues that speak ill of you here I am tempted to blame her for all that has happened, but who am I to judge any one? And the worst I wish for her is that she may soon become a God-fearing girl.

"Margret Neilsen is just as she always was, a twisted

bough with plenty of sap in it, and the Factor would be well enough but for a bad hip. He too, like your father, is much oppressed by worldly cares and taking it ill that they should fall so fast upon him in the evening of his days.

"And now I have to tell you of your little Elin that she is as well as can be, and she has cut two front teeth and her hair is curling over her forehead. She is the best child that ever was born, and when she smiles she is so like somebody that it nearly breaks my heart to look at her. Margret is as good to the darling as if she were her own mother, and your father and the Factor can hardly see the sun for her. As for me it fills my heart brimful to think how God in His goodness has sent us old folks this little angel after our late troubles, for she is like the spring after a hard winter when the snow and ice have stayed so long that we think surely we shall never see the grass or hear the rivers again, and then all at once there are the green fields and the shining streams and all the gladness of the flowers.

"And now, though you are getting on so well, you must not be angry with your mother for sending you a little present. Maria has been all day in the kitchen packing your college box, and goodness knows what things she may have put in it. But I am knitting you a pair of stockings out of old Maggie's brown wool, and I hope you will not be ashamed to wear them, for they will keep your feet warm in the cold weather, when the English socks must be so thin and cottony. Then I remember how fond you used to be of our smoked mutton, so I am telling Maria to put in some of that too, and a few rolls of Rullapilsa.

"I dare not let the Governor know I am sending the mutton—he would think it foolish and unnecessary—and of course, with so many good things to eat and drink I do not expect you to offer it to your English friends, but perhaps you can hide it in a cupboard somewhere and take a slice when you are quite alone.

"And now I must conclude for Magnus is coming to the end of his paper. It makes me happy to think your bedroom is comfortable and I wish I could thank your landlady for being so kind and motherly. I may never see her in this world, but we shall meet in heaven some day and *then* I will thank her.

"And now, my dear son, in the midst of your great prosperity, do not forget that all good things come from God and remember to put your trust in Him. To His care I commit you, for He knows all our wants and all our troubles and all our secrets and His eye ever watches and His heart never sleeps.

"Your affectionate mother,

"ANNA."

IV

WHEN Oscar received his mother's letter he was living in a slum in Westminster. It was called Short Street, and it was a typical example of the mean streets which nearly always, and in all countries, lie near to a great minster, like sea-wrack at the foot of a rock.

Short Street was a cul-de-sac, whereof one end was a ginpalace and the other an archway to the railway depot of a suburban necropolis. Late at night the inhabitants were kept from sleep by the quarreling of tipsy men who had been turned out of the public-house, and early in the morning they were awakened by the rumbling of the hearses that rattled the corpses over the cobbles of the street.

Oscar's home in Short Street was at Number One, a grimy house with a soiled card in the fanlight above the door, saying, "Lodgings for single men." Besides himself, there were four lodgers, three of them being porters at the funeral depot and the fourth head barman at the public-house. The barman had the parlor floor, and he generally brought home a number of noisy companions at closing time to play cards and drink beer.

Oscar's bedroom in this house was not so much a room as a stifling closet of miserable aspect, in which the refuse furniture seemed to make an effort to range itself in order —a threadbare carpet, an iron bedstead without foot or head, a painted washstand, a broken-lipped water ewer, two or three rickety chairs, a table that was safest when it rested against the wall, a few pictures of race-horses on the remains of a dirty wall-paper, and a looking-glass blotched by damp, like a sheet of ice spotted and scabbed by thaw.

His landlady lived in the basement and was never seen

except on Monday mornings, when she went round for her lodgers' rent some two or three hours before the collector called for her own. The only person whom Oscar saw constantly was the landlady's servant, Jenny, a typical cockney girl of the humblest class, untidy and unclean, but as bright as a London street sparrow, and with a big soft heart in her vulgar little breast.

Jenny had conceived a certain affection for Oscar, based on no grounds more personal than that he did not shout at her down the pairs of stairs, or take liberties, or use bad language, and that he always raised his hat when he passed her in the street.

The only effect of this sentimental attitude on Jenny's part was that she always dressed in her clean "print" on the days when Oscar happened to be at home to tea, and it was on one of these afternoons that she came knocking at the door of his bankrupt garret and said, "Letter for you, sir."

It was so long since Oscar had received a letter of any kind that he leaped up with a kind of fear, and on taking the envelope out of Jenny's hand and seeing it was addressed in Magnus's writing, and had been sent on from his former lodging, he turned pale and trembled.

"Is it bad news, sir?" said Jenny. "I wouldn't 'a' brought it up on no account if I'd knowed."

"No, no! Leave me, Jenny," said Oscar, and when the girl had gone and he had opened the letter with nervous fingers, he read it with eyes that were wet with tears while his cheeks were flushed with shame.

When he came to the end his heart was beating wildly and he was asking himself if it would not be the brave and manly thing to write at once and say that all this story of his prosperity was a miserable fiction, that he had never been otherwise than wretched, that he was living in a common way among common companions, doing common work which he dare not think of, and that no words could express the secret agony of his soul at having sunk so low. But deep as was the degradation of that bitter hour it was not so deep as that of the following morning when Jenny came lugging his college box up-stairs, and chattering gaily as if she had brought him a fortune.

" The railway man said as 'ow it was as 'eavy as lead, so I give 'im twopence for 'isself—I 'ope I did right, sir."

" Quite right, Jenny. Here's the money. You can go now."

" Can I 'elp ye to unpack it, sir? There ain't no sort o' box as I can't unpack. My! what a long way it must 'a' come!"

" It came from Iceland, Jenny."

" Fancy that now! Pat Looney, the lorry man, 'e come from there, and the neighbors says it's a pity 'e don't go back. They never says that about you, though. ' He's so perlite,' they says."

Oscar allowed the girl to open the box and empty it of its contents, and as she did so she chirped away like the street sparrow that she was, while he sat with the mist of his boyish associations floating up to him from the happy past.

" Well, I never!" she cried, sitting back on her heels as she knelt before the box. " Polonies! And sausages! And pickled tongues! And hams! Why, you won't 'ave to buy nothin' to eat for months! Isn't that lucky now? Just when you're ' out' too! Is it a present?"

" Yes, it is a present, Jenny."

" They must think somethin' of ye as sends ye a present like this," said Jenny, and then, after a moment, in a fluttering voice, " Is it a laidy, sir?"

" It's my mother," said Oscar.

" Your mother!" said Jenny, in a tone of relief. " Well, that's what I *do* call a mother—being good to anybody like this."

" She has been good to me all my life, Jenny, and all my life I've treated her badly."

Jenny looked at him strangely as if something surprised and pained her.

" *You* have, sir?"

" Shamefully, Jenny, yet she has forgiven me again and again."

Jenny was silent for a moment and then she said, " Mothers *is* like that, isn't they? Now there's Jim Cobb, the shandry man, 'e knocks 'is mother about somethin' cruel, but she never 'aves 'im up for it, never! Mothers is proper good!"

" Is your mother good to you, Jenny ? "

" Me ? I'm an orfling," said Jenny, and then, lowering her voice to a tone of confidence, she added, " I don't mind tellin' you, but I am! I always tells the other lodgers as my mother was one o' them girls as ye see at the Aquarium at nights covered with silks and diamonds."

" And was she ? "

A look of dejection crossed Jenny's face. " I don't see as she could 'ave been, because they say at the Orflinage as I was born in Holloway when my mother was doin' time."

By this time the contents of the box were ranged on the table and chairs, and Jenny was sitting back on her heels again to look at them.

" There! They're as pretty as a 'am and beef shop! And I do believe as that's what your mother meant 'em for too. Jim Cobb, 'e wanted me to set one up with 'im, but not me! Not as I 'ave any objections to the 'am and beef business, and if anybody else thought of starting it——"

Jenny's hint was interrupted by the sound of a vehicle stopping suddenly outside the house.

" Now, I bet ye I know who that is," she said with a wink. " It's that blessed Jim Cobb again. He's always a-wantin' me to go for a ride in 'is shandry."

But going to the window she cried, " Goodness! It's a handswim cab! And there's a laidy a-gettin' out of it ! "

" A lady ? "

" You can't see 'er now—she's on the steps. There she is," cried Jenny, as a rat-tat came to the street door, " and me not 'ad time to comb my 'air yet ! "

With an indefinable feeling of mingled fear and hope which there was yet no cause for, Oscar stood on the landing and listened while Jenny ran down the stairs. When the street door was opened he heard his own name in a voice that sent the blood to his head and made him reel with dizziness. A moment later Jenny came back with a face that looked white even under the smudges that soiled it, and she said in the same fluttering voice as before:

" I thought as much. It's you she's askin' for. I've took 'er into the barman's parlor—'e won't be 'ome till tea."

Oscar went down-stairs slowly, but when he got to the bottom his breath was coming and going in gusts, and his heart was beating against his breast as with the blows of a hammer. The parlor door stood ajar and a perfume he knew was coming out to him. After a moment he pushed the door open and then she whom he expected to see was standing before him, she herself, more radiantly beautiful than ever, with something soft and white about her neck and a face shining with smiles.

How much he lived in that moment no one could say. A hundred emotions coursed through his soul like the flash of flame—joy, delight, pain, shame, the rapture of seeing her, the humiliation of being found in such a common place, the degradation of being ill-clad and obviously poor, but above all love—the uncontrollable love that leads men on to happiness and victory or to ruin and death. His face broke up, tears burst from his eyes and holding out both hands he cried—

"Helga! My God! Helga!"

V

HELGA appeared to be not less excited than Oscar himself. She was genuinely moved to see how the joy he had in meeting her affected him, and when he had kissed both her hands she kissed one of his and tears which she could not keep back came to her eyes also. There was a shiny leather-covered sofa in the room and they sat on it side by side and hand in hand.

"I have never, never been so glad," he said.

"And I am glad too," she said. "Let me look at you again, Oscar. A little paler, and perhaps a little thinner, but otherwise not changed in the least."

"Yet *you* have changed a great deal, Helga."

"Grown older, have I?"

"Grown lovelier and more beautiful than ever."

At that she leaned her face toward him and he kissed her, and for some moments they could not restrain their fondness. Helga was the first to recover self-possession.

"And now let us talk seriously," she said, but Oscar was

still quivering with excitement and, having brushed away his tears, he laughed hysterically.

"How long have you been in London?" he asked.

"A month—a month to-morrow," she replied.

"And to think that I have never known it until now! But how did you come to leave Copenhagen?"

"That's just what I am trying to tell you. My father, for some unknown reason, elected to reduce my mother's income by half, so something had to be done. Then I remembered Neils Finsen and the wonderful things he used to say about my voice."

"Finsen!" repeated Oscar, in a graver tone.

"So I wrote to him, and he answered that if I would come to London he would have experts to hear me, and then they would see what could be done."

"Well? Well?"

"Well, I came, and the experts heard me, and they concluded that my voice was quite unusual—the most promising soprano they had found for years."

"And now?"

"Now I'm at the Royal Academy of Music, and by and by I am to go to Paris for two years, three years, perhaps four to study under Marchesi or Bonby and to attend an acting class, and finally I am to be taken to Monte Carlo or Nice in representations of "Faust" and "Romeo," as a first step toward taking London by storm as Marguerite or Juliette—there!"

"And Finsen is doing all this for you?"

"Well, yes, so to speak, I suppose I must say that."

"Is he to pay your expenses?"

"I really don't know who is to pay them, but I've signed a contract to come out under his management and to refund everything when I am fairly launched. And now about yourself, Oscar?"

"About me?"

"It's nearly a year since I saw you last. What have you been doing?"

Oscar made a clumsy laugh. "Oh, I'm like the lilies of the field—I toil not, neither do I spin."

But his forced gaiety broke down badly, and he said more soberly, "Don't ask me what I've been doing, Helga."

Helga's eyes wandered around the room for a moment and then she said, "I know! Neils told me something about it, and he wished me to say——"

Before she could finish Oscar had risen to his feet. "If you come from Finsen I know what your errand is, and I would rather die——"

"*No, no, no*," said Helga, clinging to his nervous hand. "Sit down. It's not that at all. Listen!"

He sat and the sweetness of her look banished all his fears.

"They're giving what they call promenade concerts at Covent Garden, and a few days ago there was some difference with the leader of the orchestra. It seemed desirable to make a change and the question was who the new leader ought to be. Naturally I thought of you."

"Of me?"

"Why not? Didn't I see what you could do with those hundred and fifty numskulls at Thingvellir?"

"But Covent Garden!"

"My dear Oscar, I've seen every leader they have here, and while they are all your superiors in knowledge and experience, there's not one of them with a tittle of your magnetism and genius. So I said, 'Neils, if you want the finest leader that London has ever seen let me go and fetch him!'"

"But you can't know, Helga—you can't imagine—if you had the least idea of what I've gone through to live—merely to live——"

Helga looked around the room again and she said, "Can't I see? Haven't I got eyes? But if you were to tell me that nobody has had any use for you in the meanest work that is ever done by the commonest men, I should still say what I said to Finsen."

Oscar's throat was hurting him. The thought of Helga's faith and championship broke down his self-control. He never allowed himself to think there could be any selfish ground for it.

"What do you wish me to do, Helga?" he asked.

"To meet me in Finsen's office at eleven o'clock to-morrow morning."

"But I vowed I could never set foot in the place again."

" You didn't know then that *I* should ask you. And I *do* ask you, Oscar."

He remembered the promise he had given to his father; he reflected on the danger of reopening a page of his life which he had crossed out and turned down as for ever; he thought of Finsen and his interest in Helga and the hold he would have of her through her hopes and ambitions; and his will was like a broken withe, for the controlling destiny of his life was leading him on.

" You *will* be there, will you not?" she whispered, and Oscar answered:

" Yes."

She leaned her face forward again, and again he kissed her and then she rose to go.

" Where are you staying?" he asked, and she told him. It was in a fashionable apartment-house on the edge of the Green Park.

" Does Finsen live there also?"

" Well, yes, he lives in the same building. And you must live there, too. I shall want to see you constantly. There are a thousand things I want you to do for me. But now I must be off."

He could not let her go, and they renewed their caresses. " It will seem like a dream when you are gone," he said. " I shall hardly be able to believe you have been here, or that you will ever come back again."

" Don't say that. I told you in Iceland that I should come to you if you didn't come to me, and I've kept my word, haven't I?"

" My dear, dear Helga!"

" It wasn't quite good of you to go away without giving me an opportunity of seeing you again."

" I know, I know!"

" You had a certain duty to me, you know, after what had passed——"

" Hush, dear, hush!"

" But I'm willing to believe it was the fault of other people."

" Don't let us speak of it, Helga," said Oscar, and his arms, which had been about her in a close embrace, slackened away and fell.

It was easier to part with her after that, but before he opened the door he kissed her again, and when he helped her into the hansom he put her fingers to his lips.

He stood bare-headed on the pavement oblivious to all surroundings until the cab had rounded the corner of the public house and Helga had waved to him through the glass. Then he became aware that the sight in that sordid slum of so lovely a girl, so beautifully dressed and with a hansom waiting for her, had brought the neighbors to their doors, and that the women were thumbing their apron-strings and grinning to each other across the rails.

When he reentered the house Jenny passed him in the lobby with a stealthy and guilty air which seemed to say that her poor tortured little soul had not resisted the temptation to listen and to watch.

He returned to the parlor for a moment and the perfume of Helga's presence was still to be felt there over the odor of dead ale and tobacco. Never had he envied the barman before, but at that moment he would have given all he possessed to keep this room for the rest of the day, that he might sit on the sofa where Helga had sat, and lay his hand on the table where her hand had rested and kiss the carpet where her feet had trod.

He was like a man moving in a dream, and when he went back to his own apartment he was not conscious of his squalid surroundings. The dirty wall-paper, the threadbare carpet and the blotched looking-glass humiliated and compromised him no longer. His body was still in his bankrupt garret, but his soul was far away. It was in another world —a world that was bright with Helga's eyes as its sun and stars, for he was going over again the time he had spent with her, every word of it, every tone, every look, every gesture.

This lasted the whole of the day and when darkness fell a curtain seemed to have fallen on the life he had been living during the past twelve months. The mire and slime of vulgar associations, the degradation of common companionship, the sense of loneliness, of friendlessness, of being nothing and nobody, the deep remembrance of being homeless and hopeless and helpless and useless—all this had gone. That passage of

his life was over now, and never, never, never would its pain
and shame come back to him again. He had passed through
it because he had sinned; but if he had sinned he had suffered,
and God Himself had seen that he had suffered enough.

His eyes were wet when he lay down on his soiled pillow,
but he fell asleep in a blissful condition and in the first dream
of the night he was back with Helga. Once in the dark hours
he awoke and heard the deadened hum of the barman and his
friends at their cards and ale; and again he awoke in the
dawn and then he heard the hearse of the necropolis thundering up Short Street and rumbling under the archway at
the top of it.

At eleven o'clock that morning he went to Covent Garden,
and again and again at eleven the following mornings he
went there. On the tenth morning he called to Jenny, who
had grown shy of him and was leaving his breakfast on a
tray outside his door, and said:

"Jenny, I wish you to tell your mistress that I shall be
leaving this lodging in another week."

Then Jenny's white and wistful face broke down utterly,
and with a crack in her voice, and the ghost of a smothered
sob in it, she said:

"I knowed as it 'ud come to this. The minit I set eyes on
'er I said as she'd take ye away from me—*an' she 'as.*"

VI

THE Governor never knew that Oscar had broken faith
with him.

When the time came for the next session of Althing, a Bill
for the reform of the Constitution, reenacting the abolition
of the Governorship and the appointment of a Minister, was
passed by a large majority. But an Act involving a constitutional change had to be voted by two Parliaments and therefore a dissolution of Althing became necessary. The time
of dissolution was at the discretion of the Governor, and he
might have delayed it until the fever for reform had passed.
Instead of doing so he decided to dissolve immediately, thus
feeding the agitation and precipitating his own fate.

Many things befall the man whose day is done, and the measure of the Governor's errors was not yet full. When the time came to select the candidates it was found that the constituency for which Oscar had sat—the capital—was once more without its man, and to everybody's astonishment the Governor himself, in order to secure a voice in the popular assembly, determined to stand for it.

This unusual step on the Governor's part created great excitement, but the fever increased tenfold when it was announced that the Factor intended to oppose him.

Never had popular feeling run so high as on the night when the Governor and the Factor had to confront each other on the same hustings. The better people stayed away, being sorry and ashamed that these two friends of fifty years should claw each other face to face like eagles, but the baser sort were reveling in the prospect of that spectacle and the Artisan's Institute was crowded.

"You learn a lot when your servants quarrel," they told each other, and they were not to be disappointed.

The Sheriff was in the chair, and it was clear from the beginning that his life-long rivalry of the Governor did not prompt him to restrain either candidate from making a fool of himself. Bad luck is a quick voter and the Governor played into the Sheriff's hands without suspicion and without delay.

The once silent and dignified man had lost all reticence and self-control, and when his time came to speak he flung innuendoes on every side. If you hate a man all his deeds are hateful, and coming at length to the Factor's business life the Governor said:

"Never is selfishness satisfied, my friends. Will you commit the care of your public purse to one who in order to grasp all is losing all and hurling himself into bankruptcy and want?"

This thrust was received with ironical cheers and counter cheers, not unmixed with derisive laughter, and when the Factor's turn came he said with a humorous leer over a face that was white as death:

"A blunt knife should seek the joints and not hack at the solid bone. But if it comes to asking conundrums I'll ask one also: Will you commit the care of your public purse to one whose son was banished from the country because he was a forger and a thief?"

This charge against Oscar, often whispered, but never before publicly uttered, fell on the reeking crowd with the effect of a thunderbolt, and before the audience had recovered from its astonishment the Governor was on his feet again, against all rule and order, saying in a loud voice:

"And will you commit the charge of your public morality to a man who in his youth contracted an alliance with an abandoned woman and only married his mistress after his first daughter had been born a bastard?"

This was the climax of sensation. The chewing and spitting crowd were silent, save for the sound of their audible breathing which was like the hissing in-wash of an ebbing wave. The Factor was pallid and speechless, as if the Governor's cruel word had struck all sensibility as well as sneering out of his face, while the Governor faced him with bloodshot eyes and blazing cheeks and lips that quivered convulsively.

Thus the two men stood for a long moment with scarcely a yard's space between them, and then a big man was seen to be parting the people at the back of the platform and coming forward with great strides. It was Magnus, and he was making for his father as if to take him forcibly away.

But before the Governor had seen him, or could be conscious of his presence, another hand, an unseen hand, had been laid upon his shoulder. With a blow on the brain that was like a stroke from heaven, the Governor had realized that in returning the insult of the Factor, in his mad wrath and blind passion, he had outraged the memory of Thora, and that Thora was in her grave, and he had loved her better than any human soul that was not of his own flesh and blood.

Then the noisome place in its ghastly silence spun round him, and with a low whine like that of a poisoned dog he fell heavily to the floor. Magnus took him up and carried him home—he had a stroke of paralysis.

There was only one nomination for the capital, the Factor was returned unopposed, and when the writs came back from the country it was found that the reform party had a larger majority than before.

The Governor made a slow recovery, but he was moving about by the time that Althing was next in session and when the constitutional question came up again he hobbled down to Parliament House on two sticks, in spite of all remonstrance, and took a seat in his little room overlooking the legislative chamber.

The debate was short and not exciting, and no one looked toward the alcove in which the Governor sat in his faded uniform, a doddering shadow of his old authority, but many cruel sallies of clumsy wit were aimed in that direction. The Governor grew more and more indignant, and at length he rose, frothing at the lips, to protest against unmerited insult, and was put down by the Speaker, who had formerly been his own private secretary.

The Act was passed by acclamation; there was much cheering, with the usual nine hurrahs after " God save the King," and then the fallen man was carried home.

In the middle of the night he had a second seizure, and he never left his room again. But as soon as he had recovered his speech he occupied his time dictating petitions to the King praying him not to give his sanction to an Act that was designed to degrade his servant.

After a few weeks Magnus came to persuade his father and mother to leave Government House and make their home at the farm.

" It's of no use to resist Parliament, sir," he said. " The new Minister will be appointed presently, and why should you wait until he turns you out? Come to Thingvellir—I'm strong, I can work for all of us."

But his father flew at him in a fury. " How dare you make such a proposition?" he said. " And how dare you show your face in this house? Don't you know that *you* have been the cause of everything? If it had not been for what *you* did at the beginning none of this mischief would have happened. As for the new Minister, if he comes here to turn me out tell him to bring my coffin with him—do you hear me?—tell him to bring my coffin."

The idea that Magnus was really to blame for all that had occurred, being the first cause and origin of the trouble, grew upon the Governor day by day, so that Oscar seemed to be

18

without fault and even came to be regarded as a martyr. He called upon Anna to read Oscar's letter to him again, and when he had heard it a second time he was so seized by the idea that the Prime Minister of England was a friend of his son's that he had himself propped up in bed in order that he might write to Oscar with his own hand calling on him to defeat his father's enemies.

" You have great influence now, Oscar, and you must save your father from the machinations of these malicious scoundrels, of whom the worst and most devilish is the Factor."

That was what he thought he was writing, but his poor brain was far gone by this time and the paper he scribbled on over the counterpane was merely covered with unintelligible curves and strokes which Anna could not send on to Oscar.

When it seemed certain that the intensity of the Governor's wrath would kill him, and that he would die with nothing in his heart but hatred of the Factor, Anna and Aunt Margret put their heads together and thought of a way to soften his feelings and sweeten his end. It centered in the child as before. " A little child shall lead them," they said.

They took little Elin to the Governor's bedroom, and left her to play on the floor. She had grown to be the sweetest thing, with an angel's face, a little beam of spring sunshine that ran about the room and talked. But the only effect of her presence was to make the sick man stretch his arms to a safe near the head of his bed and take out a roll of papers.

Nobody knew what the papers were, except that they were old and that they crinkled in his stiff fingers. He kept them under his pillow at all times save when his bed was being made and then he smuggled them into the breast of his nightshirt.

When the women talked of Elin and all her pretty ways and sweet mysteries of childish make-believe, the Governor talked of Oscar. Although his memory was confused about recent events it was wondrously clear about distant ones, and he had countless stories of Oscar as a child. Some of them were humorous and he would laugh at them as well as he could with his distorted face, but all were meant to show that Oscar was not like other children, and when he had come to an end he would say:

"My son is a great man now, as I always said he would be, and when he gets my letter you'll see what he will do."

Meantime the Act had been sent over to Denmark and the Sheriff had been called across to Copenhagen. There was only one thing that this could mean, and in the absence of telegraphic communication the little capital sat waiting for the return of the steamer that was to bring the Sheriff back. She was due on a Sunday night, and the bell-ringers of the cathedral stood ready to ring a peal in honor of the new Minister.

The Governor heard that the "Laura" was expected and he conceived the idea that Oscar was coming with her to bring the King's veto and to scatter his father's enemies. He was very ill that day, and Doctor Olesen had said he might not last until morning. But he would have nobody to nurse him, and Magnus, who had come at his mother's call, but dared not show his face to his father, sat on the stairs outside the door.

Aunt Margret was coming and going during the whole of the day, and toward evening the Factor himself was seen tramping to and fro outside the house, looking up at intervals at the Governor's windows with a face in which the madness of love and fear was fighting with the greater madness of pride and wrath. At length Anna went out to him and said:

"Oscar Neilsen, come into the house to see your old friend."

"Not till he asks me—not till he asks me," said the Factor; whereupon Anna went indoors again and whispered over the bed of the dying man:

"Stephen, the Factor is outside, and he only wants to be asked to come in."

"He must come in on his knees then," said the Governor, and that was the end of everything.

The steamer did not arrive that night, and the bell-ringers went to bed. But at daybreak, when the fishing-boats in the bay were breaking through a veil of mist and the sunlight was glistening on the mountain-tops, the bells began to ring merrily, for the "Laura" was sailing up the fiord with flags floating from stem to stern.

Magnus heard the bells, and then a shuffling movement in his father's bedroom. A little later he heard the hurrahs of people cheering in the streets, and then a smothered echo of the same sound at the other side of his father's door.

"Hurrah!" "Hurrah!" cried the people outside.

"Hur-a! Hur-a! Hur-a-a-" echoed the voice within.

At the next moment the house shook as with a heavy fall and Magnus burst into his father's bedroom. His father lay in his night-shirt on the floor. He was dead, but his face was smiling and in his withered hands were the crinkled papers on which Oscar in his boyhood had scribbled his childish compositions.

Later the same day Magnus wrote to Oscar: "This is to tell you that our father died this morning. I think he died happy."

But the mail did not leave until the end of the week, and under Magnus's message Anna wrote for herself: "He loved you to the last, and we hav berrid him next to our dere Thora."

VII

WHEN Oscar received the news of his father's death he was near the close of what he had believed to be the happiest period of his life. His success as a leader of orchestra had been substantial and immediate, and when the concerts at Covent Garden came to an end he had been offered engagements in other quarters.

"There! Didn't I know what I was talking about?" Helga said. "But this is nothing to the reputation you will make when you consent to appear as a composer."

"Ah, that is past praying for!" Oscar answered with a shake of the head, but all the same he was pleased and happy.

On leavng his dismal lodgings in Short Street, he took rooms in the same house with Helga and Finsen at the corner of Piccadilly and the Green Park. There the three friends lived the innocent lives of children, observing few of the restrictions which society imposes on the manners and conduct of men and women.

Helga's sitting-room was the general rendezvous, and the

men used it with the utmost freedom. Oscar. in particular, was nearly always to be found there, except in the mornings when Helga was at the Academy and in the evenings when he was himself at the theater.

No hour was too early and hardly any hour too late for Oscar to call on Helga. He ate with her, played with her, sang with her, read with her and helped her with her lessons. Mozart, Cherubini, Ouseley, Macfarren, Parry, and again Mozart—their work was all play and their play was all music.

Helga was more than satisfied that Oscar should be always with her, always assisting her, always praising and encouraging and inspiring her, and he on his part was entirely happy to devote himself to her service. To think for a moment that this was all she wished for, all she wanted with him, was more than his heart was capable of.

On their off days and nights they went to other concerts and opera-houses; attended the English cathedral services and the masses at Catholic Oratories; heard the old masterpieces over and over again; became familiar with nearly every new opera, oratorio, symphony, and voluntary, and studied the methods of most of the great singers and players who appeared in London. It was one long feast of music eaten at the table of love.

They had their social pleasures too, and kept open house on Sundays. Sometimes they supped or dined at restaurants with their new friends, who were chiefly Finsen's friends, and then brought their hosts back to Helga's rooms for cards and conversation until one, two, or three o'clock in the morning. It was a reckless, irresponsible, unconventional life, a little like the life Oscar had lived at college, a little like the life Helga had lived with her mother at Copenhagen, and more than a little dangerous, though they never thought of that.

Oscar found only one cause for uneasiness and that concerned Finsen. A certain pride which he felt at first in Finsen's interest in the girl he loved, the girl who loved him, soon gave place to jealousy. He was jealous of Finsen's hold over Helga, his control of her career, his power over her destiny. Little by little this became a gnawing anxiety until at length every pleasant word Helga exchanged with Finsen, and every smile she gave him, seemed to go to Oscar's heart like a stab.

He spoke to her on the subject, and she only laughed at him for his folly. Her endearing words and caresses dissipated his uneasiness for a time, but it always came back. Sometimes it seemed to him that Finsen presumed on his position as the one who was finding the ways and means, and that Finsen's friends interpreted this attitude according to the morality of the atmosphere they lived in. At length to ease the secret gnawing at his heart Oscar proposed that they should marry. Why not? There was no longer any impediment, and there would be an end of damaging misconceptions.

Remembering the past he thought Helga would have received his proposal with delight, but times had changed since they were together in Iceland and a cheerless smile hung about her lips as she shook her head. She showed him how fatal marriage at this stage would be to a girl in her position, —fatal to her aims, her ambitions, her standing with the public, and above all with the men to whom she had to look for favors—until he felt almost as much ashamed as if he had proposed a guilty thing.

"But why should *you* be jealous?" she said, approaching him to embrace him. "If *he* is so there may certainly be some cause."

She put her arms about his neck and added, "Business is business, you know, and I may have to do things in the future which neither of us could wish—unless," she whispered, laying her head on his breast, "my bad boy will at length consent to be true to himself and to his genius and promise to write the great works I know he *can* write, and let me sing them all over the world. Then," she cried with passion, while her eyes shone and her arms clutched his neck, "then he will see what I can do."

To this, and such as this, Oscar answered, "No, no," or, "It's impossible," or "Don't let us talk of it;" but Helga's endearing words and caresses, again and again repeated, were like the water from sunny streams which trickles between the snow and the frozen rock and brings down the avalanche at last.

The days passed—they kept no count of them—six months,

a year, a year and a half, and at length the time approached when Helga, according to the program which had been mapped out for her, was to leave the Academy of Music and begin her lessons in Paris. The prospect of an early separation was a constant nightmare to Oscar, who was striving in vain to devise schemes to prevent it, when that secret play of fate which men call chance, helped out by the blind strivings of human passion, brought him unexpectedly to the end he aimed at.

One day Finsen came dashing into Helga's sitting-room with his mouth full of news. The syndicate which held the theater and Casino in one of the principal towns of the Riviera had applied to him to recommend a leader of orchestra who should be capable of controlling a season of opera; he had recommended Oscar; his recommendation had been accepted, and it had been left to him to conclude terms with the company's servant and to despatch him without delay.

If a desire to separate Oscar from Helga had been a part of Finsen's plan his hopes were instantly frustrated, for Helga herself cried:

"Splendid! But if Oscar is to control the opera season why can't I go also? He can put me into small parts under an assumed name in that distant place where I can never be recognized, and that will be better practise for the stage than all the acting-classes in Christendom."

"Admirable idea!" shouted Oscar, and Finsen—not half-convinced—was compelled to agree.

It was while Oscar's heart rode high on this last freak of fortune, while he was preparing for his flight to the Riviera and while Helga was writing to Paris to postpone her lessons, that the letter came from Iceland and fell on him like a thunderbolt. The sight of a black-edged envelope addressed in Magnus's handwriting sent the blood rushing to his head. It was long before he could gather courage to open it. Feeling numb and faint he put the letter in his pocket and went out into the park to breathe and to think.

He had not written to his mother since the early days in his first lodging, being afraid to write from Short Street from dread of disclosing his poverty or from Piccadilly from fear of saying anything about Helga. As a consequence he had heard nothing from home since Anna's letter; the only news that had reached him had come through Finsen by way of his father and concerned public matters chiefly—the fall of the barter trade, the passing of the new Act and the progress of the elections.

Some one belonging to him was dead—who could it be? For no other reason than that little Elin was the youngest and frailest he concluded that it must be the child. His poor motherless darling! He reproached himself with having thought so little of her amid the appeals of an absorbing passion. Yet he *had* thought of her: he had thought he would go back for her some day, as it was his right and duty to do, and so make amends to Thora in the care and love he would bestow on her child. But perhaps that atonement was impossible now and his sweet child was with her mother in heaven.

Oscar thought that of all disasters that could befall him at home the death of his child would be the worst, but when at length he opened his letter and found that it was his father who was gone from him his grief was greater still. His dear father who had loved him better, perhaps, than any one else in the world, and whom he had rewarded the worst! He remembered the forgery and felt choked with shame; he thought of the promise to break with Helga and felt crushed by remorse. His father, who had pampered him and cherished such high hopes for him that should never be realized, never justified now, was dead far away in Iceland, and had loved him to the last!

Sitting on a bench under a tree he was trying to read again, as well as he could for the fading light and the blinding mist in his eyes, the written sob of his mother's misspelled postscript, when a park-keeper touched him on the shoulder to say the gates were closing, and then the dull hum of London's burrowing mazes fell on his ear again.

Helga had expected him in her room that afternoon to make the last arrangements for their journey, but the sun set, the evening closed, the night fell and he did not come. Next morning he walked in with drooping head and a dejected step and she saw that something had occurred.

"You have had bad news. Oscar—what is it?"

"My father is dead," he answered, and after that they sat for some moments without speaking.

Then Helga recovered herself—her brain had been going like a fly-wheel—and she said, scarcely above her breath:

"Well, what do you intend to do?"

"I intend to go back," said Oscar.

"Back to Iceland?"

"Yes—to my mother and my child."

He lifted his eyes and looked at her, and at the sight of her face, so full of pain and disappointment the blood rushed from his heart, and he said:

"Helga, why shouldn't you go with me? Why shouldn't we marry and go back together? I know it is a good deal to ask, dear, but we should be everything to each other, and I should make up to you for any sacrifice by my devotion and love. What matter if we have to forget our cherished dreams and aspirations? Life is the fulfilment of duty, and our duty is at home—mine is at all events—and if you will share it, if you will go back with me——"

He stopped suddenly and dropped his head on his hands and his elbows on his knees. With every word he uttered the impossibility and folly of what he proposed forced itself upon him, and the blood that had flamed up to his head fell back to the depths of his heart.

Helga sat a moment without speaking; then she said in a steady voice:

"I'm sorry, very sorry, but it's impossible! If I had nothing and nobody else to think about I should have to think of Neils. He has spent money upon me and I have given him a contract, therefore I can't run away from him like that."

Oscar drew deep, gasping breaths and answered, "Then I must go alone. It will be hard, terribly hard, but I *must* go. There is the mortgage—I must take up that burden now that my father is gone—I can not let anybody else be borne down by it. And then there is the child—I've not done too much for her hitherto, and it is my duty, my sacred duty——"

"The child is all right, Oscar. Aunt Margret is taking care of her. Nothing you could do for the little mite would be half as good as is being done for her already. As for the mortgage, you can bear that burden just as well in England as in Iceland! Better—far better! You'll earn more money here—ten times, a hundred times more. And then think of the difficulty of beginning over again under the old conditions. Everybody must know everything by this time. They do—I know they do!"

She rose, and standing over him she stroked his hair—the uncombed curls of his fair hair—and said, softly:

"No, no, dear! You can never go back to Iceland until you go back rich and famous. And you may! I say you may! And then I, too, perhaps——"

But he covered his ears with his hands, for what Helga was saying sounded like mockery.

"Meantime you can not think of leaving me—especially now when I want your help so badly—and when everything depends upon it—my work and my future."

She dropped to her knees by his side and put her arms around his neck.

"Say you will not leave me, dearest! Say you will not!"

She loaded him with caresses, she addressed him by every endearing name, she conquered him. He felt that the impulse to go back to Iceland—the impulse of duty—was overcome by the rapture of love, and that he must stay where Helga was, whatever happened.

"I belong to you, body and soul, Helga—do as you like with me," he said.

"And you will go to the Riviera?"

"Yes."

If he had known what he was saying he would rather have called upon the river to carry him to its lowest depths and count him in the death-roll of its damned. But none of us can foresee the future. We must all bow before the Unknown.

VIII

The engagement on the Riviera was completely successful and Oscar covered himself with honor, but when the opera season came to an end he declined all offers to come back.

Finsen was there. Under cover of professional and fra-

ternal interest he had made frequent visits to Oscar and
Helga during the course of the season, and at the close of it
he was staying at the same hotel. Oscar was nervous, fretful,
and unhappy. The secret gnawing anxiety which had oppressed him in London had returned with redoubled force.

Helga's love of the gaiety and grandeur of the life of the
Riviera was only too evident, and Finsen set himself to feed
it. He fed it by every art and resource of a full purse and
an open hand. Races, regattas, fêtes, flowers—he gave her
everything that was being enjoyed by other women living in
abundance. Oscar protested, but she laughed at his protests
or tried to coax him out of his jealousy. Her caresses and
endearments were beginning to fail of their old effect. In
spite of himself he was beginning to feel a certain contempt
for her, and at some moments even a sort of hatred which
tore his heart to pieces.

For his own part Oscar hated the life of the Riviera. What
nature had done for the place was good, but what man had
done was bad. The soft air, the blue sky, the deep blue sea,
the smiling gardens, the flowers, the oleanders, the orange
groves, the scent of the resin and then the still nights and
the nightingale—could anything be more enchanting? Yet
this paradise of nature, this God-blest corner of the earth was
degraded by every gross desire that was at war with beauty
and art and genius and the everlasting laws of life.

But Oscar's hatred of the Riviera was due to a cause more
personal than his moral revolt—a poignant memory of the
past. In the Casino which stood in the middle of the gardens,
beyond the brilliant hall and the noisy orchestra, there was an
inner room, guarded by keen-eyed door-keepers and watched
by spies, where men and women sat about a green-topped
table in a dusky and clammy silence; and at the end of that
room, in the darkest part of it there was an alcove, almost
covered by palms, where two persons could sit unseen. Helga
and he had once sat there, and she had pleaded with him to
do something that his soul shrank from, and he had done it.
" Why not? " she had said. " He will never hear of it, and it
will only be a matter of form. My luck *must* change, it
must, and then we will pay back this money and everything
will be wiped out. Do, Oscar, for me, please! "

From fear of reviving this memory Oscar had avoided the Casino during his present visit. That was easy enough to do while the opera season lasted, but when it was over, and his work no longer wanted him, it was hard to see Helga go off with Finsen night after night, and to wander round the Casino like an uneasy spirit that could find no rest while they were inside of it. The jealousy that was rankling in his breast could not bear that ordeal long and when Helga said, "What nonsense! You needn't play—why should you?" he followed her into the gambling-house.

He saw the usual sights there, and found the usual company gathered about the tables—all middle-class whatever their rank and station—the middle-class financier, the middle-class millionaire, the middle-class baron, the middle-class peer, the middle-class duchess smoking her cigarettes, and then the prostitute in her feathers and the black-leg in his diamonds, as well as reputable men and virtuous women, for the gambling-house knows no distinctions of means or morality or intellect and is the high court of the devil's democracy.

On the night of Oscar's first visit Helga played and lost; and seeing the strained look in her face his very soul felt sick and he walked out into the gardens. On the second night she lost again and he saw her borrow from Finsen who stood behind her. On the third night it was Finsen who played and he won largely, and then Helga, who sat by his side, seemed to be intoxicated by excitement and delight.

Next day she showed him a costly jewel which Finsen had bought for her out of his winnings. "For luck!" she said, and when Oscar protested against the present, she said:

"But why shouldn't I take it? Every penny he spends on me makes me more necessary to him for the future. Come, dear, don't be jealous. Didn't I tell you that I should have to do things that neither of us could wish?"

At this, and such as this, Oscar's sense of shame was choking him. His feeling for Helga was now in a perpetual alternation between love and hate. He loved her, he hated her, he despised her, he was proud of her, and this red riot in his blood was driving him to despair.

At one moment he thought her nature was utterly selfish, and that she would sacrifice anything and anybody to gain

her ends; at the next moment he believed she loved him with
an unselfish love, but that her disposition was such that she
had to struggle between her love for him and her love for luxury and success, and therefore she was as much an object for
pity as himself.

Sometimes, when he walked in the gardens of the Casino,
he remembered how Thora had suffered as he was suffering
now; and then, while the nightingale sang unseen above his
head and the peace of the night soothed his soul, he told himself he was rightly punished. As he had done so he was being
done by, and now the manly thing was to leave Helga and go
away; and then if she loved him she would suffer, too, and
that would be his best revenge.

But at other times, when he saw Helga wearing the brace-
lets and brooches which Finsen had given her he felt that
flight was impossible; that he must fight this man with his
own weapons and subdue this woman on her own terms.

Yet how was he to do it? When he asked himself that
question one answer, and one only, came back to him with
every breath he drew in that atmosphere of gamblers, the old,
delusive, mocking answer—he must do it by means of play.

But while he had money enough for his own needs he had
none for the gambling-table, and it was not at first that he
saw a way to the means with which to begin. Suddenly an
idea came to him—he would make the man himself find the
means—and without waiting to consider this, without pausing to count the cost, with his pulses throbbing painfully
and his heart leaping with a devilish joy, he hurried into the
Casino and drew Finsen aside to the alcove covered by palms,
and said, in a false and tremulous voice:

" Old friend, do you remember the first time I called on you
at Covent Garden ? "

" When you said you were starving—perfectly."

" You offered me something if I would sell you some compositions of mine that are buried in Iceland."

" And you said you would die in a ditch first."

" Would you still be disposed to take your chance with
them ? "

" Why not ? My father is Minister now—there ought to be
no difficulty."

" And you would be prepared to pay me the money at once ? "

" Certainly—as soon as you are ready to sign the necessary authorization."

" I'm ready to sign it now," said Oscar in the same tremulous voice.

Within ten minutes everything was settled, and Oscar was pocketing the notes that were being paid on Finsen's account from the treasury of the Casino. His hands were trembling, his lips quivering, and his face was white.

" So you're caught by the fever at last, old fellow," laughed Finsen. " And what you wouldn't do before to feed your stomach, you are doing now to feed your luck."

" Just so, to feed my luck," said Oscar.

That night Oscar played carefully and won. The following night he played more freely and won again. On the third night he took the bank and won once more. He took the bank on the fourth, fifth, sixth, and many succeeding nights with the same result. Such a rapid and unbroken run of luck had scarcely ever been seen. The manager of the Casino, a plausible person with a rubicund face, congratulated Oscar. The " house " had rarely had a banker so popular as well as so fortunate, and it rejoiced in his success.

Meantime Oscar was never for a moment his own man. He seemed to be laboring under a wild intoxication of soul. In a fortnight he had become rich, but he had no love for money for himself and he heaped it upon Helga. There were presents to outshine Finsen's, excursions in steam launches and in automobiles and even some social entertainments. The winsome and remarkable-looking young leader of the opera, with his handsome if reckless sister-in-law, became objects of attention. They gave one or two dinners in the restaurant of the Casino, where the rich of all nations ate their food in the glitter of a thousand diamonds and to the music of an orchestra in red coats and black silk stockings.

Then the change came—the inevitable change. One night it became evident that the tide of Oscar's luck had turned. He did not flinch—he doubled his risk and played on. The ebb set in with frightful rapidity, and every night he increased his stakes, and lost his money with a smile. At the end of a week Helga, who had been transported with rapture became pallid with alarm.

"Your luck is leaving you—hadn't you better stop?" she said, but he would not listen.

He touched bottom at last. Sitting in his usual seat he called for fresh counters, and said with a laugh, "Life or death—this is my last."

"Do you mean that?" said Helga, and he nodded and laughed again.

Finsen had been punting silently at the other side of the table, and now Helga went over to him and stood behind his chair. It was only the straw that told how the wind was blowing, but Oscar saw it and his twitching face grew red.

The inscrutable gods of chance seemed to hover over the table. A greater risk than that of money depended on the issue of the next *coup*, and both men knew it.

When the cards had been cut Oscar served them slowly, very slowly, and when he came to the last card his trembling fingers seemed loath to turn it. He turned it at last with a rapid movement and at the same moment he rose from his seat and laughed.

He had lost, and the clammy silence was broken.

"Are you going?" asked Helga, in a listless tone, with wandering eyes.

"Certainly. And you?"

"Not yet—Neils is winning splendidly."

Then in a moment, as in the twinkling of an eye, his month-long intoxication of soul left him and he saw where he was and what he had done. He had taken money from Finsen to permit the grave of his wife to be opened, and he had gambled with that money and lost it!

When he saw things in this way he could scarcely stand upright, but with an effort he walked out of the gambling-room, down the corridor where the spies were watching, past the restaurant where the sluggards were smoking, through the hall where the band was playing and out into the garden.

There he looked for a dark place and sat on a bench under a tree. The night was clear and quiet, the stars were out, and the sea was singing in the distance, but he could hear nothing except an owl that was hooting somewhere in the eaves. Oh, for the snows of his own country to cool his hot forehead! Oh, for the storms of Iceland to silence the babel in his brain!

When he thought of his conduct he hated himself, and when he remembered his temptation he hated Helga also. The one hatred counteracted the other or he would have destroyed himself. He must live, if only to subdue Helga, to bring her to his feet and then to cast her off forever!

How was he to do this? There was one way, but it was closed to him—closed by the vow he had made when he stood by the open coffin of his wife and, in punishment of himself for having neglected her and sinned against her, he had sworn before God to bury his ambitions in her grave and never write another line of music as long as he lived.

If he could only wipe out that vow, if he could only begin again, if he could only say to himself some day, "Oscar Stephenson is dead!" But that could never be and Oscar Stephenson must go on to the end, trailing the slag of his burned-out life behind him.

Deciding to return to England immediately, he walked back to the hotel and asked for his bill. When it was given to him he found that the money remaining in his purse was hardly sufficient to discharge his debt and pay the expense of his journey. Without a moment's thought he sat down and wrote to Helga:

"DEAR HELGA:—I want to go back to London by the midnight train and I find I am a little short for my railway ticket. Send me a hundred francs by the messenger who brings you this letter, and for mercy's sake do not keep him too long waiting—I can not live in this place another night.
                                                                "OSCAR."

He had lavished so many presents upon her that he never dreamt she could refuse him, but this was the answer that came back:

"DEAREST OSCAR:—How unlucky! I've just this very minute lost my last sou, and you don't like me to borrow from

Finsen. But, you bad boy, you can not be in earnest about going off at midnight. It's impossible! Your devoted
"HELGA."

Oscar had nothing that he could turn into money except his watch, and that was his father's gift and all he had to remember him by, but after a sharp struggle he called for the manager, and parted with his keepsake.

When his bill was paid and his luggage ready, the clock across the gardens was striking eleven. He had still an hour to spare, and bitterly as he felt toward Helga he could not go away without saying good-by to her, so he walked for that purpose by the shore road to the side door of the Casino.

It was there that his fate encountered him.

IX

As he was going into the Casino he met the manager, who greeted him effusively.

"Ah, Mr. Stephenson, they told me you were going away—I'm glad to see it isn't true!"

"It is quite true, sir," said Oscar.

"Why should you? The season isn't at an end yet."

"But my money is," said Oscar; whereupon the manager laughed, put his arm through Oscar's and walked back with him toward the baccarat-room, whispering:

"Mr. Stephenson, I told you the house liked to see you take the bank. The game is good when you are in the chair. Now there are a few gentlemen here to-night who would play high if they had the proper inducement. Don't go, Mr. Stephenson."

"But I'm penniless—don't you understand me?—penniless."

"Come this way."

They were in the baccarat-room by this time and the manager was drawing Oscar toward the alcove.

"I must ask you to excuse me. I have a lady to speak to, and my train to catch," said Oscar.

19

"Listen for a moment," said the manager, and then with a glance toward the company who stood absorbed and silent under the bright light in the middle of the room, he added, in a low voice, "Mr. Stephenson, I suggest that you return to the table and take the bank. When you call for counters they will be provided. If you lose your first coup the loss will be the loss of the house, and if you win the gain will be your own."

Oscar laughed, and chopping the air impatiently with a pair of gloves which he carried in his hand, he said, "Do you run this house on philanthropic lines then?"

"Hush! At your second coup you will call for fresh cards as you have a right to do, and when you receive them you—you will win. You understand me? *You will win!*"

The impatient chopping ceased and Oscar stood looking steadfastly at the man's eyes.

"At your next coup and your next you will call for cards as before and at the end of your fourth coup you will rise from the table."

"And then?"

"Then you will divide your earnings with the house, and be richer than you have ever been in your life."

Oscar had listened first with astonishment, then with indignation, and finally with ungovernable wrath. "How dare you? What do you take me for?" he said in a loud, choking voice, and lifting his hand he smote the man with his gloves across his ruddy and smiling face.

The unexpectedness of the attack compelled the manager to utter a startled cry, and in a moment the people from the table were crowding round, asking, "What is it?" What's happened?"

But the manager recovered himself in an instant and said: "It's nothing! The gentleman misunderstood something I was saying to him. I beg of you to resume the play."

Helga had come up with the rest, and when the others had returned to the table she drew Oscar into the alcove and said: "Tell me what occurred."

He told her, and still trembling with unsatisfied anger, he added: "This is what I have come down to, Helga—that a man can think it safe to make a proposal to me like that!

Can you wonder that I want to get out of this place—this atmosphere of cheats and cheating? And yet people talk of the honor of the gambling-house! They might as well talk of the morality of hell."

Helga was sitting with her head down and her fingers—which sparkled with some of Oscar's presents—interlaced upon her knee.

"You might have spared me one of these, Helga," he said, touching her rings. "We could have replaced it some day, whereas I've had to part with the watch my father gave me, and I can never replace that."

"I didn't want you to go, Oscar, that's why I didn't send you the hundred francs—I didn't want you to go away without me."

"Do you mean that, Helga? Really mean it? You do? Then come with me now! I came to say good-by, but how can I leave you behind in a place like this? It will destroy you as it has destroyed others. It will sap away your health and spirit and talent and charm and everything a woman wants to keep. Helga," he said, rising to his feet, "I am nearly distracted by what has occurred to-night, but I know what I am saying. If you will throw in your lot with me—with me only—I will devote my whole life to your welfare, and do everything you wish. If there is anything you want me to do for you I will do it. Do you understand me, Helga?"

"Yes, Oscar."

"Then let us go back to London—to our own world, our own work, Helga."

"I should like to—dearly like to."

"Then why not?"

"If I throw in my lot with you—with you only—I must break with Finsen—and I'm in Finsen's debt.

"I know! Oh, I know!"

"If I could only repay him somehow! But I have nothing!"

"You have your jewels, Helga."

"They are not enough. And besides, how could I part with a present of yours, Oscar? But if there were any other way of getting money——"

"Helga, what are you thinking of?"

"I am thinking that if this is an atmosphere of cheats and cheating perhaps *you* have been cheated also."

"Helga!" His voice was tremulous with protest.

"Would it be so very wrong to do to them as they have done to you, Oscar?"

"Helga! Helga!" His tremulous voice was breaking into gasps of helplessness.

"I suppose it would, but how happy I should be if we could go back together, and live for each other and our art, and have nothing and nobody else to think about!"

Oscar was standing by her side and quivering like a frightened horse. There were some moments of silence in which nothing could be heard but the call of the croupier in the middle of the room. Then a waiter went noiselessly by the mouth of the alcove carrying an empty tray to his own quarters, and by a sudden impulse, in a thick croupy voice Oscar called to him:

"Garçon! My compliments to the manager! Say I am sorry for what occurred just now, and if he is still of the same mind I will take the bank."

A few minutes later Oscar, who had thrown off his overcoat and hat, was taking the banker's chair at the baccarat-table. The people seated about it welcomed him with nods and smiles, and when he called for counters and received a huge pile of ivory ones a bald-headed man with a sinister face said, "I congratulate you, sir! It isn't everybody who can revive his credit as quickly as that."

"What does it mean?" whispered Finsen to Helga, whereupon Helga whispered back:

"Don't ask me yet," and then she walked up to Oscar and stood close behind his chair.

There were a few strange faces about the table, including an English lord and an American financier. The manager of the Casino stood watching from the back. Stakes were high for the first coup and the bank lost it.

"I'm afraid the luck is still against you, sir," said the bald-headed man.

"I'll try again," said Oscar. "Fresh cards, please!"

The stakes were higher for the second coup, and the bank won it.

"That's better," said the bald-headed man.

"Another pack of cards, please!" said Oscar.

When the money was on the table for the third coup it was seen to be double what it had been for the second. The bank won once more.

"But this is like your old luck, sir," said the bald-headed man.

"Another pack!" cried Oscar, and he swept all his winnings into the bank.

The money for the fourth coup was four times what it had been for the third. The bank won again, and then Oscar rose from the table.

"But aren't you going to give us our revenge, sir?" asked the American.

"This is mine," said Oscar, as he left the chair.

Helga's face was quivering with excitement and delight. There were tears in her eyes as she congratulated Oscar, and she looked as if she were going to kiss him.

"If you will step this way, Mr. Stephenson—" the manager's suave voice was saying, when all at once a commotion broke out behind.

"Croupier," said a voice with a nasal accent, "I will trouble you to examine them cards," whereupon the manager swung round with an aggrieved expression.

"Surely, sir, you do not mean to say, to imply——"

"I can only say I'll trouble the croupier to examine them last three packs of cards."

In the confusion that followed Finsen came up to Helga, who was now trembling by Oscar's side and said: "You had better let me take you out of this."

Oscar saw Helga hesitate, then take one step away from him and stop, but when somebody in the throng about the table cried excitedly: "The bank ought to be impounded," he saw her drop her head and follow Finsen out of the room.

"Come this way, Mr. Stephenson," whispered the manager, and while most of the company were still crowding about the croupier he half-led, half-pushed Oscar through a small door to a private corridor, and a moment afterward there was a roar from the other side of it.

"Stay here. Leave everything to me. I'll do the best I can," said the manager, and then Oscar found himself alone in a small room, quite dark and silent, save for the glimmering of lamps in the garden and the deadened rumble of the tumult he had left behind.

How long he stayed there he never knew. It seemed like an hour, but it could hardly have been more than a few minutes. The tumult grew louder, then there was the report of a pistol-shot, and then the noises frayed off to silence.

Unable to restrain himself any longer, and delirious with a wild desire to face the consequences of his conduct, whatever they might be, Oscar was opening the door of his room when the manager returned to it, bringing his hat, overcoat, and gloves.

"I've done the best I could for you," said the manager, panting and gasping. "I have told them you have shot yourself, and your friends have supported that explanation. You must get away at once. You must catch the midnight train to Paris. You've only four minutes, but you'll do it if you run. Here is a second-class ticket to London. Good night! And remember," said the man, as Oscar was passing through a private door to the garden, "remember—*Oscar Stephenson is dead.*"

X

Oscar was just able to control his faculties long enough to reach the railway-station, find the train, and search out an empty second-class compartment and then he collapsed utterly. He was like a beast that has been smitten in the shambles and is shattered in every sense and nerve.

Looking up at the lamp in the roof and seeing smoke floating above it, he thought at first the carriage must be afire, but looking again the smoke was gone and then he knew his sight had suffered and he supposed he must be going blind. There was a roaring noise in his ears and he thought it was the roaring of the train, but when the train stopped the noise continued, and then he knew that his hearing was injured and he supposed he must be going deaf. Two officials came into the carriage to examine the tickets, but though he saw their lips moving he could not hear what they said, or rightly grasp what they wanted, until they were turning to go, and then the noise in his head slid off for a moment and he heard one of them say to the other, " Drunk, poor devil ! "

This lasted through the dark hours of the night, and when the morning dawned his experiences were yet more terrible. At the first gleam of light his stunned soul awoke, and with a sharp pain like the after-pain of a bullet wound, he realized where he was and what he was doing. He was flying from the consequences of perhaps the most base and infamous conduct a man could be capable of—conduct the more base and infamous because there was no law to punish it.

Low as he had sunk hitherto he had never sunk so low as this. This was as low as man could go and live in the face of other men and the eye of the light. And *he* had descended to this depth, he, Oscar Stephenson, son of the Governor of his country ! When he thought of his father he thanked God that death had taken him before this disgrace befell.

Every artery in his body seemed to bleed, every tendon to be torn. When the sun rose on him in his ghastly solitude it seemed to sere his very brain and he pulled the blind down to shut it out.

Then the women passengers began to move about the corridor of the train and he thought of Helga. Although it seemed so long ago as almost to belong to another existence, he could still see her frightened face as she sidled away from him last night and left him standing alone at that hideous moment when it seemed certain that he must pay the penalty of the offense to which she had tempted him. He despised her for her cowardice; he loathed her for her treachery; he hated her for herself; and he told himself that never again as long as he lived should love of Helga hold dominion over him.

At one moment he found himself cursing her. At the next he found himself weeping. Could it be Helga whom he was thinking of like this ? Helga, who had been so much to him during so many years, who had come so very close to him, nearer than his father, nearer than his mother, nearer—Heaven forgive him!—than his wife or child? Helga, who had been with him early and late, a soft voice always at his ear, a sweet presence always at his heart, a spirit, a support, an inspiration? Helga, whom he had loved and should always love, let her do what she would with him, let him do what he would with her? God pity him! God help him!

Yet his tenderness and tears were stronger than his hatred and rage, and he resolved that for her perfidy and selfishness, Helga should be punished, and that he should punish her. There was no longer any need to ask himself how this was to be done. The words that had rumbled in his ears like the roll of a muffled drum when he ran from the gardens of the Casino were rumbling in his ears still. *Oscar Stephenson is dead!* At first he could not be sure that the manager had really spoken them, so exactly did they echo the wish that had been bubbling within his own breast. But Oscar Stephenson was dead indeed, and the words that might have crushed him with shame moved him more than a trumpet.

If Oscar Stephenson was dead, then the vow he had made in Thora's death-chamber was dead also! That vow had been intended to punish himself for his infidelity and for all his failures of love and duty, by denying himself the gratification of his greatest pride, the realization of his highest hopes. But what pride could be gratified and what hopes realized to Oscar Stephenson if his name was wiped out, his identity lost, and he was dead to all the world except himself?

The feverish soul in its hour of suffering found the reasoning sufficient, and Oscar thought he saw as in a glass everything that he had to do. He had to take another name, to bury himself in London and to set to work on the only task he was fit for! He had to write an opera, as he was now free to do, since Oscar Stephenson was dead, and he was living in the name of another man.

The scene was to be in his own country, among the lonesome grandeur of its untrodden glaciers and the stark sublimity of its burned-out plains, and the story was to be from one of the fiery Sagas of the same stern old land. And when, after many days, many months, perhaps years, eating the bread of poverty in loneliness and obscurity, he had finished his task, and had sent it out like a dove from the ark, men were to know that a new voice had come among them and the name of Iceland was to be on the lips of the world.

Then when people asked each other, who was he that in the darkness of years of labor had learned all the art and mystery of music, he would give no sign because his lips would be sealed, but there would be one who would read his secret. It would be Helga, and she would come back to him in shame if not remorse and throw herself at his feet and cry: "I did wrong, forgive me, and take me back to your heart!"

And then he would answer and say: "You came between me and my sweet young wife; you persuaded me to the act that broke her heart and killed her; you tempted me to the crime that ruined my father and to the offense that destroyed myself, and then you left me to bear my punishment alone. Therefore, I have wiped you out of my life; I have cut you off as I would cut off a rotten limb that threatened to drag the whole body down to death. I love you—yes, I can never cease to love you—that is the punishment I shall always bear—but there can be nothing more between us— we part now forever—your course lies that way, mine this. Farewell!"

As the train rolled along he found a delirious joy in this prospect, which began and ended with the idea that Oscar Stephenson was dead. In the light of that thought he looked back on the past of his life and many things that had been hard to understand became plain. Again and again he had tried to stop on his downward course and he could not do so. Before he could rise out of the degradation of his past life he had had to drink his cup to the dregs, to go down to the depths, to be covered by darkness and the shadow of death! But at last Oscar Stephenson was dead! Thank God! Thank God!

How strange that at the moment when Helga was tempting him to the infamous act, which if it had succeeded would have made him her slave and the slave of sin forever, she was leading him by one of Death's terrific strides to life and liberty! How mysterious and how mighty, aye, and how cynical also, were the powers of Destiny, whose supernatural wings hovered over the lives of men and women and moved their little motives of love and hate and revenge and selfishness like pawns on the chess-board of Fate!

It was in this mood he reached Paris, and having some three hours to wait before his train started for Calais, he walked through the streets until he came to the center of the city, and then sat outside a café to eat a roll of bread and drink a cup of coffee. It was six o'clock, and the news-vendors were crying the evening papers. He bought one to beguile the time of waiting, and had not yet opened it when he saw his own name standing out from the front page as if it had been printed in a different ink.

For some moments thereafter a mist seemed to float between the newspaper and his eyes, but he read the paragraph at last.

It was a telegram from Nice, headed: "Suicide in a Casino," giving a mangled version of the events of last night, clearly inspired by the manager to protect himself and his house, and closing with the words:

"The deceased, who was from Iceland, is understood to be a son of the late much-respected Governor-General of that country."

XI

THE paper slipped from Oscar's fingers and his transport of rapture passed. He told himself that this report would go far, that it would reach Iceland, that his mother would hear of it, and that his child would be told that she was fatherless.

Little Elin was too young to feel grief, but could he allow his mother to believe that he was dead and to weep for him as for one who was lost to her forever? That would be too cruel; it would be impossible; he would write to his mother immediately; he would write privately saying he was still alive and that part of the report was untrue.

But then came the chilling thought that though he might dispose of the fiction of his death he could not get rid of the fact of his offense, and that when his mother pictured him as one who was flying from the consequences of his conduct, skulking in a slum and hiding his face from the faces of his friends, there would be something in the shame of that end more bitter than death itself, and even his own mother would wish that he had died.

He had not thought of this before, and in the confusion and pain of it he got up from the table at the café and began to walk the streets again. After a while he found himself ascending the steps of the Madeline, hardly knowing what he was doing, except that he was trying to pass the time by following a stream of people into the building.

It was the hour of Benediction, the most beautiful, the most tender, the most moving of all the offices of the Catholic Church. The congregation were chiefly women, and among ladies in silks, whose carriages stood outside, were some flower-sellers from the flower-market round the corner, for there is only one caste in the commune of the Cross. One poor woman who took a chair and knelt close beside Oscar, had the sad and storm-beaten face that the Cross draws to it in every church in the country, for its empire is the empire of the oppressed and bereaved and broken-hearted.

"*Somebody's* mother," thought Oscar, as she crossed herself and sighed. But when she raised her weary eyes to the figure of the world-mother above the altar, her sad face softened and smiled and it was almost as if an angel had come down and whispered to her.

Then as the sweet music swelled through the great church the hard lump rose to Oscar's throat, and thinking of his own mother so far away, he told himself that if she believed he was really dead the angel of Death would comfort her. His faults would be forgiven, his errors would be forgotten, and the dust of death would cover all his transgressions. She would be happier in his death than she had ever been in his life, and though it was a sore thing to think of that, the pain would be his, not hers, and her poor heart would be at ease.

He thought of Magnus, too, how his hatred would be appeased when he heard that his brother was dead, and all the flames of his rage extinguished. Then he thought of his enemies at home, how they would cease to revile him, and how he would pass out of shame, reproach, and contempt into the charity of silence and the peace of forgetfulness. Finally he thought of his little Elin, his sweet motherless daughter, how she would hear no more hard words spoken of her father, but would grow up to think of him merely as one who had died early. Oh, blessed and merciful death which can make those who hate us hate us less and those who love us love us more!

It was bitter to comfort himself with the thought that he was dead—dead in disgrace and in a foreign country, with no mother's tears falling on his face and no child weeping by his side, that tragic consolation of the dying. But just at that moment the music ceased, the bell tinkled at the altar, and raising his eyes as the priest elevated the host the awe deepened about him, and he told himself that it was not he who was dead at all but only his sin and misery, and that he might rise, if he would, out of the shadow of death into another and better life.

Then, almost before he knew it, the thought had become a prayer, and he found himself praying that he might be permitted to begin again, to put the past behind him, and to think of the lost days of his life hitherto as seed that was not dead though he had trampled it into the clay. Out of the heart came the only songs that went to the heart, and out of his shame and suffering in that future he had foreshadowed for himself the voice might come that would speak to other souls as stained with sin as his.

Yet who was he to speak to any one? Only a prodigal in a far country who had wasted his substance in riotous living, and having come to himself at last, now that no man would give to him, was turning his eyes homeward and crying, "Father, I have sinned against heaven, and before thee, and am no more worthy to be called thy son!"

The service came to an end and the people rose to go. As Oscar rose, too, he told himself that in actual fact he would go back home some day. A little longer, only a little longer, and he would return to Iceland. His father would be gone, yes, his poor father would be gone, but his mother would be there, and he would make amends to her for everything she had suffered for his sake and wipe all tears from her eyes. His child would be there also, and he would claim her as he had always intended to do, and though she might not even know his face, she would hear the voice of nature calling her and she would come to him and he would be a father to her, guiding and protecting her, and she would be a daughter to him, cheering and comforting him, and her love would be his solace for all the pains of life. A little longer, only a little longer!

When he came out of the great church he felt himself lifted into a purer air, where he was no longer a fugitive from the vengeance of his fellow-men, but a pardoned soul born again in a blessed resurrection; and when he had settled in the train for Calais he set himself to consider what other name he should be known by in that new existence which he had just begun.

It had to be a name that would sufficiently conceal his own, yet one that would be characteristic of his country, and, after much beating of the wings of memory, he decided on Christian Christiansson as a name which not only answered to the conditions, but possessed an added nobleness of meaning and associations that would forever forbid the lowering of the flag of his purpose.

But after he had concluded that Christian Christiansson was to be his name in the future, it cost him a pang to think that Oscar Stephenson was to be his name no longer. Stephen had been his father's name and his poor father had expected him to carry it on from strength to strength and from glory to glory. Oscar had been the name his mother had known him by, and it came back to him now in the tones of her voice with the happiest memories of his boyhood. He could hear it in Thora's voice also in the tremulous happiness of her bridal chamber, in the tender joy of her motherhood, and in the pleading accents of her despair. It was like burying something of himself to bury his name, but Oscar Stephenson was dead, and that name could be his no more.

It was early morning when he reached London, and returning to it after six months' absence he felt like one who had been dead and was alive again. As the empty streets echoed to his footsteps his spirits rose and he looked to the future without fear. Though he was coming back friendless and nearly penniless, he saw himself as he would be some day—Christian Christiansson, the composer, rich, respected, honored perhaps, and perhaps beloved. It might be months, it might be years, but God willing, it should come! A little longer, only a little longer!

He had at first intended to look for a lodging where he would be quite unknown, but in his present elevation of feeling it seemed unnecessary to do so, and he determined to return to his old home in Short Street. When he came to Westminster Bridge, he stopped for a moment to look down at the houseless wretches who were still asleep on the benches of the embankment, and to remember the night when he had been one of them, and to think of the other night that was soon to come when the first-fruits of his new life would be in his hands.

He could see it all as in a glass that revealed the future. The curtain would be down on the new opera and there would be a great demonstration in the crowded opera-house. Again and again the singers would be recalled and then there would be loud cries for the composer. The cries would rise to a deafening clamor, and the whole audience from the royal box to the top-most gallery would be calling for the unknown man who had breathed his suffering soul into an old Saga and made the dry bones live. But the Unknown would not appear; he would not be there. Where would he be? He would be down here—here under the night sky, weeping for joy and gratitude, emptying his pockets among these homeless outcasts in memory of the night when he, too, was homeless and an outcast, and vowing never again to forget the friendless and the fallen or to be hard on the sinner and the prodigal. He could see it happening as plainly as if it had already come to pass. It *should* come to pass! A little longer, only a little longer!

When he reached Short Street the hearse of the Necropolis had just turned the corner and was rattling up the archway. Nearly all the window-blinds of Number One were still down, but as he hesitated at the foot of the front steps the door opened and a young woman in curl papers came out with a mop and pail. She stared at him as if he had been a stranger, but he knew her instantly.

"Don't you remember me, Jenny?" he said.

At the sound of his voice Jenny's face assumed a look of bewilderment; this was followed by a smile of recognition.

"Well, I never! Mr. Steevison! Is it you, sir? Ye'r so changed I wouldn't 'a knowed ye, an' when ye spoke ye might 'a knocked me down with a feather."

"Can I have lodgings here again, Jenny?"

"Certingly ye can, sir. An' ye've come in the nick o' time, too. We buried the barman a week come Wednesday and 'is room 'as been just cleaned out. Come in, Mr. Steevison!"

"Hush, Jenny! That is not my name now."

"Isn't it really?" said Jenny, with a puzzled look, and then, as by sudden enlightenment, "Well, I'm married myself and I've changed my name, too. I'm Mrs. Cobb now, an' I've took over the 'ouse since the missus 'as been down with the stroke, an' my 'usband's asleep in the cellar."

They had stepped into the lobby by this time and putting down the pail Jenny cried over the banisters of the basement stairs:

"Jim! Jim Cobb, you bone-lazy thing, come up an' see an old friend."

"Don't disturb him now! Another time! I'm tired."

"Ye look it, sir. Ye really do. I'm afraid she's been 'a treatin' ye cruel. I knowed she would. It's always the way with them women. Ye'd better.'a stayed with me, sir— I'd 'a been real good to ye in them days and never 'a wanted nothink.— But go inside, sir, and I'll get ye some brekfist. The kittle is just on the boil an' ye'll have a cup o' tea an' a rasher afore ye can say 'Jack Robison.'"

Jenny went scurrying down the stairs like an old slipper, and Oscar stepped into the barman's parlor and sat on the shiny leather-covered sofa. He remembered that he had sat there before, he remembered who had sat with him, he remembered all that had happened since, and then for one brief moment his visions of the future failed him; his hopes and intentions sank away; everything was blotted out except the sweet and bitter memory of the woman he had loved and lost, and he broke down utterly.

XII

IT takes a long time for the truth to travel from a distance, but a lie flies on the wings of the wind. The report of Oscar's death in a gambling-house on the Riviera reached Iceland by the next steamer.

Three days before the steamer's arrival Magnus and his mother were sitting in front of their farm at Thingvellir. Anna was spinning and Magnus was making rope by a twister turned by a small boy a dozen yards away, for it was just after the wool-plucking and a little before the hay-harvest.

The sun was setting behind the crags of the Almanagja, the blueberry ling was reddening over the green waters of the chasm, and there was no sound in the evening air save the plash of the Axe waterfall, the lowing of kine and the cry of curlew. Then over the hum of the wheel and the wis-wis of the twister came the dull thud of horses' feet on that hollow ground and Anna stopped to listen.

"That must be the post coming," she said, and Magnus answered, "Perhaps," without turning to look at the road, which was still empty as far as to the top of the cleft, where it opened on to the plain.

"I wonder if there will be a letter from Oscar?"

"Why should you wonder, mother? Has he answered your letter of three years ago? Has he had the decency and humanity to reply to the news of his father's death? No!"

"Still, I can not give up hoping. He must know by this time how you are placed with the farm, and perhaps he is only waiting until he can send you some assistance."

Magnus made no reply, but the wis-wis of the rope was louder.

"It's true he doesn't know everything. He doesn't know that his father left nothing behind him but the debt to the bank, and that the bank has been so hard——"

"Mother, if you go on talking like that I shall never get

this rope finished. I don't want anybody to help me to pay my way, and the bank shall have its money every Christmas if hard work can make it."

"You'll work yourself to death—that's what you'll do, Magnus. You sent Asher away in the winter, although he was so good at feeding the beasts when the snow was on the ground, and now that the hay has to be cut and the lambs killed, you're discharging Jon Vidalin."

"We'll have to thin down somewhere, and the sooner we begin the better—it's too late to spare when you see the bottom of the meal-barrel, you know."

"That's what *you* call thinning down—sending everybody away who can help you with the farm and keeping a houseful of women who are of no use for anything."

"Why, which of them is of no use, mother?"

"Gudrun for one. She only milks the cows in the morning and the ewes in the evening, and I could do both myself and save her keep and wages."

"Nonsense, mother! You're not young enough now to get up at four o'clock winter and summer and I won't hear of it for a moment."

"Then there's Maria—*she's* old enough for anything, and what's the use of her?"

"Maria's been in the family since before I was born, and we can't turn her away now because she's old and rheumatic."

"And here's Eric," said Anna, dropping her voice and glancing at the boy who was turning the twister.

"Eric? Poor little chap, he's lost his father, and he only gets a lamb for his wages anyway."

"It's to be a sheep this year, remember, and then there's his food— But if it's an orphanage you want to keep, or a home for invalids——"

"Helloa! Here's the post! And who's this he has got with him? The Rector! The Rector and two strangers!" cried Magnus, as a canvas-covered wagon, drawn by four ponies, rumbled over the bridge above the waterfall and galloped up to the Inn-farm.

"Welcome, Rector," said Anna.

"Thanks, Anna. These are friends from America, trav-
20

eling to see the country. We should like to sleep here to-night and go on to Geyser in the morning."

"With pleasure! Maria! Gudrun! Jon Vidalin!" cried Anna, and while the strangers were being taken to the guest-room and the horses to the stable, the Rector went indoors with Anna and Magnus and they sat and talked around the hall table.

"You look hale in spite of everything, Anna."

"And you, too, Rector!"

"Ah, yes, old wood burns slow! But I sometimes wonder if it's well to live long. Better go to bed early than sit up too late, I say."

"Any new trouble in town lately?"

"The Factor is down at last, poor fellow."

"You mean that he's——"

"Bankrupt, and about to be sold up—business, office, everything."

"Poor Margret Neilsen!"

"What about the child?" asked Magnus.

"I think he would part with it now. To tell you the truth, he is feeling bitterly about Oscar just at present. 'A dove doesn't come out of a raven's egg,' he said yesterday."

"He said that?"

"So the new Minister says—but then it was the Minister who made him bankrupt."

"But I thought they were such friends; and when poor Stephen was petitioning the King——"

"Then you haven't heard what happened about Thora."

"Thora?" said Magnus.

"Poor Thora's grave, I mean. It makes the blood run between my skin and my flesh to think about it."

"Tell us," said Anna.

And then the Rector told them how the Minister, acting under instructions received from abroad, had ordered Thora's grave to be opened and certain musical compositions which had been buried in it to be taken out; how this had been done and the papers despatched to England; how the Factor had heard of it, and, being furious, had threatened an action against the Minister; and finally how the Minister, to cut the ground under the Factor's feet, had caused the bank to make him a bankrupt.

During the progress of the Rector's story Magnus sat without saying a word, but every moment his cheeks grew whiter and his eyes glared and his lips quivered. Meantime Anna covered her face and said:

"It must have been Neils who did that. I never liked the boy—he was always too much like his father—and now that he is——"

"It wasn't Neils, Anna. It was Oscar."

"Oscar?" said Magnus, and his hands clutched the corners of the table.

"Oh, dear! Oh, dear! I couldn't have believed it of Oscar. But who knows how he may have been tempted? Perhaps he was poor, yes, perhaps after all he was in want and they offered him money. There are such ups and downs in these foreign countries—perhaps he was starving in the streets of London——"

"He wasn't in London at all, Anna. He was at Monte Carlo, or Nice, or somewhere."

"Then you mean he only wanted the money to—the same as before, when he—I won't believe it!"

"Be quiet, mother," said Magnus, with the hoarse croak of a raven, and then turning to the Rector, "Who did it—the work itself, I mean?"

"Hans, the sailor—they could get nobody else, it seems."

"Hans, the sailor," repeated Magnus, in the same hoarse croak, and while the table creaked under the clutch of his great hands, his face grew hard and ugly.

During the remainder of that day Magnus went about without speaking to any one, and next morning, after the strangers had started on their journey, he saddled Silvertop and rode off toward Reykjavik. Anna saw him go, and calling to Jon Vidalin, she said:

"Take the fastest horse and ride to town by the low road and find Hans, the sailor. Tell him to fly before Magnus comes and never to come back again."

XIII

WHEN Magnus returned to the farm three days afterward he was like another man. His face was no longer hard and ugly, it was as soft as a tender woman's, and he was smiling down at something that looked like a huge bundle which he carried on the saddle in front of him. Anna saw him crossing the bridge, and she ran out to meet him.

"Goodness me!" she cried. "Is it the child?"

"Yes, it is the child, mother," said Magnus, and out of a mountain of rugs and shawls came little Elin, now in her fifth year, and she was dropped into Anna's arms.

"The darling! What a great girl she has grown! So she has come to see her gran'ma?"

"Yes, gran'ma," said the child.

"And here are her clothes—all of them," said Magnus, swinging a satchel off his shoulders.

"Then she has come for good! And she is going to live with her gran'ma and Uncle Magnus!"

"And Silvertop and the sheeps and the doggies," said the little one.

"So she shall, bless her! Jon Vidalin, see to the master's pony. Eric, where are you? Ah! that's a good boy—carry the satchel into the house. Maria, did you *ever* see anything so bonny? But, Magnus, how ever did the Factor come to part with her?"

"He wouldn't at first, for all his worries and the hard things he had been saying. And when he came to it at last he wanted me to promise that if Margret Neilsen died before himself he should have the child back again."

"You didn't agree to that, Magnus?"

"I said the girl should choose for herself if she was old enough, and at last he consented."

"But what about Margret Neilsen?"

"That was harder still. 'I promised her mother I should keep her as long as I lived,' she said."

"Ah, poor thing! She didn't know what was to happen."

" 'I wouldn't part with her to anybody in the world but Anna,' she said."

"I always said Margret Neilsen was as good as gold."

" 'And I wouldn't part with her now,' she said, ' only Anna is in such trouble.' "

"Trouble?"

"Give the child to Maria and come into the house, mother."

The sunshine died off Anna's face; she saw what was coming.

"Here, take her in and give her some barley cake and syrup, and for goodness' sake, woman, don't sniffle as if you had a cold. What is it, Magnus? Am I the only one who doesn't know? Tell me plainly—is he in disgrace again?"

"Have courage, mother," said Magnus.

She looked at him and understood everything. "Wait," she said, and she went down on her knees in the hall and prayed for some moments. After that she got up, pale but calm, and said:

"Now tell me everything—I am ready."

Magnus told her what he had heard and all that had happened: how he had gone to town with murder in his heart, intending to punish Hans, the sailor; how some one had warned him and Hans had taken refuge in a schooner that was to sail for Norway; how he had hired a boat to follow the man when the mail steamer dropped anchor in the bay and somebody shouted from the deck that Oscar was dead, and it was the same as if a hand from heaven had stopped him.

"Dead, did he say?"

"Dead in France, he said, and he threw down a Danish newspaper. Here it is, mother, but God knows if I should read you the report in it."

"Read it," said Anna.

He read it—it was the same which had appeared in Paris —and she listened without drawing breath.

"Then he died in a gaming-house—by his own hand, too— and to save himself from further disgrace!"

Magnus did not attempt to speak, and presently Anna's tears began to flow. After a few moments she wept bitterly and prayed aloud, now for Oscar, that God would forgive him; now for Elin, that God would protect the little orphan; finally for herself, that God would have pity upon her and let her die.

Magnus went over to the dresser for a bowl, dipped it in the water-crock, and gave her a drink, and after that she seemed better.

"My poor Oscar!" she said. "He wasted his life, poor boy! Such a precious life, too! Such talents! There wasn't anything he couldn't master. Everybody said what great things he would do some day. And to think it should come to this! I never expected to thank God that his father was dead, but I do now. Oh, God, I thank Thee— But what am I saying?"

After a few minutes more she began to blame herself for everything that had happened.

"I didn't bring him up properly. I could never be strict with children. And he was always so sweet, and even when he was naughty he was so loving. Everybody loved that child. Yes, it was my fault, and God ought to punish me. Almighty Father, be merciful to my poor boy, and if I was to blame——"

"Mother! Mother!" said Magnus, and she stopped in her self-reproaches, waiting for a loving word to comfort and support her, but Magnus said no more.

A few minutes later all she had suffered at Oscar's hands was wiped out of her mind and the wayward sinner had become a saint.

"He never changed to me, never, and even when he grew to be a man he always kissed me going to bed, just as he used to do when he was a boy. He was so good to his mother. Both my sons have been good to me. No mother ever had such good sons——"

"Mother!" said Magnus, and again she waited, but Magnus did not speak.

At length she checked her tears and began to comfort herself with the thought that if Oscar had taken his own life it must have been in madness, therefore God would not hold him accountable.

"And if he died in disgrace, perhaps it was only because he wanted to come back rich, so that he could pay the mortgage and make us all happy. I used to think of that and pray for it so often. But now if he could only come back poor—I shouldn't care how poor—as poor as the prodigal in the parable——"

" Mother ! " cried Magnus. " I can't hear you talk like this —I can't and I won't. Oscar is dead, but he treated you shamefully."

" Don't say that, Magnus."

" But I do say it. I say you were the best mother to him a son ever had, and the only return he made to you for your care and loving-kindness was to neglect you and forget you."

" Don't say it, my son."

" I will say it, mother. And I'll say, too, that Oscar lived in disgrace and died in disgrace, and now that he is gone I am not going to pretend that I wish he could come back again."

"Magnus ! Magnus ! "

" I don't wish it. If he came back poor, what right would he have to bring his poverty here ? And if he came back rich, what reason to expect that his money would make amends to us for the evil days we have had through him ? I don't believe in the return of the prodigal, mother, and I don't believe in the parable, either. That may be the way in the other world, but it isn't the way in this one, and it shouldn't be— I say it shouldn't be."

" Oh, dear ! Oh, dear ! "

" As for Oscar, I tried to forgive him—you know I did— but there are some crimes that seem to be past forgiveness, and when I think of this last one against Thora I'm not sorry he never came back—I shouldn't have been able to keep my hands off him. I was thinking of him when I was following Hans, and if he had returned with the ship that brought the news of his death it would have been God help both him and me."

" But, my son, your brother is only just dead, and it is your duty to forgive him whatever he did."

" He died to me long ago, mother—before he went away from Iceland—and now that he is dead indeed, I thank God he can never come back again."

"Well, the Lord knows best what He is doing," said Anna, and then her tears came again, whereupon Magnus, seeing what he had done, walked over to her and kissed her. He had never done that in the whole course of his life before, so her tears flowed faster than ever. And then he went out of the house, muttering to himself:

"Ah, well! My God! My God!"

That night when the bell in the hall rang for prayers, and little Elin sat in her grandmother's lap and the farm-servants trooped in with the awesome looks of persons who knew what shadow hung over the little house among the lonely hills, Magnus, in his quality of family priest, took up the Bible and hymn-book at the place where Anna opened for him. The chapter was from second Samuel, and it ended with the verse:

"And the king was much moved, and went up to the chamber over the gate, and wept: and as he went, thus he said, O my son Absalom, my son, my son Absalom! Would God I had died for thee, O Absalom, my son, my son."

The hymn was—

"Meek and low, meek and low,
I shall soon my Jesus know."

When the singing ended, the farm-servants went out one by one, each saying to Magnus:

"God give you a good night!"

And Magnus answered, as well as he could for the emotion that mastered him:

"And you! And you!"

XIV

IN the house of sorrow God closes the hearts of little children so that they may not break. Little Elin had been bright and happy the whole evening through. She was a merry little sprite whose laughter—like the rippling of a sunny stream—set everybody else laughing. Old Maria was at a loss to say which of her parents she resembled most. When the child laughed, Maria said: " There's a deal of the father in the little one," and when she listened and looked up sideways Maria thought there was a deal of the mother, too.

Anna put her to bed, and while she was being undressed her little tongue went like a shuttle. Existence had gone rapidly since she arrived, and she was full of stories: how she had gone to the chasm with Maria to pluck blueberries, and two big, black ravens, sitting on a crag, had looked down at her and croaked; how she had gone to the cow-house with Eric to see the cows milked, and Gudrun (to her infinite glee) had squirted some of the milk at her; and, above all, how all alone she had found a pet lamb and it was brown, because it had lost its mother, and lived in the elt-house, because its father had run away from it, and how it put its cold nose against her face and said, " Bah! " and its name was " Maggie."

" Maggie shall come and waken you in the morning, darling," said Anna.

" Shall she come in here, gran'ma? "

" Yes, dear," said Anna, and then the sunny stream of the child's laughter rippled through the room.

" But now it's late, and good little girls must be as quiet as mice."

" Yes, gran'ma"—in a breathless whisper.

" This is to be your own little bedroom always, dearest, and gran'ma has made it nice, so that it may do for you when you grow up."

" Yes, gran'ma "—another breathless whisper.

" That is the wardrobe for your clothes, and this is your little chest of drawers, and that—up there on the wall—that is your mamma's guitar and you will learn to play it some day."

" Yes, gran'ma "—the whisper was growing a little weary.

" The next room is the guest-room, and Uncle Magnus always sleeps there, except when there are strangers, so if you knock in the night he is sure to hear you."

" Yes, gran'ma "—the whisper was getting slow and weary.

" Gran'ma wants you to be *such* a good girl to Uncle

Magnus. He loved your dear, sweet mother so much. Oh, so much, but he lost her——"

"Same as Maggie's mother?"—there was a sudden burst of wakefulness.

"Maggie's mother was only a sheep, darling."

"Oh!"

"But now God has given you to Uncle Magnus to make up to him for everything, so you must be as good as good to him."

"Yes, gran'ma"—the whisper was becoming faint.

"When you grow up to be a big, big girl, and grandma isn't here, you must love him and comfort him just the same as if he had been your own father."

"Ye—es, gran'ma."

"And if anybody ever comes and wants to take you away from him, you mustn't go—you must always stay with Uncle Magnus."

"Ye—es, gran'——"

"That's a good girl! And now climb up into bed, and grandma will kiss you and tuck you in for the night."

"And will Maggie come in the morning?"

"Yes, dearest."

"Good night, gran'ma."

"Good night, my own darling."

"Goo—nigh—gran'—ma."

PART VI

" One moment in annihilation's waste
One moment of the Well of Life to taste,—
The stars are setting and the caravan
Draws to the Dawn of Nothing—Oh, make haste!"

I

THE Danish mail-steamer "Laura," outward bound on her midwinter trip from Copenhagen to Leith, and from Leith to Iceland, carried two saloon passengers only.

One of these, a comfortable, elderly person of ample proportions, dressed in the warmest Icelandic vadmal, was an Iceland merchant returning from Edinburgh with a hundred tons of British produce. This was Jon Oddsson, formerly radical champion in politics, and now conservative leader in trade.

The other passenger was a tall, spare man apparently about fifty years of age, with large and luminous but weary eyes, long pale cheeks deeply scored with lines of thought, and a pointed beard that was beginning to be tinged with grey. This was Christian Christiansson, now ten years older than when he returned from the Riviera to London, and so changed in every feature by the strange characters which work and sorrow inscribe on a man's face with the stern hand of Time, that few or none would have recognized him.

In the interval Christian Christiansson had carried out his plans and realized his expectations. Buried in the depths of London as a man dying on shipboard is buried in the vast grave of the sea, he had lived long as one who was dead, but his hour had struck at last. For five years he had been one of the most popular of living composers. His operas, founded on the Sagas of his own country, had made Iceland familiar to people everywhere; his works had been represented in

307

every capital; his tunes had been played in every street, and it was almost as if he had breathed over Europe and set the air to song.

Meantime he had been faithful to the pledge he had made with himself. His name was a household word, but it was no more than a name, and his identity had never been revealed. No temptation had prevailed with him to disclose it, and the few who knew his secret had found it to their interest to maintain the mystery. And now he was returning to his own country rich and famous—rich as the man who strikes ore from the rock and finds it pouring down on him in an avalanche of gold, but famous only as the "hidden folk" are famous, the good fairies who leave food and drink at the doors of poor men and then steal away before they awake in the dawn.

How changed the old world was when he emerged at length into the light of open day! The telegram he sent from London, asking for a berth to be reserved for him, had almost paralyzed the captain with excitement and delight. It was the same old Captain Zimsen, who in former days had given him the best room when he was in favor, and the worst when he was in disgrace. The moment he set foot on the ship, lying in dock at Leith, the time-serving old salt had been there—hat in hand—to lead him to his private cabin.

"Do me the honor to occupy my stateroom, sir, and if there is anything you could wish—any little dainty for the table——"

"You are very good, very obliging."

"Don't mention it, sir. It is a pleasure, a privilege, to do anything in my power for the most distinguished Icelander of modern times. Do they know you are coming, Mr. Christiansson?"

"Not yet, Captain."

"What a pity! What a reception they would have given you! But they will, they will!"

If the world was changed, the man was changed also. The buoyancy of youth was gone, and over the old captivating gaiety of manner and expression, a sad gravity had fallen, as if a lilac-tree, still bright with blossom, had been borne down by snow. But after two days at sea his spirits rose, and he felt like a slave who had been emancipated, like a prisoner set free.

It was fifteen years since he had left his own country, but he was returning to it at last, as he had always hoped and intended to do. He had left it in disgrace, he was going back to it in honor; he had left it in poverty, he was going back to it with wealth. He was going back as the prodigal, yet not, like the prodigal, empty-handed and ashamed, but able to make amends, and to wipe the tears from all eyes.

Would it be wrong to permit himself to be known? If the people of Iceland, more observant than this old captain, identified in Christian Christiansson the Oscar Stephenson who was thought to be dead, would it be false to the pledge he had made with himself to submit to their recognition? Fifteen years he had lived in obscurity—was it not enough for penance and pardon? Were not the doors of his dungeon even yet broken open? Could he not believe that he was delivered from the body of the death he had lived in? He had lived, he had died—might he not live again?

II

DURING the ten years in which he had been as a dead man all channels of communication had been closed to him, and except for information casually gathered, he had little or no knowledge of what had occurred in Iceland. And now, finding himself for the first time face to face with men who had been in constant touch with his people, he had a hundred questions which he yearned to ask: "Is my mother alive? Is she well? And my little daughter—has God been good to me and let her live, or is all my labor wasted?"

But he was afraid to learn the truth too suddenly, so he waited and watched and listened for answers to the questions he dared not ask. Meantime he tried to amuse himself with the curiosity of the captain and his fellow-passengers, who were clearly at a loss to know who he was, where he was born, and what family of the Christianssons he came from. It was a perilous pleasure, a dizzy joy, to listen to the names of his family and to hear himself discussed; and sometimes, in mortal shame of the subterfuges to which his disguise condemned him, he could hardly resist an impulse to blurt out the truth of his identity, and sometimes he had to leap up from his place in the smoking-room and fly.

"You've not been home very lately, Mr. Christiansson?" said the captain, who was smoking his long pipe after midday dinner while the ship swung along in open sea.

"Not very lately, Captain," said Christiansson.

"You'll see changes, then," said the merchant.

"No doubt, no doubt!"

"The new Constitution has worked wonders for Iceland, sir."

"Worked wonders, has it?"

"The barter trade has gone, the cash business is established everywhere, and as for the fishing, it's another industry, sir."

"Another industry, is it?"

"Judge for yourself, sir. Instead of the old open boats we have sixty smacks, manned by twenty men apiece, and going as far as six days out and home again."

"Then the people were right, after all, who used to say the old trade was doomed and the water was to be the wealth of Iceland?"

"They were that, sir," said the merchant, inflating his chest and pulling down his waistcoat. "Everybody has benefited by the change, and I shouldn't be surprised if you find your own people better off than when you left them—that is to say, if they are still alive."

"If they're still alive," said Christian Christiansson, dropping both voice and eyes.

"By the way, were you at home in Governor Stephen's time, Mr. Christiansson?" asked the captain.

"Well, yes, Captain, yes, I was at home then," said Christian Christiansson, with a momentary faltering in his voice.

"In that case you must have seen the beginning of the end. The old Governor tried to resist the change, and lived with a sword over his head all his latter days, poor devil."

"A wise old man, though, wasn't he?" said Christian Christiansson—he could scarcely trust himself to speak.

"Wise?" said the merchant, with a curl of the lip. "No man is wise who will not be warned, and he had warning enough. But it was his sons who settled *him*."

Christian Christiansson looked up with a start. "Ah, yes, of course, his sons, he had two sons, I remember. What became of them?"

"One of them is living at Thingvellir still."

"Living still, is he?"

"If you call it living—up to his ears in debt."

"In debt, you say?"

"Always has been, always will be. As for the other one—Olaf, Eric—what was his name, now?"

"Was it Oscar?" said Christian Christiansson, with a catch in his throat.

"Oscar it was—what a memory you must have, sir! Oscar Stephenson! He used to think he could do a little in your line, sir, but he was here to-day and there to-morrow, and he never did anything in his life except put an end to it. You would hear what happened—it all came out in the newspapers."

"Died abroad, didn't he?"

"Shot himself in a gambling hell, sir."

"The young rascal!" said the captain, taking his pipe out of his mouth to laugh. "*I* took it out of him though. The last time he crossed from Iceland I made him sleep in the hold."

"Serve him right, the scoundrel," said the merchant.

"A scoundrel, was he?"

"He used to beat his poor young wife black and blue, sir."

"Beat his wife, you say?"

"She died of his ill-usage, anyway. He killed his father, too. The night he went away he broke open the Governor's safe and carried off everything."

"Broke open the Governor's safe?"

"That's so—the old man died a pauper."

"Died a pauper?"

"Left nothing behind him, so it comes to the same thing. Every stick in the house had to be sold to the new Minister."

"But is this true?"

"True enough, sir. Everything came out at the general

election. The Governor and the old Factor were rival candidates, and they told us the family secrets."

"And is this all they say at home of Oscar Stephenson?"

"All? Not a tenth of it."

"Then his very name must be hated in Iceland?"

"Hated? Execrated, sir. Not that anybody cares about the old Governor; he is dead and gone with the rotten system he tried to support, but as for his son, nobody can say bad enough about him."

"So that if he had lived and come back alive——"

"He would have been hounded out of the country, sir."

"Just so, just so," said Christian Christiansson, and rising with a startling gesture he stumbled back to his stateroom.

The merchant looked after him uneasily. "Who the deuce can he be, I wonder!"

"I wonder!" said the captain, pulling at his extinguished pipe.

It was impossible! The odium attaching to the name of Oscar Stephenson made it impossible that Christian Christiansson could ever reveal his identity. He had thought that the dust of death might cover his transgressions, but rumor and report had kept them alive and magnified them. Even the effort of his family to conceal the truth about his offenses had given birth to falsehood and fostered slander.

The people of Iceland must never know that Christian Christiansson was Oscar Stephenson. If they suspected, he must use means to deepen his disguise; if they questioned, he must deny.

What else had he expected? In thinking he could ever allow himself to be known in his true name and character, what secret craving of pride and vanity had he been cherishing unawares? His errand to Iceland was one of penance and atonement—at the bottom of his heart he had been looking to it as the top and high-tide of his career, the flush and crown of his success, as the hour of triumph when he was to justify the friends who had loved him, and to put to rout the enemies who had hated him, and to come off with flying colors at the last. If so, he was rightly punished. Oscar Stephenson was dead, and nothing and nobody could bring him to life again.

III

CHRISTIAN CHRISTIANSSON became more reserved as the vessel approached its destination. Every mile of the voyage was full of memories, and the sweetest were the bitterest, the happiest were the hardest to bear. He was standing in the bow when he caught his first glimpse of Iceland, glimmering white and blue like a sheeted ghost in the distance where its glaciers rose out of the sea. And then, thinking of the enchanted hopes of the days when he had first seen it so, and how many of them now were dead under ashes, he would have broken down badly but for the captain, who came up behind him and said in his cheery croak:

"There it is, sir! There's your country! That's the place you've made them all hear about!"

Christian Christiansson returned to his cabin immediately, and he was not seen on deck again until the following morning, when the "Laura" was steaming up the fiord. And then the merchant, in his shore-going hat and overcoat, began to point out the sights to him as to a stranger.

"There's the old town, sir. Bigger, I'll be bound, than when *you* saw it last. That's the new shipyard on the right, and that's the leper hospital on the left. This is Engey, the island with the eider duck—famous place for young folks courting, sir. That's the old cathedral in the middle, and that's Government House to the left of it. They're nearly hidden by the new warehouses now—I built them myself, sir."

The "Laura" cast anchor under the town, amid a fleet of smacks and coal-hulks, and remembering how he had stood there last, Christian Christiansson's emotion would have mastered him again but for the bustle that was going on around—the orders of the captain from the bridge, the shouts of the sailors who were lowering the ladder, and the cries of the men who had come out in small boats and were clambering up to the deck.

Christian Christiansson knew most of the boatmen, though some were old who had been middle-aged, and some were

21

middle-aged who had been young, and some were bearded who had been boys. But none of them recognized Christian Christiansson, as they tipped their hats to him and pushed past to the officers of the ship.

"Good morning, mate! Good morning, Captain! What passengers this time?"

"Only one, besides Jon Oddsson, but he's a host in himself—Christian Christiansson!"

"What! The *great* Christian Christiansson?"

In less than three minutes half the small boats were scurrying away to carry the news to the town, while the owners of the other half were scrambling for Christiansson's luggage to have the honor of taking it ashore.

"Easy on, my lads," shouted the captain. "Mr. Christiansson will go with me in the ship's boat, and don't you forget it."

It was a full half-hour before this could come to pass, for Christian Christiansson had first to drink the captain's health and the ship's luck in the chart-room. When at length they were going ashore, with portmanteaus piled up in the bow of the boat and the captain chattering in the stern, it was almost more than Christian Christiansson could do to control himself under the memory of the dark night on which he went the other way, with no one to see him off except his mother, who sat by his side and held his hand as if she could never part with it.

When the boat drew up alongside, the jetty was packed with people, and as Christian Christiansson stepped ashore, with the air of a man trying to escape from observation but conscious of being under the full fire of it, a little fat fussy person with asthmatical breathing—Christiansson knew him instantly—bowed deeply and began to read something from a sheet of foolscap paper.

It was an effusive address, drawn up hastily by the Chairman of the Town Board, in the name of the inhabitants, beginning, "Illustrious fellow-countryman." and going on to hail Christiansson as one who had "revived the ancient spirit and glory of a thousand years ago."

Agitated and ashamed, hardly daring to speak lest the sound of his voice should betray him, Christian Christiansson replied with a few commonplaces, and then, amid a whispered chorus of "Modest!" "The modesty of greatness, sir," he tried to push his way toward the hotel.

He had not made many paces before he was confronted by a young man in the uniform, hat, and cloak of a Government Secretary, who parted the crowd and said, in the breathless gasps of one who had been running:

"The Minister's compliments, sir, and will you do him the honor to become his guest at Government House?"

Christian Christiansson tried to excuse himself, but every eye was on him, and seeing that he could not escape without the danger of exposing himself to suspicion, he yielded and allowed himself to be led away.

The little journey to Government House was like the progress to a Calvary. Every step was sown with memories—memories of the pleasures, the passions, the darling joys, the sorrows and the tragedies of the past—but while they seemed to strike up at him out of the very stones of the street, he had to nod and smile as the Secretary, walking by his side, rattled along with explanations and descriptions of the places they passed on their way.

"This is our principal thoroughfare, Mr. Christiansson. That is our chief hotel, and this is our national bank. The large building flying the Iceland falcon is our parliament hall. That is our old cathedral, sir, and this—this is Government House."

Suffocated with shame, choking with a sense of duplicity, and trembling with the fear of detection, Christian Christiansson continued to say, "Yes" and "Is that so?" until he reached the porch of his old home. And then, remembering how and when he had passed out of it last—alone, at night, disgraced and with his father's door closed against him—it was almost as much as he could do to restrain an impulse to turn about and fly. But just at that moment his father's door opened quickly, and there on the threshold another man, in the uniform of the Governor, stood waiting with outstretched hand to welcome him.

The palpitation of Christian Christiansson's heart was almost choking him. What wild harlequinade of real life was this, that he who had been so nearly flung out of Iceland should be received back to it with open arms? What mad game of blind-man's buff were the powers of destiny playing with him? It was not for nothing that he had taken the name of Christian Christiansson. What invisible wings of Fate had been over him when he did so? And were they plumed to honor or to dishonor, to reward or to punishment, to joy or to sorrow, to life or to death?

IV

THE Sheriff made Minister was the same man still. He received Christian Christiansson with suavest politeness but without a trace of recognition.

"Welcome!" he said. "Welcome to Iceland! My wife is in the drawing-room—she will be delighted to see you. We may go this way—this way through my bureau—do me the honor to follow me. Don't knock against the stove—strangers do sometimes. A ramshackle old house, sir, for which my predecessor was responsible—I'm building a better in another part of the town. You've not yet dined? How fortunate! In these high latitudes we keep up primitive customs, Mr. Christiansson. We dine in the middle of the day, and you are just in the nick of time. I was holding a meeting of my executive when the news of your arrival reached me, and I took the liberty to invite one or two of my colleagues. This is the drawing-room—have the goodness to step inside."

Muttering monosyllables only in reply to the Minister's explanations, Christian Christiansson followed him through the house that was as familiar as the palm of his hand until he came face to face with his hostess and the friends who had been invited to meet him.

The hostess was an acquaintance of his school-days, grown middle-aged and matronly, and the friends were the Rector of the Latin School, looking elderly and iron-grey, and the Bishop, looking white and old. They received him with the utmost cordiality, but, like the Minister, without a sign of recognition.

Christian Christiansson bowed but scarcely spoke. He was no longer in fear of discovery, for now he knew that unless he wished it otherwise he could pass through Iceland unknown; but standing there in the old home, with the traces of his boyhood about him, his heart swelled and his throat thickened, and it was as much as he could do to control himself.

After a moment a servant announced dinner, and the Minister led the way to the dining-room. It was the same old room, with the same furniture, and hardly altered in any particular. But it was full of ghosts in the eyes of him who entered it again. In one rapid glance Christian Christiansson took in everything—the chair his father used to sit in, his mother's place, Magnus's, and Thora's. And remembering that all these were gone; that everything connected with his own people had faded away; that the old house was inhabited by others now, and nothing remained except himself and he had neither part nor lot in it, the palpitation of his heart nearly choked him again, and he sat at the table like a guilty thing.

But if Christian Christiansson was silent the Minister talked incessantly.

"You will find that Iceland knows all about you, Mr. Christiansson—all about you! Speaking for myself I may say that in addition to the ordinary channels of intelligence I have some private sources of information. My son—you know my son, I think?"

Christian Christiansson bowed.

"My son has kept me constantly informed, so you will find me abreast of all your movements. Certainly, I take it amiss that he did not warn me of your coming—but perhaps he didn't know. He didn't? I thought as much. Not that he would have told me if you had wished it concealed. Neils is discretion itself, sir—discretion itself. For instance I could never persuade him to tell me who you were. I tempted him —I confess I tempted him. But no! 'Business is business, father,' he would say, and I was forced to be content."

"Iceland is honored that you show yourself first in your own country, sir," said the Rector.

"Indeed it is, Rector, and Mr. Christiansson will find that his fame is no empty bubble here."

"There isn't a student who doesn't sing your songs, sir," said the Rector.

"Nor a girl of fourteen in a farmhouse who doesn't play your music," said the Minister's wife.

"Wonderful!" said the Minister himself. "It's perfectly wonderful! But I always say the musician is the international artist. Other artists—the poets for example—require their translators, but the musician needs no go-between. He uses the one universal language, and when he speaks the whole world may hear. What a gift! What a thing it must be to be among the great composers! Perhaps it has its penalties, though. What does the poet say? They learn in suffering what they teach in song. What a thought that is! I wonder if it's true? I wonder if every great song, every great symphony, every great opera is born of the suffering— the actual real life suffering, and perhaps in some cases the sin and sorrow—of the man who created it! What should you say, Mr. Christiansson?"

"God knows," said Christiansson, and after that there was silence for a moment.

"Poor Stephen!" said the Bishop suddenly, and then everybody raised his face from the table.

"I was thinking," said the Bishop, "that if sin and sorrow, added to the gift of genius, go to the making of great music, somebody was born in this very house who should have left immortal works behind him."

Christian Christiansson had looked up with the rest, and now the Minister leaned across to him and said in an undertone, "A sad story, sir—a son of my predecessor who made shipwreck of his life, poor fellow."

"You mean Oscar Stephenson?"

"Yes, indeed. But can it be possible that you knew him?"

"We talked of him on the steamer."

"Ah, of course, certainly! And then he was a kind of humble confrère of yours, and conducted at Covent Garden. What a tragedy! What a scandal! When the dreadful news came from Nice everybody here felt ashamed. Such a well-known Iceland name, and the son of a former Governor! It was almost as if Iceland had been dishonored in the eyes of the world, sir. So different, so entirely different, from the effects, the glorious effects of your own magnificent achievements."

Christian Christiansson was quivering from heart to eye-lids, but the same mysterious impulse that compels the lamb to confront the dog forced him to go on.

"His mother is alive, isn't she?" he said.

"Anna? Yes! She's alive—that's nearly all you can say about her."

Christian Christiansson's voice deepened and shook. "Is she sick?" he asked.

"Sick in fortune at all events. When the old Governor died she went to live with her other son at Thingvellir, and he is in trouble again, poor creature."

"In debt, isn't he?"

"Yes, he is in debt to the Bank for the interest and prin-cipal of some money which his father borrowed on mortgage to keep his brother out of prison."

"And what is the Bank going to do with him?"

"Sell him up immediately."

Christian Christiansson sank into silent reverie again, and when the conversation at the table had taken another turn, he said unexpectedly:

"He left a child behind him, didn't he?"

"Who, sir? Oh, Oscar Stephenson? He did—a girl."

"She's living, too, isn't she?"

"She is, sir—that is to say, for all I know to the contrary. Rector, Oscar's little daughter is still alive, is she not?"

"Alive and well and hearty," said the Rector.

Christian Christiansson's eyes brightened visibly. "That's good news, at all events," he said.

The altered tone startled everybody, and nobody spoke for a little while. Then the Minister said:

"It is really very good of you to take an interest in the family of your poor dead confrère, and if I'd had the least idea you wished to hear more about them it would have been so easy—I might have invited the banker."

"I'll see him to-morrow," said Christian Christiansson, and then, breaking through his reserve, he talked for the next half-hour on other subjects.

He talked well and the company were delighted, for there was no one to know that his vivacity was nervousness and his laughter something like shame. When the dinner was at an end the Bishop, who had fixed his eyes constantly on Christian Christiansson, rose and held out his hand to him.

"It has been a great happiness to have seen you, Mr. Christiansson," he said, "and I trust we may meet again. I know nothing of music, sir, but I rejoice to see that the noble musician is only another name for the noble man, and I pray God to bless you body and soul."

Christian Christiansson could not trust himself to reply, for the Bishop's praise added a new bitterness to his remorse, so he stooped over the old man's hand and kissed it.

The Bishop was pleased and touched. "How charming he is! How perfectly charming!" he said, as he put on his overcoat in the porch. "He reminds me of some one I've met somewhere."

"Me, too," said the Rector.

"Those beautiful manners, that captivating smile, and that voice that goes through and through you!"

"Does he resemble—or is it only because we have been talking at table——"

"You mean poor young——"

"Yes."

"Ah me!" said the Bishop as he opened the door. "What brave things he might have done if Heaven had willed it!"

"He might have been another Christian Christiansson by this time," said the Rector.

"Poor Stephen!" said the Bishop.

"Poor Anna!" said the Rector, and the two old friends went heavily down the path.

Meantime the man they were talking of, though they did not know it, was going through an agony of self-reproach. The duplicity of winning his way to the love and esteem of his people under the cover of a false name was suffocating him. It was necessary, it was inevitable, it was a part of the conduct that was forced upon him by the errand that had brought him home, but if they who welcomed him in the ignorance of their enthusiasm could know who he was, how their hearts would turn from him; how their sympathy would change to loathing and their admiration to contempt!

The evening was one of prolonged suffering to Christian

Christiansson, for everything that happened in that house, every trivial object that met his eye, seemed charged with the power to torture him. As soon as he could, he excused himself, and asked to be shown to his room.

They showed him to the bedroom that had been occupied by Thora!

That was the last drop in his cup. He felt like a man who had stumbled into a hidden grave, and he wanted to say, " Give me any room in the house except this." But he dared not speak, lest his slightest word should betray him.

When the door was closed, he flung himself in the armchair before the stove, and then one after one, as by flashes of lightning, he saw over again the scenes of his life with which that room was associated. He thought of his wedding night, when with a fluttering heart he came on tiptoe into the cosy nest of his bridal chamber, and heard Thora's tremulous breathing behind the curtains of the bed. He thought of the joyous morning when her pale face shone like sunshine, and the air of the room was full of auroral radiance, because a child was born to them. He thought of the dark day when he found her lying dead, and of the heavy hour when he took his last look at her, and buried his compositions in her coffin.

Oh, miserable mummery! Oh, broken and senseless vow! Yet not senseless either, save to his own violated intention, for now he knew why he had taken the name of Christian Christiansson. In the blind spasm of his accusing conscience he had thought it was merely in order to deny himself the fame which his works were to win for him, but the inscrutable and ironical powers of Destiny had sterner purposes than that.

It was in order that, being dead as Oscar Stephenson, he should yet return to Iceland; in order that he should see the accumulated consequences of his conduct; in order that he should follow, as if with bare feet on the hot ground of a geyser, the footsteps and the funeral of his youth; in order that the living might torture him with gratitude, and the dead with memories; in order that God's right hand of Justice should fall on him as it had never fallen before, and everything he had done should be paid for.

This was why he had taken the name and won the fame of Christian Christiansson. And the martyrdom of his new life was beginning.

V

As soon as the Bank opened in the morning Christian Christiansson called on the manager, and was received with extravagant politeness.

"I must take the liberty to introduce myself," he began.

"Quite unnecessary," said the banker with a bow, "all the world—I say all the world, sir, has been introduced to you."

"You would receive a letter from my banker in London——"

"We did—it came with the mail that was brought by the 'Laura.'"

"I think it asks you to honor my signature up to two hundred thousand crowns."

"That is the amount, sir—two hundred thousand. And if you wish to draw any of it immediately——"

"I do," said Christian Christiansson, and taking a large pocket-book from his breast-pocket he drew out a cheque-book and took up a pen.

"Mr. Palsson," he said—the banker started at the mention of his name, then bowed and smiled—"I was much touched by a case of distress which the Minister spoke of at dinner yesterday, and I could wish to be of some assistance."

"You are very generous, Mr. Christiansson, and if I can be of the slightest use to you—I say if I can be of the slightest use, sir, pray be good enough to command me."

"It was the case of the family of the late Governor—I understand that they are in debt to the Bank and that the Bank is in the act of distraining."

"Unhappily true, sir, but the Bank has been very indulgent—I say the Bank has been very indulgent—it was impossible to hold back longer."

"I think that the debt is for interest on a mortgage on the Inn-farm at Thingvellir, and that the money was borrowed by the father of the present owner?"

"That is so, sir, but the interest is long in arrears, and

the mortgage—I say the mortgage itself, sir, is the reverse of a good security."

"Mr. Palsson," said Christian Christiansson, "if I were to pay you the interest out of my own pocket would that stop the proceedings?"

The banker's breath seemed to be arrested. "You are very good, sir," he said after a moment. "But the interest is large; you can hardly be prepared for the amount of it."

"What *is* the amount of it?" asked Christian Christiansson.

"Eight thousand crowns at least, sir—I say at least eight thousand. And in any case I should be unable to receive it. Things have gone too far. The deed of execution has been served, the advertisements of the auction have been published, and the whole matter is now in the hands of the Sheriff."

"When is the auction to take place?"

"Let me see," said the banker, consulting a newspaper, "this is the last day of the year, the auction is advertised for to-morrow, sir."

"Did you say to-morrow?" said Christian Christiansson, rising suddenly.

"To-morrow at nine in the morning, sir."

Christian Christiansson resumed his seat and sat for some moments nibbling the top of the pen. Then he said:

"Mr. Palsson, I have been many years abroad, but I seem to remember that when landed property has to be sold by the law in Iceland three auctions are necessary—two at the office of the Sheriff, and the third on the estate itself."

"That is so, sir, but unfortunately this is the third—the two others have taken place already."

"So the Inn-farm must go to the hammer in any case?"

"It must go to the hammer in any case."

"You think there is no help for it?"

"I am sure, sir—I say I am sure there is no help for it."

"Ah, well—if it must be, it must be," said Christian Christiansson, and then, as by an after-thought, dipping the pen in the ink, "The interest is eight thousand crowns, you say?"

"At least eight thousand, sir. With legal and other expenses probably ten—I say probably ten."

"And the principal is——"

"The principal is one hundred thousand, sir."

"Poor souls, poor souls!" said Christian Christiansson. He began to write his cheque, but the banker went on talking.

"I am sorry for the mother, sir—I say I am sorry for the mother. She belongs to a generation which is rapidly passing away, but there are still many in the town who remember her. A good, motherly soul, sir—it is a pity misfortune should fall so fast on her in the evening of her days——Blotting paper?"

"Thank you."

"I am sorry for the son, too—I am very sorry for the son. An Ishmael, sir—always was and always will be—but he seems to have had a terrible time of it. To tell the truth the farm was frightfully over-mortgaged at the beginning, and if he had thrown it up fifteen years ago it might have been better for himself and the Bank and everybody. Apparently he wished to hold on to it for the sake of the family, and to give the poor wretch his due he has made a splendid fight for it—I say he has made a splendid fight for it."

Christian Christiansson had written his cheque and was tearing it out of the cheque-book.

"Then, as you say, sir, the mortgage was not made by himself, and everybody knows the conditions under which the first debt was contracted. Ah, if that scapegrace brother could only be here to-day! When a man does wrong he seems to think the consequences of his crime will end with his own action, but they are like snowballs rolling in the snow—I say they are like——Two hundred thousand crowns, sir?"

Christian Christiansson had handed his cheque to the banker, and the banker, fixing his eye-glasses, was reading the amount of it.

"Do you really mean that you wish to draw the whole sum at once, Mr. Christiansson?"

"If you please," said Christian Christiansson.

The banker began to laugh. "Certainly we have no highwaymen in Iceland, sir—I say we have no highwaymen—but unless the money is wanted for immediate purposes——"

"It *is* wanted for immediate purposes, Mr. Palsson."

"In that case, of course—certainly—may I ask you to wait a little?"

It took half-an-hour to find the money for Christian Christiansson's cheque, and when it came it was in three banknotes of fifty thousand each, signed specially by the Minister, and fifty other notes of a thousand. Christiansson put the whole of them in his pocket-book, and they filled it to its utmost capacity.

"I've given you a great deal of trouble, Mr. Palsson."

"It has been a pleasure, sir—I say it has been a pleasure. I only regret that I was unable to help you in that other matter. If you had come to me two days ago I should have sent a messenger to the Sheriff, and perhaps he——"

"Who is the Sheriff in that case, Mr. Palsson?"

"The Sheriff of Arnes, sir. He lives at Borg."

"How far is that from Thingvellir?"

"Only some thirty to forty miles, sir."

"About as far as from here to there?"

"About the same, sir, but in this country of no roads and no railways that is sometimes a long day's journey."

"Just so! Good day, and thank you, Mr. Palsson!"

"Good day to you, Mr. Christiansson," said the banker, and looking after him he thought, "What does he want with two hundred thousand crowns at once, I wonder? And why —I say why did he wish to pay the interest for Magnus Stephenson?"

"Thank God I've come in time!" thought Christian Christiansson.

And going out of the Bank he told himself, with a thrill of hope and joy, that the inscrutable powers of Destiny, which seemed to have made him the plaything of chance and error, could not be wholly evil if they had brought him back to Iceland at the moment of his people's greatest peril, that he might succor and save them at their utmost need.

VI

THE morning was heavy and cheerless. Dark woolly clouds were rolling over the mountains, a cold wind was coming up from the east, and the voice of the North Sea was loud and shrill.

"We shall have snow before the year's out, sir," said one of a group of fishermen who were stamping their feet and beating their arms at the bottom of the Bank steps.

"No time to lose!" thought Christian Christiansson. "I must send for horses immediately and start off without delay."

But before going to Thingvellir there was something to do in Reykjavik, and that was the most important thing of all— by some excuse or subterfuge he had to see his child as a first step toward claiming and recovering her. She had been ten years at the farm, but he thought she was still at the Factor's, and he bent his steps in that direction.

Of the Factor himself he knew no more than he had been able to glean at breakfast without betraying a particular interest—that he was still alive, that enough had been saved out of the wreck of his fortunes to enable him to keep his house, and that he lived the life of a misanthrope, blaming the whole world for his misfortunes and all the trouble of his days.

Christian Christiansson might have walked to the Factor's blindfold, but the house itself when he came in front of it seemed strangely unfamiliar. The once bright little villa looked like a witless man who has lost his place in the world and all hope and all respect for himself. The white paint of the walls was cracked and dirty, the windows were smeared with the salt which is borne on the breath of the sea, the garden was wild, and the cobbled path was overgrown with grass.

It was hardly like a house a young girl might live in, but after he had rung the bell he listened for a light step in the hall. The door was opened by a withered old woman in white ringlets, with her gown tucked up in front. It was Aunt Margret, but the little old maid, once so pert and dainty, had the neglected and frightened look of a cat in an empty house, left behind and forgotten.

Her face was the first he had yet seen of the faces of his own people, and so hard did he find it to play his part that he had mentioned her name before he was aware of it, and she had started perceptibly, as if at the sound of a familiar voice.

"Is your brother at home, Margret Neilsen?" he asked.

"He is always at home," she answered, "but he never receives anybody now. Who shall I say wishes to see him?"

"Say that Christian Christiansson would like to speak to him."

Aunt Margret, who was not wearing her spectacles, seemed to listen for a moment as to a voice that came to her from afar, and then she asked him into the house.

As he passed through the hall he listened, in his turn, for the silvery voice he wished to hear, but he heard nothing save the sound of his own footsteps, for the house echoed like a vault. The sense of change made him forget for a moment the object of his visit, and when he stepped into the sitting-room and found the familiar room so different from what he remembered it, so bare, so bleak, so stamped with the seal of poverty (with its scrap of worn carpet on the floor and its two broken firebricks in the cold stove), he felt as if the ironical powers that controlled his fate had brought him there not to see his child but only to torture him.

After a moment the Factor came in with the old fire in his eyes and the old spirit in his step, but wearing a threadbare skull-cap over a threadbare suit that had once been black, and looking like a grey rock in a green place when the sun has gone from it, leaving it grim and hoary.

"I heard of your arrival, Mr. Christiansson," he said, "and I suppose I ought to thank you for your call, but I am an old man who has lived past his day, and I can't think why you wished to see me."

Christian Christiansson had his subterfuge ready. "Coming from London," he said, "I thought I might be able to tell you something of your daughter."

"Helga? You know my daughter Helga?"

"I used to know her, but our ways have parted, and we have met only once in ten years. Nevertheless I know all about her, and can tell you what has happened."

"What *has* happened, sir?"

"She has become a great singer."

"A singer, has she?"

"A great opera-singer."

"Then she's rich, I suppose?"

"In the way of being so, perhaps, but famous at all events, and a favorite all over Europe."

The Factor was silent for a moment, leaning on his stick; then he said:

"Well, that will suit her mother, I daresay. As for me I don't think it matters. It's ten years since Helga Neilsen left Iceland, and I've never seen the scribe of a line from her since. If she's rich I'm poor and she doesn't care anything about it. What I call a daughter is one who remembers her father when he is old and past work and the world has got its heel on him. I had a daughter like that once, but they killed her between them—they killed her between them, I say."

Th old man's voice was breaking, and thinking to comfort him Christian Christiansson said, hardly knowing what he was saying:

"I heard of your trouble, Mr. Neilsen."

"When did you hear of it? Helga couldn't have told you. She had too much to do with her sister's death to talk of it. Did you, perhaps—in those days you speak of—did you know my daughter's husband?"

"Yes," said Christian Christiansson, for in that heart-quelling moment there seemed to be no escape from it.

"Then you knew a scoundrel, sir," said the Factor.

Christian Christiansson dared not flinch, though the Factor's lash had cut him to the bone. With a throttled utterance he tried to plead for charity. "Oscar Stephenson never ceased to reproach himself for his share in Thora's death or to mourn——"

"It's a pretty way to mourn for one daughter to corrupt another," said the Factor.

"Corrupt?"

"What else was it? He hadn't been a year in London before he persuaded Helga to follow him."

"Mr. Neilsen, I have no right to speak for the man we are talking of, but Helga is your daughter, and if it is any comfort to you I tell you that you are wrong—I know you are wrong——"

"*How* do you know—he lived in the same house, didn't he?"

"Nevertheless I—I believe in my heart that whatever his failures of duty to your daughter Thora while she was alive, when she was dead he reverenced her memory too much to——"

"Was it reverencing her memory to sell the right to violate her grave, and then waste the money at the gaming-tables?"

The perspiration was breaking out on Christian Christiansson's forehead and he had forgotten the object of his errand, when the door opened and he looked up in the expectation of seeing Elin. It was only Aunt Margret again, but now washed and oiled, and wearing her spectacles.

Christian Christiansson placed a chair for the childless woman, and began to talk about the child.

"The man we are speaking of had his faults, God knows, but if you had heard him talk about you, sir, and your sister and his daughter—especially his little daughter——"

"He talked about his daughter, did he?"

"Constantly—he seemed to be always thinking of her."

"He never did anything else, then. He left me to bring her up and never sent a penny toward her support."

"He was poor himself perhaps—indeed I know he was poor."

"Then what about the letters he wrote to his mother, bragging of his business and the fine friends he was making?"

Christian Christiansson dropped his head.

"And when my own business was broken up, did he offer to relieve me of my burden?"

"That was afterward, Oscar—you are confusing the dates," said Aunt Margret.

"Hold your tongue, Margret Neilsen—I know what I'm saying. No, sir, when the ingrate at Government House made me a bankrupt and I didn't know if I should have a roof to cover me, it was the father's brother who had to take the child off my hands."

"Magnus?"

"Magnus Stephenson, and he had his mother to provide for already."

22

"Then Elin is at Thingvellir! And Magnus has been bringing her up all these years! How good of him! And now he is a broken man himself, poor fellow!"

"Serve him right if he is," said the Factor. "I've no pity for him either—he was the beginning of all the trouble."

"But when a brave man who has borne other people's burdens——"

"A brave fool, you mean, sir. Fortune comes to every man once, sir, and it came to him, but he wouldn't have it. Look at this room, sir. You may not believe it, but I used to have four assistants eating and drinking with me here, and Magnus Stephenson was one of them. He had good ideas in those days, and if he had stayed with me we should have kept out the free traders, and he would have been the first man in the west of Iceland by this time. I gave him every chance, too. I was willing to make him my partner and marry him to my daughter Thora. But no, grasp all lose all, he insulted my girl and turned up his nose at my contract. And now he's down, but he's not done yet. What gets wet on a fool gets dry on a knave, and Magnus Stephenson will be worse than a bankrupt before we've heard the end of him."

"Mr. Neilsen," said Christian Christiansson, who was breathing heavily, "you are wrong again, and you ought to know it."

"Who says I am wrong, sir? And what am I wrong in?"

"You are wrong in thinking that when Magnus Stephenson refused to marry your daughter Thora he did so from selfishness."

"If it wasn't selfishness, sir, what was it?"

"It was unselfishness—sublime unselfishness."

"So?"

"Thora had found that she loved his brother Oscar, and to make her happy Magnus was willing to give her up to him. But the contract was made, and you had built all your hopes on it, so to save your daughter from your displeasure he allowed it to appear that he refused her, although he loved her dearly and his heart was breaking."

The Factor rose to his feet with a wild lustre in his eyes. "But is this true?" he said.

"It is God's truth, sir."

" Who did you have it from? "

" From one who should have told you himself fifteen years ago but dared not."

The Factor turned rigidly to his sister. " Margret Neilsen, do you hear what he is saying? "

Aunt Margret, who was breathing audibly, merely bowed her head.

" I don't know what to say to you, sir. If what you tell me is true I've been hating the wrong man for half a lifetime. And yet people talk of Providence! "

" God veils His face from us, Factor. We are only His little children. He has His own plans and purposes."

" Good Lord! sir," said the Factor in a husky croak, " what purpose can there be in blinding a man for fifteen years and letting him break up all his friendships? "

He was walking to and fro to calm his nerves under the shock as of a moral earthquake.

" If I have been wrong about Magnus I may have been wrong about Oscar, also. I got frightened when he signed my name, so I helped to send him out of Iceland. And now he is dead! "

Christian Christiansson's head was down—his throat was surging.

" His father is dead, too. We quarrelled about our children, and now it seems it all began with a blunder! He was my friend for fifty years, and I've never had another. There's no such thing as making an old friend in your old age, sir, and when your friends are gone the world gets lonely. Perhaps I was hard on Oscar, too. He was my godson. I liked the boy in spite of everything, and he always came to see the old man the minute he set foot in Iceland."

Christian Christiansson wanted to throw off all disguise and cry, " And I'm here again, godfather," but he could not and dared not speak. He rose to go, and the Factor took him to the door.

" I'll come again before I leave the country," he said at the last moment, " and then perhaps I'll have something to say to you."

When the Factor returned to the sitting-room, looking like the same grey rock but with clouds enveloping it, Aunt Margret, who had scarcely moved, said in the frightened voice of one who has seen a ghost:

"Do you know who that was?"

"What do you mean?"

"That was Oscar Stephenson."

"Margret Neilson, you are mad. Oscar Stephenson is dead."

"Then he came to life again. That is Oscar Stephenson as sure as I'm a living woman!"

VII

CHRISTIAN CHRISTIANSSON left the Factor's house glowing with excitement. Oh, for the hour when he could lay aside the armor of duplicity! When he could say to his own people, "I am Oscar Stephenson. Let the world think me Christian Christiansson, but at least you must know me for who I am."

It was necessary and inevitable that he should reveal himself to his own family! How else could he carry out the plan he had formed of buying the farm at the auction to-morrow morning and giving it back to his brother? And how, except by right of blood, by right of parentage, could he claim the child and take her away with him when he returned to England?

In this mood he went back to Government House and announced his intention of going on to Thingvellir.

"Thingvellir!" said the Minister. "It's only natural, sir, that you should wish to see our great historic meeting-place, the scene of so many of our Sagas. But why go there to-day? It isn't every day the old town is alive, but this is the last of the year, you know, and before midnight we shall have many interesting ceremonies. Why not stay until to-morrow, and then I shall be happy to go with you?"

"I have a particular reason for wishing to go to-day," said Christian Christiansson.

"That's a pity, and our townspeople will be wofully disappointed. To tell you the truth, I've done nothing all morning but receive deputations asking me to offer you a public banquet. Every class of the community is excited, and the students are talking of a torchlight procession."

" That settles it, Mr. Finsen, I *must* go now in any case."

" You are too modest, Mr. Christiansson. But perhaps you don't know the way. And then look at the clouds—a snowstorm is coming."

" I know every inch of the way, and the snowstorm, if it is not too heavy, will only add to my pleasure."

" If it is not too heavy! Believe me, there's nothing in the world more miserable than being caught in a blinding snowstorm on the Moss Fell Heath. But if you must you must, sir, and if you have a particular reason for going it is not for me to keep you back."

" It is late, Mr. Finsen, and the days are short—I must get off immediately."

" I'll send for ponies without delay, sir. You'll want two— one for yourself, the other for your pony-boy. You'll be back in a few days, I trust, so you'll leave your baggage behind you."

The pony-boy with the ponies came round at noon, and by that time, the report of Christiansson's departure having passed through the town, a number of the townspeople had gathered at the gate to see him off. Among them were Palsson the banker, Oddsson the merchant, Zimsen the captain, Jonsson the chairman of the Town Board, and (most surprising of all) the Factor.

There was a tingling atmosphere of unsatisfied curiosity in the little crowd, for rumor of the two hundred thousand crowns had passed from lip to lip, and people were asking who the stranger was, who his father had been, and what he could want with so much money. When Christian Christiansson, in his long blue ulster and close-fitting fur cap, came out of the house, and parted from his host and hostess at the porch, he seemed to be in high spirits, for he saluted everybody at the gate, and mentioned most of the company by name.

This intensified the curiosity, and amid a running fire of chaff and laughter the bolder ones began to probe with questions.

"You'll put up at the Inn-farm to-night, Mr. Christiansson?"

"No doubt, Mr. Jonsson, no doubt."

"But there's to be an auction there in the morning, you know—I say there's to be an auction in the morning, so you'll be turned out to-morrow,"

"Unless," said the captain, with a wink in his weather eye, "unless Mr. Christiansson buys up the old place and turns farmer and innkeeper."

"And why not, Captain Zimsen, why not?"

"Hard work early and late, sir."

"Well, no man ever won the day by snoring."

Christian Christiansson had swung to the saddle, when the Factor came up to him with his rheumy eyes shining, and said:

"Don't be surprised if I follow you to Thingvellir. Life is short, and before I die I have something to say to Magnus Stephenson."

"We talked of *him* on the ship, sir, didn't we—him and his rascally young brother?" said the merchant.

"We did," said Christian Christiansson, and then at the last moment, the pony-boy being mounted, and everything ready, a spirit of recklessness came over him, and he added, "But you made one mistake, Mr. Oddsson."

"And what was that, Mr. Christiansson?"

"You said Oscar Stephenson had never done anything in his life, except putting an end to it, but he did one thing once, I remember. He stood for parliament when I was at home, and gave a dreadful drubbing to the dunderhead who opposed him. Good-bye!"

When he was gone it was the same is if a spell had been broken. Something in his last word, something in his laugh, and something in the lifting of his cap as he cantered up the road, had struck a vague consciousness of his identity into the gossips at the gate. For a moment they stared into each other's face in blank bewilderment and then the merchant said:

"Who the deuce can he be then?"

"Shall I tell you who my sister says he is?" said the Factor.

" Who ? "

" Oscar Stephenson himself."

It fell in their midst like a thunderbolt.

" Well, that would explain something,—I say that would explain something," said the banker, and he told the story of Magnus Stephenson's interest.

Within half-an-hour the word had gone through the town with the rush and rattle of the holme wind. Christian Christiansson was Oscar Stephenson! Almost in as many words he had said so himself, and there could not be a doubt about it!

That night at the Artisans' Institute there were a hundred stories of Oscar Stephenson. Some of them were good, and they were told with tears; but some were bad, yet they were received with peals of laughter. In the smoking-room of the hotel the students sang Oscar's songs until the lamps went out, and then they bellowed them through the darkness in a dozen different keys, while the windows rattled with the vibration of their lusty voices.

Meantime a group of sedater citizens had taken their surmise to the Minister, and he had said with his shy smile:

" We cannot uncover his nakedness, you know, but we can go on with the arrangements for the banquet, and so tempt him to reveal himself."

They went on with them immediately. The banquet was to be at the Templars' Hall the night after the stranger's return to Reykjavik. The Minister was to propose, " Christian Christiansson, Iceland's favorite son and heir!" Then the students were to sing Oscar Stephenson's patriotic hymn, " Isafold! my Isafold! great land of frost and fire." And after the guest had spoken the cathedral choir were to give Christian Christiansson's stirring anthem, " Who shall ascend into the hill of the Lord, who shall rise up in His holy place? Even he who has clean hands and a pure heart, and hath not lifted up his mind with vanity! "

Everything else was forgotten! The odium attaching for ten years to Oscar Stephenson's name was gone! The dishonor which Death itself could not kill had disappeared before the blinding light of genius, the glittering shrine of success!

VIII

MEANTIME the man himself was on his way to Thingvellir. The clouds might be low, but his heart was high; the sea might break on the black beach with a monotonous moan, but his whole being sang a song of hope. A wild activity of thoughts, imagination, feelings, and impulses possessed him, and for the first time since he returned to Iceland he was entirely happy.

God had permitted him to come in time to save his people from being made houseless and homeless! He had sinned and he had suffered, but the sacred duty of atonement was not to be denied him! The Inn-farm, which had been mortgaged to save him from the grip of the law, was to be given back unburdened to his brother! Two hundred thousand crowns were in his breast pocket, and they were to buy the old place at the auction to-morrow morning!

As he cantered up the road that led out of the town his soul careered like a leaf in autumn under a bottom wind of hope and joy. He saw himself arriving at the farm in the dusk of the evening and meeting his mother and Magnus and his daughter Elin. He heard himself saying, "Mother, don't *you* know me? I am Oscar, and I have come back to make amends." And next day, when the auction would be over, the Sheriff gone and everybody crying for happiness, he saw himself taking Elin between his knees—Elin with the eyes of Thora, yet with his own face looking at him as in a glass— and saying, "You are to come with me now, my dearest, and if you have gone short of anything as a child I will make it up to you as a woman!"

The pony-boy caught the contagion of his high spirits, and as they cantered along he sang snatches of the Elf-song:

> "Dance by night and dance by day,
> Life and time will pass away,
> Love alone will last alway."

He was a tall lad of eighteen who must have resembled his mother, for he had the pink and white face of a girl. They nad passed the hot springs and the Ellida river, and risen to the heights of the first hill on their journey before the sunshine of the boy's spirits began to be overcast. Then as they rested their ponies and tightened the girths, he said in a frightened whisper:

"Do you hear it, sir?"

"Hear what?" said Christian Christiansson.

"The Peak," said the boy, pointing to a rock of rugged outline that stood on the topmost line of the mountain to their right, with a dark cloud, that was like a great monster of the air, poised above it.

"What about it, my boy?"

"The storm and the Peak are friends, sir, for they always talk together before the wind comes down. When people hear them talking they tremble, because they know the storm is coming."

"Let us get on then," said Christian Christiansson.

In half-an-hour they had come to the bleak and barren country of the Red Hill, the Red Lake, and the Deep Tarn with its dark waters and gloomy shore, and by that time the great cloud which had been poised above the Peak was broken into many parts, and each part seemed to be fighting the others in the sky, for there were volleys of sound like thunder.

"Hadn't we better stop at the farm at Middale, sir?" said the boy.

But Christian Christiansson thought of his mother, of Magnus, of Elin, and of the auction to-morrow morning, and he determined to push on.

They were on the edge of the Moss Fell Heath when the snow began to fall. It fell at first in big flakes like dead butterflies, for there was yet no wind on the ground, although the clouds were still scurrying across the sky and the noise overhead was deafening.

Christian Christiansson remembered what the Minister had said, that of all the miseries of life the worst was to be caught in a snowstorm on this desolate moor, and for one moment he asked himself if he ought not to go back to Middale and wait there until the storm had passed. But at the next instant he told himself that the devilish powers which had dogged his steps since he landed in Iceland were trying to keep him back from the good work he meant to do, so he must go on in any case.

"You're not afraid, my lad?"

"Not to say afraid," faltered the boy.

"Let us gallop, then."

The Heath itself when they came to it was a white wilderness within the embracement of black rocks and mountains. They were only able to find the road by following the beacons, which were like white-headed sentinels in single file, with their backs to the storm, going on and on over the wide waste.

The sense of desolation was appalling, and a voice seemed to say, "Go back while there is time to do so." But again Christian Christiansson thought of his mother, of Magnus, of Elin, and of the auction to-morrow morning, and he urged his horse through the deepening snow.

They had not gone much farther when the wind came down and hurled itself in their faces. The snowflakes were pelted and slung at them like splinters of flint. It seemed as if every flake would cut through their skin. Then the cold became intense. Ice gathered over their eyes, and at every other minute they had to stop to break it away.

Finally the darkness descended upon them, the deadly, implacable darkness of the wind and snow. A wild torrent of whirling snowflakes swept over the moor and concealed them from each other. It became so dark that they could only see a few yards on either side, and they had to cry out at intervals in order to keep together.

They were now in the mighty grip of the storm and could no longer think of going back. The wind hissed and howled and wept; the snow pelted and cut. There was no shelter of rock or tree or bush on any side; there was nothing about or above them but the wide wilderness and the thickening darkness.

Christian Christiansson was sorry for the boy, but thus far his own spirits had risen with every fresh phase of the tempest. He had a sense of fighting a fierce duel with the elements. At the other end of his journey were his mother and Magnus and Elin, and if he could reach them before morning he would be able to succor and save them. It was a race as for life, for the lives of his nearest and dearest, against the wild wantonness of elemental powers. Nature herself, with more than her usual heartlessness toward man, was at devilish war with his effort to save his people. But he would conquer her! Let it snow or blow or hail or thunder, he would reach home in time for the auction!

The ponies were the first to fail. The one that Christian Christiansson rode was a strong mare of mature age, but the boy's was a young one, newly broken, and it seemed to be suffocating in the snow and the wind. After a time it turned its head from the storm and refused to go forward, and then the boy had to alight and walk in front of it and tug it along by the bridle. In a little while it stopped altogether and slid down on its side, and could with difficulty be raised to its feet again.

"He's only four, and this is his first journey," said the boy in a whimpering tone, as he laid the lash on the pony's back.

Then the boy himself began to give in. He wore bag gloves (with two thumbs but no fingers), and in tugging at the bridle he lost one of them. As a consequence his bare hand got frost-bitten and was soon quite powerless. In walking before the horse his clothes had frozen stiff, and he was hardly able to put one foot before the other. His voice became weaker and his speech more broken, and when his companion called back to him he could scarcely send forward his reply. At last in a faint voice he cried:

"Come and fetch me, sir—I have no strength left."

A little later he became delirious, talked of his mother, and tried to strip off his clothes as if he were going to bed.

Christian Christiansson experienced deep anguish of mind at the thought of the sufferings he had inflicted upon the lad, but he lifted him to the saddle with his back to the horse's head, and comforted him as well as he could in his awful situation.

"Courage, my boy, courage! The House of Rest cannot be far off. We'll shelter there. The storm will pass."

A vision of the little house of basaltic rocks, which he had entered with Helga, had been floating through his mind like a dream of the Calenture. How long it took him to get there and with what desperate exertions he never knew, but walking in front of the young pony and leading the mare beside him, he reached the little house at last.

As soon as they were under cover, the boy dropped to his knees, and, with a gibbering accent, as if speaking through half-frozen lips, he began to repeat the Creed, " I believe in God the Father Almighty." He thought he was saying his prayers.

The House of Rest was badly provided, but it had hay for the horses, and they began to munch it immediately. There was no lamp, and when the door was shut to keep out the driving snow, the place was in pitch darkness.

After a while the air became warm with the breath of the ponies, and the men's clothes melted. This made them very cold, and they had to beat their arms under their armpits to keep their bodies from shivering and their teeth from chattering. Then the atmosphere grew hot, for the ponies began to sweat, and the boy stripped off his outer garments, and lay down with the young horse, boy and horse side by side, as if they had been human companions.

Christian Christiansson threw himself upon the wooden platform prepared for travelers, and listened to the storm outside. The wind was howling and hissing around the corners of the house, and he had the sense of the snow becoming deeper and deeper about it. If the storm continued the little place might be buried before long, and then it would be difficult or impossible to cut a way out.

His heart fell low. He began to feel appalled by the awfulness of his position. The devilish elements were beating him. He was only half way on his journey, and if he could not make the rest of it before morning, his mother and Magnus and little Elin would be homeless. Yet the storm showed no sign of abating; the ponies were spent, the boy was done, and it seemed impossible to go on.

Suddenly a new thought came to him and he raised himself and cried:

" My boy, my boy! do you know the road from Borg to Thingvellir? "

" Yes, sir," said the boy's drowsy voice in the darkness.

" What sort of road is it? "

" Awful, sir."

" Worse than this? "

" Ten times worse—over the Hengel mountain and past the boiling pits, sir."

" Thank God! " said Christian Christiansson, and he lay down again with content, telling himself that the same storm that was keeping him back must keep back the Sheriff, and therefore there could be no auction to-morrow morning.

The storm still hissed and howled and wept in the wild wilderness outside, but the tempest had now lost its terrors. The boy and the young pony had fallen asleep and were breathing heavily, the mare was munching the last of the hay, and Christian Christiansson, with his heart at ease and a sense of safety, had settled himself for the night and was dropping off into unconsciousness when there came a thud on the roof of the little house.

He started up and listened, and again he heard the thud-thud over his head. The mare also heard the strange sounds, and ceasing to eat she came across to him, as if in fear, and laid her head upon his legs. It was not at first that he realized that the sounds were human footsteps and that somebody was walking on the roof, but as soon as he did so he cried out to know who was there, and a voice that was like a voice out of a grave answered, " Let me in."

He removed the saddles with which he had barricaded the door and opened it. There was then another doorway of the snow that had fallen since he entered, but in a little while he had cut it away with the spade that hung on the wall for that purpose. At the next moment a man crossed the threshold— a man and a horse.

IX

" Oh, God! What a night," said the stranger. He seemed to be scared and awe-stricken by the uproar he had come out of.

When Christian Christiansson had closed and barricaded the door afresh the darkness seemed denser than ever.

" Have you any matches? " he asked.

" No—yes—that is to say, I'm afraid they're damp," said the stranger. He struck one and it spluttered out.

"Take care then. A boy is lying asleep on the floor. Bring your horse this way."

"Thanks! How lucky I heard you! I had lost the road, and was wondering what hollow ground I was walking on when you shouted from below. It nearly frightened my life out."

It was a young voice; the stranger was clearly a young man, probably a young farmer. They talked together in the darkness, neither being able to see the other's face.

"Who are you, my lad?" asked Christian Christiansson.

"I am Eric Arnasson. I come from Thingvellir. Who are you, sir?"

"I am a traveler, and I'm on my way there."

"Going to the sale, I suppose?"

"Yes."

"Then I have just come from the house you are bound for."

"Are you a farm-servant at the Inn-farm?"

"Used to be, but the hands are all gone now. I was the last to leave, sir."

"Where are Gudrun and Jon Vidalin?"

"Farming Korastead these ten years, sir."

"And Asher?"

"He has gone too. We thinned down fast when the master got into trouble. I was with him from the time I was a little chap, but he paid me off this afternoon."

"Where's old Maria?"

"Dead long ago."

"Is there nobody left then?"

"Nobody but the master and his old mother and his young daughter."

"Daughter?"

"Well, everybody calls her so, but she's only his niece."

"Is there nobody else in the house to-night?"

"Not a soul that I know of. And *they* will not be there another night, I suppose."

"But the sale can not take place to-morrow, my lad. The Sheriff will never be able to get there to-day. He has to come from Borg, and the road over the mountain is even wilder than this."

"The Sheriff is there now, sir."

"Now?"

"I left him in the kitchen when I came away, making a list of the house property, and he was to sleep at the Parsonage."

Christian Christiansson's hair seemed to rise from his head. There was no escape from the terrible journey. He must go on in spite of the storm. His limbs felt like lead, and when he tried to move them he could only do so with a tremendous effort. But he shook off his torpor and began to saddle his mare.

"What do you think is the time, my lad?"

"I don't know, my watch has stopped. And then I have no light either. It must be seven o'clock at least. But you're not thinking of going on to-night, sir?"

"I must."

"You'll never get to Thingvellir, sir. It was bad enough for me with my back to the storm, but it will be ten times worse for you with your face to it. You'll be lost. Your friends will see no more of you."

"Good night! Take the boy back to Reykjavik in the morning."

Out on the snowfield again Christian Christiansson was conscious of nothing but a headlong impulse to go on. The saddle was damp, and he had a sensation of riding in cold water; the snow was deeper than before, and sometimes his horse stumbled up to its girths; the darkness was now the darkness of night, and it was with difficulty that he could follow the line of the beacons; the wind hurled itself against his body, the snow slung itself against his face, but still he strained along, for a new and inspiring thought had come to him.

The Almighty was fighting on his side in his fierce war with the elements! The devilish powers of Nature had been trying to keep him back from saving his people, and when he reached the House of Rest they had lulled him into a false repose, but God had sent the farm-servant to warn him that his dear ones were still in danger, and that if he stayed there until morning he would arrive at his journey's end too late! Thinking so, his heart grew strong, for he felt himself in the immediate presence of Him who was greater than the greatest tempest.

But after some two hours had passed the sacred fire of this theory began to fail him. He was growing faint, and the beatings of his heart were suffocating; he was also losing his way in the deepening snow, and when his mare stumbled into the drifts he was scarcely strong enough to drag her out of them. Then, before he was aware of it, the voices of Nature were speaking to him again.

"Why did you leave the House of Rest? The Sheriff may be at the farm, but no buyers can get there to-night, and without people to bid there can be no auction."

Just as this thought came to him he saw a red speck gleaming through the darkness, and he turned his horse's head in the direction of the light. It proved to be in the window of a farm-house, and finding the door he shouted, and presently a man came out to him.

"I've lost my way," he cried, over the wailing of the wind. "Tell me, please, what place this is?"

"This is Korastead," the man cried back, and then a woman came into the hall-way and stood behind him. The man was Jon Vidalin and the woman was Gudrun, but neither of them knew him.

"Where were you going, sir?" said Jon.

"To the auction at Thingvellir."

"You are not so far out of your road, then. Bear to the right until you cross the river, and then follow the stones until you come to the Chasm."

Christian Christiansson hesitated. "I'm tired, having ridden from Reykjavik, and it doesn't seem much good going farther. Nobody else will be fool enough to travel in weather like this, and without people to bid there can be no auction. So if you can give me shelter and a shake-down——"

"You are welcome to the shelter, sir, but if you want the place you had better go on and get there."

"Why so?"

"Because it's a Sheriff's sale, and he'll sell in any case."

"How can he sell if there's nobody to buy?"

"He'll bid for somebody himself, sir, and we all know who that is."

"Who?"

"Somebody at Government House who has wanted the farm these fifteen years."

" So you think the Sheriff will hold the auction to-morrow morning whether anybody is there or not?"

" Sure to, sir. The fewer there are to bid the better he'll be pleased, and the bigger the Minister's bargain."

" I must go on then, I suppose," said Christian Christiansson.

" Come in and melt yourself first," said Jon. " The wind is going down—it will be quiet presently."

A few minutes later Christian Christiansson was drinking hot coffee in the elt-house, while Jon and Gudrun talked of the family at the Inn-farm.

" We were servants with the family for ten years, so we know them well, sir," said Jon.

" Poor old Anna!" said Gudrun. " She would be welcome to anything I have, but with the boys growing up we haven't a bed to spare in the badstofa."

" There's an adopted daughter, isn't there?"

" There is, sir, and anybody would be glad to have her for a helper, but the master won't hear of letting her go. ' Elin shall be servant to nobody,' he says."

" It isn't Magnus Stephenson's fault if misfortune has overtaken him," said Jon. " He has the strength of Samson and has done the work of six men."

" How does he bear his troubles?"

" Badly," said Gudrun. " He never goes to church now or reads the prayers at home either."

" Yes," said Jon, " he has lost his religion, poor fellow, and when a man loses that he loses everything, you know."

" People are afraid of him," said Gudrun. " He looks like a man with no luck, and he is always beating his arms about him and driving away the good spirits that walk by a man's side."

" And what do people say is the cause of the change in him?"

" The Bank and bad times," said Jon.

" And a bad brother," said Gudrun. " His brother is dead and the old mistress has made a saint of him, but she daren't mention his name before Magnus, or he gets up and goes out of the house."

" Does he hate him so much then?"

23

"There was a time when I believe in my heart he would have killed him," said Jon.

Christian Christiansson started up and prepared to go on to Thingvellir, although his half-frozen limbs would scarcely cross the saddle or his swollen fingers hold the reins. Again his heart had fallen low, and the hope with which he had begun his journey—the hope of a joyful reunion at the end of it—was now gone.

The intensity of Magnus's feeling made it impossible that he should reveal himself to his people. If he rode up to the door and said, "I am Oscar, the report of my death was false, and I have come back rich and prosperous," what would Magnus say? He would say, "Your father is dead, your wife is in her grave, your mother and your child have gone through poverty and perhaps want, and all the consequence of your transgressions—do you think that your miserable money will make amends?" And then his brother would fling him back into the road.

Not to-night could he make himself known—not to-night at all events! Perhaps to-morrow, when the sale would be over and the Sheriff gone, and he had smoothed the way and made sure of his welcome! But now he must go to the Inn like any other traveler who had come there to be present at the auction and to bid for the estate.

Seeing his course clear in this way, his heart rose again and he pushed on with a better will. The storm had subsided, and when he came to the sudden mouth of the Almanagja the wind dropped altogether, and it was almost as if some vast volcano in the sky had poured its lava over the earth in snow.

The Chasm itself was full of memories—memories of the day of his triumph, the day of his disgrace—but icicles hung from where the flags of the nations had floated, and drifts of snow, like mighty mushrooms, were lying in the holes where the tents had been. He remembered the witch who had said "Beware of your brother," and he thought of the white face that had broken in upon the dancing. In the breathless calm the sky came out and it spanned the brant walls like a majestical roof studded with stars, but he stumbled in the darkness on to the frozen surface of the drowning pool, and almost rode up to the spot where he had sat with Helga.

At the bridge that crossed the frozen waterfall he caught his first sight of the lighted windows of the Inn-farm, and then his heart seemed to stand still. His mother, his brother, and his little daughter were there, and he had been ten years preparing to join them, but now that he was so near, he could hardly bring himself to go on.

Would his mother recognize him—she who had read his features first and known him from the cradle up? He was afraid she would, and then, in the tumult of his tossing heart, he was afraid she would not. Nobody in Iceland had known him hitherto, and now he was aware that he was less like himself than ever, for, seeing his face in a glass as he came out of Korastead, he saw that his lips were swollen and his eyes bloodshot with the heavy labor of that awful day.

He had crunched through the broken ice of the river below the bridge and reached the silent snow of the pathway to the farm, when the door opened and two men came out of the house. " The Sheriff and the Pastor," he thought. He drew rein and they did not hear him, but when they had taken the path to the Parsonage, the dogs inside began to bark.

The palpitation of his heart was almost choking him, and it would have taken little to make him turn about and fly. How long he stood there—whether five minutes or ten—he never rightly knew. A hundred thoughts, more wild than the whirling snow, were tossing within his brain. But thinking at length that Almighty God who had brought him through the perils of that fearful day—defeating the designs of the devil and of the elements, and driving him before His mighty will as before a greater hurricane—could not have led him there at last to any end save a good one, he urged his horse to the foot of the steps and raised his whip to the window.

X

MAGNUS STEPHENSON had indeed lost his religion. For
fifteen years he had believed with all the strength of his soul
that everybody in this life was treated according to his deserts; that if you did right you were rewarded sooner or later,
and if you did wrong you were punished. But experience of
the world had little by little, and year by year, inflicted upon
his profound faith in the rule of conscience the most inex-
plicable contradictions. The man who lived a good life was
not being rewarded, and the man who lived an evil one was
not being punished. What, then, was there left to believe?
That there was no God in the universe at all, or that if there
were a God He did nothing!

Magnus Stephenson had tried to do what was right. He
had taken up the burdens which others laid down and he had
struggled on with a strong heart. For fifteen years he had
labored like a slave, and though his arrears of debt constantly
accumulated, he had never allowed himself to believe that
the end was coming on. The mortgage was monstrous, the
interest was exorbitant, and the Bank would come to see
that more than he got out of the land and stock it was impossible for man to make!

But the deed of execution had been served on him at
length, the advertisements of the sale had been published, and
the two preliminary auctions had been held. Then, as if in a
moment, the man's religion had disappeared and his soul had
sent up that sublime if blasphemous cry, which since the
beginning of the world has borne to heaven the lamentation
and protest of humanity against the misery of man: "I
have obeyed Your laws; I have lived a good life; I have
assisted the poor and helped the oppressed; I have shared
my bread with the orphan and protected the widow—what
have *You* done for me?"

In the grim silence which follows that ghastly question, it
is more than a man's religion that disappears, and Magnus
Stephenson's belief in right and wrong, his faith in justice,
in conscience, and in virtue had gone down together, leaving
nothing but the fierce convulsions of his animal nature.

From the moment the Sheriff arrived to make the inventory he had done little but sit in the hall and drink. He sat there all day long, with his coarse snow-stockings over his boots, his sullen face to the stove, his hands deep in his trouser pockets, his broad forehead heavily wrinkled under the rough stubble of his iron-grey hair, his massive jaw resting on his breast, and his mighty loins making the chair creak as he moved and turned.

At intervals during the day his mother tried to comfort him.

" Don't be too downhearted, Magnus," said Anna. " The stars shine when it is dark, you know."

" Isn't it dark enough yet? " said Magnus, and he laughed bitterly and drank again.

At intervals Elin came to him also. She was a tall girl now, nearly sixteen years of age, with a whisper of womanhood in her face and form, but coming in her short blue skirt and buckled shoes she would slide into a seat on Magnus's knee and, slipping one arm about his neck, put the other hand on his hot forehead, and try to soothe him in her motherly little way.

But " There, there! That will do. Go to your grandmother. I'm tired," he would say.

Early in the day he had been tormented by thoughts of the travelers who might come from a distance to stay over-night in order to be present at the auction, and in his mind's eye he saw the Inn-farm full of them, with their indifferent talk and heartless laughter, and himself in his impotent rage itching with a desire to fling them into the road. But when the storm broke his fears on that head were appeased, and while the wind and snow wailed and wept about the house he sat for hours alone in a gloomy and tragic peace.

Besides the Sheriff, the only person who visited the house that day was the Pastor, and he came as late as ten at night to take the Sheriff back to lodge with him. By that time all that was left of the broken household had gathered in the hall, where Magnus still sat before the stove, while the Sheriff, with Anna and Elin, stood by the dresser making an end of the inventory.

" Ugh! What a night! " said the Pastor, stamping the

snow off his stockings. "You're not likely to be brought out of bed by travelers on a night like this—that's some consolation, isn't it?"

He was a garrulous old man, with a shallow heart and a shallow head, who chewed the cud of his humdrum livelihood with content on his stipend of fifty pounds a year.

"So this is to be your last night in the old home, Anna! What a pity! Well," tapping his snuff-box, "naked came I out of my mother's womb, and naked shall I return thither! Blessed be the name of the Lord!"

Magnus moved his chair impatiently and made contemptuous noises in his throat.

"I've known the old house through all its days of joy and sorrow for forty-five years, Anna. Ever since your poor father that's dead—I buried him myself, God rest his soul!——"

"God rest his soul," said Anna.

"Ever since the day he gave you away as a bride. And a nervous, blushing, tender-hearted little bride you were, too!"

Again Magnus shuffled in his chair and made noises in his throat.

"I remember it so well because it was the same year that your father's big barn was burnt down, and his cousin Jorgen was found dead in the Chasm. What a sensation that made! What inquiries! What examining witnesses! Your predecessor had something on his hands in those days, Sheriff."

The Sheriff muttered some commonplace and Magnus kicked at the smouldering wood in the stove.

"Suspicion actually fell upon your father, you remember, and because he had been drinking and was such an ungovernable man when he was drunk——"

"Oh, for the Lord's sake let's have done with this," cried Magnus.

"Magnus Stephenson," protested the Pastor, "if we *are* in trouble let us behave like God's rational creatures——"

"Rational hell!" growled Magnus, whereupon the Sheriff, to avoid further friction, closed his book with a bang, saying he had finished and was ready to go.

Magnus sat quiet while the Sheriff—a sharp-featured man

with the eyes of a ferret—put on his snow-shoes and cloak, and then with a tremor in his voice and a somber fire in his eyes he turned and said:

" Is it all over, sir? "

" Yes; it was a long job, but it's over at last," said the Sheriff.

" I mean," said Magnus, " is it certain that the auction must take place? "

" Quite certain. There has never been any doubt of it that I know of."

" Look here, sir," said Magnus, heaving up to his feet. " A Sheriff can do a good deal if he cares to use his influence. Give me another chance, and you shall have everything I owe. I've had five bad years in succession—no wonder I fell into arrears. Last spring I lost forty lambs in a single night, and next morning two heifers and a calf. The floods came in the autumn, too. And half my hay was swept into the lake. But weather like that can't last forever. We are sure to have a run of good years next. Give me four years more, sir—and you shall see what I can do."

" The thing is past praying for," said the Sheriff.

" Don't say that, sir. Listen! My people have farmed this place for a hundred and fifty years, and a man doesn't like to be the one to lose it. My own flesh and blood are in the land too—the strength of my muscles and the sweat of my brow. Give me three years more, sir—just three."

" Impossible! " said the Sheriff.

" Sheriff, come this way," said Magnus, drawing the man aside by the arm and speaking in a low voice, so that the women might not hear. " I don't care a straw about myself— I'll get along somehow, and if I don't it doesn't matter—but there's the child. She ought to inherit the farm, and she's an orphan, but she'll get nothing. Give me a chance for the child's sake, Sheriff. Don't be hard on me. Sell up half my stock to pay part of the interest and let me have two years more—only two."

" You know quite well that the mortgage is on the loose property as well as the land," said the Sheriff. " How can I sap away the security? As for the girl, she's young and strong; let her go into service."

Magnus bit his lip in an effort to control himself, and then he said, " You are quite right, sir; the girl and I can take care of ourselves, but there's the old mother. She was born in this house and she expected to die here. I shouldn't so much mind if she were gone, and to tell you the truth she's not well now, sir. Give me one more year, Sheriff—one single year."

" It's no use wasting words," said the Sheriff. " Matters have gone too far. The only thing I can do now is——"

" What, sir? "

" If you can pay me the whole of the interest before nine o'clock to-morrow morning I can stop the sale on my own responsibility."

" Eight thousand crowns! " said Magnus, raising his voice to a cry of derision; " you ask me to find you eight thousand crowns before nine o'clock to-morrow morning? You might as well ask me to find you the moon! "

" Then let us say no more on the subject. The Bank has been very patient, very indulgent——"

" The Bank! " cried Magnus, in the wild defiance of his despair. " Has the Bank got a mother? Has the Bank got a child? No! The Bank is a great, grinding monster without bowels of compassion for anybody. God damn the Bank and all its fools and flunkeys! "

" Magnus Stephenson," said the Pastor, raising his little fat hand, " I will ask you to remember that a clergyman is in your company, and if you take God's name in vain——"

" Take God's name in vain! *You* do that often enough— you do it every Sunday."

" I'll not pretend to misunderstand you, Magnus Stephenson, for I know you are deeply tainted with skepticism, and since you ceased to come to church——"

" Church! You pray to God in your churches, and what does He do for you? What does He do for any one? What has He done for me? "

" If your life had been straight and pure God would have watched over you."

" And hasn't it? Haven't I tried to do what was right? And yet God is seeing me sold up and turned out, and my dear ones left to die in a ditch."

" God chastises His own, and if we only have faith in Him——"

"Faith in Him? Where is He? Is He in the North-lands? I have never heard of it. Is He in the Southlands? I've never seen Him here, though I've seen the devil often enough. He's in the clouds if He's anywhere, and that's no use to me."

"Magnus Stephenson——"

"If God is on the earth let Him do something. Here's His chance. You call the poor His people, don't you? Well, I've fed and sheltered His people for fifteen years, and now I want feeding and sheltering myself. I want eight thousand crowns before nine o'clock to-morrow morning, and if God can do anything in the world let him find me the money and save my mother and my child from starvation. But He can't do it! He can do nothing!"

"Magnus Stephenson," said the little clergyman, raising his little fat hand again, "when you come to stand before the great white throne God will have something to forgive you."

"Pastor Peter, when I come to stand before the great white throne I shall have something to forgive God, it seems to me."

"Blasphemy! Blasphemy!" cried the Pastor, and as he followed the Sheriff out of the house Magnus sent a ringing laugh of contempt after him into the darkness of the night. At the same moment two sheep-dogs that had been lying at the door with their snouts on their paws, as if anxious to join the uproar, began to growl and bark, whereupon Magnus (who had always been a lover of animals) kicked them savagely and then reeled back to his seat by the stove.

The strangers being gone and the little family alone, Elin, who had been standing by the dresser, went over to Magnus and slid into her seat on his knee and said:

"You must not think about me, Uncle Magnus. Wherever you have to go I will go too, and what is good enough for you is good enough for Elin. And then, who knows what may happen before the Sheriff comes back in the morning? This is New Year's Eve, you know. All good things come at New Year—miracles come at New Year, Uncle."

But the sweet buoyancy of her girlish spirits, which had been the sunshine of his life for so many years, was failing him at last, and putting her aside with petulant expressions he got up and went out to the back.

Then Anna, who had been sitting in silence by the table, took the Bible and four hymn-books from the corner cupboard and rang the bell for prayers.

"I wonder why I did that?" she said. "I forgot that Eric was gone. I hope he found shelter somewhere, poor boy—I should pity a dog that had to be out of doors on a night like this."

And then Elin, in default of Magnus, read the lesson which Anna had marked for her. It was the psalm beginning, "The Lord is my Shepherd, I shall not want." And when the short chapter was finished the two women stood up and sang a hymn—Elin in the silvery treble of youth and Anna in the husky tones of age, they two only in the lonely house among the solitary hills, with nothing about them but the darkness and the snow—nothing but that and the immeasurable wings of God.

> "Happy the man whose tender care
> Relieves the poor distressed;
> When he by trouble's compassed round
> The Lord will give him rest."

Anna sat down when the hymn was ended, but Elin continued to stand by the table, and closing her eyes with her innocent face uplifted, she said a little prayer for herself.

"O Father," she said, "bless Uncle Magnus, so that he may fear no evil. Show me how to help him, so that I may not be a burden and a care. Dear Jesus, send the miracle that will save Uncle Magnus and grandma and me. It will be such a little thing to you, but such a great, great thing to us, and we shall all be so happy and dwell in the house of the Lord forever. For Christ's sake. Amen."

Then she opened her trustful eyes and said, "I'm *sure* He will, grandma," and kissing Anna she said "Good night" in a cheery voice and went off to bed.

Prayers being over, Magnus returned to the hall and began to rake out the stove for the night. The clouds hung heavier on him than ever, and thinking to banish them Anna talked of Elin.

"She grows more and more like her mother, and sometimes I think it can only be a dream that our dear Thora is dead.

If you had heard her praying for the miracle it would have filled your heart brimful. She has gone to bed quite certain that the miracle will come before morning."

"It would *have* to be a miracle to help us now, mother," said Magnus. "And miracles don't happen—except such of them as we make for ourselves."

"What do you mean by that, Magnus?" said Anna, lighting the candles.

"I mean—if I had to live my life over again, I shouldn't try to do what is right, mother."

"You wouldn't do what is wrong, would you?"

"There is no wrong and no right, mother; there is only what is best, and if I had to begin over again, I should do what was best—best for myself and for the people about me."

"You don't know what you are saying, Magnus. There are moments when it might *seem* to be best to rob, even to kill——"

"And why not?" said Magnus—he was bolting the door. "If a man came to this house to-night with eight thousand crowns in his pocket, do you think I should hesitate to take them?"

"My son, you don't mean it."

"I do!"

"You are driven to despair, Magnus, and a despairing man's words belong to the wind. If I thought you meant it I should die—I should die this very minute."

She was crying and there was silence for a moment, and then Magnus said:

"Never mind, mother. It doesn't matter whether I meant it or not, the temptation isn't likely to come to me. Give me the candle and let us go to bed."

"You have borne a terrible burden, Magnus, and if I could only have helped you to bear it——"

"You have, mother. If it had not been for you and Elin I should have gone under ten years ago."

"Your father knew he had robbed you of your inheritance, and perhaps that helped to kill him in the end."

"It wasn't father's fault altogether. *He* tried to do what was right, too. But the poor wretch who comes after the prodigal gleans in a barren field, you know."

With their candles in hand they were turning to go—Anna to the badstofa above, and Magnus to the guest-room off the hall—when the dogs, who had risen again, and were snuffling at the bottom of the door, began to growl and bark.

"There's somebody coming," said Magnus.

A moment later there was a sharp knock at the window, as with a metal end of a riding-whip, and a tremulous, high-pitched voice outside, making the customary Icelandic salutation, "God be with you!"

They looked at each other in blank surprise, while backward thoughts galloped through their minds, and then Magnus, forgetting to give the customary reply, walked back to the door, and threw it open.

There was a dull thud of heavy feet on the outside steps, and at the next moment a man stood on the threshold. He seemed to be an old man, for his eyebrows, beard, and mustache, and as much as could be seen of his hair under the peaked hood of his ulster, were white with snow. One moment he stood there as if breathless after his journey, looking from Magnus to the mother, and from the mother to Magnus. Then he said, in the same tremulous voice as before:

"Can I have a bed here to-night, and shelter for my horse?"

It seemed to Anna that he spoke to her, but instead of answering immediately, she looked across at Magnus with helpless eyes that were full of inexpressible fears. Magnus looked back at his mother and hesitated for an instant, while he held the door open with his hand. Then:

"Come in, sir," he said, and the stranger stepped into the house.

PART VII

" The ball no question makes of ayes and noes,
But right or left, as strikes the player goes;
And He who tossed you down into the field,
He knows about it all—He knows—HE knows."

I

" THE little mare is hot—she'll want a rub down and a rest before you give her a feed."

" I'll see to that, sir," said Magnus, and he went out and pulled the door after him.

Christian Christiansson had taken two paces into the hall, and was standing there like a man who is dazed. His heart was thumping against his ribs, and his pulse was beating violently, and he felt that he would fall if he took another step forward. So often had he pictured himself in that place that he could not at first believe in the reality. Coming out of the darkness, the light of the candles dazzled him, but he looked round the room, trying to remember. At one glance he took in everything—the old portraits on the wall, the old Bornholme clock in the corner, the stove and the armchair in front of it—and, fresh from the warm comfort of Government House, the Inn-farm seemed bare and bleak. This sent a chill pang of remorse to his mind, and the pain of conscience increased when he looked at his mother.

Her hair was white that had once been dark, and her face, which had been full of the loveliness of love and the beauty of happiness, was scored deep with lines of suffering. His heart yearned over her, and notwithstanding his determination not to reveal his identity until morning, it was as much as he could do to restrain himself from saying as well as he could for the emotion that was mastering him, " Mother, don't you

357

know me? I am Oscar," and then throwing his arms about her dear neck as he had always meant to do.

Meantime Anna, who had recovered her self-control and was lighting the lamp that swung from the ceiling, glanced across at the new-comer and thought, "He's nearly frozen stiff, and no wonder." With that thought she bustled about to rekindle the stove, and called on him to remove his snow-covered clothing.

"Won't you take off your cloak and boots, sir?" she said, and though the question was so commonplace he could not answer immediately, for his voice would not come.

"Your cloak and boots, sir, and I'll put them to dry by the stove."

"Ah yes, of course, certainly."

She stood by him while he threw off his ulster and shook the snow from his hair and beard, emerging a younger and stronger man, but she only thought, "A stranger, I suppose. Why does he travel in this weather?"

When he had pulled off his riding-boots, she brought him a pair of Magnus's slippers and said:

"You must have had a terrible ride, sir."

"It was pretty bad certainly," he said, and after that he got on better.

"A gentleman must have been anxious to get on with his journey to travel on a day like this."

"I was—I had something to do at the end of it."

"Have you come far, sir?"

"Altogether? Yes, very far."

"From Reykjavik perhaps?"

"Farther than that—from England."

"From England!"

"From London."

As he stooped to put on the slippers he thought his mother was looking at him, and he trembled between fear and hope of being recognized.

"I suppose," he said—his head was down—"I suppose you've never been as far as that, landlady?"

"No, sir."

"Nor any of your family?"

He could not resist the temptation to say this, but his

mother did not seem to hear him—she was on her knees, breaking sticks into the stove.

" Sit up and warm yourself, sir. My son raked out the fire, but these sticks will burn presently. You are here on business, I suppose ? "

" Yes, I'm here on business."

Anna thought of the auction and waited for the stranger to speak of it. When he did not do so she said, " Travelers come from England to buy sheep and ponies, but they don't often come in the winter, sir."

Still he did not speak (he was thinking of Elin and looking round for any trace of her), and rising from the stove Anna said:

" But you'll be hungry after your long ride—what can I give you to eat ? "

" Anything at all—anything you have ready."

" I'm afraid I have nothing ready—that is to say, nothing that is good enough for the like of you, sir."

As soon as he could find his voice after that he said, " Don't you always keep smoked mutton in an Iceland house ? "

" Well, yes, if that will do, sir."

" I should like it above all things."

There was a moment's silence, and he thought his mother was looking at him again. " Then perhaps you are an Icelander ? " she said.

" Yes, I'm an Icelander," he answered.

" What is your name ? "

Another wild impulse to reveal himself immediately to his mother, nearly swept down his fears, for he was choking with a sense of duplicity and his conscience was fighting in contrary ways, but after a moment his prudence conquered, and with a gulp in his throat he said:

" They call me Christian Christiansson."

" Well, it's lucky you found us up, sir. We were on the point of going to bed."

" I suppose the other members of your family are gone already ? "

" There's only one besides what you've seen—my grand-daughter—and she had just gone off as you came in, sir."

He looked at her as she was crossing in front of him, and

saw that she was wearing the brooch which he had given her when he came back from Oxford. That sent all the blood to his head again, and he was saying, before he was aware of it—

"Do you know, landlady, I've slept in this house before?"

"It must have been a long time ago then—I don't remember you."

"It *was* a long time ago. That," pointing to the portrait of Anna on the wall, "that is a portrait of yourself, isn't it?"

"It used to be, but I was younger when it was like me, sir."

A sudden softening came into his voice as he replied, "It was exactly like you when I saw you last, landlady."

"Then you've not been here for ten years at least, sir."

"Quite ten years," he answered. "And that," pointing to the portrait of the Governor, "is a portrait of your husband."

"It must be more than ten years since you were here, sir, for my husband is more than twelve years in his grave."

"It *is* more than ten years. In fact it is sixteen years— nearly sixteen."

She looked fixedly at him for a moment and something in her memory seemed to stir, for her bosom heaved perceptibly, but she only said, with a deep sigh, "We've seen trouble since you traveled in these parts before, sir."

"Ah, yes, I've heard of it—I heard of it in Reykjavik. You had a son——"

"That was my son who opened the door to you."

"But you had another son—a younger son."

"Yes, but—we never talk of him now, sir."

"Who's portrait is that in your brooch, landlady?"

"It's his—he is dead."

"Died in disgrace, didn't he?"

"Who knows that, sir? Man sees the deed, they say, but God the circumstance."

"They think hard things of him in Reykjavik, though. They say he robbed his father of every penny when he went away, and never sent anything home toward the maintenance of his child."

"It needs no skill to wound the defenceless," said Anna, bridling up. "The father robbed himself to save his son, if you want to know the truth, and as for never sending anything home for the child the poor boy had nothing to send, for he was poor himself, sir."

"So you found that out, did you?"

"After he was dead we did—one of his father's English friends wrote to tell us so. And all the time he had been writing letters to me to say how busy he was and how well he was succeeding—just to keep up my heart and save me from fretting."

The mother's lingering fondness for her prodigal was rising in her eyes and breaking in her voice and she was trying to turn away, but he could not let her go.

"What a pity his father didn't live long enough to hear that! It would have softened his heart toward him, perhaps."

"It didn't need softening, sir—not at the end at all events."

"His father forgave him, did he?"

"He died thinking his son had become a great man and had justified all his hopes and atoned for everything. It was only a delusion, sir, but it made him very happy."

"Your son was a musician, wasn't he?"

"Yes, sir, and from the time he was a child he used to scribble things and call them his compositions. The pieces of paper always disappeared and I never knew what had become of them, but when his father was lying dead I found out where they were."

"And where were they?"

"In his poor father's hands."

Christian Christiansson had gone on and on, while the hot blood throbbed in his brain, struggling between the desire to reveal himself and the fear of doing so, but he was drawn up at last by a stifling sense of his own unworthiness, and before he knew what he was doing he said:

"The man who could do wrong to a father who loved him like that must have been a scoundrel—a bad-hearted scoundrel, and he deserved everything that happened to him."

"He was nothing of the kind, sir," said Anna. "He may have done wrong—I'm not defending him—but a better-hearted boy was never born into the world. Everybody loved him, and he loved everybody, and as for me——"

Christian Christiansson recovered himself at the sound of Anna's faltering words. "God bless her!" he thought, and

24

his heart danced to a new song, but he only said, with a perceptible lowering of his voice, "I beg your pardon! Naturally his mother cannot think so, but this is the first time I've heard a good word for him since I came to Iceland."

"I hadn't meant to speak of him at all, sir. I never do when my other son is near—Hush! He is coming back."

But the noise which they heard behind them was that of the opening and closing of a bedroom not a kitchen door, and it was followed by the light footstep of a girl, whereupon Anna said:

"Elin! I thought you were in bed and asleep, my child."

"I was, but I awoke and heard you had a visitor, so I got up to help, grandma."

Christian Christiansson trembled from head to foot. The silvery voice at his back seemed to come to him from across a wide abyss—for it was a familiar voice but vague as with the mist of dreams and dim as with the clouds of night.

"This is my granddaughter, sir," said Anna. And then Christian Christiansson turned and saw her—a young girl as tall as a woman, with fair complexion, a soft smiling face, and beautiful blue eyes. She wore a laced bodice, a turned-down collar, a hufa, a tassel, plaited hair, and looked like the living picture of what her mother had been when he came from college.

It was his daughter, his little Elin, whom he had traveled so far to see, but it seemed to him as if all the cruel years had rolled back in a moment, and it was Thora returned to life.

II

"WELL, now that you are here, you had better lay the table," said Anna.

"Yes, grandma," said the girl.

"Put on the smoked mutton and the Rullapilsa and the Rikling, while I go to the elt-house to make coffee."

"Yes, grandma."

"Make yourself at home, Christian Christiansson—my granddaughter will wait on you."

"I will," he tried to say, but his voice would scarcely come.

Anna being gone, he sat for some moments looking at Elin while she tripped from dresser to table, and in and out of the pantry, spreading the cloth, and laying the plates and the food. The girl was so simple, so natural, so free from self-consciousness, that she seemed to be hardly aware of his presence, for she hummed to herself softly as if some song-bird in her breast could not be kept quite still. His heart swelled and throbbed as his eyes followed her about, and when she left the room the light seemed to fail in it, and when she came back the air seemed to become warm. In the dizzy happiness of that hour he felt as if he had lost a daughter in every one of the fifteen years he had lived without her, and now that she was near, so close, his hands burned and itched to hold her. He wanted to take her in his arms and say, " My child! My child! Doesn't something tell you who I am? I am your father, and I have wanted you so much and thought of you so often, and now I have come to fetch you and we shall never be parted again!" But between fear of frighten-ing her and dread of disclosing himself, all he could do was to conquer the fluttering in his throat and say:

" Your name is Elin, isn't it?"

" Yes, sir," said the girl.

" What a beautiful name it is, too—Eleen! Your father chose it, didn't he?"

" I have never heard that, sir. Did grandmother say so?"

" Grandmother and I," he stammered, " have been talking of your father. You don't remember him?"

" Oh no, sir—he died when I was quite little."

" What a loss that must have been to you, my child!"

" I can't say that, sir," said the girl, " because, you see, Uncle Magnus has been the same as a father to me all my life, and I have never known any difference."

" What a loss to your father himself then! How happy you would have made him, and how proud he would have been of you!"

" I can't say that either," said the girl again, " because he lived five years after I was born, and it seems he never took any notice of me."

" Did grandmother tell you so?"

" Oh no, sir. Indeed no! Nor Uncle Magnus neither.

But everybody knows all about my father, and even the **girls** at school knew that."

A feeling of mortal shame came over him, and the warm pulsing place in his breast grew still and cold.

"So you are not sorry your father is dead, Elin?"

"It wouldn't be right to say that, sir."

"At all events you feel no love for him?"

"I never knew him—you can't love somebody you never knew, can you? Perhaps if he had lived longer and returned home I might have come to love him. But I don't see how I could if what people say about him is true."

"What do they say, my child?"

"They say he was unkind to my mother, and that that was one of the reasons why she died so early."

"Then you never wish you could have seen and known your father?"

"How can I? If he wasn't good to my poor mother, why should I think he would have been good to me? But see, your supper is ready. Grandma will bring the coffee presently; won't you begin with the meat, sir?"

He sat down to the table but his hunger was gone. For a moment he almost wished himself back in the black night from which he had come. The girl's simple words had been ringing the death-knell of his expectations. He had left her all these years to the keeping and care of others—could he expect to come back now and find the affection he had forfeited? Ah no! He had come too late—too late! But just as one part of the plan he had formed for himself was becoming vague and shadowy a gleam of new light was shot into his brain, and his heart rose with a bound.

"Didn't grandma call you Christian Christiansson?" asked the girl.

"Yes," he answered. "Ever hear that name before, my child?"

The girl turned to him with a face glowing with excitement and said, "Everybody in Iceland has heard it, sir. It is the same as the name of the great composer who lives in England."

A deafening tumult of joy was rising within him, and he said, "So you—*you* have heard of him, have you?"

"I sing his songs, sir. They are beautiful! I think they are the most beautiful songs in the world. Would you like me to sing one of them while you eat your supper?"

"Will you?"

"I should like to," she said, and before he could catch the breath which had been suspended she had slipped off like a shaft of moonlight and was back like a ray of the sun, bringing a guitar in her hands.

"This was my mother's guitar, and now it's mine, and it's such a good one," she said, and with the utter freedom from self-consciousness which is the charm of children she sat and began to play. After a moment she stopped, with her head aside, and said:

"Which should it be, I wonder? But perhaps you know them all and would like me to sing something in particular?"

His face was down, the waves of emotion were surging through and through him. "Sing—sing anything you like, my darling," he replied.

The fluttered earnestness of his words startled her for a moment, but she only smiled with a new sweetness and began to sing, first in low, clear half-tones, and then in a high, tremulous treble that was like the peal of a lark at the gate of heaven.

Christian Christiansson could not eat; he could only rest his elbows on the table and cover his face with his hand. His own child was singing his own song to him in a voice that was like her mother's voice and like his own voice too!

When the song was done she turned to him again with eyes shining with unshed tears and said, "Isn't that beautiful?"

"It was beautifully sung, my child, beautifully!" he said. And then, after a moment, "Elin, would you like to hear something of the man who wrote that song and how he came to write it?"

Elin's eagerness was heart-breaking. "Indeed, indeed I should," she said. "Do you know your namesake then?"

"I have known him all his life, my child."

"Tell me about him. Oh, do tell me. One who has such beautiful thoughts and feelings must be so good and noble."

"He is neither the one nor the other, Elin, but only a poor wayward sinner like ourselves. In early life he did wrong by

his young wife and she died. Then he did wrong by his
father and he had to fly from his country. After that he
went through many sufferings and was guilty of many sins,
but he came to himself at the end, and then he remembered a
little daughter whom he had left behind him. He wished to
return to her immediately, and be a father to her at last, and
make it up to her for all that he had done amiss to her
mother who was dead. But there were many things to do
first, for he was like one who was buried under an avalanche
which he had brought down on himself, and he had to work
his way back to life and the world. So when he was far away
and his heart was hungry for the love of his little girl, and he
didn't know what was happening to her, and he wanted so
much—oh so much—to go to her, but could not do so yet
because he had sinned and must pay his penalty, he wrote
that song, and it was the cry of his soul to the mother in
heaven to comfort and care for their child on earth."

As Elin listened to the story of Christian Christiansson the
tears which had been standing in her eyes rolled down her
cheeks, and her bosom under her laced bodice slowly rose and
as slowly fell again.

"How beautiful!" she said. And seeing how much she
was moved by the sorrows of the man who was not her father,
the new light came to him and he asked himself why, if she
could not care for him in his true character, she should not
love him as Christian Christiansson.

There was a shadowy ghost of pain in that thought too, but
he put it aside. After years of hope and heavy labor he had
come home to claim his child, and what he had dreaded had
come to pass—her heart had been poisoned against him. But
while he loathed him as Oscar Stephenson she loved him as
Christian Christiansson! Oh, beautiful, blind, pathetic fal-
lacy, could he not let it be?

In a tumult of heart and brain that was like a whirlpool in
a dark river, he had risen to go to the girl, hardly knowing
what he was to do or say, when Anna came back with a smoking coffee-pot in her hand, saying in a cheery voice:

"Here it is at last! The fire had gone out in the elt-house,
and I had work enough to kindle it."

And then, having both in the room at one moment—his

mother and his daughter—his feelings almost mastered him again, and he had as much as he could do to keep himself from blurting out everything and so being done with further torture. But just as the words of his confession were trembling on his lips he thought, "Not to-night; to-morrow morning; and then what joy, what happiness!"

Almost at the same moment Magnus returned to the house and said, "The little mare was nearly done, sir, but I've rubbed her down and given her hay, and she shall have a mash before I go to bed."

"Let us have a bottle of brandy first," said Christian Christiansson, and a few minutes later Elin was carrying away the dishes to wash them, Anna was going into Magnus's bedroom to make it ready for the guest, and the two brothers were sitting at opposite sides of the table with the bottle between them.

III

THEY were less like each other now than ever before—the elder with his matted, black beard, his strong features, and the vertical lines in his low brow under the upright stubble of his iron-grey hair; the younger with his luminous brown eyes and delicate face, his full round forehead, and his thin, silken, light hair brushed backward to the crown.

Christian Christiansson was quivering to the core at this first encounter with the brother whom he had wronged and ruined, but he tried to bear himself bravely and to see how safe it would be to reveal his identity when the time came to do so.

"It's good of you to give up your room to me," he began.

"That's nothing—nothing at all," said Magnus.

"And perhaps you ought to know why I'm here to-night."

"Please yourself, sir—please yourself."

"To tell you the truth, then, I'm here to attend the auction to-morrow morning. I only heard of it in Reykjavik yesterday, having arrived by the 'Laura' the day before."

"So that was the business that brought you, sir?"

"It was. I've been abroad for fifteen years, and I've made

some money, and now I've come home to invest it. So knowing this was a good farm——"

"None better in Iceland, sir, if it only had a chance, and
if you can afford to buy it out and out——"

"I think I can—I've money enough in my pocket at this
moment to buy the place to-morrow and leave some for something else. I'm sorry for you, though, and if it's painful to
you to hear me talk like this——"

Magnus, who had been rolling in his chair like a man whose
mind as well as his body was uneasy, began to laugh im-
moderately. "Not at all, sir! Not at all!" he said, filling
his glass. "It's pleasant to hear of anybody having more
money than he wants. For my part, I've never had enough
to pay my debts, sir. For sixteen years I've been ploughing
the waves and now," raising his glass and draining it, "I'm
reaping the breakers, b—— them!"

Christian Christiansson trembled to his very heart at the
sound of Magnus's laughter—the bitter laughter of rebellion
and despair—but he tried to cover up his fear and to carry
it off with a cheery tone.

"Don't be too depressed," he said. "Nobody knows what
the future has in store for him. It's a pretty dark night
outside, but all the same the sun will rise to-morrow morning. Besides, there's always a sunny side to misfortune if
we'll only allow ourselves to see it. Life is sweet, my friend,
whatever happens."

"You think it is, sir?"

"I know it is, so why should we sit down on our little
handful of thorns?"

"Because some of us have nothing else to sit upon," said
Magnus, and he laughed again—the same cold, quaking
laughter.

Christian Christiansson shuddered, but struggled on.
"You think you've failed, but I know some that have
succeeded who would be glad to change places with you
any minute. They've got their gold or their fame or both
pouring down on them like an avalanche, and nothing to do
with it, nobody to share it with—so it is only so much Dead
Sea fruit being piled on their backs. You are not like that.
Even if you have to lose your land, you've got your health,

and a good character and a clean conscience, and your dear ones left to you, haven't you?"

"That's why!" said Magnus. "You don't suppose I'm thinking of myself, do you? It's just because I've got my dear ones left to me that this accursed ill-luck is so hard to bear. What's it to me to have my houses full of lambs, if the floods have come and they are floating on the lake? You talk like a man who has never known misfortune, sir."

Christian Christiansson felt dizzy. "Perhaps I haven't— perhaps I have," he said in a faint voice, "but I've known despair, and I know that no man can live by that. We can only live by hope—not what is, but what is to be—and if we cannot believe, when the clouds are dark, that the world is ruled in righteousness——"

"And is it?" said Magnus. "Does the bad man suffer in this world? Do his sheep die of the rot and his cattle tumble over the rocks, or do they increase faster than anybody else's? No, sir," he said, turning away in his seat, "if you're a rascal ready to rob your own father, the chances are you'll prosper in this world, but if you're an honest man trying to do good to everybody, as likely as not you'll do no good to yourself or to anybody about you."

The dizziness which had seized Christian Christiansson was increasing every moment, but he said:

"The world has its own way of punishing offenders, and even if they escape in life, death is always waiting for them——"

"Death?" said Magnus, swinging round in his creaking chair. "Death is a blind, blundering monster who strikes down the young and leaves the old, the happy and leaves the miserable, the innocent and leaves the guilty, the poor helpless betrayed one and leaves the betrayer! We have all seen that, haven't we? *I* have, I know that much."

The heat and flame of Magnus's husky voice had fallen to a thick whisper that was like a broken sob. Christian Christiansson dared not raise his face, but he tried to say:

"God brings out all things well in the end. I have always found it so. The march of the world may be enveloped in darkness, but it tends toward justice in the long run."

"What is the long run to me, sir?" said Magnus. "I'm

only here for a few years and I want justice *now*. I want to see the bad man punished in the present, not in some future generation. Justice, you say! The sins of the fathers visited on the children—that's the only justice I see in this world. A poor child left penniless because her father gambled or drank the money he didn't make—do you call that justice, sir? I don't!"

Magnus's thick voice was breaking again, and there was silence for a little while.

"No, no, sir! Don't tell me we get our deserts in this world—any of us—good or bad. Life gives the lie to that old story—always has, always will do. If you are a cheat or a profligate, or a prodigal, you may live in luxury and travel as far as the sun, but if you are a poor devil staying at home and working your fingers to the bone you'll get thrown out into the road. But what's the good of talking? The evil day is coming. Let it come!"

Never before had Christian Christiansson felt so little and so mean. The sources of pride were dry in him and he was brought very low in his own esteem. In the presence of the brother who had borne his burdens and broken down under them he saw himself as an abject and pitiful thing. He could not raise his head, for he felt as if his shame were written on his forehead; but he struggled to say something, and the only words that came to him seemed to scorch his tongue and parch his throat.

"I can not dispute with you," he said. "You've suffered more than I have, and no doubt your present troubles are the legacy that was left to you by the prodigal brother your mother was talking about."

Magnus's manner changed instantly at the mention of his mother. "She was talking about him again, was she?" he said.

"Does she often talk of him then?"

"Too often, and she seems to think of nothing else. He was the foundation she built her house upon, poor soul, and it fell, but she holds to him all the same."

"God bless her!" said Christian Christiansson involuntarily. "God bless all women, I say. They're always on the side of the sinners and the sufferers. They'll get their com-

pensation somewhere—they must,"—he was thinking of to-
morrow morning.

"I see no sign of it in this case," said Magnus. " She was
the best mother to him a man ever had, and he knew it, but
he repaid her with neglect and contempt."

" Contempt ? "

"What else would you call it ? He lived five years abroad
and wrote to her only once in all that time. Yet every night
she used to stand outside the door until the post passed,
winter and summer, dry or fine, waiting for the letter that
never came."

Christian Christiansson felt as if his very soul were shriv-
eling up with shame.

" She forgave him for that, though, and when he died—you
know *how* he died, everybody knows it—she thought that all
he had been trying to do when he fell into that foul dishonor was to get money enough to come back home and make
amends."

" She thought that, did she ? "

" She still thinks it."

Christian Christiansson had a sense of hysterical oppression at his heart. Again he wanted to tell all, and he dared
not. "But if it had been true," he said—" I don't say it was,
but if it had been—if your brother had really been trying
for years to make money solely in order to wipe out the debts
he had left behind him—if he had come home with the fortune in his hands——"

Magnus's dark face darkened ominously, and bringing his
great fist down on to the table he said, " There would have
been a *curse* on every coin of it, and I should have flung it
in his face."

Christian Christiansson did not ask him why. He knew
too well what Magnus meant. In an instant, by such a flash
of the lightning of the mind as must come to the guilty soul
on the Day of Judgment, the past of his life lay open before
him, and the most awful fact of it stood out with naked vivid-
ness—the desecration of his wife's grave.

It was impossible to plead that this had been only the act
of a moment; that he had repented it a thousand times with
bitter tears; that he had derived no profit or advantage from

it, and had endured for ten years its fearful penalty in the death of his identity. Again and again he had soothed himself with such excuses, but he could not cheat his conscience now. Why was he Christian Christiansson? How had it come to pass that he had two hundred thousand crowns in his pocket and that his works were known all over the world?

All the miserable sophistry and false reasoning which had made him what he was, the owner of fame and fortune, had been riddled through and through by Magnus's terrible words. All the mocking vanity which had lured him onward to that hour with promises of the great surprise, the great dénouement, when he should say, "See, I am here; I have justified all expectations," lay stark and dead and cold.

No, he could not reveal himself to his family to-morrow morning. He could not reveal himself at all. Having once become Christian Christiansson, he could never again be known as Oscar Stephenson. Thus did the dead punish him, and the desecration of his wife's grave had but rendered the vow he made to himself perpetual and registered the oath he made to her in heaven.

Christian Christiansson was feeling as if all the world had gone away from him when Anna came out of the guest-room, saying:

"There, sir! Your room is ready and you can go to bed at any time."

Magnus got up to go to the elt-house to mix the mash for the pony, and then mother and son were together again.

IV

In the confusion of that heart-quelling moment he was asking himself how he could carry out his plan of rescuing his family from their misfortunes if he could not tell them who he was, and how he could claim his daughter and take her away with him, if he could not say, "I am her father, she is mine," when chance and a commonplace word—those twin sisters of invention and wisdom—showed him what he was to do.

"I shall want to be awakened early in the morning, land-lady, for I suppose the Sheriff will come soon."

"The Sheriff, sir?"

"I've just been telling your son that I intend to bid for your farm at the auction to-morrow morning."

"So that was what you had to do at the end of your journey?"

"Yes, it was what I had to do, landlady."

She looked at him for a moment, and then asked, "What can a gentleman like you want with a farm like this?"

He did not reply, so she said, "You can not think of living in such a lonesome place as Thingvellir."

Still he did not speak, and she said again, "You might let the farm certainly, but it is hungry land, I assure you, and everything depends on how you work it."

She busied herself about the table as if trying to find something to do. "My son," she said, "is the only one who has ever been able to work it properly, and if he has got into difficulties at last it wasn't his fault, for there isn't a man in Iceland who would have been able to keep his head above water."

She waited for him to say something, but he gave no sign. "His difficulties are not so very serious, either. Eight thousand crowns arrears of interest—that is all, in sixteen years, sir."

Again she waited, but he was still silent. "When the Sheriff went off this evening, he said if my son could find the money before nine o'clock to-morrow morning, he wouldn't go on with the auction."

Christian Christiansson had rested his head on his hand and seemed to be listening intently.

"If my son could only find somebody to lend him the money——"

There was a ring of appeal in her voice which startled herself, for she stopped, and looking nervously round at the stranger, said:

"I'm sure he would never regret it, sir. Magnus would work his fingers to the bone to repay every penny. He has always been a boy like that, and with better seasons and a little luck——"

It was then that the new scheme came to Christian Christiansson and he covered his face with his hand to think of it, whereupon Anna, mistaking the meaning of the altered gesture, faltered and began again.

"I'm taking a great liberty, sir, but I'm not thinking of myself—I'm thinking of my son. In one sense I'm to blame for all that has happened to him. He doesn't know it and I daren't tell him, but I am."

Christian Christiansson looked up at her.

"It was all my fault that his father took the mortgage."

"*Your* fault?"

"Yes, sir. My husband loved the poor boy who is gone, but he was the Governor of Iceland and every eye was on him to see that he kept his own house in order, and but for me he might have let the law take its course. I pleaded and prayed with him, thinking that we ourselves would be the ones to suffer. But I only ruined one son in trying to save the other —and I didn't save him."

Christian Christiansson dropped his head, for the waters of bitterness were falling over him in a flood, and Anna, thinking she had touched him, went on more eagerly:

"Then there's the girl, sir, my granddaughter. You've seen her yourself, and you'll say she doesn't look like a servant, but if the auction comes off she'll have to go out to service. They treat girls shamefully in some farmhouses, and my son can not bear the thought of it. Neither can I, for I can't help thinking of her father. Whatever else he may have been he was a gentleman, and to think of his daughter being a drudge to somebody——"

Anna's voice was faltering again, but after a moment she went on bravely.

"As for myself, I'm an old woman, and a little misfortune more or less doesn't matter to me now. My time is short in any case, and I shall be glad to go when I'm called. Most of my loved ones are gone already—my son and my granddaughter are all that are left—and if I could feel that I was leaving them happy and comfortable——"

Christian Christiansson could bear no more. "Landlady," he said, "I had set my heart on buying the farm— I had a particular reason for wishing to buy it—but instead of doing so I'll lend your son the money to pay the interest."

Anna's eyes opened wide in astonishment, and now that her prayer was answered her breath seemed to be suspended. " You *will*, sir? " she said.

" I will, on one condition."

" Oh, never mind the condition, let me go and tell him."

" My condition is that you give me the girl to adopt as my daughter."

" Ah! "

" I'm a lonely person, too, though I'm not so old as you are, and when I'm in England I haven't wife or child or mother or brother to share my life with me. The girl's sweet face would be a great comfort to me there, and I'm ready to pay this interest if you are willing to let her go."

The light had died out of Anna's eyes—her head was down.

" I should give you every guarantee that she would be taken care of. I am rich, as men of my class go, and she should want for nothing."

" But I didn't think your condition would be like that, sir," said Anna.

" Why not? Are you thinking of the girl or of yourself, landlady? "

" I am thinking of my son. No man was ever so wrapped up in a child. He has had her nearly all her life, and he is very, very fond of her. When she was little and the snow was deep as it is to-day he used to take her to school on his shoulder, and at night when she was sleepy he would carry her in his arms to bed. If she were his own he could not love her more dearly. It is like fatherhood to him, and he will never be a father now, because——"

Anna hesitated as if trying to say something which she was afraid to say, and then through her gathering tears she blurted out her secret.

" To tell you the truth, sir, he cared for her mother, but gave her up to somebody else and she died, and from that day forward all the best years of his life were wasted in a cruel longing for something to love. Then the child came, and it was almost as if the mother herself had sent her little one to comfort him. *She* could not love him, for she loved the other one to the last, but the child might, and she has—God bless her, she has!"

Christian Christiansson was wrung to the heart, but he struggled on. "So you think he could not part with the girl even for her own welfare and happiness?"

"I don't say that, sir; and perhaps if it were put to him properly——"

"Put it yourself, landlady."

"I daren't! He might suppose that I was thinking of myself."

"And if he did, would that be such a serious matter? Can it be nothing to him that his mother will be saved from being homeless if no harm is to come to the girl? And no harm shall come to her—you may take my word for that."

Anna thought for a moment and then she said, "You would tell us where she is to go, and what she is to do, and how she is to be brought up?"

"Indeed I would."

"She might write to us constantly and come to see us sometimes, perhaps?"

"Certainly she might."

"After all, it would just be like going into service."

"Just."

"Only she would be a lady, not a servant?"

"Only that."

"You would be good to her? Something tells me you would. And you would, wouldn't you?"

"I should be as good to the girl as if—as if I were her own father," said Christian Christiansson.

Anna dried her eyes and said:

"I don't know what to say, sir—I really don't know what to say to you."

"Say nothing to me—speak to your son, landlady."

"You will lend him the money to pay the interest immediately?"

"Immediately."

"Eight thousand crowns—you can find it all by nine o'clock to-morrow morning?"

"See," said Christian Christiansson, taking the pocket-book out of his breast-pocket, "there's enough in this purse to pay the interest twenty times over. And I'll not *lend* the money to your son—I'll *give* it to him if he will give me the girl instead."

"He will be sorry to part with her, but after all it will be one mouth less to feed, and when I'm gone that will be another, and then perhaps, having no burdens and no embarrassments——"

"Speak to him—he's here," said Christian Christiansson, and just at that moment Magnus returned to the hall carrying a wooden bowl of smoking bran.

Then in a low and trembling tone, hardly daring to raise her eyes to his face, Anna told her son of the stranger's offer, dwelling chiefly on the advantages to himself when Elin would be provided for, and she herself would be under the earth, and he, no longer crippled by grinding debt, would be able to pay his way and win back his lost inheritance. But as she went on her voice faltered, and her words became confused, for he was looking down at her with a lowering brow, and at last she stopped altogether, saying:

"I didn't mean any harm, Magnus. I only thought——"

"You thought I could sacrifice Elin to save myself, mother," said Magnus, and at that hard word Anna sank into a chair and sobbed.

Then Magnus turned to Christian Christiansson and said, "I'm much obliged for your offer, sir, but my niece is not for sale."

With that he was passing out of the house, when Christian Christiansson, who was quivering from head to foot, cried, "Wait!"

"Well?"

"You have decided for yourself fast enough—have you thought of anybody else?"

"Who else is there to think about?"

"Your mother for one. If you refuse my offer and the house is sold over your heads to-morrow morning, what is to become of her?"

Magnus flushed as if an invisible hand had smitten him across the face.

"What is to become of the girl, too—have you thought of
25

that? Have you a right to send her into service—to be a drudge to somebody?"

Magnus was shuddering visibly—even the bowl was trembling in his hands.

"No doubt you are fond of the girl and have been good to her, but if she were your own daughter she would be a separate being, and in a case like this you would have no right to speak for her."

"Then she shall speak for herself," said Magnus, and putting the smoking bowl on the table he crossed to the inner door and cried in an agitated voice, "Elin! Elin! Elin!"

In a moment the girl came running into the room with a look of alarm, saying, "What is it? Has anything happened?"

"Listen!" said Magnus, and Christian Christiansson could see that though his voice shook as if his soul were shaken he was trying to speak calmly. "This gentleman," he said, "has told your grandmother that he wishes to adopt you as a daughter, and he offers to pay my debts if I am willing to let you go."

"Uncle!" cried the girl.

"I have told him you shall speak for yourself, and so you shall, and whatever you decide to do your grandmother and I will agree to."

"But, Uncle!"

"Don't speak yet, my child. It is only fair that you should hear everything. Elin, I am a broken man and I have no longer a home to offer you. After the auction to-morrow morning I don't know what is to become of grandmother and you and me, or where we are to go or what roof is to cover us. But this gentleman is rich, and he promises to provide for you all your life, and to give you all you need and everything you could wish for. If you stay with me you may suffer privations, but if you go to him you will never know a poor day again as long as you live."

His deep voice had all it could do to support itself, but he bore up to the end, and then Anna, whose eyes were filling as fast as she could wipe them, said:

"Isn't it wonderful, Elin? Isn't it like a miracle? Like an answer to your prayer, my child, just when we were so low and downhearted? The gentleman will satisfy us that you are going to a good Christian home and that you will be properly brought up and cared for."

And then Christian Christiansson himself, though he could scarcely speak for the contending emotions that shook him to the soul, stepped forward and said:

"Let me tell you who I am, Elin. We spoke of Christian Christiansson the composer, and you sang his song to me and said you would like to hear something about him. *I* am Christian Christiansson."

The girl made a little involuntary cry, and his voice faltered for a moment.

"Yes, I am he, and the story I told you was the story of my own unhappy life, only—I have lost my daughter since I wrote that song, and now I am quite alone. Will you not come and take her place, my child? You shall be just the same to me as my own daughter, and you shall never know the difference. You will return with me to England and live my life, and whatever I do you shall do, and wherever I go you shall go also."

"Think of that, Elin!" said Anna. "You love music— you take after your poor father that way—and you will travel about just as your dear mother used to do!"

"It would be beautiful!" said Elin.

She had been standing all this time by the table with one hand resting lightly upon it, while her sweet face reflected the changing lights of alarm and pain and surprise and joy.

"I can't think of anything in the world I should love so much, but—I can not, I must not."

"Elin!"

"Grandma, didn't you tell me yourself when I came here long ago, and you put me to bed the first time, that I was never to leave Uncle Magnus, and if anybody ever came to take me away I was not to go? I was a little mite, but I gave you my word, I remember, and I am going to keep it."

"But I was thinking of somebody else then, Elin. I couldn't know that this gentleman would come—at a time like this, too——"

"But that makes no difference, grandma. Besides, if I were to go to this gentleman and he were to treat me as if I

were his own daughter, I should have to think of him as if
he were my own father. Would you like that, grandma?
And would Uncle Magnus like it?"

"We should sacrifice ourselves, honey, we should sacrifice
ourselves that you might be well off and happy."

"But I don't want to be well off if you and Uncle Magnus
are going to be poor. And I shouldn't be happy at all—I
should be miserable."

"Oh, dear! Oh, dear!" moaned Anna, unable to say more.
And then the girl turned with a smile to Christian Christiansson, who was throbbing with pride and pain, and she
said:

"It is very, very good of you, sir, and there isn't another
girl in the world who wouldn't be glad to go; but I can't,
you must see yourself I can't—I must stay with my uncle.
Grandma is going to do so, and why shouldn't I?"

"He would be better without either of us, Elin," said
Anna.

"Don't say that, grandma."

"I do say it, my child, and if you only knew how cruel
the world is——"

"But God isn't, and He will not separate us now after we
have been together so long. You said so yourself, you know,
when I talked of going into service. You said He would
find another way, and He will—I'm sure He will."

It wrung Anna's heart to have her own teaching coming
back to reproach her, yet thinking of Magnus she made one
more effort. "But don't you see, dear, that if you stay with
Uncle Magnus he will lose the land, whereas if you go with
this gentleman he will be able to keep it?"

Then the innocent young face which had been so full of
beautiful trust in the greatness and the goodness of God to
triumph over all perils and privations clouded over for one
moment, and she said, "Do you *want* me to go, grandma?
And does Uncle Magnus want it?"

Neither of them answered her, and she looked from one to
the other—Anna brushing her eyes with the back of her
wrinkled hand, and Magnus standing motionless with a white
face broken up like the melting snow—and then the cruel
swelling in the girl's heart subsided and her eyes shone like
the sun.

" I *know* you don't," she answered herself. " You are only thinking about *me*."

And then the brave little soul tossed up her head with a proud look and said, " As for the land—if it comes to losing that or losing me, I know what Uncle Magnus will say. He will say—I *know* he will—' Let me keep my little Elin and the land—*the land may go!* ' "

" And so I do, my darling," cried Magnus, and he opened his great arms to her, and she ran into them and was gathered to his breast.

At the next moment Anna had joined them and Magnus had put his arms around both, and it was just as if they had conquered a great temptation—as if some dark shadow which had threatened to separate them had passed away—for they were clinging together and crying like children.

Christian Christiansson stood aside for a moment and looked on at their happiness, feeling himself without part or lot in it, and then, fearing that he might cry out and betray himself or break down altogether, he turned away and fled into the guest-room.

V

HE threw himself face downward on the bed, and the waters of Marah went over and over him. Sight of the happiness he had lost the right to claim was the hardest experience that had yet come to him, and he wept bitterly. " My child! My dear, dear child! " he had wanted to cry, but those were words of proud endearment which he might never use except in the voiceless chambers of his empty heart.

But this mood lasted only for a few moments, and then a fierce and almost savage jealousy took possession of him, and he dried his eyes and sat up in contempt of his own weakness. What right had any one to rob him of his child? Elin was flesh of his flesh, and no man should take her away. Even the law would recognize his right to his own offspring. He had merely to say to the Sheriff, " She is mine," and the Sheriff would have no choice but to deliver her up to him.

Then calmer moments came, and he saw that he could

only assert his legal right to his daughter by disclosing his identity, and that was out of the question. And even if it were possible to carry his daughter away by force, it would be a poor triumph to take her body if he could not also take her soul. Every man wished his children to love him, and unless Elin could love her father, what was the good of claiming her?

He opened his eyes to calm the deafening tumult of his conflicting thoughts, and saw a little faded photograph in a stand on a table that stood beside the bed. It was an old photograph of Thora, and he remembered it immediately, for it was the same that in the better time belonged to Aunt Margret and stood on the drawers beside her door. He took it up in his shaking hand and held the candle to look at it, and then, in a moment, by that magic the Almighty knows, he was back with Thora in the birth-room at Government House, and she was saying, in the tremulous joy of her young motherhood, " Kiss me, Oscar! Put your arms about both of us, dearest! That way—so! "

Something of the tenderness of Thora's sweet heart returned to him with that haunting memory, and along with it came a new and thrilling thought. If Elin belonged to him by right of Nature, then Nature herself would speak for him. He had only to say to her, " I am your father; you are my daughter," and she would come to him—she could not help herself—because Nature is a mighty thing and none of us can resist the mysterious call that comes to our blood from the blood that gave us birth!

He would do so; he would find the girl alone and speak to her; he would whisper the secret of his life in the ear of his own child, and then the marvelous Mother of us all would do the rest.

When he returned to the hall, Elin was shaking out the cloth and removing the last of the supper things—all except the bottle and glasses, which she left on the table. " It must be now," he thought, and though his heart quailed at coming to this last throw in the game he had played for life and love, he put his fortune to the test.

" It was very brave of you, my child," he said, " to choose poverty when you might have chosen wealth. But you did well, for wealth is only of this world's making, and the angel that brings us happiness does not ask us if we are poor or rich."

His voice faltered when he came to what he had to say next, but he rallied and went on:

"It was very sweet of you, too, to remain with your uncle and your grandmother, instead of coming to a stranger, for being of your own flesh and blood they have naturally the first claim upon you. But if—if, instead of Christian Christiansson, I had been *your own father*, would you—would you have come to me then?"

Elin did not answer him immediately, and he looked steadfastly into her face, feeling that all hope of happiness for the remainder of his life hung on her reply.

"Would you?"

The sweet young face looked troubled for a moment, and then slowly—very slowly and sadly—Elin shook her head.

He felt like a man who had been sentenced to death, but while his face clouded and fell, the girl's rose and became beautifully calm.

"I don't see how that could make any difference," she said. "I couldn't feel as if you were my father unless I had known you as long as I could remember, and longer even than that. What I call a father is one who has nursed you on his knee when you were a little thing, and kissed you and coaxed you when you were sick, and thought of you and cared for you always, not one who has been away from you all your life, who has never cared for you at all, and whom you wouldn't know if you met him in the road."

"But don't you feel, dear, that there is something in the relation of a child to her father, however he may have neglected her—something intimate and sacred—something she can never know in her relation to anybody else, however much he may have done for her—don't you feel that, Elin?"

Again the girl thought for a moment, and again she shook her head.

"But if I were to say to you, 'My child, my dear, dear child, I may have done nothing for you, but still I am your father, and you are the only one who is left to me now, and I want you to come to me and be my daughter, and we shall never be parted again '—if I were to say that to you, would you still hold to your uncle?"

The tremulous fervor with which he spoke these imploring words brought tears to the girl's eyes, but her heart stood firm and strong.

"Yes," she said, "I couldn't help it, because Uncle Magnus has been my real father after all."

It was all over. His last hold of the girl was lost. Again he felt as if the world had gone away from him, as if the dark column of hope which had shown its bright face for a moment had turned again, and now all was hopeless darkness.

He had thought Nature would speak to the girl, but it had not spoken. Nature was a great, inexorable instrument in the hand of God, and God's hand was on him. *As he had done, so he was being done by*—as he had taken the love of Thora from Magnus, so Magnus, after many years, had taken the love of Elin from him. It was right, it was inevitable, and he must bow his head in speechless submission before the justice and the vengeance of God!

He must leave the house as he had come to it, not only without revealing himself to his mother and brother, but also without his child. It would be the bitterest moment of his life, but he must meet it and go on.

"You are quite right, my dear—quite right," he said. "A child's love is like a flower in the window—it cannot grow without somebody to water it. Your uncle has done everything for you, and he is entitled to all your affection. It wouldn't be fair if your father could come back, after all these years, and take you away from him. Cling to him, Elin, love him, and comfort him, and may God bless you for your loyalty and trust!"

He had tried to speak bravely, but his voice broke and he stopped. After a moment he said calmly:

"Can you give me pen and ink and a sheet of writing-paper?"

She brought them instantly, and he sat at the table and wrote a line or two. Then he took out his pocket-book, opened it, and put the paper inside of it, and closed it up again.

"Elin, will you do me a great favor?"

"Oh yes, sir," said the girl.

"It is late, and I've had a long day, and I may not be up when the auction begins in the morning—will you take this pocket-book and give it to the Sheriff the moment he arrives?"

"With pleasure, sir."

"You will not open it or show it to anybody else, but you will carry it to your room at once and put it under your pillow, and to-morrow morning you will be up early and give it to the Sheriff before he begins the sale—will you do this for me, my dear?"

"Indeed I will, sir."

"Thank you! And now you must go to bed. Good-by, my child!"

"But I'll see you in the morning, sir?"

"Who can say? We may both have other things to think about by that time, so we had better say good-by to each other now."

"But am I not to see you again?"

"Who can say that either! I have come a long way, you know, and now I may have to go—" he hesitated, and then turning away he said, "I may have to go still farther."

"You have been so kind to me, sir—I am sorry I can not go with you."

"Ah, God forbid!—I mean, you can not—I see you can not! But if you *could* have done so I should have been so fond of you, and we should have been such good friends together."

"I shall never forget you, sir."

"Nor I you. I shall always think of the brave little girl I met once—only once—and then could see no more."

"You are only a stranger to me, sir, but—but——"

"Yes, I am only a stranger to you, my child, but we have come together on the great ocean of life, and now—now we must say good-by and part."

"Good-by, sir!"

"Good-by, little girl, and God bless you!"

The girl stepped to her bedroom door and then stopped and turned and looked back at him. Her eyes were full—she knew not why. Nature was saying something to her at last—she knew not what.

He was looking after her with all his hungry soul in his quivering face, and when she turned he stretched out his arms to her.

"Elin!" he whispered, and she came back to him, and he folded her to his heart and kissed her on the forehead and on the lips. Ah, sweet, soft, warm lips, he felt them to the last!

A mist floated before his eyes; he heard footsteps going away from him; he heard a door open and close, and then— his child was gone.

.   .   .   .

Christian Christiansson was alone. He felt that he had come to the lees of his life and saw nothing but a blank where he might crawl to die. Could he go back to Reykjavik? That was impossible, for the Minister and his people would be preparing their banquet in honor of his visit, and to go through such rejoicing would be a scorching martyrdom at which the devil himself would laugh. Could he return to England and resume his old life as the unknown composer? That was impossible also, for he could never write as he had written before, because the old impulse was gone, the fire was burnt out, the life that had inspired him was dead, and because the foundations of his fame were broken up by the new consciousness that he had no right to it, by the sense that his career and all that had come of it had been built on the desecration of his wife's grave, and by the certainty that his success had been paid for as by the sweat of his very soul.

What then was before him? Old age? What was old age without friends, without children, without love, without respect and with memory—that last joy of a man's declining days—like a poisoned river running through a wasted land?

Was there nothing before him then? Yes, there was one thing—one only—and as he lay in that room alone with his head over his hands on the table, he had the trembling, thrilling, palpitating sense of supernatural wings hovering above him, and of an awful voice that seemed to say, "THE WAGES OF SIN IS DEATH!"

At that moment he became aware of other voices—more human and homely voices—murmuring about him, and one of them said, " He has fallen asleep, poor gentleman," and another, " He has drunk too much, perhaps." Then a hand touched him on the shoulder and somebody cried in his ear:

" Hadn't you better go to bed, sir?"

It was his mother, with Magnus behind her, and looking at both he could see that they supposed he was intoxicated. In the wild laboring of heart and brain, it suited him that they should continue to think so, and indeed the strain of nerve had been so hard that when he rose to his feet he staggered like a drunken man.

" Heigho! What's this?" he laughed. " Your brennie-vin must be pretty heady, landlady. But no matter! It will be a good nightcap and make me sleep the sounder. I'm tired, very tired, but I'm going to have a long sleep at last—a long, long sleep at last."

" But to-morrow will be New Year's Day," said Anna. " The bells ring at daybreak, and the Sheriff will be here soon after, so you'll have to be stirring early if you want to be ready for the auction."

" Why, so I shall—I had forgotten all about it—and since we can not agree about the girl I must buy the farm whatever happens. I told you I wanted it for a particular purpose, but I didn't say what it was. It's my secret, landlady, but I don't mind telling you. I want it for my mother."

" Your mother?"

" That's so! She was born in these parts, and the poor old thing would like to end her days here."

" So she tells you to buy up my farmstead?"

" Not she! She doesn't know anything about it. That's to be my surprise. I've not been a good son, but when I go away never to come back again I want to feel that the dear old soul is happy and comfortable and has a roof to cover her."

He laughed, with the same sense as before of an hysterical oppression of the heart, and then turned to Magnus and said:

" Sorry to buy your house over your head, but business

is business, you know, and anybody is at liberty to bid who
has money to pay."

Magnus moved aside with a contemptuous expression.

"Don't look so glum, my man. You think you've been
badly treated and perhaps you have, but you're the luckiest
man in Iceland if you ask me. You think because you've
done well you ought to be rewarded, but what right have poor
wretches like us to expect reward in this world? You think
because a man is rich he is to be envied, but what's the use
of having your pocket full if your heart is empty? And you
think because Death kills the innocent and the happy it is
a cruel monster, but there are worse things than Death, and
Life is one of them when you've nobody to care whether you
live or die. Then cheer up, old fellow! You've got your
health and your good name, and your mother and that sweet
girl to love and to love you, so what the devil have you got
to complain of? Nothing at all!"

Saying this with a mixture of real emotion and its mocking make-believe, a touch of the boy came back to him for a
moment and he put his arm across his brother's shoulder as
he used to do in the old days, but Magnus shuddered and
shrank away.

"Your candle is burning in the bedroom, sir," said Anna
coldly.

And then he saw that his mother also looked black at him,
as one who had come to turn them out of house and home,
and as one who had tried to tempt the girl away from them,
and as one who could laugh at their condition and have no
thought except for himself. And thinking that this was the
last he would see of her; that it was so different from the
parting he had expected; that all hope of pardon and reconciliation was lost; that his mother would never hear that
her lingering faith in her prodigal had been justified and
never know that he had been and gone, he had as much as
he could do not to break down and betray himself even at
the end.

But gathering up his clothes which had been drying by the
stove, he turned toward the bedroom, saying with another
laugh—a laugh that went to Anna's heart like a sword:

"Don't look so downhearted, landlady. When things are

at their worst they can't move without they mend. You've had your troubles, but you shall drink my health under my mother's roof-tree to-morrow morning. Good night!"

And then he reeled into the guest-room.

VI

THE stranger being gone, mother and son looked into each other's faces. Then they spoken in whispers.

"Did you hear him?" said Anna.

"About his mother's roof-tree?" asked Magnus.

"About the auction—about everything. The man can have no feeling—no pity."

"None."

"'Business is business,' he said, when he talked of buying the place over our heads. And when he spoke of his mother ending her days here he never once thought of me."

"He never thought of Elin either. He would have taken the girl away from us without a moment's hesitation."

"He would," said Anna. "'There's enough in this purse,' he said, 'to pay your interest twenty times over.'"

"Did he say that?"

"He did. He took his pocket-book out of his breast-pocket and——"

"His breast-pocket, you say?"

"Yes, 'and I'll *give* the money to your son,' he said, 'if he'll give me the girl instead.'"

Anna talked on in an innocent, helpless way without knowing what bad work she was doing, but suddenly, mysteriously, at the mention of the purse a change passed over Magnus's face and it grew ugly with evil passions.

"He must be rich," said Anna.

"Richer than anybody has a right to be," said Magnus.

"Surely God can not mean that anybody should be as rich as that while other people are so poor."

"God!" said Magnus, and his distorted face quivered.

"If he would only lend us enough to satisfy the Sheriff in the morning!" said Anna.

"What's the good of expecting a man to help us to keep the farm when he has come to buy it for himself?"

"It's hard, though, cruelly hard, to be turned out of house and home by the first person who comes along with more money."

"That's what I was thinking," said Magnus.

Down to this moment Anna had only been trying to sympathize with Magnus's mood, but now something in his tone made her suspect that she had awakened a devil, and she looked at him in terror.

He took up the bottle and drank; he drank out of the neck; and there was a new devil in every drop. His eyes began to gleam with a feverish luster, and Anna trembled. She remembered that Magnus had not taken any strong drink until to-day since the day of Thora's funeral, and then she thought of her father, and a sensation of extreme cold crept over her.

"Let us not talk of it any more," she said, as she tried to put the bottle away, but Magnus held on to it.

Mother and son looked at each other again, and then Anna went over to the stranger's door and listened.

"Has he locked it?" asked Magnus.

"No, I'm afraid—   No, no, he has not."

"What is he doing?"

"The candle is out—he must be in bed already."

"Then," said Magnus, "he has thrown himself down without undressing and the pocket-book is on him still."

"Magnus, what are you thinking of?" said Anna—her teeth were chattering.

"Would it be so very wicked?"

"What?"

"To take as much as would satisfy the Sheriff in the morning?"

"Magnus! I didn't mean that."

"He would never miss it—never know it was gone—and it would enable us to keep the farm and so save us from starvation."

"Oh, dear! What have I done?"

"He's a prodigal himself, it seems. Very well, let prodigal pay for prodigal."

She could not breathe freely—she could only look at Magnus in speechless surprise. He took up the bottle again and gulped down the last of the liquor.

"He has drunk a good deal—he will sleep heavily—and he won't awake until the auction is over."

"Let us go to bed," said Anna.

"Go yourself," he growled, for the furies that march in the brain of the drunken man had mastered him.

"Magnus," said Anna, "if you will not go to bed I shall stay up all night with you."

Then the devil that had changed Magnus into a cunning, savage beast, showed him what he had to do.

"Very well, let us go to bed," he replied.

He bolted the outer door again and raked out the stove, while his mother extinguished the lamp and re-lit the candles. She thought the evil impulse that had come to him had been conquered, and she talked of other matters.

"I've made up Eric's bed for you, and you'll find everything comfortable," she said.

As she passed Elin's door she opened it gently and held her head aside to listen. The sound of the soft and measured breathing came out to them for a moment and then the door was closed again.

"Poor child! She would lay her head on her pillow full of faith in the miracle that is to happen before to-morrow morning. Of such is the kingdom of heaven!"

They parted at the door of the badstofa, and a few minutes afterward the little house lay silent and dark in the arms of the hills and on the breast of the snow, but the wings of Death hung over it.

.   .   .   .

Magnus did not go to bed. He threw himself on the eiderdown and went through a fierce fight with God as represented by God's vicar, his conscience. A vision of the pocket-book in the stranger's breast-pocket danced before his dark heart, and he told himself that come what would he must take enough of the stranger's money to pay the interest in the morning. If he did not do so the man would buy the farmstead and Elin and his mother would be turned adrift.

On this thought came compunctions. To take the man's money would be to steal, and Magnus had never stolen. But faith being already gone, morality followed, and he wrestled with his conscience and overcame it. What he was going to do was what men did every day, only they called it business, and they did it to wrong the right, whereas he would do it to right the wrong. Magnus marshaled his reasons and justified himself. Here was a man so rich that he would not know to-morrow morning that he had lost what was sufficient to make his dear ones happy. That man was going to expose them to poverty and destitution. Surely it was right, it was necessary, it was his duty to prevent him.

In the mad tangle of his disordered brain he saw everything that had happened that day in a sinister light, and it seemed as if fate had thrown the man into his hands. He might have gone to lodge at the Parsonage—he had come there! He might have concealed the purpose of his coming —he had revealed it! He might have said nothing of the pocket-book—he had shown it with childlike simplicity! Surely this was the way out of his difficulties which Destiny had marked out for him, and not to take it would be to cover himself with self-reproaches when his dear ones came down to want.

Having persuaded himself that he could not help but take as much of the stranger's money as was necessary to pay the interest, he began to ask why he should take so little. If the pocket-book in the man's breast-pocket contained enough to pay the interest twenty times over, why not take enough to buy the farm out and out? That would enable him to leave to Elin the inheritance which he had lost through his brother's extravagance and crime. This man was about to take it away from her—he must not and he should not do so!

Stage by stage he pushed back the bulwarks of conscience until he came to ask himself why he should not take all. His mind was clogged and numb by this time, but he knew well what that meant. It meant taking the stranger's life. There was at first an indescribable horror in the thought of killing a human being, but after a moment it passed away. This man alone stood between his dear ones and shelter—why shouldn't he? This man threatened to take their lives by exposing them to starvation—why shouldn't he take his life instead?

A momentary qualm came with the thought that he would be attacking one who had trusted himself to the hospitality of his house, a defenseless man in his sleep. But he thought of the stranger's heartless laughter, his callousness to their condition, and recalled what he had said of his mother, and pictured her sitting there surrounded by every comfort while his own mother, born in that place, was turned out to perish, and then his gorge rose again and his heart knew no pity.

He began to ask himself how it could be done. It could be done quite easily. Nobody except themselves had seen the man; nobody else would ever know that he had been to their house. He could tell his mother and Elin that the stranger had gone away in the early morning. They would believe him, and even if they did not they would hold their tongues, for his interest would be their interest, and all he would do would be done for them.

A new and awful light illumined his gloomy mind, and he saw himself doing everything. No other eye would see, no other ear would hear. It was freezing hard to-night, and if it was found in the drowning pool when the ice melted the story would be that the stranger had lost his way in the snowstorm and stumbled over the rocks.

Having satisfied himself that he could defeat this world's judgment, the tortured man in the toils of his temptation began to think of the judgment of the next. But fear of that vanished in a moment. Nothing was known in the other world of what took place in this one, and God interfered but little in the affairs of men!

At the thought of God a singing noise came into his ears like water in the ears of a drowning man. It was his conscience going down after its last gasp, for he was telling himself that murder though it might be, and contrary to God's law, God had done nothing for *him*, and therefore he was not called upon to do anything for God. He had been a good man all his life, yet God had left him in the lurch. God and the world were letting his mother and Elin perish, therefore he must fight the world—and God!

In the last convulsion of his human nature he remembered
26

that once before the impulse to kill had come to him, and that
he had suffered the tortures of the damned whenever afterward he had thought of it. But that was different, that was
in the whirlwind of outraged passion, and if he had carried
out his threat it would have been the worst of crimes, the unpardonable sin, the sin against the Holy Ghost—a brother's
murder! A thousand times he had thanked God that Oscar
had not lived to come home, but how strange were the ways
of fate—another man, another heartless prodigal, had come
there, and if his dear ones were to be saved from starvation
and the consequences of Oscar's crimes, he knew what he
had to do!

"Let prodigal pay for prodigal," he thought again, and
then he leaped up from the bed.

His brute nature, goaded on by the flattering devil of drink,
had conquered his conscience, yet his knees knocked together
as he went on tiptoe by his mother's room, and when he came
to Elin's door he could hardly breathe. Their pure souls
were sleeping in the protecting atmosphere of prayer; and
when he asked himself what he was to say in the morning if
they wanted to know where he had got the money, his mind
was so clogged and numb that he could find no answer.

But this thought, with the vision that came after it of how
his mother and Elin would look at him with searching and
suspicious glances—of how when all would be over and he
hoped to be at rest he would find them sitting together in
silence, staring at nothing—nearly broke down the brute in
him and his whole body was shaken by a kind of tearless sob.
Nevertheless the flash of human light on his dark heart only
made the blackness more profound, and after a moment he
went on with his preparations.

When he stepped on tiptoe into the hall, the two sheep-dogs
who had been sleeping on the mat by the door got up and
stretched themselves and yawned, and lest they should make
a noise he took them out and locked them up in a shed.
After that he went over to the stable, which was at some
distance from the dwelling, and saddled and bridled the
stranger's mare, and then with a sharp cut of his whip he sent
her galloping and whinnying into the darkness. A breath of
icy wind was coming down the valley as if day were stirring

in its morning sleep, and a faint pink and white light in the eastern sky, with a glint on the western glaciers, seemed to say that the dawn was near, but the drink was in Magnus's eyes and he could not see clearly.

No snow had fallen since the traveler arrived, and returning to the front of the farmstead Magnus made backward tracks from the porch to the river, partly in order to obliterate the stranger's footsteps and partly to conceal his own when he should come out again, carrying a heavy burden. The man was gone by this time, and Magnus was like a night-bird hovering about his own house and thinking of his prey.

When he returned to the hall there was no sound there except that of the ashes slipping in the stove, and of the clock ticking in the darkness the deliberate seconds. He took off his boots, leaving on his snow-stockings only, and then he picked up a large cushion from the arm-chair and stepped to the stranger's door and listened.

But heaven as well as hell is in the heart of every man, as long as life is with him, and the tearless sob came back to Magnus and shook his whole body, as he thought at the last moment of the awful pity of the thing he had to do. Yet telling himself again that God did nothing in this world, and saying once more, " Let prodigal pay for prodigal," he turned the handle and opened the door.

Then he stepped softly into the guest-room and bolted the door behind him.

VII

ANNA, at that moment, had awakened from a frightening dream. On first going to her room she had been troubled by the memory of what she had done to awaken evil thoughts in Magnus, and visions had come to her of how, if anything happened, Magnus might say, " You put it into my head, mother." To banish her self-reproaches she had said a prayer for forgiveness, telling God she had never once thought of theft or violence, but only of Magnus and Elin and the inheritance they had lost through her importunity, and how cruel it seemed that while other people had so much more than they wanted, such hard times should come to her dear children.

Then she had gone to bed, and the voice of the stranger, which had teased her all the evening through with memories she could not fix, haunted her again, and the light being out, and her eyes no longer disturbed by sight of the stranger's different face, she knew whose voice it reminded her of. It was a voice very dear to her, a voice always near to her, Oscar's voice, which she was never to hear again.

When, with a thrill of the heart, this thought came to Anna, it altered the stranger altogether. His laughter ceased to be cruel, and what he had said of himself not being a good son became touching. And when she thought of his poor mother waiting for her prodigal and so soon to see him home again, and pictured her joy when he should say, " Mother, mother! I'm here at last, and we shall never, never be parted again! " her heart overflowed with sympathy, and she was sorry she had not been kinder to him when he was going to bed.

Then she went to sleep and the dream spirit took her back to the good time when she had two boys in her house, a dark one and a fair one, and the father had punished the dark one unjustly, and his stern and gloomy soul, with its sense of wrong, would not suffer him to explain, but the fair one was sobbing out a confession—" It was not Magnus, it was me, papa "—and a moment afterward two happy little heads were on the same pillow side by side, and both were laughing merrily.

In the shifting kaleidoscope of her dream this picture had hardlly gone when Anna awoke with the clearest consciousness of Oscar's voice crying, " Mother! Mother! Mother! " She thought it must have been the stranger calling in his sleep, for the china ornaments on her dressing-table seemed to ring, but when she listened there was no other sound.

Then the memory of Magnus's temptation came rolling back on her like a thundercloud over a clear sky, and she got up to go to her son's room to make sure that he was in bed.

Magnus had not been to bed!

With candle in hand, and still in her night-dress, Anna hurried to the hall, crying in a whisper of only half-realized apprehension, " Magnus ! Magnus ! "

There was no reply.

She listened at the stranger's door and thought she heard a movement inside the room, but she dared not enter or knock.

" Magnus ! Magnus ! " she whispered again, but no answer came back to her. She heard the neighing of a horse that seemed to be running round and round the house and her flesh began to creep, for that sound in the night was like the cry of a disembodied soul. Then there came the deadened noise of dogs barking, and she knew they were their own dogs and that they must have been shut up in an outhouse. This started a new thought, and she ran to the outer door to see if it had been opened.

The door was unbolted !

She was about to open it and cry again when she heard a noise behind her. It came from the stranger's room, and putting her ear to the door she distinctly heard the sounds of sobs. Some one inside was sobbing.

She knew the low, stifled voice. It was Magnus. He was on his knees or prostrate on the floor, and he was sobbing as if his heart would break. At that Anna boldly tried to open the door, but found it fastened on the inside.

" Magnus ! Magnus ! " she whispered, but he did not answer.

She was now sure that the awful thing she had thought of had come to pass. Her suspense had deepened to fear, but pity and love conquered every other feeling, and going down on her knees in her night-dress, she whispered through the key-hole :

" Magnus ! Magnus ! Open the door. It is only mother ! It was all my fault, dear ! Let me come in ! "

But the smothered sobbing inside continued, and no other sound came back to her. Then in the silence of all else she heard the sound of sleigh-bells outside. At first she thought this must be a ringing in her ears, but the bells grew louder and came nearer, and then the dogs in the outhouse barked again.

Fear deepened to terror, the necessity for concealment flashed upon her, and she knocked at the bedroom door and cried in the same affrighted whisper:

"Magnus, there is some one coming. Wait till he has gone. Don't stir. Don't come out. Only tell me you hear me."

The sobbing ceased, but Magnus did not speak. Meantime the sleigh-bells came nearer and nearer, with the cracking of a whip, the whoop of a driver, and the hiss of runners in the soft snow.

"Magnus! Magnus!" cried Anna loudly, in a last effort, but she was stopped by the near shout of some one outside, "Helloa! helloa there!"—and she rose to her feet with an intention of bolting the outer door.

Before she could do so there was a metallic knock on the window-pane, a voicě crying, "God be with you!" and footsteps hurrying up the outer steps. Then Anna turned about and fled back to her bedroom.

While she dressed she heard the outer door thrown open and the sound of many persons trooping into the hall. They were very bright and happy, for they laughed merrily and talked all together, and the house was full of noise.

When she came out of the badstofa she met the postboy on his way to the elt-house to boil water to give his ponies a hot drink, and on returning to the hall she found the door and the shutters of the window open, the daylight streaming in, and the postman himself there with several passengers, including the Factor, who was muffled up to the eyes, and Margret Neilsen, who was unrolling herself from the folds of a white bearskin.

"Helloa!" cried everybody, and the postman said, "Here we are at last, you see! We couldn't come yesterday by reason of the snowstorm, but the Factor actually got me to start away as soon as it stopped at eleven o'clock last night—eleven!"

"Well, we don't kill a pig every day, do we?" said the Factor, and while the men laughed and winked, Margret Neilsen said:

"And how's Anna?"

Anna was speechless and ghastly white, so the Factor said,

"We seem to have startled her out of her senses, for she looks as if she had seen a ghost. But where's Magnus?"

"Magnus? Oh—somewhere about," said Anna.

"And how's my precious Elin?" said Aunt Margret.

"She's not up yet," said Anna.

"Then I'll go and waken her. Which is her room—this one?" said Aunt Margret, making for the guest-room.

"No, no," said Anna, intercepting her and standing with her back to the guest-room door. "That one," and Aunt Margret went into Elin's bedroom.

"And now," said the Factor, with winks all round him, "what about the other one?"

Anna looked at the Factor in mute terror.

"The new-comer, you know? Not stirring yet, I suppose?"

"New-comer?"

"Well, guest, friend, whatever you choose to call him."

"What friend?"

"Why, the friend who came last night, of course."

Anna, who had never lied in her life, wanted to lie now, but she could not do so. "I don't understand you, Factor," she said faintly.

"Well!" said the Factor, and then, as if by an afterthought, "I thought he wouldn't wish to startle you, having been so long away and supposed to be dead. But don't you know yet who he is?"

Anna trembled and said, "Of whom are you speaking, Oscar Neilsen?"

"Of the tall fair man with the pointed beard who came to lodge at your house last night."

Anna was now speechless with terror, and the company, misunderstanding her silence, became suddenly very grave. "Can it be possible that he lost his way in the snowstorm?" said one. "But he knew every inch of the road, and could find his way blindfold," said another. "Such a night, though," said a third. "He got as far as the House of Rest." "But the boy there said he would never see the end of his journey."

"Well, this is serious," said the Factor. "The Minister wanted him to stay at Government House over-night, but he seemed so anxious to see you——"

"To see *me!*" said Anna.

"Naturally, after his long absence. Strange! very strange! But do you mean to say that *no* traveler came here last night?"

A vague shadow of the Factor's meaning had flashed upon Anna's mind, and the terror of a moment ago had deepened to horror. What had Magnus done in the blindness of his passion and despair? But even then the desire to save her son was above all other emotions, and she was about to deny all knowledge of the traveler, when the door behind her was opened and a voice over her shoulder said:

"Yes, a traveler *did* come here last night, but he went away again in the early morning."

It was Magnus, and when Anna turned to look at him she drew a deep breath of relief, for she knew he was telling the truth. His face, since she saw it last, had undergone a mysterious and miraculous change. The gloomy arrogance of despair had gone, something had carried light into the darkness of his soul, and he looked like a man who had come as from the immediate presence of his God.

"But this is stranger than ever," said the Factor. "It was known that he had taken a large sum of money out of the Bank, and everybody supposed he meant to buy up this place at the auction."

"Yes," said Aunt Margret, coming out of Elin's bedroom, "to give to his old mother."

And then Elin's soft voice was heard to say, "Has the Sheriff come yet?"

"Who is asking for the Sheriff?" said the Sheriff himself, coming forward at that moment.

"The gentleman gave me this pocket-book last night, and told me to deliver it to you before the auction began this morning."

"It's not for me, though," said the Sheriff, who had taken the pocket-book to the table and opened it, and was reading the writing on the sheet of paper which fell out first, "'For Elin, Oscar's daughter, from Christian Christiansson.'"

"A present for Elin, perhaps," said the Factor.

"A thousand-crown note!" cried the Sheriff.

The gaiety of the company was breaking into loud congratulations, when the Sheriff, who was still opening the folds of the pocket-book, said, " Wait! There's more than that—much more! One—two—three—fifty thousand—another—and another—and "—then the rapid rustling of bank-notes, followed by the delighted cry, " Two hundred thousand crowns! "

" The very sum he took out of the bank! " said the Factor.

" Kiss me, my precious! " said Aunt Margret.

" Me, too, granddaughter," cried the Factor.

Anna looked stunned, and Magnus like one who wished the earth to swallow him. But the Factor rattled along with shouts and laughter.

" Now I understand everything. He has given the money to the girl, but left it to her friends and relations to advise her as to what she is to do with it."

Elin's blue eyes being still full of bewilderment, the Factor kissed her again and said, " Now who do you think has left you this great fortune, little one? "

" Christian Christiansson," said the girl.

" Certainly! But don't you know who Christian Christiansson is? No? You neither, Anna? "

Anna was trembling on the verge of discovery. " Who? " she said, but rather with her lips than with her voice.

" Why, Oscar—your son Oscar, who isn't dead at all, and has come back and made amends to everybody! I always knew there was good stuff in my godson! "

The truth burst on Anna in a whirlwind of joy—joy that her son was alive, joy that he had come home and justified her faith in him, joy, too, though with a twinge of pain in it, that he had gone away again and further trouble with Magnus was averted. A prayer gushed from her heart and she wanted to go down on her knees.

" My son! " she said in a breathless whisper.

" My father! " said Elin, with a tenderness the word had never had for her before.

The company were now cackling and crowing again, but the two women—the old one and the young one—looked round for Magnus. He was standing at the back, his strong face all broken up and melted. It was not at this moment that the truth had first burst on him. That had come like a blinding blow of light the instant he had entered the guest-room and realized that God did something after all in this world for His children.

"Mother—Elin!" he stammered, and he opened his arms to them.

"It's the miracle, isn't it?" said the girl.

It was the miracle indeed.

.   .   .   .

There was no auction in Thingvellir that day, and when the bells rang for service the company went to church. The little wooden tabernacle was full of worshippers, for it was New Year's Day, and the farmers had ridden over with their families from all the country round about. They sat, in their thick mufflers and snow-stockings and the mist of their smoking breath, as far up the church as the square rail enclosing the communion table, on stools about the octagonal pulpit and even among the refuse, the lumber and potted-meat barrels that were stored in the gallery.

The Factor was there, very loud in his responses, fixing up the figures on the tin plate which announced the hymns; Elin, too, with the wonder not yet gone from her innocent blue eyes; Anna with her tempered happiness and a heart overflowing with thanksgiving, and (most strange of all) Magnus himself, a changed and humbled man.

Everybody looked at Magnus, in surprise at seeing him there, but Magnus looked at no one. While the Pastor read the lesson ("All we like sheep have gone astray"), while he gave out his text ("This day shalt thou be with Me in Paradise"), while he preached his homely sermon on the conversion of the dying thief on the cross, showing the shortness of time, the power of redemption, and the certainty of death's sundering, and even while the deacon chanted the anthem ("Weeping may endure for a night, but joy cometh in the morning"), and the congregation sang the closing hymn, and Elin's silvery young voice ringing up to the round ceiling reminded him of her mother's, Magnus sat with his face toward the picture on the wall above the communion-table.

It was a picture of Christ in white robes and among warm eastern foliage, healing the blind man by the wayside, and while he looked at it a great softening of the heart came to him, for he thought of the blessed but awful moment, only just passed, when the scales fell from his own eyes, and his naked soul stood face to face with its Maker.

That was the moment when, with murder in his mind and a spirit of war with God, he had entered the stranger's bedroom and bolted the door behind him, and then found that his victim had been snatched out of his hands and heard a fearful voice which seemed to say, "Stop! or the voice of thy brother's blood will cry unto Me from the ground!"

When the service was over there was much handshaking and well-wishing outside the porch, for rumor of what had happened in Anna's household had passed from mouth to mouth, but Magnus took his old mother on his arm and walked home with her alone, except for Elin, who tripped through the crisp snow by their side, humming a little of the last hymn.

The young people were racing the ponies to and fro in their joy of the first snow; the old ones were gossiping in groups on the exciting news of the day; and the Factor, who was swinging along in his plaid-shawl, with a contented expression, like an old cow going home in the evening with her udder full, was saluting everybody, and inviting all and sundry to the Inn-farm for a cup of coffee.

It was more than a cup of coffee he had had prepared for them, for assuming command while Magnus seemed paralyzed by surprise, he had ordered a lamb to be killed, and Aunt Margret remained behind to roast it.

The dinner was a large and long one, for everybody was welcome to it, and before it came to an end the Factor rose to propose a toast.

"Every snow-cowl has an end," he said, "and I am happy to inform you all that the cloud that has hung so long over the Inn-farm, over Anna Magnusson's family and over my family, is now gone for good. 'Show the man and not the table,' says one of our Sagas, but in this case we have had to show you the table and not the man. He will be on his way to Reykjavik by this time, I suppose, and, if prophecy is the wise man's guess, I guess he will get such a rousing welcome there as no man ever had in this old island before.

"Brothers and sisters, I give you a health—Anna's long-lost son, *our* long-lost son, Iceland's long-lost son—Oscar Stephen-son!"

The toast was received with shouts and the jingling of glasses, but Anna did not drink, and Magnus dropped his head.

VIII

On the east of the plain and the lake of Thingvellir there is a pass going over the mountain of Hengel to the little trading station of Eyrarbakki. It winds through a number of geysers and mineral springs which seem to be always smoking against the bare side of the fell. They are little pools of simmering water in the crusted yellow earth, some of them white and sparkling as a star, some round and deep-blue as a woman's eye, some oval and blood-red, like the living heart of some monstrous animal.

You walk warily on the path between, for the earth is hot and thin under his feet, and sometimes it throbs like the lid of a boiling kettle, and sometimes there is a smothered roar beneath you as of mighty battles in the bowels of the earth, and then the pools begin to boil and send up spouts of foaming water and tongues of liquid flame, and the air is full of sulphurous vapor.

An awful, evil, and devilish place, looking like a cauldron over a circle of hellish fire. But higher up the pass the snow lies white and calm and crisp, and higher still are the glistening glaciers, and there, while the mountain quakes in its volcanic throes, the avalanche comes down in winter so suddenly that no man can hear or see it, for it is loud as the crack of doom and swift as the shaft of death.

At daybreak that day Christian Christiansson was crossing this pass on his way to Eyrarbakki, intending to take ship to Norway. Although it was only two hours since he had pushed open the guest-room window and left the Inn-farm, he was already a stronger and braver man. Then he had thought of nothing but ending everything, and the shadow of self-destruction had floated before him, but now he saw clearly that until God ordained he should die it was his duty to live. As he had sinned so he should suffer. He must pay his penalty to its last pang, its uttermost moment. His penalty was to live on without the love he had forfeited, the happiness he had lost the right to claim. It was hard, but it was just, and he must face the end without flinching. Welcome life, then, as long as it lasted! Welcome death when it was due!

After he had passed through the heat and smoke and come out on the clear heights beyond he paused to look back. The world around was all white and stark under the snow of last night's storm, but a crimson shaft from the sun which had not yet risen was crossing the topmost peaks, and the lowlands were still sleeping in a veil of mist. He thought he could hear the ringing of the church bell, and that sweet human sound came winging its way up to him through the vapor of the sulphur-pits as the singing of a star might rise through the clouds of the world to the ears of the souls in heaven.

Presently the sun strode up and the mist fell back, and then he saw in the valley far below the little church itself and the home he had left behind him. He had left happiness there, and love, and warm comfort, for that was his reparation to the dear ones he had injured, and now for his atonement to God he was going out alone, stripped of everything and unknown to any one.

It was as much as he could bear to think of that, but he smiled to himself sadly while he pictured the surprise and joy of the happy scene when the girl would come out with the pocket-book and the auction would be stopped. He thought, too, of his mother in church, with a soul full of gratitude, and saw Elin with a ray of sunlight from the lead-lighted window on the heart-breaking sweetness of her smile. It was not thus that he had expected to leave them when for ten years he had worked by the sweat of body and spirit that he might come back and be forgiven. But it was not in this world that the prodigal could be taken back; not here that any earthly father could run to meet him and throw his arms about his neck. What he had sown he must reap, and not all his penitence and tears could undo what he had done.

It was long before he could take his last look at the home he was leaving forever, and when at length he drew a deep breath and went on, he had to comfort himself with the thought that Thora would be pleased with him for giving up their child to Magnus. Her voice from the other world seemed to come to him and say, "Well done! Poor, brave, wounded heart, God's angels rejoice over you!" But it was hard to find solace in heavenly cheer while his blood ran warm and yearned for human company.

Before he was aware of it he was at the foot of the glaciers, those great lone homes of Nature never trodden by the foot of man or animal, where no bird sings and no flower grows, where only the wind moans over motionless billows of ice and the sun rises in a blank barrenness on chasms of the frozen deep. Looking back from this place he could see nothing of the valley and the houses of men, or of anything but a wide circle of mountain peaks, all silent and white, in which he was the only living thing. And then the feeling of being cut off from the rest of humanity amid these grand but grim surroundings elevated his senses and affected him like music, like composing, with a sort of ecstacy which was part rapture and partly pain.

In this ecstasy of emotion he asked himself if his life had been wasted, if happiness was gone from him even if, because he had sinned, there was nothing before him now but renunciation and suffering. And then the teaching of his childhood came back to him with a new and sublime significance, and he saw for the first time the lesson of life and the meaning of death. The lesson of life was Duty—to do right without expectation of reward or fear of punishment; and the meaning of death was to bring to the sinful, penitent soul the pardon the world can not give.

Then thank God for life, but thank God for death also! Whatever a man's sin, Nature could not forget it, and the laws of life could not forgive, but the mercy of God was without measure of guilt, and the gates of heaven were wide!

God veiled His face from His creatures, and to man's questioning eyes the infinite wisdom was as blank as these white walls of ice and snow, but two thousand years ago a simple Galilean had read this riddle of life as no man before or since has read it. He had read it for all men, good or bad, but most of all for wayworn sinners like himself, for whom the world has no pity, and no forgiveness. And though he was the guiltiest of the guilty, and his sin had found him out, and as the price of his repentance he had had to give up everything in life that he held most dear—the love of his child and the hope of pardon and reconciliation—yet love and pardon and reconciliation were waiting for him still when God's own voice should call him, and "this mortal should put on immortality."

By this time he was in that mood in which a man of his temperament finds it difficult to distinguish the real from the imaginary, in which he hears the sounds of Nature and mistakes them for voices from the other world. He had wandered without knowing it from the path of the pass, which was marked by stones standing upright out of the snow, when the volcanic fire in the womb of the mountain began to shake it with mighty throbs, and then suddenly the awful stillness was broken by a crash and a resounding rumble as of echoing thunder coming down from the snow-capped heights.

Oscar Stephenson did not see or hear or feel anything. He was only conscious of a burst of heavenly music, of a sense of ten thousand angels singing an anthem, a triumphant pæan or praise that grew louder and louder every moment; a sense of blinding light, and of traveling at a terrific velocity into the realms of the sun; a sense of the Day of Judgment, of the life of the world being over, its busy throngs gone, its pageants finished, its honors, distinctions, castes, gold, wealth, and fame passed into nothingness; a sense of being outside the great Judgment Hall with an infinite multitude of kings and beggars, good men and bad, the guilty and the innocent, and of kneeling there among the meanest and most ashamed; a sense of a spirit stooping to him and taking his hand and saying, "Come," of looking up into her face, and seeing it was Thora, and of his breath coming so fast and short that he could scarcely breathe; a sense of stumbling along with his head down and the spirit leading him forward and singing as they ascended; a sense of an overwhelming Presence somewhere in front of him, of the music dying down and becoming fainter and fainter, and then of an awful hush and of a blessed Voice which said:

"FOR THIS MY SON WAS DEAD AND IS ALIVE AGAIN, WAS LOST AND IS FOUND."

. . . .

A moment afterward there was no one on Hengel mountain, the great lone home of Nature was calm and white and silent.

(1)

THE END